THE CANDY SHOP WAR

CARNIVAL QUEST

OTHER TITLES BY BRANDON MULL

THE CANDY SHOP WAR

CARNIVAL QUEST

BRANDON MULL

Illustrations by Brandon Dorman

SHADOW
MOUNTAIN
PUBLISHING

© 2023 Creative Concepts, LLC

Illustrations © 2023 by Brandon Dorman

Visit us at ShadowMountain.com

Library of Congress Cataloging-in-Publication Data

CIP on file

ISBN 978-1-63993-088-3

Printed in the United States of America

1 2 3 4 5 LBC 26 25 24 23 22

For my beautiful Erlyn,
who makes everything better

Map illustration by Garth Bruner

CONTENTS

CONTENTS

MOZAG

Mozag stepped into Marcelo's Italian Restaurant and paused to enjoy the ambiance. The smell of cooked tomatoes hung in the air like a promise. Pictures of popes and vintage cars adorned the walls. The lights were low enough to make almost anyone look good.

A hostess approached—the charming one, Carissa. "Hello, Mister Mozag. Your table is ready."

Whenever he called an hour before coming, his table was always waiting—the round one in the corner beneath the painting of a carousel. If a guy came in regularly and tipped at least fifty percent, the staff was always happy to see him.

He sat down, and a server promptly appeared. Raymond. Tall and thin. Maybe twenty, with a quick smile and efficient service.

"Are you here for the gnocchi?" Raymond asked, filling a

glass of water. Marcelo's only made gnocchi on Wednesdays, and Mozag was a fan.

"Not today," Mozag said. "Meat lover's calzone."

"Always a good pick," Raymond said. "Just the water?"

"Yes," Mozag said. "And a caprese salad."

Mozag rested his hands on the red-and-white-checkered tablecloth. The blinds over the windows were all closed, keeping the darkness out and the coziness in. This place wasn't expensive, but it was hard to find better Italian food in Chicago. Mozag liked that the clientele was ordinary people with the sense to find excellent food at a fair price. It was the kind of eatery the locals didn't tell too many people about, or it would get overrun. Marcelo's already verged on more business than it could handle.

Nobody at Marcelo's knew he was a mage, and that suited him fine. He flicked the brim of his Cubs cap. His lair was only three blocks up the street, but he never left it without his trusty hat. As a mage who had policed some of the most dangerous living magicians, he knew payback was coming sooner or later. Like magical karma. So you had to build an enchanted fortress and stay inside if you wanted to survive.

But his Cubs cap functioned like a portable lair. Strictly speaking, it was more like an umbilical cord, letting him connect to the protection of his lair from a distance. Sort of like a diver with an air hose.

The caprese salad soon appeared alongside a basket of fresh bread. The house-made mozzarella was perfect, as always. Mozag wondered for the thousandth time where they sourced such tasty tomatoes.

A tremor ran through the ground, rattling the tableware and the pictures on the walls. What was that? An earthquake? In Chicago?

Then he heard an explosion from somewhere outside. The ground shook again. The water in his glass swayed. He heard shouts, and another explosion farther away. What was going on? This was a safe neighborhood.

Something exploded right outside the front windows. The blinds rippled and snapped as glass turned to shrapnel.

Ears ringing, Mozag fell flat. Customers screamed. One guy flipped his table over to make a barricade.

"Get down!" Mozag called, and others hit the deck.

What was this? Organized crime?

Mozag scowled. Was this about him? It was difficult to imagine any mage would set off explosions, especially in the middle of a mortal community.

Closing his eyes, Mozag sought his magical senses, but all elements of his power were strangely elusive. Was somebody blocking him? Who was that powerful?

A moment later, Victor Battiato crouched at his side. He wore a dark suit with silver pinstripes and held a crossbow. His thick eyebrows were knitted together. Mozag knew the Battiato twins were working security for him today, and he was glad to see Victor responding so quickly.

"What's happening out there?" Mozag asked.

"Hard to say," Victor said. "Explosions, obviously. Bunch of clowns putting on a show."

"Do you know their agenda?" Mozag asked.

"Not yet," Victor replied. "But they're putting lots of attention on this restaurant."

"Are they after me?" Mozag asked.

"We see no other viable targets," Victor said. "Better get you out the back."

Fire roared through the broken window, flowing over the ceiling. Had somebody brought a flamethrower? Or was it a spell? Mozag felt frustrated. He should be able to sense the difference.

The flames took hold on part of the ceiling and one of the walls. Hanging photographs curled and blistered. Tear gas cannisters shot through the window and thumped to the floor, hissing as they emitted a yellowish fog.

"This way," Victor said, pulling Mozag to his feet and keeping his thick body between the mage and the front windows. Mozag pressed a fabric napkin over his nose and mouth and kept his head down, eyes squinted. They moved in a crouch to the rear hall, past the bathrooms, to where Ziggy Battiato stood at the back door.

The restaurant staff guided patrons into the kitchen. Mozag didn't want to go that way. Whoever was behind this attack was probably after him. Staying with the crowd would turn them into human shields.

Ziggy held up a beringed hand to suggest they pause. Holding a sleek tranquilizer gun, he lunged out the back door into the alleyway.

Mozag braced for an attack, but it remained quiet.

"Boss," Ziggy said, poking his head inside. "You better see this."

Mozag nodded, and Ziggy pulled the door wide.

Beyond the doorway, daylight shone down on tawny dunes that stretched to the edge of the horizon. A saddled camel stood in the foreground, chewing, lower jaw swaying from side to side in circular sweeps.

"A desert?" Mozag asked. "Are you kidding me?"

"No alley," Ziggy reported. "No mobsters or mages. Just the camel."

"Strange landscape for Chicago," Mozag said. "Last time I checked, it was evening, not midday."

Heat washed into the hall as the fire spread in the front dining room. A thunderous explosion reverberated through the building.

Victor held up his compact crossbow. "We can't stay here. Looks like we're making our escape across the desert. Wish we had a jeep."

"Who can say whether this unexpected desert is any safer than the attack out front?" Mozag asked.

"It's our safest way out," Victor said. "Must be magic."

"Not magic," Mozag said calmly. "I should feel magic. We're being herded. This must be a dream."

"It's no dream of mine," Ziggy grumbled. "We're in a great restaurant, and we can't enjoy the food."

"What's our move?" Victor asked.

The fire was spreading down the hall, together with tear gas fumes. Another explosion rocked the building. Victor supported Mozag as he staggered. Support beams creaked overhead.

"All right," Mozag said. "We'll try the desert."

Ziggy led the way onto the sand, floundering in his wing

tips. Mozag came next, followed by Victor, who closed the door behind them. The day was scorching hot, the sun blazing overhead, the sand uncomfortably warm even through Mozag's shoes. He turned to look back at the restaurant, but only the door remained. As he watched, the frameless door toppled backward like a single large domino, landing flat on the sand.

Victor crouched and then lifted the corner of the door high enough to peer beneath it. "It's just sand, boss. Marcelo's is gone."

"The attack was unbelievably severe," Mozag said. "Hopefully my departure will calm the assault, and the good people who work there will remain safe." He wiped his lips. The taste of tomatoes and mozzarella lingered on his tongue. "Gentlemen, we are stranded in a wasteland."

"With a camel," Ziggy added.

Mozag stared at the huge dromedary, taking in the long legs, knobby knees, and bulbous eyes. "Don't let it run off."

Ziggy approached the camel slowly and gathered the reins. He turned with a smile. "He likes us. Boss, you ride, we'll walk. Obviously."

Mozag gave a nod, wiping his brow under his baseball cap. Heat radiated down from above and up from the sand. "You boys are going to fry in those suits."

"They cover us up," Victor said. "Give us some protection from the sun."

"We'll walk in the camel's shadow," Ziggy said.

"Not a bad thought," Mozag said. "Though this time of day might mean walking directly beneath the brute."

Mozag shuffled on the sand. Closing his eyes, he summoned his power, but felt . . . nothing. No energy anywhere.

"Are you going to summon water, boss?" Victor asked.

Mozag opened one squinty eye. "I have no power. It's like I've been unplugged. It was like that in the restaurant too. This has to be a dream." He took his Cubs cap off and fanned his face. "This hat is just a hat. My watch is just a watch. None of my talismans have their potency."

"The cap is still good for shade," Ziggy said.

Mozag nodded. "That it is," he said, replacing the cap on his head.

"We're literally in a dream?" Victor asked. "Can we wake up?"

Mozag put his hands on his hips and frowned. "It's no normal dream. I feel far too alert, but I don't see how to awaken."

Ziggy pinched himself.

"Hey, lay off," Victor said, rubbing his own arm in the same spot. He slapped his own face.

"That smarts!" Ziggy complained.

"Stop being teenagers," Mozag said. He knew that each twin felt what the other twin experienced.

Digging the toe of one shoe into the sand, he flipped a spray of particles into the air. He marched over to the camel, brought his face close to the neck, and sniffed the fur. "The camel smells so real."

"I feel wide awake," Ziggy said.

"Me too," Mozag agreed thoughtfully. "But the restaurant's back door led to a desert and then lost all connection to the real world. That's bizarre, even for a dream." Mozag folded his arms. "My powers are dead for no perceivable reason. I normally keep my abilities in a dream. And the explosions were overdone. Who bombards a restaurant like that? Where were the cops? We weren't in a war zone."

"Yeah, what was with the explosions?" Victor asked. "It felt heavy-handed."

Mozag bent down, scooped up a handful of the sand, then let it trickle through his fingers. "Yet here we are with this camel. The sand is hot to the touch. I'm starting to sweat all over. And the minutes are ticking by."

"So where are we?" Victor asked.

Mozag hoisted himself into the saddle. "Let's go find out." The camel sidestepped, and Mozag patted it. "Easy. Easy."

Ziggy gave the reins a tug. "You be good for the boss. No shenanigans."

"Which way?" Victor asked, popping a breath mint into his mouth. Since each twin tasted only what the other consumed, he handed Ziggy one as well.

Mozag scanned the surrounding horizon. "I have no idea. My sense of direction feels confused. We could be anywhere."

"Or nowhere," Ziggy said.

"Or nowhere," Mozag echoed quietly, considering the possibility. "We'll pick a direction and stick with it."

Shielding his eyes, Victor squinted upward. "Sun is pretty high for navigation."

"It'll get easier as the day wears on," Mozag said.

"Should we bring the door?" Ziggy asked.

"What are we going to do?" Victor mocked. "Knock until somebody answers?"

"Hold it up," Ziggy said. "Shield us from the sun."

Victor shook his head. "I'd rather walk under the camel."

Ziggy shrugged and pointed with his chin. "This way then." He trudged forward, the camel in tow.

They went up one dune and down the far side. It was slow going. As Mozag watched the Battiatos wading down the sandy slope, he was grateful for his ride. When they crested the next dune, Mozag called for a pause.

"What is it?" Victor asked, panting.

"We need to change directions," Mozag said, peering at a neighboring dune.

"Tell me you see palm trees and piña coladas," Ziggy said.

"I'd settle for a town," Victor tried. "I'm tired of hiking." He wiped perspiration from his brow. "My suit feels like a wet sponge."

"I'm not sure what I see," Mozag said. "Just a point poking up in the distance. A triangular point."

"Another dune?" Victor asked.

"No," Mozag said. "It's made of stone. Too geometric to be natural."

"Like a pyramid?" Ziggy said. "Are we in Egypt?"

"We're going to find out," Mozag said.

"I always wanted to see a pyramid," Ziggy said. "Didn't want it to be my final resting place though. Careful what you wish for."

"You might look good as a mummy," Victor said. "We could cover up that face."

Ziggy punched his own shoulder so his brother could feel it. "Keep it up, wise guy."

Several rises and falls later, the Battiato brothers were walking with rubbery legs and gasping for breath. The relentless sun showed little sign of budging.

"I still don't see no pyramid," Ziggy wheezed.

"Grammar," Mozag scolded.

"My grammar gets fuzzy when I overheat," Ziggy said.

"I haven't seen the pyramid either," Victor put in.

"If we stay on course, we'll see it soon," Mozag said.

"Unless it was a mirage," Ziggy mumbled.

"We'll have a good view from this next dune," Mozag assured him. "It's a big one."

"Is that supposed to be welcome news?" Ziggy asked. "We're at the bottom! Not everyone is riding a camel."

"I'm down to my last mint," Victor said. "You enjoy it."

"We should split it," Ziggy said.

"It won't split easily," Victor replied. "I'll suck on it—you taste it. Fair enough."

Ziggy stared up the long slope. "If I die on the way up, don't bury me. I'm sure a sandstorm will come along."

They started up the incline. The camel advanced tirelessly. Victor and Ziggy huffed and puffed alongside the animal. When they reached the top, a large pyramid came into sight, with only a couple of smaller dunes concealing the base.

"What do you know?" Ziggy said. "I'd rather see a Holiday Inn, but it's better than more sand."

"Maybe it draws tourists," Victor said. "Is it too much to hope that we could catch a ride with someone?"

"We can't see the far side," Mozag said. "Or the base. We'll have to approach it to know what we're dealing with."

"Think we'll find some sphinxes behind it?" Ziggy asked.

"I'd rather find a ginger ale," Victor replied.

"Onward," Mozag said. "At least we can hope for some shade before you two collapse."

"It'll take more than a little heat and some sand in my shoes to defeat Ziggy Battiato," he said bravely.

"Maybe we should have taken our chances with the fire-fight," Victor said. "Hard to go down with style hiking in the desert."

"We've survived worse," Mozag said.

"If we die, think we'll wake up?" Ziggy asked hopefully.

"Only one way to find out," Victor said, starting down the far side of the dune.

By the time they summitted the dune nearest the pyramid, Ziggy and Victor were having a hard time staying on their feet. Both had taken multiple spills, and their suits were sandy enough to prove it. Even the camel showed signs of flagging.

"It's tremendous," Mozag said, studying the pyramid. "Reminds me of the Great Pyramid of Giza. But it's all alone out here. No settlement in sight."

"Maybe all the action is behind it," Ziggy said. "The fella vending snow cones and whatnot."

The ground began to tremble. Vibrating sand shifted on the slopes below them.

Victor took out his gun, looking around. "Another attack?"

The quaking increased, and the camel got skittish, snorting and sidestepping. Staggering to stay on his feet, Ziggy gripped the reins tighter. Trickles of sand slid down the slope.

"Look at the pyramid," Mozag said in wonder. "Is it getting bigger? Rising out of the sand?"

"Now I've seen everything," Ziggy said.

"What's it mean, boss?" Victor asked.

"We're only looking at the tip of the iceberg," Mozag said. "See, it keeps growing. This pyramid extends down deep, and it has decided to surface."

"Are you sure?" Victor asked.

"My senses are awakening," Mozag said. "My power is returning."

The earthquake grew louder and more violent. A hot wind began to blow. The pyramid emerged faster, towering ever higher above the surrounding dunes.

Victor fell to his knees. Ziggy went down as well, losing his hold on the reins. The camel reared, and Mozag fell to the shuddering sand.

"My hat!" Mozag barked, feeling his hair.

The camel ran down the slope at breakneck speed, the Cubs cap in its mouth.

Ziggy and Victor tried to aim their weapons at the fleeing animal as the sand bucked and heaved beneath them. Shots rang out. A howling gale raised a stinging screen of gritty sand.

"This was a trap!" Mozag called, hands up to protect his sandblasted face. "Might have been all about the hat!"

"Never trust a found camel," Ziggy blurted.

"We're under attack, and I'm utterly vulnerable," Mozag said. "I have to take another shape." He looked to the sky. "I'm still not sure where we are."

"What should we do?" Victor asked.

"Wake up," Mozag cried. "Fight to escape the dream. We're somewhere in the dreamscape—but in some altered version I've never experienced. And we're not alone. We're being watched. I can feel it. This is not something you can protect me from. Stay alive, if you can. I gotta go."

With those final words, Mozag shrank into the form of an aardvark.

CHAPTER ONE
NEW SCHOOL

N ate awoke with a start, surprised to be in his bed. The dream had been incredibly vivid, like living inside a movie. Except instead of participating, he had simply followed the action as an observer. Mozag had fled a restaurant into the desert, and, in the end, the old magician had turned into an aardvark.

As leader of the enforcers tasked with policing the magicians of the world, Mozag was extremely powerful. The dream was probably nonsense, but Nate wished he had a way to make sure the mage was all right.

Glancing at his clock, Nate saw that he was ten minutes ahead of his alarm. Plenty of time to talk to Rocco.

Nate kicked off his covers and went to the window. The seagull stood outside on the little apron of roof. Nate opened the window, and the seagull's head swiveled his way. Nate reached into a bag on the windowsill, as the bird stepped expectantly from one foot to the other. When Nate tossed a few kibbles of Brain Feed onto the shingles, the gull hopped forward and snatched one up.

"Morning, human," the seagull said, the magical snack having restored its ability to speak.

"Good morning, Rocco," Nate said. "Any news?"

"I dunno, I dunno, seems like there was something," Rocco said, munching down a second fragment of Brain Feed. "It's all getting hazy. Sure wish I had some bread."

Nate stared down at the gull. He had experimented all summer giving Brain Feed to various animals, trying to find reliable informants. He'd learned that just because animals gained boosted intelligence and the ability to speak didn't necessarily mean they wanted to be helpful. Domestic animals were more reliable talkers, but Nate had wanted a winged spy.

Not all birds were willing to eat the kibbles. Most ignored what he sprinkled by the bird feeder in the backyard. Ducks would gobble them up, but after the temporary upgrade, each enlightened duck told him to "scram" or "get lost" and swam away. He had tried the kibbles on several seagulls, and they mostly laughed at him, hurling insults like "stupid human" or "land plodder."

Rocco had been different. He had mocked Nate at first, but when Nate pulled out a sandwich, the gull started asking for bread. An understanding had quickly followed. Even without the influence of the kibbles, Rocco appeared outside Nate's window every morning.

"I've got your merchandise," Nate said, casually displaying

a whole slice of white bread. "Do you have anything worth telling?" He moved the bread behind his hip.

"Hard to say for sure," Rocco said. "I'm so hungry."

Nate tore off a bit of crust and tossed it onto the roof. "Start talking."

"As usual, boring humans doing boring human stuff," Rocco said. "Moving slow, unless they're in cars."

Nate moved to close the window. It was all part of the act. "I'm going to go make myself some toast."

"Wait!" Rocco cried. "I might have something. I'm getting better at noticing even when the Brain Feed wears thin."

"I'm listening."

"Your friend, Mr. Stott, had a late visitor," Rocco said.

"Who?"

"A man," Rocco said. "Not old, not young. In a suit. I don't know his name."

"Did he look strong?" Nate asked.

"Pretty big man," Rocco said.

"How late?"

"Long after dark. Almost no cars out."

"That's something," Nate said, tossing a couple pieces of torn bread onto the roof. "What else?"

"Some teenage kids were getting rowdy at the graveyard," Rocco said. "One threw a bottle at me. Gave me a scare. What is the matter with humans?"

"Were they digging up bodies?" Nate asked.

"Just running around and being loud," Rocco said. "They scattered when a police car came."

Nate tossed another pinch of bread, and Rocco snatched it up.

"Anything new at the fairgrounds?" Nate asked.

"The carnies are almost done," Rocco said. "They built all sorts of strange structures."

Nate had visited the outskirts of the fairgrounds with his friends several times. They had seen the Ferris wheel, the big tents, and the Fun House take shape quickly over the past few days. It was the first time he had seen the grounds used since he had moved to Colson a year ago.

"And Diablo View?" Nate asked.

"It's been busy," Rocco said. "Is today your first day there?"

"It's everyone's first day there," Nate said.

"Not everyone," Rocco corrected. "Lots of grown-ups were there yesterday."

"Those were teachers setting up," Nate said. "No kids have gone there yet, except for orientation. It's a brand-new school."

Back in June, there had been some question as to whether the new middle school would be finished in time for the following school year. Two weeks ago, it was confirmed that many kids would transfer from two other middle schools, along with all the sixth graders within the boundaries. Going to Diablo View meant that instead of ruling Mount Diablo Elementary, Nate and his friends would be at the bottom of the pecking order, behind seventh and eighth graders.

"I'll come check it out," Rocco said. "I figure most other seagulls will be flocking to the standard haunts. I might score big at the new place."

"I'll watch for you," Nate said, tossing out the rest of the slice of bread onto the shingles. "If not, see you tomorrow."

"You bet," Rocco said, taking up the piece of bread and flying off before Nate had shut the window.

Nate flinched as his alarm started beeping. That sound always set him on edge. He turned it off and walked to the bathroom. He hoped his dream didn't mean Mozag was in trouble. He would ask Mr. Stott about it, just in case.

Who had visited Mr. Stott in the night? Could John Dart be back in town? One of the Battiato brothers?

Teeth brushed, Nate hurried downstairs. With Cheryl in eighth grade, Nate was back in the same school as his sister. Diablo View was no farther away than Mount Diablo Elementary, less than a mile from his home. Mom had made it clear she expected him and his sister to walk or bike to school, but since this was their first day, she had planned to give them a ride.

"You don't have to be nervous, Nate," Mom said as he buckled his seat belt.

"Or maybe you do," Cheryl said from her seat up front. "I remember my first day of middle school. Lots of different classes scattered all over the school. No recess. And the big kids seemed so mature."

"Don't worry," Nate said. "Someday you'll catch up."

"Very funny," Cheryl said. "Let's see how confident you are in a few minutes. It's about to get real."

"I've handled worse," Nate said.

"Like what?" Cheryl challenged.

Many thoughts flashed through Nate's mind. Using

magical candy to fight the apprentices of Mrs. White. Fracturing into three versions of himself in a race against time. Protecting a copy of the Earth from a lunatic magician.

But he couldn't discuss those adventures. Only a few people knew what really happened.

"Like building Lego Hogwarts," Nate said.

Cheryl shrugged. "I guess that might help you find your way around. I think Diablo View used the same blueprints."

Mom slowed down as the traffic on Swamp Creek Road thickened. Adults wearing orange vests stood in front of the school, directing traffic. Nate looked in frustration at kids with backpacks walking faster than their car stuck in the bumper-to-bumper drop-off line.

When the chain of cars in front of them came to a stop, Nate unclipped his seat belt and opened the door. "Bye, Mom."

He hopped out, shut the door, and joined the stream of kids moving along the sidewalk. Cheryl glared at him like he had done something wrong, but Nate figured she was just jealous he would beat her into the school.

He saw some familiar faces among the droves of kids, but he also noticed students who looked like high schoolers—boys and girls transitioning into their adult sizes. Nate wished he was taller. Trevor had grown a lot over the past year, and Summer was now clearly the second tallest in the group. Nate's dad was fairly tall; he told himself he just needed to be patient.

A stout crossing guard held up a hand for the pedestrians to wait as he waved cars forward. He was an older guy, probably retired. Nate watched his mom's car roll past, then the guard opened up the crosswalk. Nate walked as fast as he could without running. He soon found he didn't need to worry—the line of cars advanced in short bursts with plenty of long pauses. His mom and sister were still waiting to turn in to the parking lot when he reached the entrance.

A portion of the lot had covered parking topped with shiny black solar panels. The rectangular panels also crowned some of the buildings within view. Nate wondered how much of the school's power was generated by sunny days.

Having attended an orientation a few days earlier, Nate already had a list of his classes along with a simple map. First up was history. Moving between gray walls toward a building at the back of campus, he saw a freshly buzzed head about his height, atop a stocky build.

"Pigeon!" Nate called out.

His friend turned and waited. "Good morning, Nate."

"You're here!" Nate exclaimed. Pigeon's mom had been pressuring him to enroll at Elm Lake private school. It was the swankiest school in the area, and Pigeon had been invited there with a scholarship.

"I wanted to be in the same school as my friends," Pigeon said.

"Aren't you missing a big opportunity?" Nate asked.

"I already know how to learn," Pigeon said. "I follow my interests, and I read a lot. It's a lot harder to find good friends. I finally convinced my mom last night."

"Can I feel it?" Nate asked, nodding to Pigeon's buzz cut.

Pigeon bowed his head, and Nate rubbed his scalp with both hands. "It's so fuzzy!"

"Hey, guys," Summer said from behind Nate.

He turned around and was surprised at how much he had to crane his neck back to meet her eyes. She wore a white, knee-length skirt and a blue top. Her hair had some curl in it. She even had on a little makeup.

"You're a giant," Nate said.

She looked down at her wedge sandals. "My mom is trying to turn me into a poodle. These heels are so uncomfortable."

"You look great," Pigeon said.

"Thanks, but it isn't really me," Summer said. "Mom bought me some new clothes, so I feel a little obligated. Did you hear Zac Foster is in our school?"

"The Foster Child? The YouTuber?" Nate asked. He had seen a few of his videos.

"I would call him an influencer," Pigeon said. "He started on YouTube, but now he's on multiple platforms. He would have gone to Montrose, but all those sixth graders are coming here now."

"He's so funny," Summer said. "I hope we have classes with him!"

The bell rang.

"Five minutes," Pigeon said. "Do you two know where you're going?"

"Yep," Summer said. "See you at lunch."

"See you in English," Pigeon said to Nate.

"Cool," Nate said. English was his only honors class.

Pigeon took off, and Nate hurried to homeroom, excited to see what the day would bring.

CHAPTER TWO

ZAC

Nate's history classroom was walled with maps and posters of world monuments. He found a desk and looked around. He knew some of the kids near him, but none of his good friends were in the room.

Leaning against a bookshelf in the corner, the teacher wore jeans, a pale green shirt, and a tie. He was a lean man with a small chin and hairy arms. After the bell, he walked to the front of the room and stared at the class until everyone fell silent.

He opened with a question. "Have you ever offended someone and then later apologized? A common reply might sound like, 'Hey, don't worry about it—that's ancient history.' This response implies that the misdeed was irrelevant. To which I take mild offense, because this class is literally *ancient history*. And I am your teacher, Mr. Zimmerman."

"Good," said the kid seated in front of Nate. "I won't worry about it."

Muffled laughter percolated through the room.

A faint smile bent Mr. Zimmerman's lips. "Nobody has to worry about ancient history. Unless you want to pass this class. And unless you wish to use our shared human heritage to make sense of the present and prepare for the future."

"Why read history when you can write it?" the same kid said. He had brown hair and wore a checkered shirt and stylish jeans. He slouched back in his chair, perfectly at ease. He had a bracelet made of wooden and metal beads on his left wrist.

"What is your name?" Mr. Zimmerman asked.

"Zac Foster."

Several of the students took new interest in the kid, straining to see him.

"Ah, yes," Mr. Zimmerman said. "Have you been writing history?"

"Recording it more than writing it," Zac said. "Sharing my life. Making people laugh."

"Videos can be fun," Mr. Zimmerman said. "The civilizations we will study did not have the technology to make videos, but they left many other clues that enable us to decipher much about how they lived."

"How I live is no secret," Zac inserted.

Several students chuckled.

"My kids enjoy your videos," Mr. Zimmerman said. "A lot of the content seems like you narrating as you play video games."

"Depends on the account you're watching," Zac said. "And on my mood. Video games contain some of the best narratives of my generation. My fans like to live our stories more than read them."

Mr. Zimmerman nodded. "Everything each society produces helps reveal who they are," he said. "YouTube is one of the journals of our era. Makes me wonder what the ancient Greeks would have recorded with that technology."

"They would have documented their toga parties," Nate said, earning a laugh.

Mr. Zimmerman nodded. "Possibly, though toga parties were popularized by modern frat houses more than by ancient cultures. The Greeks might have captured events from the ancient Olympics. Or publicized philosophical debates." He bobbed his eyebrows. "Methinks I spy a potential project."

Many in the class groaned.

"It's bad karma to talk homework in the first five minutes of class," Zac said.

"And it's bad form to talk out of turn," Mr. Zimmerman said. "Let's raise hands to make comments."

Zac raised his hand.

"Mr. Foster," Mr. Zimmerman said.

"Can I record in class?"

"Absolutely not," Mr. Zimmerman said. "It's against school policy. Too many liability issues."

Zac shrugged. "I was hoping we could make some history while we learn about it."

Mr. Zimmerman straightened his tie. "Let's make it through introductions first. This will be your homeroom. That means it is like every other class except we get an extra five minutes for announcements. They usually hit the loudspeaker a few minutes in."

"Doesn't sound like a homeroom to me," Zac said. "In a home, I would know I'm loved."

"Foster Child," a boy toward the front of the room said behind his hand.

"'Nobody loves me,'" a girl added, parroting a catchphrase Zac sometimes used on his channel. The whole class was giggling.

The overhead speaker crackled to life. "Good morning, Diablo View students. Welcome to your first day at this brand-new school. I'm your principal, Mrs. Jackson . . ."

Zac turned around and grinned at Nate. "Toga party wasn't bad," he said, raising a hand for a high five.

Nate slapped his palm gently. "You have to let a few jokes fly on day one. Set the precedent."

"I like how you think," Zac said, turning to face forward.

* * * * *

By lunchtime, Nate was hungry. After being on a summer-time schedule, he wasn't used to eating breakfast so early and having such a large gap before lunch. There were two lunch periods at his school, and he was in the second. Nate hurried to the cafeteria, an echoey room with tile floors and rows of long tables, and got in the food line.

"Nate!" Trevor called, catching up to him.

"Sorry, no cuts," Nate said, pulling his friend behind him.

"Whatever," Trevor said. "Have you seen the tacos? They actually look decent."

Nate looked at the kids leaving the front of the line with tacos on their trays and heading to a station with lettuce, cheese, tomatoes, and other extras. "I'll believe it when I taste it," Nate said. "They probably recycled old corn dog meat."

Craning his neck, Trevor went onto his tiptoes, making him even taller than usual. "Is that John Dart?"

"Where?" Nate asked.

"Working the lunch line," Trevor said. "Is this happening?"

Nate couldn't find a good angle that allowed him to see. "He must be undercover. Rocco mentioned that somebody visited Mr. Stott last night. Might have been John."

As the line inched forward, John Dart came into view, an apron tied around his powerful torso, a black skullcap hugging the contours of his cranium. He spooned taco meat into a pair of shells, then handed the plate across the counter.

"Keep it moving," John said, raising his voice enough for the line to hear. "Not much to think about. If you don't want delicious tacos, there are some nasty chicken nuggets in animal shapes down at the end. Or, if you're truly desperate, salad."

The line advanced noticeably faster after his remarks.

As Nate and Trevor approached the front, John glanced their way.

"Here are a couple of familiar faces," he said warmly, looking down the line at them.

"Aren't you the guy who wrestles enemies into submission?" Trevor asked. "And now . . . tacos? Really?"

"You became a lunch lady?" Nate asked.

Several kids in line snickered.

"Watch your mouth," John said. "Respect the name tag."

Nate squinted, barely discerning the letters at his current distance. "Lunch Lord," he read.

"That's right," John said. He gestured to his co-workers. "I run the kitchen with the help of my able staff."

"Since when are you in the food business?" Trevor asked.

"Off and on for years," John said, continuing to add meat to taco shells. "As a youngster, my school lunches were usually garbage. I wanted to do a solid for the kids in this area. When this school opened up, I put in the lowest bid and guaranteed the highest-quality food."

"Is that good for profits?" Nate asked.

John shook his head. "I'll lose a little money, but not enough to matter. I have plenty socked away." Nate and Trevor came even with John. "You're having the tacos, I hope?"

"Sounds like we better," Trevor said.

"I sourced excellent meat," John said, filling two pairs of shells. "The primary offering will always be good. Occasionally outstanding. The secondary options will taste exactly how you would expect a chicken nugget shaped like a lion to taste."

"Like neither a chicken nor a lion," Trevor said.

"Keep the line moving," John said, pointing ahead with his big spoon. "We have lots of fresh toppings you can add."

"Any news?" Nate asked quietly.

"Only this," John said, leaning forward and lowering his voice. "Nobody is touching the pickled jalapeños. They are missing out."

Nate took the hint and kept going. He wondered what John might have added if there were no eavesdroppers.

"Whoa," Trevor said. "They have guac. And it looks real." He scooped two spoonfuls onto his shells.

Nate added grated cheese, lettuce, tomato, and sour cream to his taco. He considered the pickled jalapeños but couldn't bring himself to do it.

"Have you seen Summer and Pidge?" Nate asked, scanning the room.

"They should be around," Trevor said. "I heard all the sixth graders have the second lunch period, along with half of seventh grade."

They browsed the tables, looking for their friends. Nate heard Zac's voice rising from a cluster of people at the end of one table.

"Ladies, please, hands off. I'm not a children's museum."

A couple of girls huffed away while some other kids laughed. As the cluster dispersed, Nate saw Summer and Pigeon sitting at the table near Zac.

Summer waved. "Nate, we saved you seats."

Zac pointed at Nate. "I know that guy. He likes toga parties."

"And you're making history," Nate said.

Zac put a hand over his chest. "Finally, somebody understands me."

Nate wedged himself onto the bench beside Summer, while Trevor settled in beside Pigeon.

"Are my taste buds broken?" Zac asked. "Or are these tacos actually good?"

"They're delicious," said a baby-faced blond boy sitting across from Zac.

"I have hope for the food this year," Nate said. "Now that we have a lunch lord."

"I saw that guy," Zac said. "He looks like a bouncer."

Nate and Summer shared a look.

"I know him a little," Nate said. "He's even tougher than he looks."

"This is Nate and Trevor," Summer introduced. "And this is Zac and Benji."

"Just Z-A-C," Zac said. "The K was deadweight."

"When did you guys meet?" Nate asked Summer.

"Math class," she said.

"Math is a great time to make new friends," Zac said.

"I thought Miss Monroe was going to throw you out," Summer said.

"She will before the end of the week," Zac said. "I'll push until she does. It helps me figure out her boundaries."

"Is school a social experiment to you?" Pigeon asked.

"Every interaction is a social experiment, no matter what," Zac said. "I just try to keep things interesting."

"He has major ADD," Benji said.

"Undiagnosed," Zac said, raising a finger. "I don't want meds. Whatever my chemistry is works for my videos."

"How many followers do you have?" Trevor asked.

"Depends on the platform," Zac said. "YouTube? Around 1.3 million—give or take. Some of the view counts blow my mind."

"You're quite a sensation," Pigeon said.

"That makes me feel like a new soda," Zac said. "I'm glad you guys are sitting with me. The Internet thing is weird. Lots of kids want to meet me, but then they don't know what to say. At Montrose, it was often just me and Benji."

"He pays me to laugh at his jokes," Benji said.

"How much?" Trevor asked. "I like to laugh."

"Mostly Doritos," Benji said.

Trevor nodded. "I could live with that."

"Is it stressful to know millions of people watch your clips?" Pigeon asked.

Zac shrugged. "I just act like myself. My dad is the marketing guru. He did the Foster Child stuff as a side project, and it blew up."

"Do any actual foster children get offended by the name?" Nate asked.

"Maybe some do," Zac said. "Most actual foster kids know everything I say is ridiculous. You'll catch on. My big goal now is to die at the right time. Think about it—James Dean, Marilyn Monroe, Tupac. They all died when they were still popular, so they never faded away. I don't want to be a footnote in my own story."

"What about George Washington?" Pigeon asked. "He died at sixty-seven. We remember him just fine."

Zac nodded. "Washington obeyed a different principle. Affiliation. He affiliated himself with the right group. He was the first president of the United States, and since the United States is still a thing, so is he. Thomas Edison gets credit for inventing the light bulb. As long as light bulbs matter to us, so does he."

"Who do you affiliate with?" Nate asked.

"You guys," Zac said. "Online? Whoever wants to sponsor me and isn't a jerk. My dad handles most of that."

"Do you make a lot of money?" Trevor asked.

"Enough to buy Doritos for Benji," Zac said.

"He makes more than our teachers," Benji said. "His dad saves most of the earnings for him."

"Invests," Zac corrected. "If you want to make money, go after brainspace. That's the actual real estate. Claim your share of brainspace, and the rest comes easy. Ask Facebook or Disney. Ask Nintendo."

"Brainspace?" Nate asked.

"It's a term I use with my dad," Zac said. "If people are thinking about you, the money follows."

"What do you put in the brainspace?" Nate asked.

"Jokes," Zac said. "Little slices of life. I make fun of video games while I play them, or shows while I watch them. I tease my mom. I mess around with my dog. And while I have people's attention, I share information about my sponsors. This week, it's the new carnival."

"The one here in town?" Pigeon asked. "Aren't your clips watched all over the world?"

"Sure, but my biggest following is in the Bay Area," Zac said. "The carnival people worked out an arrangement with my dad. I can get us a bunch of free tickets if you guys want to go. I'm scheduled to make at least three videos inside the carnival."

"Free is the best price," Trevor said.

"They're doing a parade Saturday morning," Zac said. "It ends at the fairgrounds and then the carnival opens."

"Are you in the parade?" Summer asked.

"It's part of the deal," Zac said with a shrug. "Have you guys ever been in a parade before? The only thing worse than watching one is being in one. If you've seen one cheering by-stander, you've seen them all."

"I like when the people on the floats throw candy," Trevor said.

"Note to self—fill pockets with candy," Zac said. "If you want to meet me after the parade, we can check out opening day."

"That would be so fun," Summer said.

"Perfect," Zac said. "I'll finally get to feel like somebody loves me."

CHAPTER THREE

CANDY SHOP

When Nate came through the door, Mom called to him from the kitchen. "Welcome home! How was your first day?"

"I didn't get any wedgies," Nate replied.

"Did you walk home with Cheryl?" Mom asked.

"I didn't see her," Nate said, tromping into the kitchen and setting his backpack by the counter. "She probably had detention."

"Yeah, right," Mom said. "I bet she was catching up with friends."

"I did that while we walked home," Nate said. "Some of us are planning to meet over at the candy shop. Is that okay?"

"How is your homework situation?"

"I don't think I'll have homework this year," Nate said. "It's a new school. They need good reviews."

"And the real answer?"

"Only a little," Nate said. "It was mostly introductions today. I have a few papers you're supposed to sign."

"All right," Mom said. "Say hi to Mr. Stott. Don't bother him if he's got customers."

"I'll buy a mint or something," Nate said. "Then I'll *be* a customer."

Nate hopped on his bike and rode to the jogging path at the bottom of his circle. He followed the asphalt trail to where it ended near the Sweet Tooth Ice Cream and Candy Shoppe, then parked his bike in the rack out front. Summer's pink bike was already there.

A bell jangled as Nate passed into the air-conditioned store. The black-and-white-checkered floor was polished to a semi-reflective sheen. Nearly all of the chrome-legged tables were full of kids and teens, and even a few adults. Most were eating ice cream, but others had candy. Mr. Stott had devoted more of the long, L-shaped counter to ice cream and added sweets to the bright library of candy along the walls.

Summer sat at a table with Lindy, the girl who had once owned the candy shop. Watching Lindy's animated expressions as she talked, it was hard to believe she used to be the magician Belinda White. Back when Mrs. White was trying to take over the town, Nate had slipped her a drink that made her young and erased her memories. Mr. Stott promptly adopted Lindy and became her legal guardian.

Nate crossed to their table. Lindy smiled up at him. "How was your first day?"

"Could have been worse," Nate said. "How was yours?"

She shrugged. "Dad is a good teacher. But I would rather go to public school with you guys."

Nate shared a glance with Summer. Mr. Stott had insisted Lindy be homeschooled until he felt sure she wouldn't turn into a weapon of mass destruction.

"I've always dreamed about being homeschooled," Nate said. "Of course, in those dreams, I outfox my parents and play video games all day."

"There is no avoiding the work with Dad," Lindy said.

"Where is your dad?" Nate asked.

"In the back," she said. "Donny has been manning the counter all day."

Mr. Stott had hired Donny toward the end of the summer. He was twenty, with shaggy hair and a relaxed personality. Donny worked thirty to forty hours a week at the candy shop but had not yet seemed to notice or wonder about any of the supernatural aspects of Mr. Stott's other confections. Nate and his friends typically waited until they were outside the shop before eating candy and jumping over houses.

Usually, Mr. Stott worked out front with Donny, but when there was a large order of candy to fulfill, he stayed in the back.

Nate lowered his voice. "Has John Dart been by?"

Lindy nodded. "Dad wants to talk to you about that."

As a mother and young son left the candy shop, Trevor came through the door. He strode straight to Nate.

"Pigeon is down in the creek again," Trevor said.

"More rocks?" Nate asked. Pigeon had been on a geology kick over the last few weeks of summer.

"You guessed it," Trevor said. "I told him to hurry."

"Sure, after he finds his weight in quartz," Nate said.

"Have you gone rockhounding with him?" Summer asked. "It's pretty fun."

"I've tried," Nate said. "All rocks look the same to me when they're jumbled on the ground."

Pigeon came through the door. "Sorry I was slow," he said as he approached. "I thought I saw some lizardite, but I think it was schist."

"Let me get this straight," Nate said. "You were walking along, minding your own business, and from a distance, you noticed lizardite down in the creek?"

"I may have strayed from the path to do a quick inspection of the creek bed," Pigeon amended. "Then I saw the mottled stone."

"Bigger question," Trevor said. "Is lizardite made of lizards?"

"I think the name implies it looks like lizard scales," Pigeon replied.

"You can't stop looking for rocks," Nate said. "You're addicted. Do we need to stage an intervention?"

Pigeon shrugged. "Ever since I realized there is treasure sitting around in the open, waiting for somebody to notice it, I've had trouble resisting."

"Hello," Mr. Stott said, emerging from the back. A robust man of seventy years old, the former ice cream truck driver had a gray beard with a pair of symmetrical dark streaks running the full length down to his chest. "Lindy, bring your friends and come join me."

The five kids followed Mr. Stott through the door to the back of the candy shop. His ongoing experiments topped the counters and worktables—multicolored potions bubbled in clear flasks, sugary crystals dried on racks, and a bright-green gelatinous mass prowled inside a terrarium.

Mr. Stott escorted the kids to a table where five tall glasses awaited, each filled with a milky white beverage.

"Shakes?" Summer asked.

"Banana," Mr. Stott replied. "Try them."

Nate quickly took a sip. Anything Mr. Stott made was a safe bet, and this drink was no exception. More the consistency of a smoothie than a shake, it was frosty and creamy, with just the right balance of banana and vanilla. And a hint of honey.

"This is epic," Trevor said. "I don't even like bananas, but you're changing my mind."

"Is this hard to make?" Pigeon asked. "I have to give my mom the recipe."

"The only prep is freezing half a banana," Mr. Stott said. "Combine that with a whole ripe banana, two small scoops of vanilla ice cream, one cup of milk, and a drizzle of honey. Blend well and enjoy."

"Are there other bells and whistles you sometimes include?" Nate asked. Mr. Stott often had alternate versions of his concoctions.

Mr. Stott gave a nod. "You can use coconut ice cream instead of vanilla. Or try adding your preferred chocolate mix and a spoonful of peanut butter for a richer and more complex result."

"Why is John Dart our new lunch lady?" Trevor asked.

"Lunch Lord," Summer corrected.

Mr. Stott's demeanor became more solemn. "He's worried about the carnival."

"Does he get sick on the spinny rides?" Nate asked.

"First off, the fairgrounds have been powerfully warded," Mr. Stott said. "That seems to indicate the carnival is a magical lair."

"A lair for who?" Trevor asked.

Mr. Stott shrugged and splayed his hands. "We don't know. The Dreams and Screams International Carnival has made appearances in Europe, Asia, South America, and most recently in Texas, but we still don't know who runs it."

"Does this carnival have a reputation?" Pigeon asked.

"Nothing of significant interest until Texas," Mr. Stott said. "The Council had been monitoring the carnival but only considered it a minor threat until last month."

"What happened last month?" Summer asked.

"There were numerous unreported disappearances after the outfit left Texas."

"Of people?" Nate asked.

"Yes."

"How do you know about the disappearances if they were unreported?" Nate asked.

Mr. Stott popped a malt ball into his mouth and crunched it. "For 'normal' disappearances—people who run away or who are abducted—those events tend to get reported. For disappearances that *aren't* reported, the Council investigates because those usually involve magic. Enchantments that make

38

people forget or not notice what is happening. And *dozens* of people vanished while the carnival was in Texas. Children, adults—even a few entire families."

"Could they have run off and joined the carnival?" Pigeon asked.

"The operatives we sent to investigate never returned," Mr. Stott said. "Talented, dependable people. We're still trying to figure out what happened."

"And now the carnival shows up here," Lindy said.

"Has anyone local vanished?" Trevor asked.

"I don't believe so," Mr. Stott said. "If disappearances are being magically cloaked, they're fooling me too. But there are baffling reports from around town. An orangutan was spotted in an oak tree at Hillcrest Park. And John Dart saw a stage-coach and a full team of six horses sitting idly in the Safeway parking lot yesterday."

"I saw that on social media," Pigeon said.

"My mom was there," Summer said. "She wondered if they were filming a commercial or something."

"Nobody claimed the coach," Mr. Stott said. "Or the horses. The police showed up, and some people from animal control. The authorities couldn't figure out where any of it came from. There wasn't much precedent for how to handle the situation."

"Was the stagecoach from olden times?" Trevor asked.

"John reported that everything was in good repair," Mr. Stott said. "As if it were new. Could it have slipped through time to get here? Not a bad theory."

"What happened to the orangutan?" Summer asked.

"It's still at large," Mr. Stott said. "Multiple people reported seeing it at the park. But then nobody could find it, including John."

"It's coming to my house," Pigeon muttered. "I know it."

"Did the orangutan escape from the carnival?" Nate asked.

"The carnival claimed all their apes are accounted for," Mr. Stott said.

"I thought circuses had stopped using animals these days," Summer said.

"Apparently the Dreams and Screams International Carnival has permits for just about everything," Mr. Stott said.

"They're going to have protestors," Summer said.

"Let's hope so," Mr. Stott said. "This carnival is up to no good. Any resistance they encounter will be welcome."

"I need some good candy in case that ape shows up," Pigeon said.

"Too bad our stamps wore out," Trevor said.

Nate nodded. It had been two weeks since the last of his stamp powers faded away. Having the strength of a tank or the flight abilities of a jet had been handy. The ink pads and stamps had been confiscated by the Council after Jonas White was incarcerated.

Mr. Stott scrunched his brow. "If I remember correctly, you still have some Shock Bits, several Moon Rocks, an ample supply of Brain Feed, a fair amount of Peak Performance gum, and at least a few Ironhides."

"An Ironhide would probably do the trick in an orangutan attack," Pigeon said. "He wouldn't be able to dislocate my limbs or tear me open or shatter my bones. But he could haul me off into the hills and wait for the candy to wear off."

"Could be a 'she,'" Summer said.

"And she might never show up again," Trevor said.

"I want to be ready," Pigeon said.

"I'm not sure I have anything better than what you already possess," Mr. Stott said. "I'm in the final stages of developing a trick candy that I call Sour Stink. It's sour candy that will leave you smelling worse than a family of skunks crushing rotten eggs in a garbage dump. The effect lasts a few hours, but while it does, the odor should drive off any living creature."

"Would I smell bad to myself?" Pigeon asked.

"Yes," Mr. Stott said. "Chances are good you would throw up uncontrollably. I may need to dial it back a little."

"I'll take it," Pigeon said. "I'd rather puke than become an orangutan's chew toy."

Mr. Stott opened a drawer and handed Pigeon two black cubes of a gummy substance. "Don't use this as a trick on anyone besides a mortal enemy. The effects are currently too extreme to employ Sour Stinks as a prank."

Pigeon saluted. "I'll only use these on myself or the devil."

"We were planning to go to the carnival on Saturday," Nate said. "Opening day. We even scored free tickets."

"Be wary," Mr. Stott said. "I doubt much inside will be free."

"Should we still go?" Pigeon asked.

"Up to you," Mr. Stott said. "No magical operatives or magicians can enter. We cannot be separated from our magic, and the lair is sealed against our powers. I've tried to see inside, but to no avail."

"You need us to go in," Nate said.

"I wouldn't encourage it," Mr. Stott said. "I'm convinced the carnival is dangerous. But if you end up going, I'd love a report."

"We'll do some spying for you," Summer assured him.

"Carefully though," Mr. Stott said. "We don't want you joining the ranks of those who have vanished."

Nate tipped his glass back, swallowing the last of the banana drink. He wiped his lips. "We also don't want the carnival to kidnap people while we do nothing. If they're up to no good, we should monitor the situation. Ignoring evil lets the bad guys carry out their plans."

"I would appreciate anything you can learn," Mr. Stott said. "So would John. But we will have no way to help you if things go sideways."

"We'll watch out for each other," Summer said.

"Can I go too?" Lindy asked.

"Absolutely not," Mr. Stott said.

"I'm not going to turn back into an evil old lady," Lindy said. "I don't even remember being her."

"That isn't the main problem," Mr. Stott said.

"Then how come I can't go?" Lindy challenged.

"Their parents have no idea how dangerous this could get," Mr. Stott replied. "Your dad does."

CHAPTER FOUR

PARADE

The wooden railing of the boardwalk creaked as Nate leaned against it. The buildings along Main Street were designed to replicate an old western town. Raised wooden sidewalks and barrels as trash cans lined the street. He stood in front of the Main Street General Store beside Summer, Trevor, and Pigeon. Other onlookers lined both sides of the street, two or three deep in some places.

"What's worse than a parade?" Nate asked.

"Tell us," Summer said.

"Waiting for a parade to start," Nate said. "Early on a Saturday morning." He looked up and down the street. "I can't believe so many people came."

"This carnival has been heavily advertised," Pigeon said, rubbing sunblock onto his forehead. "It will draw visitors from all over the Bay Area."

"The Foster Child has been pushing it hard," Trevor said. "Not that I follow him."

"He better throw me extra candy," Nate grumbled.

"Parades can be fun," Summer said. "You don't know what's going to come next."

"Local beauty queens waving from fancy cars," Nate said. "Or a marching band. Maybe a float."

"This is a carnival parade," Pigeon said. "There could be animals."

"Try not to freak out if there is an orangutan," Nate said.

"I'm worried there will be clowns," Trevor said.

"I hope not," Pigeon muttered somberly.

"Why is everyone scared of clowns?" Nate asked. "They're weird and funny."

"Clowns are a disturbing kind of funny," Pigeon said. "Their happiness is contrived. It's all paint and giggles. You never know when they'll snap."

"When was the last time you saw a nice clown?" Trevor added. "They're all fighting Batman or living in sewers."

"I don't mind clowns," Summer said. "They're kind of corny, though."

"Aren't clowns more for circuses than carnivals?" Nate asked.

"This carnival has a big top," Trevor said.

"Sounds like clown habitat to me," Pigeon said.

The rumble of a huge drum sounded in the distance. After a brief pause, another enormous boom followed. Then another, like the footfalls of an approaching giant. Each beat thrummed with deep vibrations that Nate felt in his chest.

The bystanders had all gone quiet. Somewhere above them, a crow cawed.

A huge clockwork elephant lumbered into view down the street. Sudden, urgent percussion filled the gaps between the steady booms. The gilded elephant plodded forward, its exterior built like an ornate cage, leaving the internal gears and cogs visible.

"No way," Nate said. "How big is their budget?"

"Magicians," Pigeon muttered. "Remember, the carnival is a lair."

Four people in metallic-colored bodysuits moved through the interior of the elephant, working levers and turning cranks, apparently powering and controlling the bizarre creation. They climbed from one internal platform to another, pulling chains and pumping pedals to make sprockets rotate and belts whir. The elephant's bejeweled head tilted back, and the trunk extended skyward, trumpeting brassily.

The mechanical pachyderm pulled a sleek wagon holding a colossal drum. A woman in a dressy tweed suit operated a small crane that swung a wrecking ball to produce the deepest thrums. A variety of other drummers in the wagon pounded out the rest of the percussion on kettle drums, snare drums, tambors, bongos, and cymbals.

"You have to admit that is cool," Summer said as the clockwork elephant approached.

"It's impressive," Nate agreed.

"Looks like four people are working the elephant," Trevor said. "We have to find a way to take it for a joyride!"

Behind the wagon came figures on towering stilts. One

looked like Uncle Sam, his red-and-white-striped pants descending all the way to the street. There was also a police officer, a firefighter, and the Statue of Liberty. Behind them came others on stilts doing tricks with enormous yo-yos. At the rear was a fake donkey with four superlong legs. Nate figured there were two people inside the donkey, rather than one individual with stilts on hands and feet.

Next came a procession of performers in vibrant and colorful costumes.

Nate watched a woman tilt her head back and slide a long, slender sword into her mouth to the hilt. She had close-cropped hair and a studded leather vest that bared her toned, tattooed arms.

Another woman held aloft handfuls of writhing snakes, some of them hooded like cobras.

Jugglers in motley tossed rings, balls, and blades into the air, some working in groups to keep elaborate patterns of thrown objects from touching the ground.

Three bare-chested Middle-Eastern men in shimmering pants blew geysers of fire from their lips.

A white-faced mime seemed to ascend four or five invisible steps at a time before dropping back to the street.

A family of acrobats in skintight apparel did numerous flips and tricks on a large, rolling trampoline. One of the sons looked barely older than Nate, and one of the daughters, her hair in a tight little bun, looked a bit younger. Other acrobats balanced atop balls or traveled inside of rolling hoops.

A slender contortionist being pulled on a platform somehow folded herself down into a clear cube no taller than her knees.

A long, bargelike float followed, hauled by eight live camels. The float featured numerous animals on platforms of different heights, including several monkeys, a crocodile, a python, an emu, an ostrich, several chimpanzees, a gorilla, a black bear, a warthog, and, in a cage at the apex, a magnificent lion with golden fur and a thick, dark mane.

"How do they get away with exploiting these animals for entertainment?" Summer asked.

"At least they look healthy," Nate said.

The lion growled and heaved against the side of his cage, making the whole enclosure rattle. It roared, showing huge teeth.

"That sound made my heart stop," Pigeon said.

The lion slammed against the cage again, and it fell apart, bars clanging as they toppled. Onlookers screamed as the lion bounded down from the float. The bear and gorilla vaulted off the float as well.

Mothers snatched their children, pulling them away from the street.

Nate was about to retreat into the general store when the wild animals came to a stop. The bear, lion, and gorilla took off their heads, revealing smiling people inside the shaggy costumes.

The lion was phony. The bear and the gorilla too. Could the animals have been a mix of costuming and puppetry? Nate could hardly believe it. But just moments earlier, he had seen a strand of saliva connecting the fangs of the lion's gaping mouth!

Nervous laughter percolated through the crowd. Frightened bystanders who had begun to retreat returned to their places at the roadside. Others kept their distance. Some of the parents looked disgruntled.

"Not cool," Trevor said. "The lion was fake, but what happened in my underwear was real."

By the time the lion, bear, and gorilla had resumed their positions, the float had passed by the general store. Workers reassembled the lion's cage. Nate could not believe how realistic the animals looked once the costumes were in place again.

A tiny car came careening down the road behind the float, honking repeatedly, some two-door model Nate had never seen, maybe from Europe. The absurd little vehicle went fast, making looping turns, doing doughnuts, and sometimes driving against the flow of the parade. At last, the car screeched to a stop in the middle of the street a few yards beyond where Nate and his friends stood, the driver hidden behind tinted windows.

The passenger window rolled down, and a tiny clown tumbled out. Then the door flung open, and a large clown was shoved to the street. He did a somersault and sprang to his feet. The driver's door opened, and more clowns began spilling from that side as well.

"No!" Trevor cried. "I should have worn a diaper!"

Nate watched in amazement as clowns continued to pour from the undersized vehicle. The trunk opened, and a sinister clown with purple makeup and long limbs came slinking out. An extremely tall clown rose from the sunroof and exited. More than a dozen clowns emerged! No, two dozen! Finally, a bulky leg protruded from the passenger door, barely fitting through. A tremendously fat clown followed the hefty appendage, the automobile rocking as he extricated himself.

Clowns scampered up and down the street, male and female, tall and short, happy and sad. One clown holding a towering cake staggered around, trying to keep the dessert from toppling. A slouching sad clown sobbed into his spotted handkerchief as others teased him. Three female clowns worked together with hoops and string to blow enormous bubbles.

The purple-faced clown prowled around in his snug, pinstriped suit, occasionally tripping other clowns. He set a bear trap in the street that clamped shut on another clown's oversized foot, leaving the victim hopping and waving both arms as he tried to shake off the clamp. The purple-faced clown approached the crowd, offering a bouquet of flowers to onlookers only to hastily withdraw the gift when someone reached for it.

Clowns stumbled over one another, provoking slapstick fistfights. The tallest clown ran in terror from a tiny poodle that chased him relentlessly. Pies were thrown. Horns brayed. Water spurted. Buckets of glitter were hurled into the crowd.

The clown with the multitiered cake collided with the fat clown, leaving both smeared with great clumps of frosting. A couple of kids darted into the street to snatch hunks of the fallen cake.

Nate's gaze returned in puzzlement to the little car. How had all the clowns fit in there? There must be a tunnel under the road, with a trapdoor or something that led into the car. Maybe a manhole? There was simply no way this small army of clowns had fit in the undersized vehicle.

Unless they used actual magic. He had to remember magicians were involved with the carnival, so legitimate enchantments were an option.

Chaotic antics complete, the clowns piled back into the little car, shoving, jostling, and wiggling their backsides. When the doors closed, the car zigzagged farther down the parade route, occasionally doubling back and fishtailing like before.

"Is it over?" Trevor asked, peering through his fingers. "I may need therapy."

"That was impossible," Summer said. "They're definitely using real magic."

"The stunt with animals too," Pigeon chimed in. "Nobody could fake it that well."

Outcries of astonishment from surrounding bystanders drew their attention back to the parade.

A muscular mountain of a man took halting steps forward, supporting a group of acrobats on his shoulders. They fanned out above him, arms and legs interlocked to form a scaffolding of humanity higher than the surrounding rooftops. The man at the base strode purposefully forward, eyes bulging, chest heaving, curly brown hair soaked with perspiration.

Nate grinned. "I have a hunch that guy likes parades even less than I do."

"He's supporting nine people," Pigeon said. "How does he keep going?"

"This is an amazing parade," Summer said.

Nate nodded. "It's unbelievable. Supernatural. Somebody in this carnival has a lot of power."

Another float trundled into view, built to resemble a three-masted sailing ship. Aerialists swung on ropes, ribbons, and trapezes around and between the tall poles, performing shocking feats of dexterity. Tightropes connected the tops of the masts, where daredevils balanced, jumped, and spun.

"There's Zac," Summer exclaimed, pointing.

Zac Foster sat on a raised seat at the stern of the maritime float, hurling candy to the spectators.

"Hey, Zac!" Trevor called, waving both hands over his head.

Zac saw him and pointed, then started heaving candy in their direction. Nearby people scrambled to share in the bounty, but Nate and his friends grabbed enough to fill their pockets before the ship of aerialists glided out of range.

"He kept his promise," Trevor said, holding up a pack of sour gummy frogs. "This is decent candy. And a good variety. Not just cheap peppermints and garbage lollipops."

"Wait, I like lollipops," Pigeon said.

After the ship came a group of bizarre cyclists. Some teetered on tall unicycles. A few rode old-fashioned bicycles with huge front tires. Several piloted strange contraptions that had six or eight or even ten wheels. One long bike featured six riders pedaling together. Many of the riders did tricks, perching on the handlebars or making the bicycles twirl, hop, or glide along on the rear wheel.

A small float crept forward featuring a man playing a white grand piano. Next to him, a woman sang opera, her voice so pure and powerful that Nate wondered for the first time if he should pay more attention to that style of music.

A group of people in red vests and yellow pants did tricks on pogo sticks and jumping stilts. Three clowns traveled down the street on a float designed as a small boat, two rowing while the other caught elaborate fish made of paper and sequins.

Another float came along covered in mirrors and slides. "Find Yourself in the Fun House" a banner across the top invited. The mirrors were positioned so that Nate saw many versions of himself, many grotesquely warped, as the float passed.

Finally, a huge catcher's mitt wheeled by on the bed of a long truck, the glove facing the back of the parade. After a long gap, a platoon of life-sized toy soldiers marched woodenly down the street in formation, keys slowly turning in their backs. Each held a heavy black rifle against its right shoulder.

Behind the soldiers rolled a colossal black cannon mounted on a carriage, at least two stories tall, the barrel longer than any of the buildings bordering the street. A man in a tuxedo sat astride a saddle toward the end of the cannon tube, yelling through a megaphone.

"Thank you for attending the parade," the man called. "This is but a sample of the wonders that await inside the Dreams and Screams International Carnival. Our ticket booths open for the first time at the conclusion of the parade. Don't miss the excitement of opening day! Come one, come all, to the biggest little carnival on Earth!"

In unison, the toy soldiers lifted their firearms to the sky, blasting spheres that burst overhead and trickled back to the ground as pink gas that smelled like bubble gum.

Nate rubbed his skin, trying to wipe away the subtle stickiness of the pink mist. He covered his nose, breathing through his fingers just in case.

With a seismic boom, the cannon fired, and a man in a

motorcycle helmet and white jumpsuit shot into the air, traveling in a long arc before landing on his back in the catcher's mitt.

"That was the best parade I've ever seen," Summer enthused.

"And going with Zac gets us into the carnival free," Trevor said.

"Don't forget it's all a trap," Nate reminded them. "This whole festival is a spiderweb waiting for flies. A magician is running this carnival and using the parade to lure victims."

"Do you think the orangutan Mr. Stott told us about was a fake?" Pigeon asked. "Like the lion?"

"Maybe," Trevor said. "Those clowns were real though."

"Did the clown rowboat have wheels under it?" Summer asked.

"It might have just been magical," Nate said.

"Let's get up to the fairgrounds to meet Zac," Trevor said.

Much of the crowd was following the cannon, walking up Main Street as an ever-growing tail to the parade. Judging by the crowd, the carnival would not want for customers today.

"Should we follow them?" Summer asked.

"That would be like deliberately driving in traffic," Nate said. "If we cut across town on our bikes, we can get there before Zac."

"Do you think the guy on the cannon was the magician?" Pigeon asked.

"The magicians I know almost never leave their lairs," Nate said. "I doubt we've seen the person who runs everything."

"Something tells me we will though, before we're done," Trevor said. "Please let it not be a clown."

CHAPTER FIVE

EARLY ADMISSION

John Dart stepped out from behind a Dumpster, barely leaving Nate enough space for him to hit the brakes. Summer, Trevor, and Pigeon skidded to a stop beside him. The kids had been traveling along a narrow road away from Main Street when John appeared. Despite the warm weather, he wore a gray trench coat.

"Thanks for the heart attack," Nate said. "Good thing I have fast reflexes."

"How did you like the parade?" John asked.

"We got free candy," Trevor said.

John gave a sniff. "Haven't you gotten into trouble that way before?"

"It wasn't magical candy this time," Pigeon clarified.

"I collected a sample of that bubblegum gas," John said. "It makes me suspicious."

"Could they have been drugging us?" Nate asked.

John shrugged. "If not, it was a wasted opportunity. You kids are heading to the carnival?"

"Yes," Summer said.

"Was that always the plan?" John asked. "Or did the idea strike after breathing the gas?"

"We were planning on it," Pigeon said. "A friend got us free tickets."

John raised his thick eyebrows. "How did you meet this generous friend?"

"He's a kid at school," Trevor said. "Kind of an Internet sensation."

"The Foster kid?" John asked. "The one chucking candy from the back of the ship?"

"That's him," Nate said.

John shook his head. "That kid is misguided to promote this carnival, but I suspect it's through ignorance rather than malice. Watch your backs in there. I won't be able to help you."

"Is there anything specific you want us to watch out for?" Nate asked.

"I want to hear that you successfully exited," John said. "The rest is gravy. Listen, I have another reason for stopping you." He reached into his pocket and pulled out a handful of crackers. "Bestial Biscuits."

"Birds?" Summer asked, looking at the shape of the crackers.

"Four falcons," John said. "Like your club name."

"You want us to become Blue Falcons?" Nate asked.

"The biscuits will enable you to perform some aerial re-con," John said. "I want to check how high the magical barrier extends. Some don't shield against entry from above, especially when protecting such a large area. See if you can fly inside. I'll get your bikes up to the parking lot."

"If we find a way through the barrier, would you parachute in?" Pigeon asked.

"Absolutely," John replied. He distributed the crackers to the kids.

"How do we switch back to human form?" Trevor asked. "I don't want to get stuck as a falcon and miss the carnival."

"The fastest way is to hold your breath until you can't stand it," John said. "But don't try that while flying."

"Is it hard to fly?" Pigeon asked.

"Helps if you're a bird," John said.

"I mean, do you have any tips?" Pigeon asked.

"Should be no problem for a kid with your name," John said. "I'm teasing. My understanding is it should be simple. Just follow your instincts once in falcon form."

"What if my instincts are to walk?" Pigeon asked.

"Then I'll carry you," John promised.

"Will our clothes stay with us?" Summer checked.

"With these biscuits, yes," John said. "Hidden until you change back into humans. All part of the package."

Nate ate his cracker in one bite. Immediately, he felt his body compress. He crouched as his head shrank and his nose and mouth combined into a beak. Hands and arms reformed into wings, and his legs became spindly, tipped with talons.

Looking up at John, he marveled at the clarity of his vision, especially for things far away. It was as if he had needed glasses all his life but never knew it. Did all birds see this sharply?

Nate's friends were all falcons now. Pigeon shifted carefully from one claw to the other. Trevor puffed out his chest and spread his feathers.

"I'm suddenly hungry for rabbit," Trevor said.

"Really?" Pigeon asked.

"He's joking," Summer said.

"Get into the air," John said. "Don't fly directly at the carnival barrier. You don't want to hit it head-on at high speed."

"We'll be smart," Summer assured him, extending one wing experimentally.

"Shouldn't Nate say something awesome?" Pigeon asked. "You know, like, 'Blue Falcons, take flight!'"

"You beat me to it," Nate said. "Let's go!"

Nate hopped forward and started flapping his wings. John had been right—in this state, flying was instinctive. He powered upward, soared for a moment, then started beating his wings again to gain altitude. He had felt ungainly on the ground, but now that he was airborne, the form of a falcon made perfect sense.

"This is amazing," Summer said, gliding beside Nate.

"It's cool we can still talk," Nate said.

"Magic has its advantages," Summer said, doing a little dive before climbing higher.

As Nate increased his altitude, he became even more impressed with his eyesight. It was like having binoculars that focused automatically. Colson sprawled out below him. As he studied the streets, yards, and rooftops, he saw nuances of color he had never noticed before.

Colson was uncommonly still, other than the steady crawl of the parade procession toward the fairgrounds. The ghostly trill of an operatic voice soaring above a throbbing percussion echoed from below.

Finding an updraft, Nate banked in a wide arc toward the carnival. Everything had been reduced to toy size—the bright tents, the food stands, the carousel, the humps of the white-washed wooden roller coaster. Was this how Rocco viewed the world? Being a bird definitely had its perks.

As Nate approached the outskirts of the carnival, he slowed and changed his trajectory so he wouldn't fly straight into the barrier. He could still see the carnival from an angle, but soon he would be over the edge of it.

"Be careful," Trevor said from above. His feathers looked ruffled. "The barrier isn't just a wall. It gives you a jolt like an electric fence."

"Good to know," Nate said. "I'll try higher up."

"We're pretty high," Trevor said. "But sure, give it a shot. Brace yourself though."

Nate flew away from the carnival, working to gain more altitude. The barrier had to have a limit, right? Unless it curved like a dome. How high could it extend? To outer space? That seemed ridiculous.

Nate climbed and climbed, pushing his wings for more strength. He used air currents to his advantage as much as possible, but he found that gaining altitude quickly was mostly about muscling upward. It got lonelier and quieter the higher he went. The whistling of the wind became the only sound. Cars shrank to the size of ants, and the carousel looked like a dime on the ground. Below him, Summer and Trevor descended in lazy spirals, while Pigeon glided to the far side of the fairgrounds.

Nate once again approached the outer limits of the carnival, tensed for possible impact. His wing tip brushed something invisible but solid, and electricity coursed through his body. Swerving away, he glided until he felt steady, then shortened his wings and dove.

Maybe the barrier really did reach to outer space.

Nate circled downward, watching his shadow grow as he neared the ground. He watched as the front of the parade reached the carnival parking lot. When Nate landed, the float with the animals was just disappearing behind a fence into a back lot staging area, with the rest of the parade in tow.

Nate alighted beside a hedge, grateful for the cover. He held his breath until he transformed back into his normal shape. He flexed his fingers and kicked his legs, trying to regain the feel of his actual body. He seemed big and clumsy compared to a falcon, but it didn't take long before he was comfortable again.

Nate caught up with Trevor, Summer, and Pigeon, who had all apparently landed before him and had gathered by the carnival fence.

"I hit the barrier even when I went super high," Nate said.

"It's bad news for John," Summer said. "But the experience of flying was incredible."

Trevor and Pigeon waved at Zac when the ship of aerialists

pulled into the parking lot. Zac signaled that he was out of candy and pointed to where they should wait for him. The float covered in mirrors was gliding into the staging area when Zac emerged from a side door.

Zac pointed at the mirrored float. "Can you imagine if that thing crashed? Centuries of bad luck!"

"Hi, Zac," Summer called.

"That was the most nerve-wracking parade ever," Zac said as he approached. "I kept expecting people to fall to their deaths. How do they hang on to those ropes for so long? My arms are tired just from throwing candy."

"Thanks for hitting us with so much," Trevor said.

"I'm glad you got some," Zac said. "People turn into piranhas when free candy is involved."

"Is Benji coming?" Summer asked.

Zac shook his head. "His family went out of town this weekend. It's just us five. Are you hyped for the carnival?"

"Who wouldn't be, after that parade?" Pigeon said.

"The whole production was more polished than I expected," Zac said. "I've never seen anything more steampunk than that mechanical elephant. I took so many selfies with it!"

"There were lots of surprises," Nate said.

"When can we go inside?" Trevor asked.

"Whenever we want," Zac replied. "The carnival won't officially open until thirty minutes after the parade ends. A lot of the people in the parade need to turn around and help run the attractions. But my access gets us in early."

"Gotta love that VIP treatment," Trevor said.

"Don't forget that I have to leave today with enough material for a video," Zac said.

"What do you have in mind?" Summer asked.

"I like to improvise," Zac said. "It's harder with a plan— you have to make everything fit together, and it starts feeling phony." He patted Summer's shoulder. "We'll figure it out once we're inside."

"Totally winging a big assignment would freak me out," Pigeon said.

Zac shrugged. "People like my weird reactions to stuff. That happens best if I stay in the moment. Low structure, high authenticity. Let's go inside. It's about to get busy out here."

The gigantic cannon was pulling into the parking lot followed by a horde of people. Zac put on a Giants baseball cap and sunglasses.

"You're going incognito," Summer said.

"It's easier to bounce back from hat hair than to face a crowd sometimes," Zac said. "Especially after an event like this parade, where attention is drawn to me."

People were already lining up at the ticket booths even though the windows were not open yet. Extending from either side of the booths was a green fence surrounding the carnival. Nate noticed a variety of signs:

UNLESS YOU ARE THE <u>ACTUAL</u> TARZAN
SHIRT AND SHOES MUST BE WORN AT ALL TIMES

NO OUTSIDE FOOD OR DRINK
WE HAVE TO PAY FOR ALL OF THIS SOMEHOW

NO PETS ALLOWED

SERVICE ANIMALS MUST BE APPROVED
ROBOTS ARE FINE THOUGH

WE RESERVE THE RIGHT TO REPRIMAND
ANY CUSTOMER FOR DISORDERLY CONDUCT
EXPULSIONS RECEIVE NO REFUND

NO OUTSIDE MAGIC
WE HAVE PLENTY FOR ALL
MAGIC YOU BRING IN WILL BE NEUTRALIZED

ALL DREAMS SPARKED BY THIS EXPERIENCE
BECOME THE PROPERTY OF
THE DREAMS AND SCREAMS INTERNATIONAL CARNIVAL
DREAM BIG!

"Lots of rules," Nate said. He glanced at Zac. "I hope you don't have any outside magic."

"I bring the magic everywhere I go," Zac said with a grin. "My sponsors count on it."

Nate wondered if entering the carnival would neutralize the magical candy he carried.

Zac bypassed the ticket booths, leading Nate and his friends to a private gate where a female security guard stood. Zac flashed a pass and pointed to his friends. "These guys are helping me out today."

The guard stepped aside, and Zac led them into the carnival.

A long wooden boardwalk formed a main path away from the entrance, fronted with bright signs to lure customers to play games and buy food. The wooden strip ended at a glittering, two-story carousel where tigers, elk, dolphins, and horses awaited riders. In the distance loomed a towering Ferris wheel, the round side facing them decorated like a spiderweb. In another direction rose the steep slopes of a whitewashed wooden roller coaster.

"First, we need to get tickets and Carnie Coins," Zac said. "You can't buy anything with normal money in here."

"Clever," Nate said. "Like needing tokens at an arcade. Use play money to hide how much actual money is being spent."

"That might be the idea," Zac said, guiding them to an octagonal booth topped by a sign that read Currency Exchange.

A sign beneath it proclaimed:

WE DON'T WANT YOUR MONEY
WE WANT OUR MONEY

Zac approached one of the windows and showed his pass.

The older man behind the glass leaned forward. "Good morning, Mr. Foster," he said. "You and your guests are entitled to one hundred tickets and ten Carnie Coins each."

"What's the difference between tickets and coins?" Pigeon asked.

The man behind the window glanced his way. "Tickets are for food, games, and attractions. Carnie Coins are for vending machines and souvenirs. There may be a few loopholes and special circumstances. Pay attention to the fine print. You'll get the hang of it."

"Thanks," Zac said, accepting a long strand of tickets and a handful of coins.

The orange tickets were linked by perforations and featured an image of a Ferris wheel on the front with a complex pattern on the back. Each ticket had a sequential eight-digit number printed along the bottom. The golden coins had a clown face on one side and the back of the clown's balding head on the other.

Zac distributed the tickets and coins to the group as they walked a few steps away from the Currency Exchange. "This should be enough for a good day. The public gets fifty tickets and five coins with a standard admission. Technically, you guys don't get more today, but I can go back for as many as I want, and there's no rule against sharing, so don't be stingy with your tickets."

"Zac Foster," declared a confident voice from behind them.

Nate turned and saw the man in the tuxedo who had ridden the cannon. With a top hat on his head, he looked dignified and comfortable despite the warmth of the day. Up close, Nate could see that the middle-aged man had a thin, debonair mustache.

"Preston Wilder," Zac replied warmly.

"Thank you for participating in our kickoff event," Preston said. "We look forward to your videos." Turning to the others, he extended a hand. "These must be your friends."

"I bought their love with tickets and coins," Zac said.

Preston flashed a gleaming smile. "That's how it works around here."

"Are you the owner?" Nate asked.

"I'm often mistaken for the owner, especially by kids, but I'm the public face of the establishment," Preston said, straightening his jacket. "Director of publicity. Emcee. Ringmaster. Your host and friend. And you are?"

"Nate. You look kind of like a magician in that outfit." Summer and Trevor glared at him, but Nate kept his attention on Preston.

Preston regarded Nate more seriously. "I may have a trick or two up my sleeve. Lend me a Carnie Coin?"

"Sure," Nate said, handing one over.

Preston set the coin faceup on his open palm. He closed his hand into a fist, then opened it to reveal two coins where one had been. He closed his hand again and opened it to reveal three coins.

"You can keep all three," Preston said. "Unless you want to try for four?"

"I'll try for another," Nate said.

Preston's hand closed, then opened again, revealing four coins. "Keep these or try for five?"

"I'll keep the four," Nate said.

"Fair enough," Preston replied. He dropped the coins into Nate's outstretched hand. "A fourfold increase is a successful investment. Want to know what would have happened if you had tried for five?"

"Sure," Nate said.

"The cost of that information is four Carnie Coins," Preston said. "You're welcome to find out whenever you like."

"I'm good for now," Nate said.

"Can I try?" Trevor asked, holding up a Carnie Coin.

"I prefer not to repeat tricks for the same audience," Preston said. "You kids have a fun day." He flicked the brim of his top hat and winked. "Around these parts, magic is always in the air."

CHAPTER SIX
FIRST IMPRESSIONS

Have you already explored the carnival?" Pigeon asked Zac as Preston walked away.

"Nope," Zac said. "That's what today is all about."

"Here's a map," Trevor said, snatching one from a pile on a shelf outside the Currency Exchange. He unfolded it, and the others huddled around. The top read "Basic Map" and listed the date.

"Where are we now?" Summer asked.

"Here's the entrance," Pigeon said, tapping a spot on the map. "So we must be by that Currency Exchange just inside. At the start of the Grand Boardwalk."

Nate looked at the wooden boardwalk stretching away from them. Beyond the carousel, he could see an orange-and-blue-striped big top, pennants hanging limp in the still air. "Lots of games that way," he said.

"And some attractions," Pigeon said. "Serpent House. Terror Castle. Bumper cars."

"It looks like the boardwalk leads to everything," Summer said. "We have to do the Ferris wheel."

"And the roller coaster," Trevor said.

"I'm impressed they have a roller coaster," Nate said. "I hope it holds together. Seems elaborate for a traveling carnival."

"This carnival is well produced compared to most," Zac said. "The rides are less rickety. More actual construction."

Nate noticed the phrase "more to come" was repeated around the edges of the map. He pointed it out. "How much more do you think they'll add?"

"Preston told me that when the carnival does well, they expand," Zac said. "If they underperform, they sometimes shrink it down or even close the run early."

"How long are they scheduled to be here?" Summer asked.

"Two weeks, I think," Zac said.

"Let's check out the boardwalk," Nate said.

They passed a game where participants could try to throw rings around bottle necks, and one where players could try to land Ping-Pong balls into bowls floating in a pool. Another game challenged competitors to pound a target with a mallet and launch a weight up a tall post to ring a bell. The cinnamon-and-oil smell of churros wafted to them from a passing cart. Nate paused at a game with pyramids of three metal milk bottles stacked on cylindrical pedestals.

"I want to try this one," he said, approaching the counter. "What's the drill?"

The guy behind the counter wore a white button-down shirt and a blue vest and had muttonchop sideburns. "One ball per ticket. Knock off all the bottles with a single throw and you win a prize."

Rows of stuffed cows hung at the side of the stall. Below them were two rows of cowbells in various colors and numerous keys on pegs.

"Are those the prizes?" Nate asked.

The man nodded.

"What are the keys for?"

"Beats me," the man replied with a wink. "You choose the prize."

Nate eyed the pyramids of bottles. They weren't too far from the counter. He was almost sure he could make contact.

"Okay," Nate said, tearing off a ticket and setting it on the counter. "I'll take one ball."

The man smiled and handed Nate a baseball, then brushed the ticket into his palm. The man raised his voice. "This will be the first throw in Colson!"

"Mind if I film this?" Zac asked Nate, pulling out his phone. "If I end up using any footage with you guys, I'll need you and a parent to sign consent forms."

"It's fine with me," Nate said.

Pigeon pulled Nate a couple of steps away and whispered. "I did some research last night. For three bottles, you want to hit them hard and low, between the bottom bottles."

Nate took out a stick of Peak Performance and put it in his mouth. If the gum was working, he should be able to waltz through these games, winning prizes with every try. As he chewed, the gum tasted right, but there was no surge of energy and focus.

Nate stepped back up to the counter, hefting the baseball. It seemed to be standard weight. He threw it hard at a tidy stack of bottles and hit the bottom left bottle squarely. It went flying, and the top bottle fell and bounced off the pedestal, but the bottom right bottle remained upright.

"Nice try," Zac narrated. "Too bad one of the bottles was nailed down."

The worker with the muttonchops lifted the remaining bottle to show there was no trickery, then swiftly rebuilt the pyramid. "Try again?"

"One more," Nate said, ripping another ticket from his strand.

His next throw hit the center of the pyramid, smacking all three bottles. The top bottle flew off, and though the bottom two tipped over, both remained on the pedestal.

"Ouch, good throw, but these bottles are clearly trained," Zac narrated.

Nate glanced at Zac. "Forget baseballs. I need a hand grenade."

"Almost had it that time," the worker said. "Go again?"

"Maybe later," Nate said, moving away from the counter.

"No help from the gum?" Summer whispered.

"It's just gum here," Nate replied quietly. "No added benefits."

From the entrance to the carnival came the sound of a crowd chanting together. "Ten . . . nine . . . eight . . ."

"Sounds like the gates are about to open," Zac said,

turning off his video and putting on his sunglasses. "Better be incognito from here on out."

The crowd continued, "Three . . . two . . . one!" People cheered, and then customers began flowing into the carnival down the main boardwalk.

"Let's head to the Demolition Derby," Zac proposed, hustling toward the bumper cars. Nate and the others followed. They snaked between the railings where the line would normally form and went to the front.

"Three tickets," said the teenage girl managing the ride. A nearby sign confirmed her request. They each handed over three tickets and then went out onto the metallic floor to choose their vehicle. A thick rubber bumper encircled each car, and a pole stretched up to the metallic grate overhead.

A sign on the wall proclaimed

STAY IN YOUR CAR
OR FACE DEATH BY ELECTROCUTION

There were about thirty vehicles. Nate and his friends had arrived first at the attraction, so they had their pick.

"Red is fastest," Zac asserted, claiming a red car. Summer and Trevor grabbed red cars as well. Pigeon went with shiny black, and Nate chose a blue car with some scratches on the hood.

"Hold on, folks," the teenage girl said. "I'll start the ride when we have more drivers."

"My car has a coin slot," Summer said.

"Mine too," Pigeon replied.

Nate checked, and next to his steering wheel was a slot for coins.

"I think they all have them," Zac said. "Hey, ride lady, what happens if I put in a coin?"

"It costs a coin to find out," she said.

"This ride doesn't require tickets *and* coins, does it?" Trevor checked.

"The cars will run without coins," the teenage girl said.

A line had formed for the ride, and several more drivers surrendered tickets and chose their vehicles.

Nate checked his controls. There was a gas pedal and a steering wheel. No brake. He fruitlessly pumped the gas pedal, eager for the ride to begin.

Finally, with about half of the cars occupied and the line empty, the teenage girl closed the gate and went to a microphone. "Please stay in your vehicle with your seat belt fastened at all times. The floor and ceiling are electric, so you could get fried if you jump out while the ride is active. Turn the steering wheel all the way to one side to reverse. No bumping other cars. Just kidding. Crash as much as you want."

She paced around the floor, checking seat belts, then crossed to a control panel. The ride hummed to life.

Suddenly pressing the gas pedal made Nate's car jerk forward. He grinned at the quick acceleration. He steered around a kid he didn't know then targeted Summer, bumping into her side. The bumpers had quite a bit of springiness, making the impact less jarring than expected, but with more recoil.

Nate turned away and started tracking Trevor when Zac came zooming at him at twice the speed of the other cars.

Nate tried to dodge, but Zac's car was too fast. After the jolting impact, Zac's car steadily pushed Nate's car sideways.

"Is red really faster?" Nate called in frustration.

"With a coin it is," Zac said, turning away to barrel toward Pigeon.

After a brief hesitation, Nate inserted one of his Carnie Coins into the slot. When he hit the gas again, his car lurched forward and quickly reached a much greater top speed. He caught up to Trevor and rear-ended him. Trevor's head whipped back. Though Trevor had been going at full speed, Nate's car was that much faster.

"Nate," Zac called from the far side of the area. "Let's play chicken."

"You're on," Nate said.

They started zooming toward each other. The two coin-enhanced bumper cars rapidly closed the distance. Nate wasn't going to swerve away, so he braced for the inevitable collision, hoping the designers wouldn't let the cars go fast enough for riders to hurt one another.

Zac didn't swerve either, and the cars crashed head-to-head at maximum speed. Nate heaved forward against his seat belt, roughly jarred as the strap dug into him. The cars rebounded several feet.

"Awesome," Zac gushed, his face red.

Soon Nate, Summer, Trevor, Zac, and Pigeon had all used coins to increase their speed. A few other drivers went for it as well. With so many zippy cars, the driving experience became more complicated. The non-enhanced vehicles seemed more like obstacles than actual participants.

Nate found the impacts jolting, especially when he got blindsided. He was delighted to discover he could go almost as fast in reverse as he could zoom forward. When the power quit and his car coasted to a stop, he wished the ride would have gone on longer.

Reluctantly, Nate exited with the others. Outside the ride, the carnival was filling up. Crowds strolled the boardwalk, trying out games and getting in line for attractions. New patrons steadily streamed in from the entrance. The parade had definitely drawn a crowd of paying customers.

"Nobody loves you," a girl with pigtails called to Zac.

"Hey, check it out—Foster Kid," a teenage boy said.

"Nobody loves me," the boy next to him repeated Zac's catchphrase.

Zac waved at them and smiled, walking purposefully forward.

"Terror Castle?" Trevor asked. They shifted in that direction.

The haunted house was set back from the game stalls, with a switchback line leading up to a two-story stronghold. A few mechanical crows with glowing red eyes perched on the battlements, occasionally cocking a head, cawing, or jerkily flapping their wings. The switchbacks were less than halfway full, so Nate and the others hurried through the empty lanes until they caught up to the actual line.

"Nobody loves you," called a kid a couple of switchbacks ahead of them.

Zac waved at the kid. "Catchphrases are bad ideas," he murmured. "Every stranger says it like they're the first one to think of it, so you end up hearing the same comment over and over. Sometimes they even want me to say it. If it were only one person, no big deal, but it gets old, time after time, day after day."

"It's why you get the big bucks," Nate said.

"I guess," Zac said with a wink.

Shutters on the second story of the castle opened, revealing a vampire. After those shutters closed, another set opened, revealing a mangy werewolf.

"That werewolf has seen better days," Zac said. "Chuck E. Cheese kicked him out of the band, so he turned to a life of horror."

"Not much is scarier than sketchy animatronics," Nate said.

"Like *Five Nights at Freddy's*," Summer added.

In other windows, Frankenstein's monster appeared, as did a mummy. The standard movie monsters were apparently haunting the stronghold.

"This looks like a dark ride," Pigeon said.

"Duh," Trevor said. "'Terror' is in the name."

"Not just dark as in spooky," Pigeon said. "In theme park lingo, a dark ride is an attraction that takes you on a tour through an interior space. Looks like the car seats four."

Up ahead, just past the open front wall of the castle, Nate could see passengers embarking and disembarking from the ride. The boxy cars had two seats in the front and two behind, with lap bars to keep the riders in place. The cars came and went fairly quickly, which kept the line moving.

Zac held up his phone and started recording selfie-style.

"We are currently at the Terror Castle," Zac announced. "Who thinks they can get through this ride without a jump scare?" His hand was already raised.

"I'll try," Nate said, putting his hand up. Summer and Trevor raised their hands as well.

Pigeon kept his hands down. "Just keeping it real. I could probably do it if we ride again."

"Anyone could do it on a second try," Zac said. "All right, we'll all be watching each other and ourselves, but if something makes you flinch or jump, you're out. Honor system rules."

When they got to the front, they each handed over six tickets. Zac split off with Summer into one car. Nate and Pigeon sat in the front of the next one, with Trevor behind them. Nate scanned the vehicle for a coin slot but didn't see one.

The car trundled forward into the ride, picking up the pace as it swung around a corner. They moved down the dismal hall of a dungeon. The air was musty and humid, and a dripping ceiling created a surprisingly authentic atmosphere. On the left side, behind bars, three mannequins were being tortured—one stretched on a rack, another strapped to a wheel where a tormentor prodded him, and the last squirmed beneath a pendulum blade. On the opposite side, cell doors rattled and clanked as inmates screamed.

Next, they entered a gothic laboratory where a harried animatronic scientist was trying to electrify a humanoid monster. The scientist stood at a control panel while fake lightning strobed through the windows. A blinding light flashed, accompanied by immediate thunder, and the monster sat up and growled.

"I already jumped," Pigeon said.

"Not me," Nate replied.

The car voyaged into a cemetery, winding among gravestones and tombs. Dry-ice fog swirled over the ground. From somewhere in the distance came the faint whistling of an off-pitch tune. Suddenly an obelisk tipped and fell in their path. The car swerved, barely avoiding it. From behind them came a loud, sudden howl, and Nate had to admit that he jumped.

As they came around a large tomb, an animatronic scene came into view—two gravediggers trying to stake a vampire. The three dimly lit figures repeated the same motions, locked in an eternal struggle.

Up ahead, the side of a pyramid came into view, and the car passed down a hallway where skittering scarabs were projected onto the wall. They reached a burial chamber full of golden treasure and big, glassy jewels. A groaning mummy emerged from a sarcophagus and came toward their vehicle.

Nate noticed other passages branching away from the burial chamber. He wondered how long those hallways kept up the illusion that they were inside a pyramid before they dead-ended into storage rooms full of brooms. Nate felt an urge to explore them.

The car progressed from the pyramid into a dark hall. Moans and gibbering became the soundtrack, and an occasional ghost swished past, projected onto a filmy screen. As the moans faded, the hall became perfectly dark.

Then a pair of headlights appeared in front of them,

accompanied by a truck horn. Nate jumped, and so did Pigeon beside him. Wind blasted in their faces well beyond what their speed should have generated, and the car veered to miss the headlights.

Then suddenly the ride was over. Summer and Zac were disembarking from their vehicle, and after a pause, the lap bars released on the car with Nate, Pigeon, and Trevor.

"Did anybody make it without a jump scare?" Zac asked, recording.

"Not me," Trevor said.

"Me neither," Nate admitted.

"I jumped multiple times," Zac said. "Especially at the end. Pretty great ride. Better than I would expect at a traveling carnival."

Nate nodded. It might be Zac's job to help sell people on the carnival, but he was also right. Nothing on the ride had looked totally real, but it had some good scares, and the scenery was way better than he had expected. The set up and take down of such an elaborate ride had to be a pain.

"In conclusion," Zac narrated to his phone, "some guys almost tortured me, a vampire tried to bite me, a werewolf wanted to devour me, and a mummy chased me down. Once again, nobody loves me." He stopped recording.

"I thought you were bugged by the catchphrase," Nate said.

"I am," Zac said. "But it's easier to say it in a clip than to hear it all the time. Like it or not, it's how I'm branded. Small price to pay if it helps me make money from my videos."

CHAPTER SEVEN
FORTUNE WAGON

Later that evening, Nate sat at a round table under a big umbrella, picking apart half a roasted chicken with plastic utensils. Trevor and Zac had opted for the giant turkey leg, which they ate with their fingers, their lips glistening with grease. Summer and Pigeon had gone in together on a one-pound hamburger the size of a Frisbee. Nate had planned to drink the free water the eatery provided, but Zac coughed up ten tickets for a big bottle of root beer they were all sharing.

Zac set down his half-eaten turkey leg and wiped his hands and mouth with paper napkins. "That does it for me today. I got the footage I need. I'll bring the media releases to school on Monday, if that works."

"You got everything you need?" Nate asked.

"Plenty," Zac said. "My dad and I will cut together something tonight. Do any of you want me to get you extra tickets before I go?" He had already provided fifty extra tickets for each of them.

"I better head home too," Trevor said. "It's almost eight."

"How late is the park open?" Nate asked.

"Until eleven," Zac said.

"My parents don't want me out too late," Summer said.

"I want to stay for a bit," Nate said. "I still have a few coins."

"I'll hang out with you," Pigeon said. "Mom said I could be home late tonight."

"Everyone dump your extra tickets on Nate and Pidge," Zac said. "Keep your coins though. I can always get more tickets, but they're stingy with coins—even with me. Today was fun. I'd love to have you back with me any day I'm here making videos. Should be twice a week."

"That would be great," Trevor said.

"Benji will probably join us sometimes," Zac said. "Too many people can get messy, but in this carnival environment, a posse works. I like the variety in this group. Nate, are you sure you don't need more tickets?"

Nate looked at the remnants he and Pigeon had inherited. "Looks like we have around twenty. That should work. I mainly just want to look around."

"You'll be all right?" Summer asked. Her eyes locked with Nate's. They hadn't encountered any obvious danger yet, but that could change at any moment.

"Pigeon and I will have a blast," Nate said.

Trevor, Summer, and Zac collected the trash onto trays

and left Nate and Pigeon at the table. Pigeon huddled close so they could talk quietly.

"Have you seen anything supernatural yet?" Nate asked.

"Everything is surprisingly high-quality for a traveling carnival," Pigeon said. "It feels more like a permanent theme park. Except for the non-PC stuff like the performing animals and 'The Hall of Oddities.'"

Nate nodded. They had only looked at the outside of the tent, which displayed posters of a two-headed lizard, a winged pony, an elephant the size of a dog, and a headless chicken that could apparently still walk around.

"I assume you want to stay so we can dig deeper," Pigeon said.

"Yes," Nate said. "Zac is cool, but it's hard to do certain types of investigating with him around. He doesn't know magic is real, and he has ties to the carnival."

"I tried a Moon Rock earlier, just to check," Pigeon mentioned. "It didn't work. Gravity stayed the same."

Nate nodded. "If they are cancelling our candy, we already have proof that something magical is going on."

"Where do you want to look?" Pigeon asked.

Nate thought about the day. They had been on a bunch of rides. At eight tickets, the roller coaster was the most expensive. The Ferris wheel cost six tickets and had taken forever. Average rides like the Tilt-A-Whirl or the rocking ship or the suspended swings were five tickets.

They had spent ten tickets each for an hour-long show inside the big top, complete with performing elephants, a lion tamer, clowns, acrobats, trapeze experts, high-wire walkers, and Preston as ringmaster. The Fun House cost six tickets, and they had been able to stay inside for as long as they wanted. There were rope swings, warped mirrors, potato-sack slides, wobbly bridges, climbing walls, foam pits, and a host of other obstacles to experience.

They hadn't noticed coin upgrades on many other rides like they had with the bumper cars. There were a couple coin slots in the Fun House—one made a circular tunnel rotate for about five minutes, while another made the labyrinth walls shift positions.

"I want to find more places to use coins," Nate said.

"Me too," Pigeon said. "It's weird that they make such a big deal about the Carnie Coins and act miserly with them, but there aren't many places to use them."

"Makes me feel like we're missing something," Nate said.

"What do you think about spending some coins on the Psychic?" Pigeon asked.

Earlier in the day, they had come across a coin-operated fortune teller in a cabinet. The figure behind the glass was an animatronic ram with bejeweled horns called Argali the Psychic. "Ask Me Anything" the front of the cabinet had prompted. Zac had put in a coin and asked if his video would be effective.

A crystal ball in front of the ram had started to glow, and the ram had waved his front hooves over the ball. Argali's eyes had started blinking mechanically, and his mouth began to hinge open and closed.

"You will reach millions," the ram had spoken. Then a

little card had dropped into an opening in the cabinet beneath the coin slot.

"You will reach millions," the card had read.

"I'm shocked," Zac had said. "The answer actually fit the question."

Nate pointed at Pigeon. "Brilliant idea. We didn't ask any questions about the carnival. That could be a great place to start without Zac."

They started walking. Pigeon's eyes stayed focused on the ground.

"Are you looking for rocks?" Nate asked.

Pigeon glanced up. "You never know where you might make a find."

"Right now, we're looking for magic," Nate said.

Long strings of lights were turning on around the carnival as the sunset began to fade. The fanciful carousel had so many bulbs it looked like a giant whirling chandelier in the waning daylight.

In a space between Mama's Food Barn and a spinning ride called the Cycletron stood a cabinet of glass and varnished wood, flanked by low heaps of fresh sawdust. Inside, the motionless ram waited to be animated by a coin.

"How many coins do you have left?" Pigeon asked.

"Six," Nate said. "Thanks to the extra ones I got from Preston."

"I've got two," Pigeon said.

"I'll use mine," Nate said. "What do we want to know?"

"Ask about the owner," Pigeon said. "Preston dodged that question."

"What if he just gives a generic answer?" Nate asked. "Like 'Eat soup when you get a cold'?"

"Then we'll know not to waste coins here," Pigeon said. "Argali seemed to answer Zac directly, which was what made me want to ask more questions."

Nate put in a coin. Lights flashed inside the cabinet. The crystal ball started to glow, and the psychic began to blink and move.

"Who owns the Dreams and Screams International Carnival?" Nate asked.

"Camilla White owns and founded the carnival, but many and any have a stake in it," the ram said. The lights went out, and the ram froze.

A card ejected into the opening.

Nate picked up the card and read the same words the ram had just articulated. "The last of the Whites," Nate said.

"We should have known," Pigeon said. "That family can't leave our town alone."

"Mr. Stott had good instincts not wanting Lindy to come here," Nate said. He fed the cabinet another coin. "Where can we find Camilla? We want to meet the owner."

The ball glowed, and the ram's mouth scissored open and closed. "Camilla spends most of her time in the Jubilee Wagon," Argali said.

Another card dropped into the opening.

Nate pushed another Carnie Coin into the slot. "What is Camilla trying to accomplish with this carnival?"

The ram waved his hooves, and the ball's glow dimmed. "That's enough questions for today."

A final card dropped into the opening.

Nate picked up the card and looked at it.

REDEEM FOR ONE CARNIE COIN

Nate held the card out to Pigeon. "At least we got a refund."

"Do you think that is what Argali does when he can't answer a question?" Pigeon asked.

"Or doesn't want to," Nate muttered. He leaned forward and tapped the glass of the cabinet. "Can you hear me?"

Argali looked like a toy with no batteries.

"The ram was done talking to *you*," Pigeon said, inserting a coin. "Maybe I can still ask a question."

Argali came back to life.

"Is there magical candy at this carnival?" Pigeon asked.

"Seek in the right places, and you will find much magic here," Argali said.

A card with the same words dropped into the opening.

Pigeon held up a Carnie Coin. "Last one." He pushed it into the slot. "What information will best help us solve the mysteries of this carnival?"

The turbaned ram blinked and waved his hooves. "*Hidden* information is needed to unravel mysteries."

Pigeon checked the printed card. "Same words." He slapped the side of the cabinet. "I wanted something specific. You took my last coin and ripped me off!"

"Hey, kid, go easy on the equipment," a gruff voice said behind them.

They turned to see a tall roughneck in a flat cap, corduroy pants, and heavy boots approaching.

"Sorry," Pigeon said, stepping away from the cabinet. "The ram gave me a bad fortune."

The roughneck huffed through his nose. "Were you expecting Nostradamus? It's a novelty. An expensive one. Scram." He took out a rag and rubbed the spot on the cabinet Pigeon had slapped.

"Come on, Pidge," Nate said.

They walked quickly away into the crowd. The sugary smell of kettle corn hung in the air. Rides rumbled. People laughed and shrieked. Hooting calliope music reached them from a distance. Many kids wore glowing bracelets and necklaces that looked increasingly bright as the twilight deepened toward night.

"Do you think that guy didn't like the questions we were asking?" Pigeon wondered. "I didn't hit the box very hard."

"I'm not sure if he could hear us, but the timing was suspicious," Nate said. "I want to find the Jubilee Wagon. Whatever that is."

"You want to meet Camilla tonight?" Pigeon asked.

"I'm not sure," Nate said. "But I want to know where she hangs out."

"Maybe it's on the map," Pigeon suggested.

A prolonged perusal by both of them identified no Jubilee Wagon.

"We'll just have to look around," Nate said.

"Let's do one full loop around the carnival," Pigeon said. "If I'm home much later than nine, my mom will give me trouble."

"Sure," Nate said, leading the way.

He soon learned that walking around the entire carnival was easier said than done. There were many branching pathways and little alleys between attractions. Nate felt like every nook and cranny needed to be investigated since they were looking for a mystery wagon.

Down one long side passage, the noise of the crowded carnival retreated, and the pathway became drenched in shadow.

Pigeon tugged on Nate's shirt. "Does this feel promising to you?"

Nate stopped, peering into the darkness ahead. "If we want to get mugged by a clown."

"Not a fun image," Pigeon said, stepping backward.

"Let's turn around," Nate said.

They started back toward the brighter end of the alley but stopped short when they saw a young woman approaching them. She wore the white shirt and blue vest of a carnival worker and carried a gunny sack over one shoulder. She halted when the boys drew near.

"Lurking in alleyways, are we?" she asked.

"Just looking around," Nate said.

"Can't fault you for that," the young woman said.

"Do you know where we can find the Jubilee Wagon?" Pigeon asked.

She scrunched her brow. "I saw some wagons behind the Fun House."

"Thanks," Pigeon said as he and Nate hurried past her.

Pigeon walked purposefully after they left the alley and

seemed to be heading in the right direction, so Nate let him lead.

When they arrived at the Fun House, Pigeon led the way around the side. Neon accents made the large building colorful but left the surroundings in shadow. Toward the rear corner of the building, they found three fully enclosed horse-drawn wagons without any horses. Each had different writing on the side:

PROFESSOR MOLASKY'S FABULOUS TONICS
WORLD-RENOWNED PALM READER MADAME ZINKA
JUBILEE WAGON

Though the wagons were in good repair, they looked dark and lifeless.

Nate approached the Jubilee Wagon.

Pigeon edged closer to Nate. "Do we really want to test our luck, just us, alone in the dark?"

"We're not trying to apprehend anyone," Nate said. "We're just asking what a Jubilee Wagon is."

A door toward the front of the Jubilee Wagon had a portable stepladder out front. Nate approached and rapped on the door. After a moment of stillness, he knocked again.

"Seems dead," Pigeon said.

"We can try again another time," Nate said. "Should we go?"

"We had better," Pigeon said. "I'm already going to hear plenty from my mom."

They made their way toward the exits. There were fewer

children at the carnival now, more groups of older teens and adults on dates.

Nate noticed several signs near the exit.

LOSE SOMETHING?
OUR LOST AND FOUND HOLDS ITEMS FOR ONE WEEK
THEN THEY ARE FED TO THE STRONGMAN

HOWEVER MUCH YOU ENJOYED YOUR STAY
IT WILL BE BETTER NEXT TIME

TAKE AN EXIT SURVEY FOR FREE TICKETS!

YOU AREN'T REALLY LEAVING
IF YOU KEEP ON DREAMING
COME BACK ANYTIME
NO STAMP REQUIRED!

Nate and Pigeon were almost past the ticket booths when a fast-talking man approached them. "Hey, kids, want to answer a few questions for some free tickets?"

"Maybe," Nate said, glancing at Pigeon. "How long will it take?"

"Just a minute," the guy said, handing each of them a clipboard with a pencil attached on a string.

"How many tickets?" Pigeon asked.

"Twenty," the man said. "You must answer every question though. There aren't many. Won't take long. Easy money."

"Any coins?" Nate asked.

"You drive a hard bargain," the man said. "For you guys? Two coins plus twenty tickets. What do you say?"

Nate looked to Pigeon.

"Sure," Pigeon said.

The first questions were simple. They just had to check boxes rating different aspects of their experience from poor to excellent. Nate checked off all categories as either very good or excellent. After that came three questions that required actual writing.

What can we do better?

Nate wrote: *Provide more places to use coins.*

How would you change any of the existing attractions?

Nate wrote: *Bigger roller coaster. I'd also add other speedy rides that do more than spin.*

What attractions do you wish we had?

Nate wrote: *Log ride. A ride that takes you straight up high and drops you. More food variety.*

Nate handed the man the clipboard.

"What did I tell you?" the man said, glancing at the answers. "It took almost no time at all."

Pigeon offered his clipboard as well.

The man gave Pigeon and Nate each a slip of paper.

GOOD FOR TWENTY TICKETS AND TWO COINS ON YOUR NEXT VISIT

"We don't get the actual tickets and coins?" Nate asked.

"Sure you do," the man said. "When you come back. What—are you gonna use them at home? Turn those coupons in at the ticket booth or the Currency Exchange and you'll have tickets and coins in hand."

"All right," Nate said. "Thanks."

"Bye," the man said. "Get home safe. Happy dreams."

CHAPTER EIGHT

GOOD BUZZ

When Nate reached the lunch line on Monday, he noticed a giant bowling ball taking up the far corner of the cafeteria. Black, with three finger holes and a smooth finish, it was at least eight feet tall.

Nate joined the crowd around the abnormality. Like many other kids, he stroked the smooth, hard surface and knocked his fist against it. How could anyone have gotten the ball through the doors? Did somebody have a size magnifier?

Pushing together, a few eighth grade boys got the massive ball rolling, at which point Mrs. Jackson intervened. "Nobody touch the ball," she ordered. "If it gets going too fast it could crush someone. Does anyone know how this got here?"

"I didn't see it this morning," a girl said.

"We've only become aware of it just now," Mrs. Jackson said. "Unless anyone knows where this ball came from, please

proceed with your regular lunch break. From here on out, anyone touching the bowling ball will be suspended."

"Make it our new mascot," one kid suggested. "The Diablo
View Bowlers."

"I'll take that under advisement," Mrs. Jackson said.
"Please, as you were. I'll get this figured out with the staff."

Back in the lunch line, Nate was disappointed to not see
John Dart working. Nate joined Zac, Summer, Trevor, Pigeon,
and Benji at the end of a long table. Lunch was fish and chips
with tartar sauce and coleslaw.

"What's with the chicken nuggets?" Zac asked Summer.
"This fish is awesome."

"I don't do fish," Summer said, dipping a vaguely alligator-
shaped nugget in ranch dressing. "What's with the bowling
ball?"

"Maybe our town has a new supervillain," Zac said. "The
Kingpin."

"It's a big calling card," Nate said.

"I got some footage with it," Zac said. "Should play well on
my channel."

"I did some quick calculations," Pigeon said. "Assuming
the same density, proportions, and volume as a fourteen-
pound bowling ball, that ball in the corner weighs around ten
tons."

"I'd get a strike every time," Benji said.

"Unless the pins were of proportionate size," Pigeon said.

"How did it get in here?" Trevor asked.

"Better question," Zac said. "How do we roll it at the
school from a nearby mountain?"

"How are you kids doing?" came a voice from behind them.

Nate turned to find John Dart standing behind him in an apron and a skullcap.

"Lunch Lord!" Zac said. "This fish beats most restaurants."

"You have discerning taste," John said. "Nate, a word in private? About the, ah, tartar sauce."

"Sure," Nate said, rising from the table and stepping aside with John.

"How was the carnival?" John asked in a low voice.

"Fun," Nate said. "Cool. No obvious magic yet, except they know how to cancel our candy. But we found a fortune-telling machine that answers questions. It said that Camilla White is in charge."

John nodded. "That confirms a hunch. You haven't seen her?"

"Not yet," Nate said.

"You left around 9:10 with Pigeon," John said. "The others departed at 8:05."

"You were watching," Nate said.

"I'm trying to do what I can," John said, handing Nate an envelope.

"What's in here?" Nate asked.

"Three hundred dollars in twenties. I don't want you dependent on Zac for carnival access. The prices could be prohibitive. Forty dollars for fifty tickets and five coins."

"Thanks," Nate said, casually tucking the envelope into his pocket. "What do you know about the bowling ball?"

"I know it didn't fall out of my pocket," John said. "If I

had some size 100 bowling shoes, I could do some serious damage."

"It would be like bowling with a wrecking ball," Nate said.

"I checked it out before it drew a crowd," John said. "Seems like a standard bowling ball. Except for the size, of course. Let's talk about this with everybody. Anything else to report?"

"Not yet."

"You're going back into the carnival?"

"Sometime soon."

"Be careful. I don't have all the answers yet, but I'm sure that carnival is trouble on a massive scale."

"The bumper cars were pretty fun," Nate said. "And the roller coaster was cool."

"Some of the best traps are baited with honey," John said. He led Nate back over to the lunch table. "Eat the fish while its warm."

"So what's the big secret about the tartar sauce?" Zac asked.

"That's classified," John said. "Here's what I can tell you. Watch for anomalies like that bowling ball. If you think you see a Siberian tiger around town, run for your life, because unlikely as it sounds, you are probably right. I tranquilized two tigers over the weekend. I also captured a zombie."

"An actual zombie?" Zac asked.

"Dead guy," John said. "Emaciated. Wanted to eat my brains. I stopped him from breaking into a house."

"Are you serious?" Zac asked. "Who *are* you?"

"I'm the Lunch Lord," John said. "And I have hobbies."

"Where is the zombie now?" Pigeon asked.

"That's for me to worry about," John said. "I've called in re-inforcements. I'm still trying to understand what is happening. Things that shouldn't be here keep showing up. This bowling ball is a textbook example."

"And the stagecoach," Nate said. "The orangutan."

"The frequency is increasing," John said, glancing at his wristwatch. "I have to go. There is a lot to supervise with fried fish. I may not do this lunch too often. Keep me informed as you learn more."

John walked away.

"Was he serious about the zombie?" Benji asked.

"The bowling ball seems pretty serious," Nate replied, pointing with his plastic fork.

"Probably a meth addict," Zac said.

"An orangutan could have escaped from the carnival," Pigeon said. "But how does a giant bowling ball get in here? There's no way it could fit through the doors."

"Maybe somebody brought it in and enlarged it," Nate said. "Or it could have been teleported."

"Right," Benji said. "Because people can make things grow and teleport stuff."

"How is the ball here, Benji?" Zac asked. "Did it appear out of nowhere?"

"It's got to be some kind of stunt," Benji said. "A promotional gimmick. Or an elaborate prank. I bet people brought in pieces and assembled it."

Nate nodded. If magic were not real, Benji had just named the most likely scenario. "You're probably right," he said.

"By the way, I have your release forms," Zac said, producing pieces of paper and handing them out. "You just need to sign them and get a parent to sign."

"What does it say?" Trevor asked, squinting at the small print.

"Mostly that I can use your faces free of charge to promote my new breakfast cereal," Zac said.

"As long as it's sugary," Nate said. "I don't want to be associated with whole grain wheat."

Zac chuckled. "In reality, it just says if you end up in my videos, you won't sue me or seek payment. They also have to be signed if you want to help me film."

"I'll get it back to you tomorrow," Summer said, already signing.

"I'll have my attorneys look it over," Nate said.

"Perfect," Zac said. "Want to see the video we're prepping for release tomorrow?"

Everybody crowded around his phone, and Zac let the two-and-a-half minute video play. As Nate watched, he realized it was edited so it looked like Zac was at the carnival alone. His best jokes and comments were strung together in a montage. Nobody else was heard speaking. There was a brief shot of Nate failing to knock over the milk bottles, but it could have been any kid—there was little to tie Nate to Zac. Pigeon, Trevor, and Summer were in the background a few times, barely as extras. Many of their comments throughout the day had been entertaining, but none made it into the video.

"That is tight," Trevor said when the video was done. "It flows great."

"Yeah, good job," Summer said. "You teased things about the carnival and made it look like a lot of fun. I bet the carnival bosses will love it."

"I hope so," Zac said. "We want to keep those free tickets coming."

"My mom is planning a family trip to the carnival next week after school," Pigeon said. "I guess she heard from a friend that it shouldn't be missed."

"My parents want us to go too," Trevor said.

"My math teacher spent the first ten minutes of class praising the carnival," Benji said.

"That's what we want," Zac said. "Good buzz."

When they finished lunch, Zac left to talk to some friends at another table. Summer, Trevor, and Pigeon decided to take a closer look at the bowling ball, leaving Nate alone with Benji.

"Did you have fun with your family on Saturday?" Nate asked.

"I guess," Benji said. "It was just a normal day."

"I thought you guys went on a trip," Nate said.

Benji rolled his eyes. "Is that what Zac told you?"

"Yeah."

Benji shook his head. "Zac asked me not to come Saturday. He didn't want too many personalities in the mix while he figured out how much he likes you guys. It was basically an audition."

"An audition to be friends?" Nate asked.

"That's how it goes with Zac," Benji said. "He has turned

his life into a show, and he doesn't want boring people around, or anyone who might hog the spotlight."

"I guess that makes sense," Nate said. "He had a job to do with that video. But it's kind of harsh he asked you not to come. Aren't you his best friend?"

"I'm the closest thing he has to a real friend," Benji said. "You'd never know from watching his clips."

"That's weird," Nate said.

"It's just Zac," Benji said. "The show is all about him. He deliberately keeps everyone besides his family in the background."

Nate thought about how the carnival video focused almost exclusively on Zac. "Does that bug you?"

"A little," Benji said. "It also has benefits. The kids who want to hang out with Zac so they can get famous soon learn that isn't going to happen, which helps keep users and fakers away. I haven't known Zac forever. I'll admit I liked him at first because of his videos. I realize he gets self-absorbed. But he's also so funny and great to hang out with, so it works for me."

"I like him too," Nate said. "Hopefully next time, we can all hang out."

"He's planning to film another video Wednesday," Benji said. "It sounded like he'd invite all of us—assuming you guys bring back the release forms tomorrow."

"I've never needed to sign a release form to hang out with a friend," Nate said.

Benji clapped him on the back. "Welcome to the club."

CHAPTER NINE

REGULARS

Nate met Summer at the carnival grounds an hour after school ended on Monday. When his mom had signed the release, Nate had exaggerated how many days he would need to be at the carnival for filming.

"Trevor and Pigeon?" Summer asked.

"They both called," Nate said. "They can't make it. Did your parents give you a hard time?"

"No," Summer said. "They think it's really cool I get to be involved with Foster Child videos. As if I won a contest or something."

"My family feels the same way," Nate said.

"I made it sound like a bunch of other girls are helping," Summer said. "That alone had my mom smiling. Do you have the money?"

Nate nodded. "It's as close as John and Mr. Stott will get to saying they need us to do this."

"Let's not waste their investment," Summer said. "We need to be good detectives today."

After waiting in line at the ticket booth for about ten minutes, Nate traded eighty dollars for a hundred tickets and ten Carnie Coins. He had expected to pay tax, but evidently it was included.

As they walked into the carnival, Nate felt surprised by how crowded it was on a weekday. If anything, it might have been busier than on Saturday.

"Is that game new?" Summer asked as they strolled down the main boardwalk. At the long counter, ten participants shot water guns at bull's-eyes. The longer the shooters kept their streams on the targets, the faster the corresponding goats climbed to the top of a mountain.

"I would have remembered the goat race," Nate said. "Look, that's different too." He pointed at a game where participants tossed darts at backlit balloons.

"I don't think any of the original games are missing," Summer said. "It's like the boardwalk stretched a little longer. Where should we go first?"

"Let's try the Psychic," Nate said. "Pigeon and I had some good luck there."

Nate showed the way, sometimes having to lead with his shoulder and weave through clusters of people. When Nate reached the space between Mama's Food Barn and the Cycletron, Argali the Psychic was gone, though the heaps of sawdust remained.

Nate turned around in a circle. "He was right here. In a big box."

"I remember," Summer said.

Nate stepped close to Summer. "I bet our questions were too good. That guy who interrupted us probably hid the machine."

"Is that a log ride?" Summer asked.

Nate turned and looked across the way. The ride entrance looked like an old wooden fort, and the letters on the sign were painted like logs in front of a splashy background.

"Yes," Nate said. "Was that there on Saturday?"

"No, I would have remembered," Summer said.

"That is so weird," Nate said. "Did you take the survey on the way out the other day?"

"Yeah," Summer said. "I got a coupon for twenty tickets."

"Did you suggest any rides on the form?" Nate asked. "I asked for a log ride, because I thought the carnival was missing water rides."

"That seems like a really complicated ride to build in a day," Summer said.

"It's no ordinary carnival," Nate emphasized.

A portly man in a bowler hat sidled up to Nate and Summer. "Say, this isn't your first visit to the park, is it?" he asked in a low voice.

"That's right," Nate answered. "We were here Saturday."

The man glanced around as if making sure he wasn't being watched. "Come over here. I've got a bargain for you."

Nate and Summer shared a glance. Summer shrugged, and they stepped closer to the man in the hat.

He led them along the outside of Mama's Food Barn to the rear corner of the structure. After checking the area, he reached into his plaid jacket and retrieved a folded piece of paper from an inner pocket. "Listen, this carnival is designed for repeat customers. There are perks for those who come often." He unfolded the paper. "This is the Regulars Map. It isn't always available, and never on a first visit. I'll sell it to you right now—ten tickets, two Carnie Coins, take it or leave it."

"Why so expensive?" Nate asked.

"This map has lots of hints and clues that they leave off the general one."

"We'll take it," Summer said, tearing off ten tickets and handing over a pair of coins.

"You spoke up just in time," the man said. "I was about to withdraw the offer." He gave her the map. "Enjoy. Pleasure doing business with you." He tipped his hat and strode away.

Summer unfolded the map. "Look, it already shows the log ride."

"This map folds out bigger than the free one," Nate said. "It has more detail."

"What are the little gold dots?" Summer asked.

"I'm not sure," Nate said. "There are lots of them."

"Here's a legend," Summer said. "The gold dots are coin slots." She pointed to the bumper cars and the Fun House.

"Yep," Nate said. "But there are so many others on different rides too. We didn't find nearly this many coin slots. Some must be hidden."

"The blue boxes with question marks inside are secret ways. What do you think that means?" Summer asked.

"We're going to find out," Nate said resolutely. "I see only four secret ways marked on the map."

Summer pointed to the map. "The nearest secret way is on the Terror Ride."

"That was a cool ride," Nate said. "But it'd be awesome if it had a secret passage!"

"Unless the secret passage leads to a lair of kidnappers," Summer said. "Could be dangerous."

"We'll stick together," Nate said. "And if something doesn't feel right, we can turn around. But we're here to uncover secrets."

"Look at this spot," Summer said. "A coin slot *and* a secret way are in this little alley behind some of the food stands. That seems promising."

"Let's check it out," Nate agreed.

They hurried to the indicated food vendors, then cut down an alley between the fried ice cream and the caramel apples. The alley elbowed, paralleling the back of the food stands. Opposite the wooden rear of the food stands ran a brick wall.

"This is where the map indicated," Summer said.

"What does a traveling carnival build out of bricks?" Nate asked.

Summer consulted the map. "It matches up with the Old Time Theater. But the marks for the passage and the coin slot are clearly in this alley."

"Was the theater here on Saturday?" Nate asked.

"I'm not sure," Summer said. "We definitely didn't go in it."

Turning in a circle, Nate scanned the dusty ground and the blank walls. "There is nothing here."

"Nothing obvious," Summer said, looking more closely at the rear wall of the food stands.

Nate began scouring the brick wall, eventually spying a metal-edged coin slot set horizontally into the grout between two bricks. "No way. Summer, check this out."

"So sneaky," Summer said, producing a Carnie Coin and inserting it.

A door sprang ajar beside the coin slot. Cunningly composed of bricks, the door had fit seamlessly into the wall. There was no knob or handle on the outside, so Nate grabbed the protruding edge and pulled the door open. A torchlit stairway descended before them. From down below came the overlapping murmur of multiple conversations.

"If evil magicians weren't involved, this would be the coolest carnival ever," Nate said.

"They would also have the best workers ever," Summer said. "Who comes to town, digs an underground tunnel, and lines it with stone?"

A tone sounded, and the brick door slowly began to close. Nate extended a hand to stop it, but the door kept moving no matter how hard he resisted.

"In or out?" Nate asked.

Summer slipped through the doorway, and Nate followed. Behind them, the door crunched shut. They paused for a moment at the top of the torchlit stairwell. The humid air smelled like wet rock, and the temperature was noticeably cooler than outside. Summer led the way down the stone steps.

At the bottom, they reached a small antechamber with empty benches against the plaster walls and an archway on the far side. Above the arch hung a weathered wooden sign.

THE GROTTO

Just beyond the archway, Nate saw a gaunt man with a bandana tied around his head and a small golden hoop in one earlobe standing in front of what looked like a podium.

"Well met, friend," the man greeted in a gruff but companionable voice. "Found the Grotto, did you?"

"Yes," Nate said, stepping forward. He could see some people at tables beyond the man. "Is this a restaurant?"

"I'd call it a hangout," the man said. "Maybe a watering hole. But if you have tickets and coins, call it what you will. Best seafood in the area, mate. Are you and your girlfriend looking for a table?"

"She's not my girlfriend," Nate said.

The man shook his head with disappointment. "Couldn't win her heart?"

"She's me wench," Nate growled in his best pirate accent.

The man slapped the podium and laughed. Summer swiftly punched Nate's shoulder.

"Talk like that leads to stormy seas," the man said, still chuckling. "You're a braver man than I. Follow me."

The sprawling room beyond the podium was broken up by stone pillars, wooden partitions, and low walls. Lit by dim lanterns and flickering candles, recessed compartments held tables where figures conversed in hushed tones. Old fishing nets hung on some of the walls, alongside harpoons, shells, and barnacle-crusted anchors.

"Most of the tables are lonely today," the man said. "How

about this one?" He indicated a booth with a table large enough for four. Two candles burned in bottles.

"Looks great," Summer said.

She sat on one side, Nate on the other. The man gave a slight bow. "I'll take my leave now."

"Are you a pirate?" Nate asked.

"Close enough, my boy," the man said. He scowled and thickened his accent. "Yer server be Mandy." With a wink, he walked away.

Nate rubbed the tabletop, appreciating the waxy texture of the timeworn wood.

"I'm going to get you back for that wench comment," Summer said.

"I was trying to blend in with the locals," Nate said.

"We're at a carnival," Summer said. "These aren't real pirates."

"It's a magic carnival," Nate said. "Who knows what kind of people we're meeting?"

"Let's not assume any of them are sexist," Summer said.

A woman with her hair tied up over her head and wearing a frilly blouse came up to the table. "I'm Mandy. What can I get you to drink?"

Nate noticed the parchment menus at the edge of the table. "What do you recommend?"

"The lime soda," Mandy said. "We also have fruit punch, ginger ale, and pickle brine."

"I'll just have water," Summer said.

"Lime soda," Nate said. "Do people actually order the pickle brine?"

"Only a few diehards," Mandy said.

"What about food?" Nate asked.

"The shrimp nachos are popular," Mandy said. "We have swordfish as a special. My favorite is the fisherman's stew. Really hearty with lots of variety. Never quite the same twice. Comes with sourdough."

"Do you have tomato soup?" Summer asked.

"Does an octopus have tentacles?" Mandy replied.

"I'll take that," Summer said. "Just a cup."

"I'll try the stew," Nate said.

"I'll get that going," Mandy said, strolling away.

"Are you even hungry?" Summer asked.

"A little," Nate said. "I usually snack after school."

"I wonder how expensive this place is," Summer said.

Nate grabbed a menu and found what he had ordered. "My stew is five tickets. Not bad. The lime soda was two. I think it's a little cheaper here than up top."

"There's deals to be had down here for sure," a young man said, approaching. He carried a three-legged stool, set it at the end of the table, and squatted down. He wore a loose white shirt and tight trousers with a rapier at his waist. "Topside is for tourists. Edward Scrum—pleased to meet you."

"I'm Summer."

"Nate."

"First time at the Grotto?" he asked.

"We just found it," Summer said. "I ordered my manservant here to bring me."

"I deserved that," Nate said.

"Are you a regular?" Summer asked.

Edward grinned and looked around. "More regular than most. You can often find me haunting these tables. A lot of secrets get traded around the Grotto."

"We know some secrets," Nate said. "I know where my sister keeps her diary."

"Personally, I'm more interested in coins than rumors," Edward said.

"We give you coins, you tell us secrets?" Summer asked.

Edward scratched his neck. "That makes me sound so opportunistic. But, yeah, those are the basics."

Nate slid a Carnie Coin to the end of the table.

"That didn't take long," Edward said, picking up the bribe. "Before you leave the Grotto, find the fountain. Toss a coin in. Make a wish out loud."

"It grants actual wishes?" Nate asked.

"Close enough," Edward said.

"We're just supposed to trust you?" Nate asked.

"If it doesn't work, tell everyone you meet I'm a fraud," Edward said. "The reason I can earn coins with information is because my tips pay off."

"Is this what you do?" Summer asked. "Hang out here collecting coins?"

"One more coin and I'll answer some general questions," Edward said. "Or I can stop disturbing you."

Summer glanced at Nate, then handed Edward a Carnie Coin.

"A fellow needs coins to explore the carnival," Edward said. "I'm here doing what all the regulars do. I'm trying to solve the mysteries. Win treasure and glory. Coins help."

"Is your sword real?" Nate asked.

"Real sharp," Edward said. "And plenty pointy."

"The carnival just opened here Saturday," Summer said. "How can you already be a regular?"

Edward laughed. "I follow the carnival from town to town."

"Does it always have a Grotto?" Summer asked.

"Before long it does," Edward said.

"How did they dig the tunnels for the Grotto so fast?" Nate asked.

Edward chuckled. "You really are new to this. The carnival tends to grow rapidly. We'll leave it at that."

"What mysteries have you uncovered?" Summer asked.

"Those answers get expensive," Edward said, raising a change pouch and jiggling it. "How much do you have?"

"I'm out," Summer said.

"Three more," Nate said.

"Then I'll leave you with some broad advice," Edward said, standing and picking up his stool. "The coins tend to open paths. Follow where they lead. There are many of us who are fully invested in trying to solve the mysteries behind the rides. If you suspect the impossible, you're probably on the right track. If you're careful, you don't ever have to leave, but if anyone official catches you topside after hours, they'll see you out. But they never press charges. It's more like playing a game of tag than actually trespassing. Are you following me so far?"

"Yes," Nate said, riveted.

"Here is a bit of advice I'll give you for free even though it's worth a whole purse of coins in importance. Don't fall asleep inside the carnival. Not unless you're positive you found a safe room. Trust me."

"What happens if we fall asleep?" Summer asked.

"Nothing good," Edward said. "Enjoy your grub."

"Are you in danger?" Nate asked. "Does your family know you're here?"

Edward smiled. "It's dangerous, but this game is voluntary."

"Do you need sidekicks?" Nate asked. "We're trying to solve mysteries here too."

Edward pursed his lips to one side. "Not at the moment. But who knows? Maybe later."

"Level with me before you go," Nate said. "Are you an actor? Hired by the carnival?"

"Want to give me another coin?" Edward asked.

"We're pretty low," Nate said.

"Probably wise." Edward grinned. "All the world is a stage." He strode away, swinging his stool from one hand.

Summer leaned across the table and lowered her voice. "What if we follow that guy? See where he goes?"

"I have a feeling he'd know," Nate said.

"This is getting more bizarre by the minute," Summer said. "How many people do you think follow this carnival?"

"It might explain the disappearances," Nate said. "And how crowded it is. If there is enough to explore, people could get addicted. Heck, I could get addicted."

"What do we do now?" Summer asked.

"We wait for our food," Nate said. "Then we go find that fountain."

CHAPTER TEN

FOUNTAIN

The fisherman's stew had large pieces of crab, lobster, scallops, shrimp, mussels, and fish mingling with bits of vegetables and stray twists of noodles in a salty, buttery broth. The accompanying bread had a firm, crunchy crust and a soft interior. Both Nate and Summer used the sourdough to mop up the remains of their soups when they were done.

"Don't miss any of those fish guts," Summer said.

"The guts are the best part," Nate replied. "Want the rest of my lime soda?" It had come in a glass along with a half-filled bottle. It was good, but a little too tart for his taste.

"Sure," Summer said, taking the bottle and guzzling what was left. "Do we leave a tip?"

"In tickets?" Nate replied. "That seems weird. But I don't want to be a cheapskate."

He slid out of the booth and crossed to the nearest

occupied table. A broad man with an eyepatch sat with a long-haired man and a thin woman with frizzy hair.

"Excuse me," Nate said. "Do we tip here?"

"If you want to give away coins, I'll lighten your load," the man with the eyepatch offered.

"No need to give gratuities inside the carnival," the woman said. "All workers get a fair wage for their efforts. Good service is expected as part of that."

"You're no fun," the guy with the eyepatch said. "He might have handed over coins!"

"The kid isn't daft," the long-haired guy said. "He was just being polite. He wanted to know the custom." The guy raised a mug in Nate's direction. "Cheers."

"Thanks," Nate said. He returned to Summer. "No tip."

"Do you think those guys are following the carnival like Edward?" Summer asked.

"I think the people eating here are mostly insiders," Nate replied. "Either employees or regulars."

Summer stood up. "Let's go find the fountain."

The Grotto was more expansive and mazelike than Nate had realized at first. They passed through entire rooms of empty tables, taking steps down into somewhat lower dining areas, and moving along narrow passages past private booths hid in shadowy alcoves. Occasionally they saw people eating or in conversation, but it mostly felt like they were traversing closed portions of the eatery.

At last, they came to a room with a tile floor and thick adobe walls. Dim lanterns and a chandelier of candles provided light. In the center of the room bubbled a three-tiered fountain. Water dribbled from a spout at the pinnacle and trickled down from one basin to the next. No taller than Nate, the fountain looked ancient, carved faces and vines almost worn away, the silty water tinted green. Lily pads covered much of the lower bowl.

"Is this the right fountain?" Nate asked.

"Edward didn't mention others," Summer pointed out.

Nate took out a Carnie Coin. "What if he is just going to come along and scoop out whatever coins we're dumb enough to throw in there?"

"That would actually be pretty clever," Summer said. "If he hopes to sell secrets, that won't last long with a reputation for cheating people."

Nate looked around. They appeared to be alone. "Maybe we should try to scoop coins out of the fountain."

"Sounds like a way to get on the bad side of a wishing fountain," Summer said.

"Good point," Nate said, craning his neck over the various basins. "Besides, I don't see any coins in there."

"What should we wish for?" Summer asked.

"World peace?" Nate suggested. "The ability to remake reality however we want? A thousand more wishes?"

"If we go too big it might not work," Summer said. "But wish for whatever you want." She took out a Carnie Coin. "I wish we could learn exactly where to find some new secret places in this carnival." She tossed the coin in the lower basin.

"You went with the bottom pool?" Nate asked. "Lucky the coin didn't land on a lily pad. I think the top tray takes more skill." He held up a coin. "I wish we had magical candy that worked inside the carnival." Nate pitched the coin into the top basin where it made a little plop.

"Well done," came a voice from behind them. They turned to find Edward emerging from a tiled niche in the adobe wall. "Very practical wishing."

"Were you there the whole time?" Nate asked.

"I was spying from a covert spot," Edward said. "That recess connects to a secret passage." He walked up to the fountain. "I pledge to see these wishes granted." Then he reached in and plucked out Summer's coin.

"Wait a minute," Summer said. "Was this just a trick to get more coins?"

"No trick," Edward said, briefly stepping into the lower basin to retrieve Nate's coin from the top one. "I'm a servant of the wishing fountain." Standing on one foot, he shook some of the water from his wet pant leg and boot. Then he held out his palm, displaying the two coins. Both were now black with no markings.

"What happened to the coins?" Nate asked.

"Have you caught on that the Carnie Coins are magical?" Edward checked.

"I guess that makes sense," Nate replied.

"The fountain really does grant wishes," Edward said. "But it can take up to one week. And each individual only gets one free wish."

"That would have been nice to know so I could have made the perfect wish," Summer said.

"Not really," Edward explained. "Had I warned you in advance you only got one wish, your wish would have been negated. Lots of little rules."

"Oh," Summer said. "Then thanks, I guess. How do you know so much about this place?"

"It's what I do," Edward said.

"How long have you been here?" Summer asked.

"You might be surprised to know," Edward said. "I've made a lifestyle of it."

"Why did you pledge to grant our wishes?" Nate asked.

"The fountain allows me one week to grant the wishes," Edward said. "If I succeed, the coin used for the wish becomes an Enchanted Carnie Coin. It looks like white gold or platinum, but with extra sparkle. I can use Enchanted Carnie Coins to make additional wishes in the fountain, or I can use them elsewhere."

"And if you fail?" Summer asked.

"If I fail," Edward said, "I have to return the coins to the fountain and I'll be cursed."

"Where else can you use the Enchanted Carnie Coins?" Nate asked.

"That's all I'm telling you for free," Edward said. "The details about the fountain were generously given to me, and now I give them to you freely, with encouragement to do the same. If you want, after your wishes are granted, you two can pledge to grant the wishes of others as well."

"Maybe if we overhear somebody make a wish that we think we can grant," Nate said. "I don't want to fail and be cursed."

"You're catching on," Edward said. "Had you asked for world peace, I would have left that wish to the fountain."

"Would the fountain have provided world peace?" Nate asked.

"Yes and no," Edward said. "I've watched this fountain for some time, and there tend to be loopholes if you wish too big. For example, you may get world peace—but only for a minute."

"But *you* can give us magical candy?" Nate asked.

"And show us other secret places?" Summer asked.

"I can," Edward said. "But we need to allow the carnival more time to open some candy stations. The magical candy will only work on kids. A lot of the magic here is like that."

"Interesting," Nate said.

"How did you know magical candy was an option?" Edward asked.

"Um, strong hunch," Nate said.

"We've used some before," Summer explained. "In other situations."

"Summer!" Nate complained. "He's supposed to pay for that kind of info."

"Exchanging information can be a kind of payment," Edward said. "When you share what you know, I'll generally reciprocate. If you've used magical candy before, you are no ordinary carnival goers."

"We want to figure out this place," Nate said.

"Your wishes are already moving you in that direction," Edward said. "You kids are in school?"

"Yes," Summer said.

"Meet me at the Ferris wheel on Wednesday at four o'clock," Edward said. "Think you can make it?"

"We'll figure it out," Nate said.

"You don't need to pay to enter," Edward said. "The booths are set up to look as if tickets are mandatory, but they're not. Of course, you'll be limited in what you can do without buying tickets or coins—or until you learn more secrets about this place."

"Four o'clock on Wednesday," Summer repeated.

"Bring tickets and coins," Edward said. "At least twenty tickets and as many coins as you can manage. The things I want to show you should exist by Wednesday."

"Because the carnival is growing," Nate said.

"It's off to the fastest start I have seen," Edward said. "People in the Bay Area are really taking to it quickly."

"It grows faster when more people come?" Nate asked.

"That's a big part of it," Edward said. "Right now, I have other places to be." He gave a little bow. "I will see you on Wednesday."

He walked over to the niche, pressed certain tiles, and a tall section of the wall slid open. He went inside and the tiles closed behind him.

"Do you think that goes anywhere?" Nate asked. "Or is he just hiding in a little closet waiting for us to leave?"

"I can still hear you," came Edward's muffled voice beyond the wall. "And yes, it does go someplace."

"I'm starting to understand why people in the Grotto talk quietly," Nate muttered.

"Probably a good policy," Summer agreed. "Let's go."

"Sure," Nate said. "If we find the easy secret places on our own before Wednesday, Edward will have to show us the *really* secret ones."

"Good thinking," Summer said. "You get a genius point for that one."

"I do?" Nate asked. "Pigeon usually gets the genius points."

"They have to be earned," Summer said. "Good job."

CHAPTER ELEVEN

SWINDLER

After exiting the Grotto, Nate and Summer found the family of acrobats performing tricks on a big trampoline in an open area between attractions. The teenage brother caught a bounce from the mustachioed dad and took off like a rocket, doing at least nine rapid flips before landing again. The dad and brother climbed down from the trampoline, and as a big finish, the mom jumped from the trampoline to land on their shoulders. And then the little daughter bounced from the trampoline to land on the shoulders of the mom.

As the crowd applauded, men in flat caps started picking up the pads and moving the trampoline.

Nate and Summer pushed through the crowd, making their way to Terror Castle. On the Regulars Map, the box with the question mark was on the ride itself. First, they walked around the exterior of the ride, scouring all surfaces for coin slots. Then they boarded the ride twice, scanning everywhere for hidden slots or other secrets. But they had no success.

"What if we have to jump off mid-ride to find the secret way?" Nate wondered.

"How do we manage that without getting booted from the carnival?" Summer asked.

"I was timing it," Nate said. "They send a new car every twenty seconds. Sometimes a little less."

"I'm sure they have cameras on the ride," Summer said.

"This feels like a dead end for now," Nate said. "Let's try one of the other locations."

The map showed a secret way at the Fun House, and a coin symbol as well. Nate and his friends had used Carnie Coins in the Fun House on Saturday, but he hadn't seen any secret passages open up.

He and Summer followed the same pattern as with the Terror Castle—combing the outside of the Fun House first, then paid tickets to go inside. They spent a couple hours roaming the labyrinthine Fun House in search of subtle coin slots. They found one behind a striped pillar that made the floor of the room spin and another one behind a painting in a hallway that engaged strobe lights through the whole area. But they found none that opened secret ways. Eventually they gave up and exited.

"The coin slots are just distractions that waste coins," Nate said.

"We're missing something," Summer said.

"Where is the last secret way?" Nate asked.

Summer unfolded the map. "It's on a smaller attraction called the Swindler."

"Small is good," Nate said. "Less to search. What's the Swindler?"

"I have no idea," Summer said. "It's on the opposite side of the park from the entrance. Should we save it for another day? It's a school night."

The sun was going down. Nate knew if they got home too late they could lose carnival privileges. "Let's hurry," he said. "We'll give it a quick look. Like fifteen minutes."

"What if we find a secret passage?" Summer worried. "That could take hours to explore."

"We'll mark it on the map and chase it down another day," Nate promised.

"Fine," Summer said. "Fifteen minutes."

They hurried down a far walkway of the carnival, past the enormous Crafts Tent on one side and Livestock Central on the other. Toward the end of the thruway, they found a compact, fancy building with "Swindler" written in cursive neon and surrounded by sparkling casino lights. Signs on the outside of the building made bold proclamations:

YOU NAME THE GAME
YOU SET THE STAKES
WE MAKE A DEAL
THEN YOU LOSE

CAN YOU OUTFOX A CON MAN?
BEAT THE BEST AND WIN BIG!

A middle-aged lady stood out front, wearing a fringed

dress with a feathered hairpiece. "Hey, you two," she called. "Want to test your skill against the best?"

"Are you the best?" Summer asked.

"No, sister, I'm just out here to reel you in," the lady said.

"Why would anyone want to challenge a swindler who guarantees he will win?" Nate asked.

"Why does anyone box the champ?" the lady replied snappily. "It brings the most glory. The best prizes. Nobody can stay on top forever."

"What are the prizes?" Nate asked.

"Best in the park," the lady said. "By far. You have to talk to him to find out. We just opened up. No wait right now."

"All right," Summer said.

"Step this way," the lady said.

Nate and Summer walked up the ramp to the bright red door and went inside. The little room was neat and clean, with a counter covered by an orderly array of games—chess, checkers, backgammon, cribbage, Connect Four, marbles, playing cards, and numerous other games that Nate didn't know. Behind the counter stood an older man leaning on a cane. He wore a dapper straw hat and a striped vest with a pocket watch.

"Are you the Swindler?" Summer asked.

"I sure am," the man said. "Have you come to lose some wagers?"

"That's not a very good sales pitch," Nate said.

"Look, son," the Swindler said, "I might be the only honest man at this carnival. Everyone here is trying to take your money through tickets and coins—you visit their attractions, eat their food, play their games. Do you think those games are designed to help players win? They want you to fail, and you usually do. I tell it straight. You can win prizes here. But you have to beat me at something."

"How does it work?" Nate asked.

"Challenge me to a game," the Swindler said. "You choose the contest. It has to be something we can do in this room, and it can't involve my bum leg, so no cartwheels. You want to bring in a game from outside, introduce me to something new, be my guest. Or try one of the many games I have here. Let's make a deal."

"What can we win?" Summer asked.

"What do you want?" the Swindler replied.

"How big can we go?" Summer asked.

Wearing a faint smile, the Swindler turned. "You see that door in the back?"

"Sure," Nate said. It was the only other door in the place, made of wood so dark brown it was almost black.

"I have access to just about any prize you can imagine back there," the Swindler said. "Try me."

"A huge diamond," Summer said.

He gave a little nod. "Be right back."

Leaning on his cane, the Swindler crossed to the wooden door and unlocked it. Nate could not see inside, because the room was dark. The Swindler limped out of view, closing the door.

"Do you think he really has treasure back there?" Summer asked. "Probably not a real diamond."

"He seemed confident," Nate said.

A moment later the Swindler returned. He closed and

locked the door, then approached the counter. He held out his hand, displaying an egg-shaped diamond the size of Nate's thumb.

"Is that real?" Summer asked.

"Oh, yes," the Swindler said, holding it up, letting the light catch and sparkle in the many facets. "And much more valuable than a stuffed octopus, or whatever you can win at the other games." He rubbed his hands together and held out two fists. "Play a simple game? Five tickets for the diamond. Which hand is it in?" His grin showed a single gold tooth interrupting his white smile.

"Sure," Summer said, tearing off five tickets and placing them on the counter. "That one," she said, tapping a fist.

The Swindler opened it to reveal an empty hand. He opened his other hand, and there was the diamond. "I always win," he said, sweeping up the five tickets. "Want to challenge me for the diamond, son?"

"How about for some Enchanted Carnie Coins?" Nate asked.

"Sure, why not?" the Swindler said, pocketing the diamond. "How many?"

"Ten," Nate said.

The Swindler reached into a pocket and produced ten silvery, glittering Carnie Coins. "What's the contest?"

"Give me a second," Nate said.

"Take a whole minute," the Swindler offered.

Nate weighed his options. He was pretty good at checkers, but he had to assume the Swindler was a master. He couldn't play any of the Swindler's games. It had to be something that put chance on his side.

"How about this?" Nate proposed. "I think of a number between one and ten, and you have to guess it."

"Hmm," the Swindler said with a little nod. "Interesting. I'll play under these terms." He reached behind the counter and withdrew a piece of paper and a pencil. "You write your number on this paper. Has to be a whole number. No decimals or fractions. If I either guess the exact number or come within one, I win. Otherwise, you win. For example, if your number is two, I win by guessing one, two, or three. The cost is ten tickets."

"More than Summer paid," Nate said.

"You have more control over the game," the Swindler said. "And I consider the prize more valuable. Take it or leave it."

The Swindler would have only a three out of ten chance. Those seemed like pretty good odds. "I'll take it," Nate said, detaching ten tickets and setting them on the counter beside the sparkling coins.

"Deal," the Swindler said, turning around. "Shield the paper however you want. Then fold it up tight."

Nate took the paper and pencil, then crouched with his back to the swindler and carefully wrote a ten. If the Swindler had to come within one, a one or a ten left him only two winning guesses. He folded the paper in half three times, then stood up.

The Swindler still faced away from him. "Ready?"

"Yes," Nate said.

The Swindler turned and looked directly into Nate's eyes. "If birds gathered in a tree, how many birds would there be?"

"I'm not going to say the number I picked," Nate said.

"I know," the Swindler replied. "But we never agreed I couldn't ask questions. How many? Then I'll guess."

"Probably one thousand and forty-two," Nate said.

The Swindler gave a nod, staring at Nate. In case the Swindler was reading his mind, Nate imagined the number four.

"Nine," the Swindler said.

Nate sagged. "How did you do that?"

"Was that your number?" Summer asked.

Nate unfolded his paper and displayed the ten.

The Swindler collected the tickets and tucked them away.

"Want to go again?" Nate asked.

"Always," the Swindler said.

"Same game?" Nate asked. "Same stakes?"

"Why not?" the Swindler said, producing a second sheet of paper. "Deal?"

"Yes," Nate said, placing ten more tickets on the counter.

The Swindler turned around. Nate crouched and wrote a five. He folded the paper twice and stood.

"Ready?" the Swindler asked.

"Yes," Nate said.

The Swindler turned around. "What's your name?"

"Nate."

"How many friends does a person need, Nate?"

Nate considered his response. "One thousand and forty-two."

"Your number is five," the Swindler said.

Summer looked at Nate.

"How did you do that?" Nate asked, unfolding the paper to display the five.

"I love to win," the Swindler said, brushing the tickets off the counter. "What now?"

"We should go," Summer murmured to Nate.

"The Regulars Map indicates a secret way is hidden here," Nate said quietly. "Maybe it's through that door?"

"That door is for me," the Swindler said. "I keep my prizes back there. If you want to know about secret ways, we could play for it. Or you can keep trying for the enchanted coins."

Nate glanced at Summer. "We'll come back another day."

"I'll be here," the Swindler said. "I'm always happy to part people from their tickets."

"I'd love to see you lose," Nate said.

The Swindler gave a little shrug. "That keeps people coming back. They always leave disappointed, but they still return."

Nate wanted to think of a contest he could win for sure, but nothing occurred to him.

"Come on," Summer said. "We can try again another time."

"Okay," Nate said. He walked to the door, then turned around. "I'm going to beat you at something."

The Swindler grinned. "I would love to see you try."

CHAPTER TWELVE

DREAM

You're home late," Mom said after Nate entered the house.

"It's not quite nine," Nate said.

"How is your homework situation?" Mom asked.

"Normal," Nate said. "I have some reading for English. I may wake up a little early to finish a few things."

"How was the filming?" she asked.

"I don't actually film," Nate said. "Zac mostly records it selfie-style."

"I keep hearing great things about the carnival," Mom said. "People sound very enthusiastic. We should go as a family this weekend."

"That could be fun," Nate hedged. "The carnival is full of surprises."

"Have you had dinner?" Mom asked.

"Seafood."

"At a carnival?" Mom asked.

"It was good," Nate said. "Tasted fresh."

"I'll believe that when I see it," Mom said.

"Either way, I'm full," Nate said. "I'll probably just lay in bed and read."

"Getting up early leaves you tired at night," Mom said. "A little different than the summer?"

"A lot different," Nate said. "Good night."

After seeing to his hygiene, Nate crawled into bed. He lay on his back, staring at the dim ceiling, but apparently, his brain had not yet received the message that his body felt exhausted.

How had the Swindler beat him at the number guessing game? Could the guy read minds? How could such a person be beaten? Was it foolish to try?

What other secret ways might Edward reveal to them? Could they locate a secret way on their own tomorrow? Nate wondered if his parents would let him attend the carnival every day. How long would the Zac excuse work? They would eventually catch on that he wasn't filming with Zac every time he went.

The carnival really was amazing. He wanted to uncover more secrets, not simply to stop the bad guys, but to uncover other mysteries too. How might the attractions change by tomorrow?

Only one way to get there—sleep. Which reminded him of Edward's warning not to sleep inside the carnival. Who would fall asleep at an amusement park in the first place?

Nate wondered what would happen if he did. Could that be how people got captured?

His eyes were getting heavy, so he closed them and continued thinking.

If tossing coins into the fountain granted wishes, might there be other places where he could use Carnie Coins besides coin slots? Maybe looking only for coin slots limited their search. What kind of magical candy might the carnival have? And would it work anywhere, or just on the carnival grounds?

At last, Nate drifted off to sleep.

* * * * *

Nate was not sure how he had arrived at the ghost town. The buildings along the main street were mostly intact but looked dusty and worn. Spiderwebs crisscrossed the interior of the trough in front of the sagging hotel. Skeletal tumbleweeds scratched fitfully over the dirt as the breeze rose and fell.

Nate strolled down the street. When the breeze whipped up dust, the wooden facades creaked and groaned. At the first intersection, he looked down the narrow side street to discover that beyond the central aisle of the town, the buildings had mostly been reduced to foundations, crumbling footprints of their former structures.

Nate heard a train whistle in the distance.

The shrill howl surprised him. The town was so dead, it seemed he must be the only living thing for miles.

Nate looked around. How had he gotten here? He wasn't old enough to drive.

"Hello?" he called. "Anyone?"

The town seemed to swallow his words, the acoustics totally flat, the opposite of an echo.

The train whistle shrieked again.

Nate realized the train might be his only way out of this place. Otherwise, his life might depend on foraging in the dry husks of forgotten buildings.

He started running toward the edge of town, in the direction the whistle had come from. A strange white shape came into view just past where the buildings ended. As Nate drew closer, he realized it was the full skeleton of a horse, crumpled on the ground beneath a cracked, sun-worn saddle. Who had left a saddled horse to decompose in the street?

The train whistle sounded again, abrasively loud. Nate could now hear the rumbling clatter of the locomotive. Up ahead, on a berm of gravel, Nate discerned the clean, horizontal line of the railway.

He picked up his pace, determined to reach the tracks before the train arrived. Prickly weeds clawed at his pant legs. Would a train even stop to pick him up without a station in view? Nate decided he would try to jump aboard if it didn't stop. The risk would be preferable to dying of thirst in a ghost town.

Did he have any magic candy he could use? Moon Rocks? Ironhides? Peak Performance? Patting his pockets, he found none.

Upon reaching the raised gravel topped by the tracks, Nate turned and beheld the train for the first time. The front looked like a dilapidated school bus. In fact, the entire train looked like it had been made by linking old yellow school buses and adapting them to ride the rails.

The engineer hit the brakes, sparks flying as the chain of buses ground to a stop beside Nate. The doors folded open like typical school bus doors. Looking in, Nate discovered that the driver was the Swindler.

"Hurry up, son, or you'll be late for school," the Swindler said.

"This train goes to school?" Nate asked.

"Sure does," the Swindler said, checking his watch. "Come on. You're not our only stop."

Nate boarded the train. The first car was nearly full. All of the kids looked older than he was. Nate recognized none of them. He walked along the aisle until he found one of the only open seats.

"Mind if I sit here?" Nate asked the strikingly pretty young woman on the bench. She easily looked old enough to attend high school.

"Suit yourself," she said in a neutral tone.

Nate plopped down as the linked buses started forward. The whistle blew, and the train picked up speed.

"That kid is trying to put the moves on Andrea," a voice behind Nate whispered.

The young woman beside Nate turned to him. "Are you trying to become my boyfriend?"

"No, I just needed a seat," Nate explained.

"Next to the hottest girl in school," a voice behind him teased. "What a player!"

Recognizing the voice, Nate turned. "Zac?"

"Don't waste time on me," Zac said. "Entertain your new girlfriend."

The train began to rattle jarringly. The speed kept increasing.

Nate found Andrea staring at him. "You shouldn't be here," she told him. "This ride is for big kids."

The track suddenly dove down, and the train accelerated wildly. Nate held on to the back of the seat in front of him as the track dipped into a sweeping turn like a roller coaster. The other kids remained seated sedately, but Nate could barely brace himself against the g-forces.

"Change of plans," the Swindler called. "We're heading to the carnival instead of school. It's high time you kids got a real education."

The train rose and then plunged. Nate felt his insides floating as the train plummeted downward. When the train turned sharply to the left, Nate slammed sideways against Andrea.

"Get off me, you weirdo!" Andrea complained. "Why did you sit by me?"

The brakes squealed, thrusting Nate against the seat in front of him. As the train screeched to an ear-punishing stop, the lights dimmed inside and outside. Looking around, Nate realized the other kids had fallen asleep—Zac, Andrea, everyone.

The Swindler stood and cried out, "Last stop! Everybody off!"

Nate shook Andrea's shoulder, but she remained slumped

in unconsciousness. A couple of the other kids were snoring. Their skin had taken on a grayish tint in the dimness.

"Last call!" the Swindler shouted.

Nate got up and hurried to the doors. They opened, and he stumbled down the stairs and into a station adjoining the carnival. His homeroom teacher, Mr. Zimmerman, stood farther down the platform, holding a clipboard.

"There you are," Mr. Zimmerman called when he saw Nate. He jotted a note on his clipboard. "I thought we might have lost you. Come with me. You fell way behind."

"There are a lot of kids asleep on the train," Nate told him.

"It's too late for them," Mr. Zimmerman said. "Every field trip has casualties."

Mr. Zimmerman led the way to a big top and lifted a flap so Nate could enter. "They're just starting musical chairs," he said. "Run for it."

Supervised by clowns, the entire sixth grade was marching around a huge ring of chairs to the tune of "Pop Goes the Weasel" in a minor key. This time Nate recognized many of the faces, though he didn't see any of his best friends. He ran and joined the procession. When the melody stopped a moment later, Nate scrambled for a seat, getting to it just before a kid named Diego.

The twenty kids who ended up without seats were escorted away. When the music restarted, a team of clowns removed twenty more chairs. This time the tune was "Three Blind Mice."

Nate watched the other kids intently stalking the remaining chairs. What was going on? Had he really just been on a train cobbled together from old school buses? Why was he playing this bizarrely huge game of musical chairs?

This had to be a dream.

The thought felt like a pure note cutting through discordant chaos.

Suddenly his unlikely circumstances made sense.

He hadn't actually been in a ghost town. Sure, the metal folding chairs under his fingers felt real. And yes, he could smell the sawdust on the ground and hear the tinkling music. But school bus trains didn't exist. Though all of this looked, sounded, felt, and smelled real, he was in a dream.

Which meant he didn't need to play by the rules. He wondered what he could get away with. Could he fly? He remembered how it felt to fly when he had the jet stamp. Trying to summon the feeling, Nate jumped, but gravity still operated like normal.

So instead, he ran away from the game. Why play musical chairs when there was a whole carnival to explore? Nate raced toward one of the flaps that led out of the tent.

With a gloved finger over an earpiece, the purple-faced clown from the parade spoke into a lapel mic, "We've got a runner."

Three of the clowns supervising the game broke off to chase Nate. One held what looked like an enormous butterfly net. A second carried a straitjacket. The third wielded a tube-like gun that might have been a grenade launcher.

Nate poured on the speed. He tried to fly again, but physics stubbornly refused.

The clown with the tubelike gun fired a weighted net that

ensnared Nate and hurled him to the ground. As he tried to untangle himself from the webbing, the other two clowns converged, seizing him roughly.

"Leave me alone," Nate shouted. "I know this is a dream."

"So do we," one of the clowns declared in a goofy voice. "Misbehave in life, and you get real-life consequences. Misbehave in a dream, and you get dream consequences." The clown looked at his associate with the straitjacket. "Wrap him up, Nobbles."

Growling in frustration, still tangled in the net, Nate punched and kicked at the clowns. They resisted his efforts, pressing ever closer.

And suddenly he was in his bed, thrashing against his covers. Relief washed over him as Nate realized he was awake and safe. The experience really had been a dream.

Sweaty and out of breath, he had awakened about ten minutes before his alarm. Nate felt relieved to be out of danger. He shut off his alarm and got out of bed. A seagull was looking in his window.

Nate opened the window and shared some Brain Feed with the bird, then offered a small piece of bread.

"Skimping on the bread today?" Rocco asked.

"Not if you have good info," Nate replied.

"Plenty of weird lately," Rocco said. "The big human who visited the candy shop goes all over town. Fighting some bear. Then chasing down a person. He is busy."

"That fits what I know," Nate said.

"Strange animals in town," Rocco said. "Not just at the carnival. I saw a rhinoceros. And an orangutan. I didn't know exactly what they were, but with Brain Feed, I have words for them."

"What else?" Nate asked.

"On my way to your place, I saw big bones down by the creek," Rocco said. "Looked like a dead horse."

Nate couldn't help thinking of his dream. "Where at the creek?"

"On the way to Diablo View," Rocco said. "You can't miss it."

Nate tore the rest of the bread into four parts and tossed them to the seagull. "Thanks, Rocco. I'm going to check out those bones for myself."

"Do humans like horse bones?" Rocco asked.

"Curious humans do," Nate said, closing the window and hurrying to get ready for the day.

CHAPTER THIRTEEN

RELICS

Not much later that morning, Nate biked along the jogging path toward school, but the creek looked normal. Maybe the bones were easier to see from the air. Nate began to worry he had passed them. As the path went up a ramp away from the creek, he caught out of the corner of his eye an odd flash of white down in the gully.

Nate skidded to a stop.

That had to be it! If he hurried, he could take a look and still make it to school on time.

Turning, Nate descended the ramp and rode off the bike path, down the weedy slope to the creek. He got off his bike and stared in disbelief at the sight before him—the full skeleton of a horse with a sun-damaged saddle still attached.

Not just any horse skeleton. Not any old saddle.

It was the same skeleton and saddle from his dream in every detail.

Nate continued to stare. What could it possibly mean? Had his dream been prophetic somehow? Was this horse skeleton important? Or was some kind of magic at play?

Time was still passing. If he lingered much longer, he would be late to school. Nate walked his bike up to the path, then mounted it and pedaled hard.

On the way to school, Nate passed a stretch where the road narrowed down to one lane. The smell of bananas grew stronger until he reached sanitation workers using brooms and shovels to clean up thousands of the fruit. Many had been crushed by traffic, but slightly overripe yellow bananas with faint brown spots were also strewn around neighboring sidewalks and yards.

Drop-off traffic was thick when Nate arrived and parked his bike. He hurried to homeroom and slid into his seat as the bell rang. He overheard kids talking about the huge mess of bananas they had passed on the way to school. Mr. Zimmerman stood at the front of the class, looking much as he had in Nate's dream.

"You had some reading assigned about Mesopotamia," the teacher said. "After announcements, we will have a surprise quiz. If you did the reading, it should be fairly easy. If not, do your best to invent some creative answers. Hopefully the experience will provide extra motivation to stay on track."

"Can we skim right now to review?" Zac asked with a hand raised.

"Sure," Mr. Zimmerman said. "Go ahead and speed-read until the announcements conclude."

Nate had forgotten about his history reading. It had seemed like the kind of assignment he could catch up on later. But he had a stick of Peak Performance gum in his pocket. He knew the magical gum optimized his skill and endurance. Could it speed up his reading? He had never used it that way.

Nate unwrapped the gum and started chewing. As usual, a sense of high alertness came over him. He opened his textbook and began hastily absorbing facts about the cradle of civilization. Never had he read so swiftly, and never had the text felt so plain.

When Mrs. Jackson started giving announcements, Nate continued to read. Multitasking was no problem, so as she spoke, he memorized names like "Tigris" and "Euphrates."

"Boys and girls, you will be happy to learn that we have organized a surprise field trip for the entire student body. On Thursday, we will attend the Dreams and Screams International Carnival."

The class reacted enthusiastically to the news.

Zac turned around to face Nate. "My video may have been a little too good."

The principal went on about permission slips going home today and needing to be back by Thursday morning. Nate could no longer cram information about Sumerians. Why was the whole school suddenly going to the carnival? That seemed like an end-of-year event. It was too much like his dream. Mr. Zimmerman started handing out permission slips as the announcements ended.

"Hey, Zac, have you had weird dreams lately?" Nate asked.

"I hardly ever dream," Zac said. "At least I don't remember them when I wake up. How come? Are you having nightmares?"

"Yeah," Nate said.

Mr. Zimmerman finished handing out permission slips. "With that out of the way, please close your textbooks and clear them from your desks. It's time for the first of many pop quizzes."

Nate smiled, still chewing his gum, confident that the facts of the chapter were present in his mind, almost as if he had downloaded them. When he received the quiz, the answers felt obvious. Nate tried not to write too quickly.

* * * * *

After school, Nate biked straight to the candy shop. At lunch, John Dart had recommended they meet there. Nate had heard odd rumors throughout the day. Nicole Ghysels had found department-store mannequins crowding her garage this morning. Noah Maldonado reported seeing three slot machines in the general store. Nate even heard a rumor that somebody's little sister had seen a unicorn.

Nate parked his bike out front, entered the shop, and went straight to the back. He found Lindy at a desk copying a diagram of a human cell out of a textbook. John Dart hunched beside Mr. Stott at a worktable. Mr. Stott was examining an old stirrup through a magnifying glass, carefully poking the leather with a scalpel. A bleached, curved horse rib rested nearby.

"Is that from the saddle?" Nate asked.

"I grabbed a couple of samples after lunch," John said. "The skeleton was right where you described."

Nate also noticed a few overripe bananas on the worktable. "Are those bananas from this morning?"

"I ate one," John said. "It tasted fine."

"These objects all appear perfectly authentic," Mr. Stott said, backing away from the worktable to look at Nate. "You saw a horse skeleton like that in a dream last night?"

"Identical," Nate said. "Same dried-out saddle, same horse bones."

Mr. Stott nodded. "That fits my working theory."

"Wait," Lindy said, looking up from her work. "That horse bone came out of a dream?"

Mr. Stott glanced at John Dart then back to Lindy. "This has to do with the carnival. I don't want you involved with that place."

"Dad, at some point you have to trust me to live my life, or I'll never have one," Lindy said. "I'm on your side. I can handle danger."

"You'll get to live your life," Mr. Stott said. "I just want you to have the chance to grow up first. We need privacy for this conversation."

Lindy rolled her eyes, picked up her textbook, and headed up to the apartment above the candy shop.

John drummed his fingers on the worktable. "We can't keep her in the dark forever."

"Of course not," Mr. Stott said. "But we also don't want her drawn into that carnival. She'll have chances to prove herself against threats that don't involve members of her family."

Summer and Trevor entered. "We saw the skeleton," Trevor announced.

"Pigeon might still be back there," Summer said. "He was examining it closely."

"Have either of you noticed objects from your dreams physically manifesting?" Mr. Stott asked.

"I dreamed last night that a school bus picked me up and unexpectedly took me to the carnival," Summer said. "That mechanical elephant was chasing me around. It was stressful, but nothing from my dream has appeared at the creek."

"Part of your dream may come true soon," Trevor said. "We're taking a field trip to the carnival on Thursday. I bet we'll take buses."

"The entire school?" Mr. Stott asked.

"It was announced today," John Dart said.

"Was this planned from the start of the year?" Mr. Stott asked.

"The first I heard about it was during the morning announcements," Nate said.

Mr. Stott looked to John. "Tell them what you have noticed."

"Carnival attendance has only increased since Saturday," John said. "I believe the carnival is exerting a powerful draw that goes beyond good advertising and positive word of mouth. The appearance of anomalies around town has increased as well."

Pigeon pounded into the room, his cheeks flushed. "That

skeleton is bizarre," he said. "Perfectly intact, except a rib had broken off. And one of the stirrups is missing from the saddle."

Trevor pointed at the objects on the worktable.

"Oh," Pigeon said.

"You're right about the horse skeleton," John said. "It's in strangely good condition."

"This rib is actual bone," Mr. Stott said. "Not an imitation. The leather saddle is genuine as well."

"That has held true for the other anomalies," John said. "Actual animals on the loose. Authentic oddities like the appearance of slot machines and the stagecoach. That enormous bowling ball at Diablo View was coated with plastic resin consistent with regulation balls."

"Why did I see the horse skeleton in my dream last night?" Nate asked. "How did a duplicate end up in the creek?"

"We are confident there is a link," Mr. Stott said. "I believe the anomalies are relics from dreams."

"Meaning what?" Pigeon asked.

"Certain objects are somehow crossing over from dreams into reality," John said.

"Our dreams are coming true?" Summer exclaimed.

"That statement is too broad," Mr. Stott clarified. "Certain objects are leaking from your dreams into the physical world."

"Can that happen?" Pigeon asked.

"Many dimensions adjoin our reality," Mr. Stott said. "The Mirror Realm is one. The Dreamworld is another."

"You mean we go to an actual place when we dream?" Summer asked.

"Your mind accesses a dimension of ideas, images, and

symbols," Mr. Stott said. "Vivid dreams can be nearly indistinguishable from our waking reality."

"But how can something jump from our minds into the real world?" Pigeon asked.

"It happens all the time," Mr. Stott said. "An architect imagines and designs a building, and then a construction team helps him execute the blueprint. Consider anyone who mentally conceives a plan, then brings it to pass, and you have examples."

"It takes a lot of work for a design to become a building," Nate said. "You can't wish a building into existence overnight."

Mr. Stott held up a finger. "It always requires work. But think about a song. A person with the right talent could sing it into existence as they create it. A lot of magic works that way. When I want to produce a certain type of candy, I first imagine it, then I use my intentions and skill to conjure the treat. An Ironhide would have no potency if I merely combined ingredients."

"So magic can make something out of nothing," Trevor said.

"Ideas have substance," Mr. Stott said. "*Something* is present after you have an idea that was not present before you had it. And this doesn't only work for magic. The more you learn, the more you will discover that imagination and intention are the real currency in this universe. We have plenty of matter, endless space, and abundant energy. The power lies in imagining what can be done with those ingredients, and in using your willpower to bring the vision into reality."

"However it works, you're telling us that objects from

dreams are materializing around us," Pigeon said. "That kind of magic could do anything.".

"The potential is staggering," Mr. Stott agreed.

"Do you know magic like this?" Summer asked.

"In small ways, perhaps," Mr. Stott said. "Nothing to rival what we are witnessing here."

"Not even Mozag can do such things," John said.

"What is Camilla trying to accomplish with her carnival?" Nate asked.

"That is what we must figure out," Mr. Stott said. "Camilla White has yet to be spotted in the carnival or anywhere near Colson. We have no clues about her objectives."

"Have you noticed the signs outside the entrance?" John asked. "One of them reads, 'All dreams sparked by this experience become the property of the Dreams and Screams International Carnival.' Let that sink in."

"I thought that was a joke," Nate said.

"I expect they rely on that reaction," Mr. Stott said.

"Why do they want our dreams?" Trevor asked.

"Maybe if we dream of treasure or other valuables, they can collect that stuff," Nate guessed. "Then they throw out the things they don't want, like horse bones."

Mr. Stott stroked his beard pensively. "I'm not sure what those who run the carnival wish to accomplish. See if you can confirm that Camilla is running the operation—we need more than the word of an animatronic ram. Then try to figure out what she is after."

"The friend we made, Edward, warned us not to fall asleep inside the carnival," Summer said.

"Who sleeps at a carnival?" Pigeon asked. "There's too much to do."

"His warning would make sense given our suspicions about dreams," John said. "Maybe the effects are exaggerated if you sleep inside the lair."

"Some people *have* to sleep there," Nate said. "Don't a lot of workers travel with the carnival?"

"Good point," Pigeon said.

"Staying awake at the fairgrounds sounds like sage advice," Mr. Stott said. "Be wary of anyone you meet, including your friend Edward. Sometimes enemies put on friendly faces, particularly if they hope to lure kids into their service."

"Edward is meeting us tomorrow to share secret ways inside the park," Nate said.

"We're supposed to help Zac and Benji film tomorrow," Trevor said. "How will that work?"

Nate shrugged. "Either we share our secrets with Zac, or some of us help him while others investigate with Edward."

"Confiding in Zac could be dangerous," Pigeon said. "Being famous doesn't make him trustworthy. Besides, he has connections high up in the carnival."

"Those connections could be useful if he helps us," Summer pointed out.

"We'll have to improvise as we go," Nate said.

"I recommend you kids avoid the carnival today," Mr. Stott said. "John is trying to procure some items that could help counter dream magic."

"The Council sees this carnival as a major threat," John said. "They are willing to commit significant resources to investigating it. Let me see what assistance I can gather. I'll meet with you kids tomorrow at lunchtime. It's lasagna day."

Nate looked at the others. "Makes sense to me. Might be smart to let my family see me at home for a change."

"Outside magic won't work inside the carnival," Summer reminded everyone.

"Which is a problem," John said. "At the very least, we'll provide tools you can use outside the carnival. At best, we'll figure out how to smuggle in some items."

"In the meantime, I made a concoction that should help suppress your dreams," Mr. Stott said. He passed out little vials of dark blue liquid. "It doesn't taste very good, but taken before you fall sleep, this solution should help you do the opposite of what the Dreams and Screams International Carnival wants. It should help you dream small."

"Sounds good to me," Pigeon said, accepting a vial.

"I'm still toying with the formula, so future batches will taste better," Mr. Stott said. "This concoction would have a minimal effect on adults but should work fairly well on you kids. I'll be interested to hear how you sleep after trying it."

"Great," Trevor said. "We're the guinea pigs testing new magical potions."

"I've already run tests of my own," Mr. Stott assured him. "The formulation shouldn't be hazardous. My main question is how well it works."

"I'll give it a try," Nate said, holding up a vial to study the viscous liquid. "I don't need any more dreams where clowns try to wrestle me into a straitjacket."

Trevor frowned. "Maybe I should drink two."

CHAPTER FOURTEEN
JUMPING

S ummer coasted to a stop in an upscale neighborhood on the far side of Colson, then wheeled her bike between two azalea bushes at the corner of Zac's property. He lived in a fancy house with a spacious, landscaped yard. Soft lights marked the walkway to the door and highlighted certain trees and bushes.

After the discussion at the candy shop, Summer had decided she would sneak out tonight. Back home, she made a figure of pillows and wadded blankets to create the illusion she was in bed. The ride to Zac's address had taken twenty minutes, so it was just after ten. About half the windows of the large house were still lit.

Summer took off her shoes and set them by the bike, then removed a Moon Rock from her pocket. Nate and the others might not love the idea, but since when did decisions have to be unanimous? By not asking for group consent, she had avoided the risk of getting her plan vetoed.

Zac had been a good friend to them. It would be hard to conduct effective investigations at the carnival with Zac still in the dark. Besides, it could be dangerous for him to have no warning about what was really going on. Instead of hiding the truth from Zac, Summer felt confident it would be better to gain his help.

She put the sugary crystal into her mouth and worked it to the side with her tongue. Her body tingled as if her blood had started fizzing with carbonation. A small hop carried her over a flower bed. She drifted to a spot in the middle of the front lawn, landing lightly. The damp grass soaked through her socks; it must have been watered recently.

Headlights announced a car coming down the street. Feeling conspicuous, she stood casually, and the car went by, pulling into a driveway a few houses down. Another hop took her to the corner of the house, where she paused.

She had no idea which room belonged to Zac. Thanks to his videos, she knew what his bedroom looked like on the inside, along with the kitchen and some other rooms in the house, but she didn't know the complete floor plan. She knew he lived with his dad and his stepmom, a younger sister, and a small, fluffy, white dog named Trouble.

The dog could be a problem. Summer didn't want to get barked at and caught by Zac's parents. Maybe she shouldn't have come in person. Was this overly dramatic? She could have simply called Zac and arranged a meeting.

But surprising him would have more flair, as long as she

could pull it off. She had to admit, part of her wanted to impress Zac.

Summer jumped to the roof, landing softly on the ceramic tiles with her damp socks and reduced-gravity weight. Accustomed to Moon Rock physics through considerable practice, she glided to the side of the roof so she would be less visible from the street. As she reconnoitered, Summer decided that the room with the big balcony in the back was probably the main bedroom where the parents slept. Creeping along like a cat burglar, she approached a dormer and pressed her face against a windowpane to view a dim office illuminated by ambient light from the hall.

Floating along with gentle steps, her toes barely touching the roof tiles, Summer headed back toward the front of the house. She found a lighted window that showed a boy's orderly bedroom. Zac sat in front of a big TV playing a vintage Mario game. He did not appear to be filming himself.

Summer knocked gently on the glass.

Zac jumped and whirled, squinting at the window. He apparently could not see well into the darkness from his bright room.

Summer leaned closer to the glass and waved.

Eyes wide, Zac crossed to the window. Once he got a good look at Summer, he went and shut his door, then came back and opened the window.

"Summer, are you sleepwalking?" he asked. "What are you doing on my roof?"

"I wanted to surprise you," Summer said.

"Congratulations," Zac said. "Mission accomplished. If I

were a few years older, I probably would have dropped dead from a heart attack. Want to come in?"

"I need to show you something," Summer said, stepping back from the window. "Come out here with me."

Zac eyed her warily. "I don't really hang out on the roof much."

"Watch," Summer said, doing a little hop, enough to rise three or four feet before slowly descending back to the tiles.

"How did you do that?" Zac asked, leaning out the window and craning his neck, as if he expected to see an apparatus with wires. "What's the trick?"

"No trick," Summer said, stepping off the roof.

"Careful!" Zac whispered loudly.

Summer landed easily in the side yard, as if she had jumped off a bottom step, then sprang back up to the roof.

Zac stared in obvious amazement. "What is going on? I must be dreaming."

"Magic candy," Summer said.

"Very funny," Zac replied. "Did you plan this with my dad or something?"

"I'm serious," Summer said. "I'm sucking on a piece of candy called a Moon Rock. Until it dissolves, I can move around like gravity is way lower than normal."

"That's impossible," Zac said.

"I know it seems impossible," Summer said, balancing on one hand. "The quickest way to get it is to try one."

"Yeah, right," Zac said. "And jump off the roof? Are you trying to kill me?"

"Try it in your room first," Summer said, returning to the

open window. "Then do what you want." She handed him a crystalline chunk of candy.

Zac looked at it. "Rock candy?"

"Just try it," Summer said. "Don't bite it, or you'll get a major jolt. Just suck."

Zac popped the candy in his mouth. "Wait. I feel weird." He pushed off the ground and launched up to his ceiling so fast he had to raise his hands to keep from hitting his head. Then he drifted back to the ground. He laughed, eyebrows raised. "Summer, are you kidding me? This actually works?"

"Come out here," she said. "If you fall off the roof it will be like dropping a foot or two."

Needing no further encouragement, Zac climbed out his window. "Are you some kind of superhero?"

"Maybe," she said. Summer leaped as high as she could, soaring twenty feet higher than where Zac stood on the roof, exhilarated by the rush of the night air. At the apex of her flight, she gazed up at the stars, then shifted her attention to the thirty-foot drop into the backyard. The landing jarred her a little, but she stayed on her feet.

"How are you not dead?" Zac asked.

"Come down here," Summer said.

"My brain thinks I'll get hurt," Zac confessed after a pause.

"You saw how far I jumped," Summer said. "This will feel like nothing."

Zac jumped, then drifted down onto his back patio, landing next to Summer. "I can barely believe it," he said. Then he jumped significantly higher than his roof, landing over by the pool.

Summer sprang over to him.

"Why isn't this stuff world famous?" Zac asked.

"It's a secret," Summer said. "There are actual magicians in the world. Some of them make magical candy."

"You know where to get more?" Zac asked.

"Yes, within certain limits," Summer said. "Last year, a magician tried to take over Colson using magical candy. Me, Nate, Trevor, and Pigeon helped stop her."

"You *are* a superhero," Zac said reverently.

"I'm just a kid who got conned into helping an evil magician because I liked her candy," Summer said. "Same with Nate and the others. We ended up defeating her. We stopped another evil magician this summer. He was running Arcadeland."

"I loved that place," Zac said. "I wondered why it closed. They had magical candy?"

"And magic hand stamps," Summer said. "They were amazing."

"I never knew there was anything supernatural about that place," Zac said.

"Now another magician has come to town," Summer said. "She owns the carnival."

"Wait, really?" Zac asked. "Dreams and Screams?"

"The carnival is bad news," Summer said. "We are working with some of the people who police the magicians. We're trying to figure out what's really going on."

"What do you know so far?" Zac asked.

"A lot of people disappeared when the carnival was in

Texas," Summer said. "We still have a lot of investigating to do."

"And you want my help," Zac said.

"We have to do it quietly," Summer said. "I also want you to keep your guard up. Have you met a lady named Camilla White?"

"No," Zac said. "Is she in charge?"

"We think so," Summer said.

Zac jumped straight up into the air and floated down. "Magical candy. It seems hard to believe, but how could I not?"

"John Dart is one of the magical enforcers," Summer said.

"The Lunch Lord? No wonder you guys seem so tight."

"He's at our school undercover. We're going to get more instructions from him tomorrow."

Zac nodded. "So filming my video will be our cover as we check things out."

"Pretty much," Summer said.

"Should we tell Benji?" Zac asked.

"Let's ask the others first."

"Do they know you told me?"

"They will tomorrow."

Zac nodded. "I'll keep the secret unless you tell me to share it. So what now?"

Summer shrugged. "Until the Moon Rocks dissolve? We jump around."

CHAPTER FIFTEEN

SANDRA

The aroma of tomato sauce and seasonings permeated the lunchroom on Wednesday afternoon. Not long after Nate entered the lunch line, he felt a tap on his shoulder. He turned to find John Dart staring down at him.

"No time for waiting today," John said quietly. "You're the last one I need. Follow me."

John led Nate down a corridor to the music room where Summer, Zac, Trevor, and Pigeon were already seated with their lunch trays. An older woman sat with them, her weathered skin slightly spotted, her dark hair streaked with silver and white. John guided Nate to an empty seat where a tray awaited with lasagna and vegetables.

"Mr. Chevsky let me borrow the music room for our meeting this period," John said. "I took the liberty of providing lasagna for each of you. It's nothing to write home about, but better than average."

"Don't worry, Nate," Zac said. "I know about the magic candy."

"How did you find out?" Nate asked.

"I told him last night," Summer said. "I figured we needed him in the club."

Nate nodded. He wished she had consulted him. "Welcome to a weirder world."

"I'm still getting oriented," Zac said. "But I like it."

"Magical candy is not a secret we share lightly," John Dart said. "The less people know, the better."

"My lips are sealed," Zac said.

"Time is short," John said. "I brought a friend for you to meet. This is Sandra Lafond. She is an expert on dreams and an active part of the magical community. As a member of the Mille Lacs Band of Ojibwe, she traveled a long way to be here to help us."

"I'm honored to be here," Sandra said. "What do you believe about dreams?"

"Sometimes objects can leak out of them," Nate said. "I didn't know that until yesterday."

Sandra nodded but made no reply, her eyes straying to the other kids.

"I've heard that dreams are how our subconscious processes the day," Zac said. "I rarely remember mine."

"My dreams get scary," Pigeon said. "I'd rather not dream at all than have nightmares."

"I have weird dreams," Trevor said. "Lots of nonsense."

"Could you give me an example?" Sandra asked.

"Once I was a shepherd for giant snails," Trevor said. "Sometimes I dream about colors mixing around."

"I like dreaming," Summer said. "My favorites are when I fly. It feels so real."

"Dreams can be extremely convincing," Sandra said. "We like to think we can distinguish our dreams from our waking lives. Here we sit around this table. Are you sure this isn't a dream?"

"Yeah," Pigeon said.

"What makes you so sure?" Sandra asked.

"I can see it," Pigeon said. "Feel it. Hear it."

Nate took a bite of lasagna. "Taste it," he said around the mouthful.

"What interprets those senses?" Sandra asked.

"Our brains," Zac said.

"What about in a dream?" Sandra asked. "How do you experience it?"

"Also in our brains," Nate said.

"From the perspective of your brain, which is more real?" Sandra asked.

"Might be hard to tell," Pigeon said.

"Except after you wake up," Nate added.

"Why does it seem easier after you awaken?" Sandra asked.

"I don't know," Nate said. "Once I'm awake, the dream seems fake by contrast. When I'm awake, things feel more complete. Sharper. Dreams get fuzzy and illogical."

"So you feel sure you're awake now?" Sandra asked.

"Yes," Nate said.

Sandra narrowed her eyes. "Are you absolutely positive? What if everything becomes illogical and dreamlike?"

Nate thought about it. "I remember waking up this morning. Last night, I took a potion Mr. Stott gave me, and I had no dreams. In a dream, I tend to accept what happens. But if I focus on whether I'm dreaming, I sometimes realize it's a dream."

"That realization can transition the experience into a lucid dream," Sandra said. "Where you have more power."

"I've had that happen," Nate said. "But right now, as I focus on this moment, I feel sure I'm awake."

Sandra looked at the other kids. "Can the rest of you relate to how Nate feels?"

The others responded with nods and affirmations.

"Except I hardly ever remember my dreams," Zac muttered.

"Fair enough," Sandra said. "Consider some ideas with me. Life is not so different from a dream. We dwell in a temporary state. This life begins when we are born and ends when we die. Our time here may seem permanent because it is tangible, but it is actually fleeting. Sometimes we only begin to understand how brief this life is as we near the end, or as we see another person reach the end. I believe when we die, we awaken to a higher, more alert state of being. In fact, I suspect this life, after death, will feel much like a dream."

"This is getting deep," Zac said, picking at his garlic bread.

"This life may be fleeting," Sandra said, "but what happens here matters. Our choices have significance. Who we become is important. The truth we learn in our life stays with us as we journey onward. Though dreams happen in an altered state, they too can be significant. Within the framework of a dream, warnings can be received. Learning can happen. Real encounters with otherwise inaccessible dimensions can occur."

"But it all fades away when you wake up," Zac said.

"Some aspects might," Sandra agreed. "But others persist. Is our waking life so different? A day may end, but certain recollections persist in our minds and spirits. And some of what happens in a dream lingers in the conscious and subconscious mind."

"I guess that makes sense," Pigeon said. "How will this help us at the carnival?"

"You must begin by accepting dreams as actual experiences that hold significance," Sandra said. "They are neither obstacles to real life nor meaningless fiction. And if they are coming under attack, you must view your dreams as an important battleground."

"Who can attack our dreams?" Zac asked.

"The magician running the carnival is an expert at navigating dreamscapes," Sandra said. "A person like that has many names: dream walker, dream traveler, dream seer, dream hunter. Unfortunately, the magician is abusing that gift. I am here to investigate what this scoundrel is trying to accomplish."

"We can fight real battles in our dreams?" Nate asked.

"The fight starts with understanding the enormous power you wield," Sandra said. "Your mind is a magnificent fortress that you control. It can be assailed, but never taken—unless you surrender it."

"My mind tends to be all over the place," Zac said. "I feel like I'm along for the ride, but rarely in control."

"Your mind is your sovereign territory," Sandra said. "You can establish total control if you choose, or you can permit others to dictate what you think and do. Why do you suppose content for television and radio is called 'programming'? Outsiders can bombard you with messages. They can scare, distract, flatter, deceive, confuse, intimidate, and persuade—but no matter what they threaten or claim, they can only take what you choose to give."

"I had a nightmare the other night," Nate said. "Clowns were attacking me. I realized it was a dream and tried to fly away, but I couldn't."

"In dreams, you can do anything you believe you can do," Sandra said. "Perhaps fear or some other distortion caused you to doubt your ability to fly. Otherwise, you would have flown."

"How do I overcome doubt?" Nate asked.

"Think of belief as a spiritual muscle," Sandra said. "It gets stronger as you use it. Belief functions in the physical world much as it does in dreams. Until you believe you can become a professional athlete, what are the chances you will put in the long hours of training that make it possible? Until you believe you can start a business, why would you hone a product to perfection and raise capital? So much begins with belief. So many doors remain closed without it."

"I never know when I'm dreaming," Pigeon said. "How can I realize I'm in a dream?"

"You all must master this skill," Sandra said. "Look for flaws in the continuity of your dreams. Dreams are often disjointed. You frequently will not know how you arrived someplace. Try to remember waking up that morning, or what happened the day before. This can trigger the realization that you are dreaming."

"My dreams get really random," Trevor said. "They are always disjointed."

"Then look for the illogical," Sandra said. "Abnormalities can signal that you are dreaming. Does the environment around you work correctly? Do mirrors cast true reflections? Try to read a book, then look away, then go back to it. Reading is often messy in dreams."

"Start checking whether you are dreaming while you're awake," John said. "It will get you in the habit of testing, and it will establish a benchmark that will be useful for comparison when you test during dreams."

"John is right," Sandra said. "Test yourself now. Can you control what happens in the next moment? Can you make your lunch tray disappear? Can you fly?"

"I'm trying," Zac said. "But my lunch tray is still here."

"That giant bowling ball felt like something from a dream," Trevor said.

"Because it was," Sandra said softly. "That is what makes this whole situation so interesting and uncertain. Relics from the dreamscape are crossing into our physical reality. Around the carnival, waking reality takes on dreamlike qualities, almost as if the physical world and the dream world are starting to converge."

"What does that mean?" Nate asked.

Sandra furrowed her brow. "That is what I hope to figure out. The entire scenario is a new experience for me. This much I know—while the carnival is operating, our dreams must be vigilantly guarded."

"How do we guard them?" Summer asked.

"Remember, you are the sole commander of your mind," Sandra said. "Decide right now to believe that wholeheartedly. When you dream, recognize your condition swiftly, and then seize control. Fend off any attackers. No matter what anyone else asserts, *you* are the highest authority in your private dreamscape."

Nate fidgeted in his chair. "If the dream world is crossing into normal life, what can we do about it when we're awake?"

"Take care not to fall asleep in strange places—especially on carnival property," Sandra warned. "And if you so choose, I can serve as a mentor. I am a dream walker, meaning I can roam the dreamscape, accessing the dreams of others. With your express permission, my right to be there increases, making it easier for me to assist in protecting your dreams."

"You could help out during my nightmares?" Pigeon exclaimed. "Sign me up!"

"I have already granted Sandra access to my dreams," John said. "I would trust her to have my back any day."

"Sure," Nate said. "I want all the help I can get. How do I make it official?"

"All I need is your permission," Sandra said.

"Yes," Trevor said. "Deal."

Everyone but Zac responded in the affirmative.

"What does this allow you to do?" Zac asked.

"You are the gatekeeper of your mind," Sandra said. "You

would be granting me access. If I am not a polite guest, you can always revoke your permission and kick me out."

"No offense, but I don't know any of you very well," Zac said. "I'd rather not give anyone access to my dreams—including my own family."

"I understand that desire, and I will honor it," Sandra said. "Let me know if anything changes. Meanwhile, I will continue to gather information and resources."

"Can you visit the carnival?" Pigeon asked.

"Not in person," Sandra said. "They have defenses against mages physically entering, but I hope that dream walking might eventually grant me access. When are you kids going next?"

"Later today," Zac said. "I have to film a video. I should start thinking up some elaborate props to include."

"That might be possible," Sandra said. "Take care inside. Anything you can learn about the individuals running the operation would be useful. And investigating your dreams could prove informative as well."

"Mr. Stott gave us a potion to limit our dreaming," Nate said.

"You should continue to use it," Sandra said. "But there may come a time when I ask you to skip repressing your dreams for a night."

Zac leaned forward. "Lady, if I hadn't spent last night doing low-gravity jumps with Summer, I'd think this sounded like the plot of a comic book. But when I combine the Moon Rocks with the huge bowling ball and the other objects appearing around town, I'm glad you're on the case."

CHAPTER SIXTEEN
CANDY

The carnival parking lot was filled to capacity, cars spilling onto side streets. Nate pedaled past the rows of vehicles until he reached the bike rack. Zac stood alone near the ticket offices, waiting in the colorful shadows cast by helium balloons. His face was partially hidden beneath a Giants baseball cap and behind sunglasses. Nate hurried over to him.

"Are we the first ones here?" Nate asked.

Zac nodded. "The more important question is, are we sure this isn't a dream? Do you remember how you got here?"

"I biked over after checking in at home."

"Can you change me into a butterfly?" Zac challenged.

Nate scrunched his nose and silently commanded Zac to transform. "Doesn't seem like it."

"And I've been trying to turn you into a penguin since I first caught sight of you. No luck. I think we're awake."

"How should today work?" Nate asked.

"We split up," Zac said. "Play our best cards. You and Summer grab info from Edward. I'll take the others to make my video and try to book a meeting with the owner. Here come Trevor and Pigeon."

The two skidded to a stop at the bike rack, then trotted over to join Nate and Zac. Benji's mom pulled up to the curb in a somewhat dusty SUV and dropped him off. Finally, Summer showed up on her pink bike.

"Sorry," Summer said. "I had to do some chores before I could come. And my mom cut these stupid bangs." She tried to push the hair off her forehead, but it fell back, hanging in a straight line.

"It's a pretty good disguise," Trevor said. "I hardly recognized you."

"Let's move on," Summer said shortly.

Nate had never seen Summer change her hairstyle. It obviously made her uncomfortable, but he thought it looked nice.

"Your hair looks great," Zac said. "Should we get going?"

Summer flushed a little and followed Zac into the carnival. Stopping at the Currency Exchange, he obtained a hundred tickets and ten coins for each of them. Nate felt rich as he jingled the coins in his palm.

The main boardwalk looked grander than before. Was it wider? Longer? A grandstand had sprung up toward the center where a brass combo played "When the Saints Go Marching In." The walls between games were taller and more elaborately decorated, and in many cases, bigger prizes had been added.

Long lines of people waited at the rides, games, and food

stands. It was a Wednesday afternoon, and the carnival was packed. Didn't the adults have jobs? What were so many people doing here?

"If they keep advertising, there won't be room for anyone to move inside the carnival," Zac said.

"I think this place will just expand," Nate said.

"Doesn't it already seem bigger?" Benji asked. "I came with my family on Monday. The bandstand wasn't here. And they didn't have that golfing game." He pointed at a golf simulator called Long Drive where players whacked real golf balls into a screen.

"Web Crawlers is new as well," Pigeon said. He indicated a tower three-stories tall. Layers of crisscrossing ropes formed a crude pyramid. A silver ring waited on a hook at the apex, just below a ticking timer. A player was climbing toward the ring, but sections of the webbing were designed to flex and pivot. As they watched, the girl fell and was trapped in lower funnels of netting.

"Summer and I are supposed to meet Edward at the Ferris wheel in ten minutes," Nate said.

"Then you better hurry," Zac said. "We'll head to the Fun House."

Nate and Summer split off from the others.

"I wish we had found more secret places on our own," Summer said.

"We tried," Nate replied. "Now we know it's hard to find new secrets without help. If Edward gives us real leads, he could be useful."

They reached the line for the Ferris wheel to see Edward

already waiting for them near a cotton candy cart. Even without his sword, his clothes looked better suited for a pirate movie than for normal life.

"Greetings, Nate, Summer," Edward said.

"Where are we going?" Summer asked.

Edward tapped the side of his nose. "The wishes you made at the fountain are about to come true. Follow me." He turned and started walking briskly away from the ride's entrance.

Nate had to adopt a shuffling jog to keep up as they passed between the Crafts Tent and Livestock Central.

"Are we going to see the Swindler?" Nate asked.

Edward shook his head. "Same building. Do you know the Swindler? Have you lost to him yet?"

"Yes," Nate said. "Have you?"

"Many times," Edward said.

"Have you beat him?" Summer asked.

"Never," Edward said. "Nor has anyone I know. It doesn't stop some of us from trying."

The Swindler's building came into view, the neon cursive less impressive in the brightness of the sunny afternoon. Ignoring the barker out front, Edward led them around to the back of the building. He pointed at a narrow, black fire escape ladder. "Did you notice the building has two stories?"

"I hadn't," Nate said, looking up. The ladder led to a wrought iron balcony. On the front side, the signage covered most of the upper story.

"Up there is a shop that sells magical items, including candy," Edward said. "It opened yesterday, and only admits kids under the age of fifteen. The candies cost coins, but don't be afraid to negotiate. Nate, I believe this will satisfy your wish. Summer, this candy shop is a secret place. You wished to discover multiple secret places, so I will share two others."

"Right now?" Summer checked.

Edward motioned for them to huddle close and lowered his voice. "The front car of the roller coaster has a coin slot. If you insert a Carnie Coin, your train will visit a different destination than normal. When you reach the secret station, trip the lap bar release and hop out. The release is on the underside of the lap bar, down on the left-hand side. You'll only have a few seconds to exit before the train will return you to the normal loading area."

"Where will the coaster take us?" Nate asked.

"You'll see," Edward said. "Here is your last secret. The Fun House is larger than it seems. To reach new parts of it, wade around the ball pit. When you find a spot deeper than the rest of the pit, search the floor for a coin slot."

"How is anyone supposed to find that without hearing the secret?" Summer asked.

"It's theoretically possible," Edward said. "Not likely though. Part of the challenge of exploring the carnival includes gathering information however you can. The Fun House gets more fascinating and dangerous the deeper you progress. Take care. The mysteries of this carnival are not for the faint of heart."

"You talked about safe places where a person could sleep inside the carnival," Nate said. "Do any of the workers stay overnight? Aren't some of them traveling with the carnival?"

"Some workers sleep here," Edward replied. "And some

THE CANDY SHOP WAR: CARNIVAL QUEST

who are trying to solve the mysteries do as well. Certain parts of the carnival are easier to explore after hours. I rarely leave."

"Where can we find safe places to sleep?" Summer asked.

"I'll share some thoughts for a coin."

Nate handed over a Carnie Coin.

Edward gave a nod and glanced around. "You won't find any of those safe zones in the regular carnival. You have to venture into secret places to locate them. The Grotto has some if you hunt around. Wherever you see a spiderweb symbol, that place is safe—a door, a room, a bed. Fall asleep anywhere else, and you won't be seen again."

"What happens?" Summer asked.

"I honestly don't know," Edward said. "Nobody who has fallen asleep in the carnival has returned to tell the tale."

"We think the carnival is somehow harvesting our dreams," Nate said.

"I suspect the same," Edward replied. "Just read the signs. I don't know how they do it, but I appreciate the results. This carnival is full of mysteries and treasure like the world has never known."

"Any examples?" Nate asked.

Edward winked. "I wouldn't sell those details no matter the price. But I've glimpsed wealth and treasure here that would make royal families jealous. A person could start a dynasty. If you investigate, you'll see. For now, I'm off on my own errands. Are you satisfied with how your wishes were granted?"

"As long as we actually get some magical candy up there," Nate said, glancing at the balcony.

"And find the secret places," Summer added.

Edward waved a hand toward the ladder. "Go live out your wishes. My Carnie Coins won't become enchanted until you do." He saluted with his forefinger.

"Now I'm curious about what riches are here," Nate muttered to Summer.

"Treasure to bait the trap," Summer replied. "Anything could be here if they can pull stuff out of your dreams. But we have to figure out why people are going missing, not chase some mysterious treasure."

"Or maybe both," Nate said with a shrug.

"John and the others can't get inside," Summer said. "If we don't figure out what Camilla is doing here, nobody will." She looked up at the fire escape ladder. "How much can we trust Edward?"

"His tips have been helpful so far, but we should still be cautious," Nate said. "Let's find out what candy they have."

Summer went up the ladder first. Nate caught up to her on the balcony in front of a small door clearly designed for kids. No signage offered clues to what lay beyond.

Nate tried the little doorknob and found it unlocked. Ducking through the low doorway, he entered a room decorated with lava lamps and art pieces made of neon lights. Reaching almost to the floor, maroon tablecloths cloaked several round tables. Drapery covered the walls in such abundance that Nate could imagine the curtains opening on any side to reveal an audience.

Preston Wilder sat at the farthest round table, black hair slicked back, shuffling cards. He wore a white shirt with jeweled cuff links and a black vest. The carnival's director of publicity did not look up but kept the cards dancing with perfect control, fanning them out, waterfalling them from one hand to the other. He spread them across the table in long rows and flipped them over, offering glimpses of numbers and suits, then snapped them back into a tight deck.

When Nate and Summer reached the table, he looked up.

"We meet again," he said, his smile slightly confused. "What are you two doing here?"

"Looking for magical candy," Nate said.

Holding up the deck, Preston cut the cards into three separate stacks using only one hand, then recombined them. "You found this place quickly. Who sent you? What exactly are you after?"

"I wished for magical candy at a fountain in the Grotto," Nate said. "It guided us here."

Preston shook his head. "This carnival could benefit from fewer shortcuts. Then again, I always use them when I find them, so who am I to judge?"

"Shouldn't you be running the big top?" Summer asked.

"I have understudies," Preston said. Cards cascaded from one hand to the other. "I play many roles at this carnival. In here, I'm the Dealer."

"Are you friends with the Swindler?" Nate asked.

"Because I do business in his attic?" the Dealer asked. "You could call me an apprentice of his. A protégé." He paused, regarding the kids. "I have limited quantities of magical candy for sale. What made you wish for such a thing?"

Nate glanced at Summer. He decided to play it straight. "Our other magical candy doesn't work here."

The Dealer nodded. "You already know that magic is real! Congratulations on being early adopters."

"What kind of candy do you sell?" Summer asked.

"How about you try to win some in a game of cards?" the Dealer asked.

"If you're anything like the Swindler, that won't go too well for us," Nate said. "We already saw you shuffling."

Grinning, the Dealer set the deck on the table. "Name a card."

"Three of clubs," Nate said.

Using one hand, the Dealer quickly cut the deck, holding up the exposed three of clubs.

"Queen of hearts," Summer said.

He divided the deck again, displaying the queen of hearts.

"You know where every card is," Nate said.

The Dealer held up a single card facing away from them. "Name a card."

"Ten of diamonds," Nate said.

The Dealer turned his card around. It was the ten of diamonds. He faced it away again. "Another card."

Nate watched the card carefully. It seemed there was very little trickery that could be done while holding a single card in plain view.

"Jack of spades," Summer said.

With a slight flourish, the Dealer turned the card around. It was now the jack of spades.

"Etcetera," the Dealer said, returning the card to the deck.

"You're not doing a very good job luring us into a game," Nate said.

"It doesn't hurt to show off a little." The Dealer shrugged. "You seem to have no intention of playing me. That's smart. You won't get much that way. If you're clever, I'd like to do business with you. What kind of candy are you looking for?"

Nate shrugged. He wasn't sure if he should name candies that would link him directly to either of the Whites or Sebastian Stott. "We've been able to give people an electric shock. Jump high. Fly. Become indestructible. Make animals talk. We want something powerful and useful."

The Dealer nodded. "You're no amateurs. Good for you. At this carnival, candy levels the playing field for kids, since most of it doesn't work on grown-ups. Here's how it works— the first samples are cheap, then the price goes up sharply."

"How expensive are we talking?" Summer asked.

The Dealer shrugged. "Your first piece of candy might cost two Carnie Coins."

"That sounds like a lot," Nate said.

"It's less than twenty," the Dealer said casually. "Or a hundred."

"For one piece of candy?" Summer asked. "That's robbery."

"We don't have to do business," the Dealer said. "You understand that this candy grants you magical powers, right?"

"We need to be able to afford it," Nate said.

The Dealer laughed. "So does everyone. Would you like to try a first piece or not?"

"Sure," Nate said. "We'll take seven first pieces."

The Dealer laughed hard. "My friend, there is only *one*

first piece. You don't get to sample the catalog. In fact, in my shop, each individual can only buy one type of candy. This allows you to specialize and keeps any single person from having too great an advantage."

Nate nodded. "So just one first piece each?"

"That's right."

"Do we get to choose what type?" Summer asked.

"Only by name," the Dealer said. "I'll cite four varieties. After you pick and pay, I'll inform you what the candy does."

"Two Carnie Coins each?" Summer verified.

"Just this once," the Dealer said. "To build loyalty. Once you know what you're getting, you'll figure out how to pay more."

"What if we each pay one Carnie Coin for the first candy?" Nate asked.

"Then you would have no deal," the Dealer said. "You can pay three coins if you prefer. Try changing the terms again and the price goes up." He picked up the deck. "You can't negotiate with the guy holding all the cards."

"What are the candies called?" Summer asked.

"Drip Drops, Cannon Blasts, Tempest Beans, and Clown Lips," the Dealer said. "Take your pick."

"Can we see them?" Nate asked.

"Not until you make the purchase," the Dealer said. "They're all among my best. I want you as repeat customers. You won't be disappointed with any choice."

Nate leaned toward Summer. "Clown Lips don't sound great."

"Neither do Drip Drops," Summer replied. "But who

knows? Maybe the silliest names are the best candies. This guy seems tricky."

Nate looked at the Dealer. "With a name like Cannon Blast, I have to try that one."

"Wonderful selection," the Dealer said. "And you, young lady?"

"Clown Lips," Summer said, awkwardly pushing her bangs to the side. "A name that weird has to be cool."

"Or the worst," Nate mumbled.

Nate and Summer both placed two Carnie Coins on the table. The Dealer passed a hand over them, and they vanished, leaving candies in their place. One looked like a set of large, bright-red plastic lips. The other was a black sphere with tiny orange flames stenciled on the exterior.

"The Cannon Blast has a hard outer shell and a soft interior," the Dealer said. "Put it in your mouth, and you will become charged with kinetic energy. Focus on where you want to go, then bite down on the candy. You'll be launched at your area of focus as if shot from a cannon. Your mass will temporarily increase by about ten times, and until you come to a stop, your anatomy will be fortified against any damage."

"I'll be an actual human cannonball," Nate said.

"Essentially, yes," the Dealer agreed. "Inspired by the carnival."

"What does my candy do?" Summer asked.

"While wearing the clown lips, you will be attired completely like a clown," the Dealer said.

Nate could not hold in his laughter. Summer reddened a little.

"I'm not finished," the Dealer said. "While you're dressed like a clown, you will be extremely difficult to harm, and you will find yourself able to perform surprising feats."

"Like what?" Summer asked.

"You'll have to try the lips to find out," the Dealer said. "Maybe it's my imagination, but if your actions are funny, the power seems to increase. The lips last until you devour them—normally two or three hours. But if you take them off, they cease working."

"That sounds pretty good," Summer said.

"Maybe," Nate said, unconvinced. At least he had managed to rein in his laughter.

"Can we get more right now?" Summer checked.

"Until you try out this candy, I will not sell you more," the Dealer said.

"We'll be back," Nate said. "And we may bring friends."

The Dealer spread his hands. "I'm not opposed to customers."

"Come on," Summer said to Nate. "We have places to explore."

CHAPTER SEVENTEEN
CAMILLA

T he Fun House has a bunch of great backgrounds for filming," Zac said. "The turning tunnels, the shrinking hall,
the room with the swirly lights, the wavy mirrors—I
underused it in my last video. Let's start there."

Pigeon tromped along between Trevor and Benji. If he
made a remark that was funny enough, was there any chance
Zac would include it in the video? Was that even worth wor-
rying about when there were mysteries to solve? It was hard
not to get caught up in the excitement of shooting videos that
could be watched by millions of viewers.

It was the hottest day since the carnival had opened. As
he navigated through the crowd, Pigeon found himself hoping
the few clouds in the sky would cross over the sun and provide temporary shade. He had made the mistake of putting
sunblock on his forehead, and now he was sweating it into his

eyes, making them sting. Pigeon kept the problem to himself, not wanting to get ridiculed.

The spiral windmills of the Fun House came into view, and Pigeon studied the building. Had it grown since the last time they had been here? Was it a whole story taller? Was it wider? It was hard to be sure, because the square, windowless structure was monolithic to begin with. The exterior was still a brightly colored hodgepodge of signage and colored lights, the entrance built into the gaping mouth of a giant clown face.

"Want to get digested by a clown?" Zac asked, filming selfie-style with his phone. "Sounds like a party to me!"

As they neared the entrance, Pigeon noticed the Jubilee Wagon parked toward the rear of the gaudy building. The door to the wagon was partway open.

Pigeon slowed his steps, studying the wagon. There was no sign of life.

Was Camilla's wagon truly open and unattended? Or could she be inside? Either way, shouldn't they check it out?

Pigeon glanced at Benji. The kid had no idea what was really going on at the carnival. It wouldn't be fair to drag him into danger.

"Zac," Pigeon said. "Trevor and I will catch up with you guys in the Fun House. I want to check out that wagon over there."

Zac glanced from Pigeon to the wagon. "It looks thrilling," he said dryly. "Have fun."

Trevor started toward the wagon with Pigeon. "What is this about?" Trevor whispered.

"Camilla White spends time in the Jubilee Wagon," Pigeon muttered. "The door is open. We should investigate."

Pigeon tried to move quietly, but the ground around the wagon was gravelly, so his steps crunched. He reached the portable stepladder leading up to the partially open door, then climbed the first step and knocked on the side of the wagon. "Hello?"

An older woman appeared in the doorway. She was of medium height, slender, with long graying hair that turned violet toward the tips. She had paired a white peasant blouse with a flowing batik skirt. Multiple necklaces of beads and crystals hung around her neck. Rings and bracelets adorned her hands.

"I wasn't expecting company," the woman said in a melodic voice. The wrinkles around her eyes and mouth deepened considerably when she smiled.

Pigeon froze. Was this Camilla? "Is this wagon an attraction?" he managed.

"Not usually, but you're welcome to come inside," she offered, stepping away from the door.

Pigeon glanced at Trevor, who shrugged. They mounted the stepladder and entered the wagon. Plentiful plants, many of them succulents, grew in boxes suspended from the ceiling by thin chains. Potted flowers took up much of the space on other surfaces. Bowls of glass beads, clear plastic thread, and a variety of clasps were strewn across one table. The smell of incense hung in the air, though none appeared to be burning.

"What can I do for you?" the woman asked, fidgeting with one of her bracelets.

"Do you own this carnival?" Pigeon tried.

The woman looked mildly surprised. "Where did you hear that?"

"The Psychic," Pigeon said.

The woman gave an exasperated sigh. "That ram blabs too much. Yes, I founded the carnival, and I own it."

"But you don't want people to know?" Trevor asked.

"I don't relish attention," the woman said, pacing as she spoke. "Paperwork makes me ill. I detest lawyers and business meetings. I abhor data and numbers. I started this carnival because I enjoy creating and playing. I wanted a place where people could have adventures and live out their fondest dreams."

"Seems like you did a good job," Pigeon said.

"Perhaps," the woman said. "It all depends on the experience you and others have here. As patrons become more involved, I begin to suspect I did something right."

"What's your name?" Trevor asked.

"Camilla," she replied. "How about you?"

"I'm Trevor, and this is Pigeon."

"'Pigeon'?" the woman repeated, clapping her hands softly. "What a delightful name."

"This carnival feels larger than life," Pigeon said. "Almost as if dreams are becoming reality."

Camilla grew still, a smile growing on her lips. "That's the miracle of a carnival. It brings out the child in everyone."

"No, I mean the carnival seems to be doing the impossible," Pigeon said. "Weird things are appearing all over town, and the carnival is growing at an unrealistic pace. How is this happening?"

Camilla pursed her lips before speaking. "I grew up in a strict household where practicality was emphasized over imagination. I'm trying to create the opposite environment here. As a child, I was taught how light refracts through water, but what I really wanted to know was how a rainbow might taste."

"Like Skittles," Trevor volunteered.

"Or frozen Otter Pops?" Camilla mused. "Or flavored mist?"

"You're pulling dreams into reality because you want to taste rainbows?" Pigeon asked.

Interlocking her fingers, Camilla reached both hands over her head and stretched her back. "People focus too much on doing what has already been done. Living life according to a tired pattern dictated by others. Imagination precedes all action. The worn templates we follow were once fresh ideas. I want to help humankind break new ground, broaden the options. People need to imagine, innovate, explore. Life should be an adventure we discover for ourselves."

"This carnival encourages that?" Pigeon asked.

"It can," Camilla said. She swept her hair behind one shoulder. "Has that not been your experience yet?"

Pigeon shrugged.

Camilla laughed lightly. "Anything that happens is therefore possible. Some who visit this carnival are surprised by what is possible. I've created an environment that ventures into territory some would consider supernatural. Few truly believe in the power of their dreams."

"Do dreams come true here?" Pigeon asked.

"Every day," Camilla said. "I'm always looking for good people to help me."

"Probably to replace the people who disappeared," Trevor muttered to Pigeon.

"What do you mean?" Camilla inquired, leaning forward.

"Lots of people disappeared in Texas when your carnival went through," Trevor said. "A lot of the missing went unreported, but some people noticed."

"Some who come here prefer this carnival to their humdrum lives," Camilla said. "They follow us wherever we go as devoted customers and co-creators. Others join us and start working here. I see it as proof that we are fulfilling our mission of inspiring people."

"Can we work here?" Pigeon asked.

"You look too young for standard employment," Camilla said. "But odd jobs occasionally arise. How serious are you?"

Pigeon glanced at Trevor. This could provide a chance to learn a lot about the carnival. "I'd start today."

Camilla gave a nod, then crossed to the door, closing it completely. The wagon became oddly silent. Normally the carnival was saturated with background noise—the steady hum of conversation and laughter, overlapping music from various attractions, screams of fear and delight from people on rides.

Camilla gestured to a little sofa. "Please have a seat."

Pigeon and Trevor perched side by side at the edge of the sofa.

Camilla knelt in front of them. "This carnival represents my life's work. But there are enemies who would love to destroy this paradise I have created. And so before you can work here, I must be absolutely certain of your loyalty."

Pigeon tried to stay calm under her prolonged stare. His mouth felt dry. It was hard to meet her eyes, knowing he planned to spy on her.

"We understand," Trevor finally said.

"Do you?" Camilla asked. "If so, all I ask is that you verbally grant me permission to access your minds while you take a nap here in this trailer. That will allow me to confirm your good intentions."

"Isn't that an invasion of privacy?" Pigeon asked.

Camilla smiled. "If I'm going to trust you as my assistants, I must be confident of your intentions. I don't require perfection. I need helpers who will be loyal and who demonstrate sufficient strength of character."

"You can measure that?" Trevor asked.

"To a degree, yes," Camilla said. "And I can test it. In your dreams. Pigeon, you rest on the sofa, and Trevor, you can recline on the futon at the back of the wagon. If you need help falling asleep, I can prepare an herbal tea for you."

"Actually, this sounds pretty intense," Pigeon said. "I didn't know the carnival had enemies. And having anyone probe my mind makes me uncomfortable. I'm not sure this job is for me."

Camilla glanced at Trevor. "How do you feel about it?"

Trevor squirmed in his seat. "My parents always say not to let strangers hypnotize me in their trailers."

"Well, this isn't hypnosis, but I understand what you mean," Camilla said. "Unfortunately, I cannot hire anyone I have not vetted. That long-standing policy is vital to the security of this carnival."

Pigeon stood up. "It was nice talking to you."

Trevor took the cue and rose as well. "We should probably get back to the rides."

"As you wish," Camilla said. "Should you change your minds, you know where to find me." She opened the door.

"Nice job on your carnival," Pigeon said as he passed, trying not to hurry down the steps.

Trevor followed.

"Boys," Camilla said from the doorway. "I offer rewards for information about people trying to harm this carnival."

"We'll keep that in mind," Trevor said.

"Have fun," she urged. "Dream big."

CHAPTER EIGHTEEN

COASTER

"Trevor!" Nate called, jumping out of line for the Fun House. "Pigeon!"

Trevor and Pigeon were coming toward the Fun House from the direction of the Jubilee Wagon. They hurried to meet up with Nate and Summer.

"We met Camilla," Pigeon said quietly.

"Wait, really?" Summer asked.

"She was in her wagon," Trevor said. "She offered us jobs."

"Did you take them?" Nate asked.

"The job interview was too invasive," Pigeon said. "She wanted us to go to sleep so she could check our dreams to determine our loyalty."

"That would not have gone well," Summer said.

"We got out of there fast," Trevor said.

"According to her, this carnival exists to help people live out their dreams," Pigeon said. "She claims any disappearances from other towns were people who decided to follow the carnival. Or even joined it as workers."

"People like Edward, maybe," Summer mused.

Pigeon shrugged. "She mentioned the carnival had enemies, but nothing she told us sounded terrible."

"Wouldn't it be great if the carnival wasn't bad?" Nate said.

"It would be a huge relief," Pigeon said. "But don't count on it. Clever villains keep their real plans deeply buried."

"How did it go with Edward?" Trevor asked.

"Summer and I each got a piece of magical candy that we can use inside the carnival," Nate said. He explained about the hidden shop above the Swindler. "You two could buy candy there as well."

"We also learned how to reach two new secret places," Summer said. "One by riding the roller coaster, the other inside the Fun House."

"Zac and Benji are in the Fun House now," Trevor said.

"If we don't want Benji involved in magical stuff, this might be a perfect time to check out the roller coaster," Pigeon suggested.

"We could just tell Benji," Trevor said.

"I still can't believe we trusted Zac this quickly," Nate said, glancing at Summer. "I hardly know Benji at all."

"Let's do the roller coaster," Summer said. "If we want to share what we find, we can."

They set off through the crowd. The enormously fat clown from the parade was creating a stir, chasing several smaller clowns with an inflatable bat. The little clowns dodged or ducked most of his swings, but when he made contact, they went flying, dramatically flipping and cartwheeling.

Nate led the way through the tight press of people at the edge of the commotion, their progress slowing to a crawl.

Eventually they made it to the roller coaster, dubbed Hurricane Hills by a sign at the front of the line. The white wooden roller coaster featured a massive first drop that plunged into a tube, dipping several feet underground before swooping up to other slopes and turns, the track rising and falling at diminishing heights before looping back to the station. The train roared down a nearby incline, the wooden framework of the coaster shuddering, passengers laughing and screaming, some with arms upraised.

Nate felt sure the roller coaster was significantly taller and longer than when he rode it the first day. The line of waiting riders snaked through several switchbacks before ending at the station. Three trains were in service at the moment—one waiting with passengers ready to disembark, one loading, and one zooming along the track.

Nate and his friends got in line. They speculated about what would happen when they used a Carnie Coin in the front car. Would the train go faster? Travel different tracks? Nate looked for places where any tracks branched from the main path but couldn't find any, except by the station where trains could be added or removed. One train stood dormant on a small track parallel to the main one. Their conversation paused whenever a train came near, resuming once the thunderous rumble passed by.

After nearly half an hour, they approached the front of the

line. The day was still hot, and Nate wished for a drink. At the moment, nothing sounded better than ice water.

"Look, there is an extra line where we can wait for the first car," Pigeon pointed out.

"Let's time it so while two of us are in the front seats, the next two are right behind us," Summer said. "No use wasting two coins when one will do the trick."

They had to wait through seven extra trains to get the front car. Pigeon and Trevor managed to sync up with Nate and Summer, securing the spots directly behind them in the same car. Once seated with a Carnie Coin pinched between thumb and forefinger, Nate searched for a coin slot.

"Here," Summer said, tapping an unmarked, horizontal slot set into the front of the car.

Nate leaned forward and pushed the coin into the opening, then settled back, pulling down his lap bar, which pressed snugly against him.

An attendant came by and made sure their lap bar was secure, then worked his way back along the train, checking lap bars as he went. When the attendant reached the back of the train, he gave a thumbs-up, which was reciprocated by a young woman in the control booth. The train started forward.

They ran along a fairly level track until reaching a steep climb. Nate and Summer rocked back in their seats as the train began the ascent, clacking menacingly. The track stretched high above them, ending with a view of the sky, only a few wispy clouds interrupting the field of blue.

Looking off to the side, Nate studied the aerial view of the carnival, the attractions shrinking below him as the train gained altitude. Turning the other way, he found Summer grinning. "This doesn't scare you?" he asked.

"I like to go fast," she replied.

Advancing slowly, still clacking, the front of the train crested the hill and hung over the long drop into the tube. The height felt surreal. For a heart-stopping moment, descending the nearly vertical track looked like a terrible decision.

Nate gripped the lap bar as the train picked up speed, hurtling downward. The anticipation over, Nate laughed at the exhilarating rush. At the bottom of the slope, the train plunged into darkness, but instead of swooping up the next wooden hill, the descent sped up. Wind blasted Nate's face as the train rocketed down a long tunnel, plummeting to unguessable depths within the earth. When the track began to corkscrew, Nate screamed in genuine surprise and terror.

As the angle of descent leveled out, the dark space around the train widened into a cavern lit by torches. The train maintained a high speed, whistling around corners and rumbling over a trestle bridge that spanned a fathomless chasm. Shadowy bats flitted into the upper reaches of the torchlight. The cool air swishing by smelled of damp stone.

The train shot forward, ever deeper. They skimmed along a subterranean river, then banked through wide, fanlike turns, the g-forces propelling Summer against Nate. At last, with little warning, the roller coaster train pulled into an underground station and came to a stop.

The simple station appeared abandoned. Globes of blue light provided faint but steady luminance, leaving shadowy pockets among the empty benches and quiet turnstiles. All around them loomed the uneven ceiling and walls of a rocky cavern, half-seen in the dimness.

Summer tripped the catch for the lap bar and pushed it up. "Go," she urged.

Nate climbed out, wondering what they had gotten themselves into. Trevor and Pigeon exited the train as well. The other passengers stared at them in astonishment, as if unable to imagine why anyone would exit the train in such an unlikely place. A moment later, the train pulled out of the station, rapidly accelerating until it disappeared into the darkness.

"What just happened?" Pigeon asked, the echoey rumble of the train fading into the distance.

"We took an alternate track," Nate said.

"Did we just trap ourselves in a cave hundreds of feet belowground?" Pigeon asked, his tone an odd kind of calm that seemed only a nudge away from hysteria.

"We found a secret place," Trevor said.

Summer walked over to a bulletin board on the wall. "Banjo lessons," she narrated. "A lost dog. A concert in three days. A shop that sells crystals. And look—topside train at midnight."

Pigeon whacked a hand against his face. "Is that the only train that takes us out of here? My mom is going to kill me."

"Let's hope that isn't the only train out of here," Trevor said.

A door to the little station marked Employees Only opened, and an older man came out. He was dressed like a vintage train conductor and had a bushy gray mustache. He stopped as if startled by the kids, then checked his pocket watch. "You from topside?" he asked.

"The carnival," Nate said.

"Right," the man said. "Up above?"

"Yes," Summer confirmed.

He raised his bushy eyebrows. "You're early. We've had very few visitors from above so far."

"Can we only get back to the surface at midnight?" Pigeon asked.

"Afraid so," the conductor said. "Only sure ride, at least. You never know when someone else from above might find their way down here. If a train comes, and there are empty seats, or a rider gets off, you can return early."

"What should we do until then?" Trevor asked.

"Explore the undercarnival, I suppose," the conductor said. "Give me a minute, and I'll switch on the guide lights."

The conductor retreated into the station, and a few seconds later, strands of bluish lights turned on, illuminating a path that led away from the station. The conductor did not return.

"Follow the lights?" Trevor asked.

"Or we could wait here for a train," Pigeon suggested. "Or maybe try to follow the tracks out."

"The track was so steep getting us here," Nate said. "It would be really risky to climb out that way."

"Maybe the track out is less steep than the track in," Pigeon said.

"Could be," Nate replied. "Or it could rise steeply and cross chasms and be totally impossible to follow. Remember the corkscrew on the way down?"

The conductor emerged from the station, walking past the kids.

"Excuse me," Pigeon said. "Are there any stairs we can use?"

The conductor shook his head. "You can't physically walk out of here. The tracks are nearly vertical along several stretches. There is no reliable path. If a train happened along while you were walking the tracks, you would be killed."

"My mom will destroy me anyway," Pigeon said. "Shouldn't there be emergency stairs?"

"In the undercarnival, we try to keep the experience reasonably safe," the conductor said. "But the truth is, once you progress beyond the ordinary carnival, everything becomes more hazardous. Higher risk. Higher rewards, too. Now, run along. I have manifests to prepare."

The conductor returned to the station.

Pigeon swallowed hard. "Well, after I get home at one in the morning, we probably won't get to hang out together for a while. We might as well enjoy the day while we can."

"I feel bad we left Zac hanging at the Fun House," Trevor said.

"Not much we can do about it from down here," Summer said. "None of us have a cell phone."

"If we had a way to call Zac, he could bring another train down," Pigeon said.

"Face it," Nate said. "We're going to get home late, and all of us are likely to get in trouble. But for now, we're in a giant cave with a lighted path to the undercarnival. We need info. Let's go see what we find!"

CHAPTER NINETEEN

UNDER

The path wound away from the station, the cave narrowing as it went. Arms outstretched, Nate could almost reach from one wall of the passageway to the other. Eventually, the rocky tunnel opened up into a vast cavern with huge stalactites pointing down from the lofty ceiling.

The four kids stopped to absorb the sight ahead of them.

A long avenue was lit mostly with paper lanterns and flanked by fanciful buildings and shops. Vendors pushed carts, jugglers tossed flaming torches, customers bargained, musicians competed for attention, suspicious figures lurked, and packs of revelers cackled. Beyond the bright avenue, merrymakers rode towering slides, floated in hot air balloons, and swished back and forth on giant swings. Nate noticed paragliders soaring up toward the stalactites above a gaping crater.

"This can't be happening," Trevor said. "We have to be dreaming."

"I'm not dreaming," Summer said, pinching her arm and flicking the side of her nose. "I know how I got here. Everything feels real. It's just . . . unbelievable."

"How did they build all this?" Pigeon asked.

"This stuff had to come from dreams," Nate said.

"Like the bowling ball," Trevor murmured.

"And the horse bones," Nate said. "And probably more things than we realize."

Summer started walking down the avenue. The other kids hurried to catch up. Many of the revelers roaming the street wore porcelain masks. Some of them were dressed in clothes that matched an older time period. A few wore clown out-fits, and a couple others hid within oversized paper-mache heads. A number of the street performers wore outlandish costumes—furry vests, velvet capes, or harlequin motley. Not many looked like they belonged to the modern world.

A short, slight man with shifty eyes approached Pigeon. "Kid, you're new to the undershow, am I right?" He spoke rapidly. "Your friends too. Let me warn you, your topside cur-rency is more valuable than the ticket swappers will let on, and they'll rob you blind if you're not careful. The coin traders are worse. I can set you up with everything you need."

"What do we need?" Pigeon asked.

"Undertickets," the man said as if the answer were ob-vious. "Deep Coins. A cave map. Have you learned about slugs?"

"Like snails?" Trevor asked.

"Like snails he says," the short man chuckled. "Nice, kid. No, counterfeit coins. They work just like Carnie Coins, but you can get ten slugs for one Carnie Coin. You can't pay a person with them, but they work in all the topside coin slots. Ten times the value! Ten times the fun!"

"You have these slugs?" Summer asked.

"Buckets of them!" the short man exclaimed. "Wheelbarrows of them. As many as you can trade for."

"And they work in *all* coin slots?" Nate pressed.

"All topside slots," the man said, one hand over his heart, the other raised as if taking an oath. "Every last one. Guaranteed. I'll give you ten times your money back if I'm wrong, or my name isn't Gentleman Marco."

"What's the exchange rate for undertickets?" Nate asked. "I have some money."

Marco shook his head. "You can't buy undertickets with paper money or plastic cards. Only gold. If you have gold, we can work some deals. But normally you get undertickets with topside tickets, and Deep Coins with Carnie Coins."

"What's the exchange rate for those?" Pigeon asked.

"Sharp question, Mister Finance," Marco said. "Sharp as a porcupine. The ticket swappers will take two topside tickets for one underticket. If you're lucky. Ticket snatchers, more like it. Ticket robbers. I'll give you *three* undertickets for every topside ticket. You could walk this cavern for days and never find such a deal. Walk it for eons."

A tall, gaunt man in a plain black suit with a flat, widebrimmed hat approached them. He was an older gentleman and walked with a stoop. "Lapo, what are you telling these children?"

"I thought his name was Marco?" Pigeon exclaimed.

"Indeed?" the gaunt man said with a wheezing laugh. He bared his yellow teeth in a disturbing parody of a smile. "He can't even give an honest name these days?"

"Marco is my middle name—" the short man started.

The gaunt man ignored him. "What deal did he offer?"

Marco motioned the kids away from the gaunt man. "Pay him no mind," he maintained. "Spend time with Walter and you'll end up in coffins."

"Marco was offering three undertickets for every carnival ticket from above," Nate said.

Walter's face became grave. "Three undertickets? For one topside ticket? Did Lapo mention that most down here prefer to deal in topside tickets? Did he clarify that in an establishment like mine you would get closer to fifty undertickets for every ticket purchased up above?"

Marco gave a weak chuckle. "We all haze the newbies. Fleece them a little. Walter does the same. He runs a gambling hall."

"Games of chance delight me," Walter said. "Maybe you win, maybe you lose. Either way, life becomes more interesting."

A woman with a pink mohawk approached them. She had broad shoulders and wore heavy makeup. "Did I hear talk of topside tickets? Those are valuable down here. Hard to get. If you kids have more than ten, you should think about protection. There are lots of shady characters on the prowl."

"We have a lot more than ten," Trevor said.

"What kind of protection?" Summer asked.

"Bodyguards," the woman said. "I can set you up with two

or three. As many as you want to pay for, really. Brings peace of mind to know you're protected."

"You don't need security," Lapo said to the kids.

"Nobody is going to mug you," Walter agreed. "We have a reputation to uphold. You're at a carnival. We need patrons."

"We'll also keep these vultures away," the woman said, indicating Walter and Lapo. "Listen, you want to deal with the providers of established games and attractions. Start talking to scavengers and they'll multiply."

"Good evening," said a stout man with a heavy mustache, tipping his hat. "Who needs undertickets? I can offer eighty for every topside ticket you wish to trade."

"No, thanks," Nate said. "We need space." He sped up his walk and moved purposefully away from the group that was forming around them, ignoring all protests. He had seen his dad use this tactic when strangers tried to hand him flyers. Pigeon, Summer, and Trevor matched Nate's pace. Lapo, Walter, and the others dispersed.

"Sounds like our tickets are valuable here," Trevor said.

"I'm not sure what to believe yet," Nate said. "Those people are liars. They may have all been working together."

"Some version of good cop, bad cop," Summer said, nodding.

"More like pushy cop," Pigeon said. "And annoying cop. And then obnoxious cop. Then another pushy cop."

They reached a structure that looked like a saloon from the old west. Carved across the top of the dark wood was the sign Brawling Alley. When they paused out front, a beefy guy in a tight, horizontally striped shirt with his hair buzzed short sauntered up to them. "Are you tough enough to challenge the champ?"

"What champ?" Trevor asked.

"Tonight? Wilson 'the Hammer' Sylvester. It's free to try, but you have to sign a waiver. Can't hold the ownership responsible for injuries. You only have to survive three rounds."

"Is he an adult?" Summer asked.

"You bet," the beefy guy replied. "Much bigger than me. You're small enough, they might let you try two-on-one."

"I'm not really a fighter," Pigeon said.

"Can we watch?" Nate asked.

"Costs to watch," the beefy guy replied.

Nate glanced at his friends. "Can we pay with topside tickets?"

The beefy guy's eyes widened. "Sure, you can! One ticket each would get you premium seats."

"Thanks," Nate said. "Maybe later." He led the others far enough away for them to talk.

"It could be fun to watch," Summer said.

"Might not be the best atmosphere," Pigeon replied.

"A boxing match would be exciting," Nate said. "But don't you want to scope this place out before we spend all our time indoors watching entertainment?"

"Depends on the entertainment," Trevor said.

"We should gather all the info we can," Pigeon said.

A piece of paper blew against Nate's leg, partly wrapping around his shin. He picked it up. Pink with black lettering, it proclaimed:

COME VISIT THE INTERCONTINENTAL MENAGERIE!
FEATURING THE FINEST ASSORTMENT OF EXOTIC ANIMALS
THIS SIDE OF TIMBUKTU!
GIANT PANDA! RED PANDA! KOMODO DRAGON!
ALBINO ALLIGATOR! OKAPI! CALIFORNIA CONDOR!
THREE-HEADED SNAKE! PANAMANIAN GOLDEN FROG!
PACIFIC WALRUS! BORNEO PYGMY ELEPHANT!
HEAVIEST ANACONDA IN NORTH AMERICA!
DON'T MISS THIS ONCE-IN-A-LIFETIME EXPERIENCE!
WHICH CAN YOU HOLD? WHICH CAN YOU FEED?
COME INSIDE TO FIND OUT!!!

"I've always wanted to see an okapi," Pigeon said, reading over Nate's shoulder.

"What's that?" Trevor asked.

"It looks like a cross between a zebra and a giraffe," Pigeon said.

"They came from opposite sides of the savannah," Trevor said in a deep, movie announcer voice. "Two different worlds. One forbidden love."

Nate folded up the flyer and pocketed it. "We need to keep moving."

They found a tall, narrow, crooked building called the Puzzle Tower. A treasure map was promised to anyone who could reach the ninth floor. Farther down the street, an archery game let players take aim at distant piñatas. Next door, a fenced garden offered a food hunt, where paying customers had fifteen minutes to gather ingredients for their meal. Nate saw diners picking berries, uprooting carrots, and gathering eggs.

Solicitors continued to offer trades as the kids progressed up the avenue, but when they paid no attention, the pitches were cut short. Outside a windowless, cinder block building labeled Freak Show, three barkers approached, two men and a woman.

"Come experience the bizarre," the first man said.

"You'll never see the world quite the same way after tonight," the woman promised.

"I don't like the idea of exploiting people or calling them 'freaks,'" Summer said.

"Neither do we," the second man said, one hand over his heart.

"The performers work on a completely voluntary basis," the woman said.

"They share in the proceeds," the first man said.

"You have to see Goat Boy," the second man asserted. "He'll eat anything you give him."

"Come behold Gerumpio," the woman said. "More than half his body has turned to wood. There is a piece of fruit growing from his elbow."

"The Alien, the Whistling Clam, the Leopardess, the Woolyman," the first man rattled off. "Talk to the Presence in the Box. Hear the predictions of the Soothsayer. Match wits with the artificial intelligence of the Robotic Titan."

"No collection of misfits and mutants begins to rival this one," the second man said.

"You have to see them to understand," the woman said. "The wonders of the world have united under a single roof."

"We'll think about it," Nate said, continuing down the street.

"This is the best attraction down here by far," the first guy assured them.

"No competition," the woman promised. "Come back before we close, or you'll miss the opportunity of a lifetime."

Trevor leaned close to Nate. "I'd pay to *not* see a guy growing fruit on his elbow."

They reached a huge opening in the floor of the cavern. A steady rush of cold wind gushed from below. On one edge of the crater, they found a game called Kite Bombers. Contestants used the updraft to fly kites with explosives up to a box kite controlled by an expert. The box kite swerved and dodged, avoiding contact with the pursuing kites. As Nate and the others watched, four competing contestants failed to destroy the box kite in the allotted two minutes, though a pair of the exploding kites destroyed each other.

Beyond the crater huddled a compound of Quonset huts, their long, arched roofs fabricated from corrugated steel. A sign out front declared the complex the Intercontinental Menagerie.

"Should we check it out?" Pigeon asked.

"I don't know," Nate said.

"We can't just investigate the attractions from the street," Pigeon said.

A paper gently slapped the back of Nate's head and stuck there, held in place by a stiff breeze. Had the current of air come from the crater? He snatched the paper and found it was another pink flyer for the menagerie.

Nate turned around, holding out the paper to Trevor. "Did you do this?"

Trevor raised both hands. "I can't summon wind."

Nate looked at the flyer. "Then maybe it's a sign. We should check it out."

"What do you think about the other people down here?" Pigeon asked.

"What do you mean?" Nate replied.

"If there is only one train back up, how many in the crowd can be normal customers? There are thousands of people down here. Do they stay here all the time? Are they even real people?"

"They seem real," Trevor said.

Pigeon shook his head. "It doesn't make sense."

"Let's think about it while we investigate," Nate said.

They walked to the front door where an old bald man with wispy facial hair sat with his legs crossed. He wore suspenders, corduroy pants, argyle socks, and loafers. "You kids want to venture inside?"

"What does it cost?" Summer asked.

"You're topsiders, yes?" the man asked. "One ticket from above for each entrant will do."

Pigeon ripped off four tickets and handed them to the man. He accepted them gingerly.

"Young and alive with your pockets full of tickets," the old man said with a grin. "You're in the salad days, that's for sure. Inside the menagerie, you can pet the baby camel and the stingrays. For a small extra contribution, you can hold a koala and feed some of the carnivores. The workers inside will clarify as needed."

Nate passed through the door into a long, well-lit room that smelled of fur, manure, and wood shavings. He saw the camels first—a shaggy Bactrian, two dromedaries, and a little one, all corralled together near the center of the space. Pens along the edge of the room held a variety of other animals. Nate spotted a pair of giant pandas on the far side of the room. He also noticed warthogs nearby, some kind of gazelle, and an elephant whose big head and ears seemed out of scale with its relatively small body. A sign on the wall proclaimed Marvelous Mammals.

"These conditions aren't great for the animals," Summer said. "Are they even allowed to have pandas?"

"Maybe somebody dreamed them here," Trevor said. "At least the pens are fairly big. They have space to move around."

"But they deserve better environments," Summer said. "Sunlight and plants and room to run."

"I like that they're so close," Pigeon said. "At a lot of zoos, the animals have places to hide and you can barely see them. Cool, there's the okapi!" Pigeon started walking toward a back corner of the long room. Trevor and Summer followed, with Nate trailing behind.

Nate analyzed the pen with the warthogs. Could there be hidden coin slots here? Were there deeper secrets?

He moved past the warthogs to the sloths, and then to the aardvarks. They were such odd animals with their long, tubular snouts. Nate was pretty sure they ate ants.

One of the aardvarks came to the side of the pen as if drawn to Nate. "We don't have much time," the aardvark said in Mozag's voice.

"Mozag?" Nate asked, crouching down.

"Not so loud," Mozag the aardvark said. "I've kept silent so they couldn't identify me. Now that I'm breaking my silence, it won't be long until they find me out."

"I saw you change into an aardvark in a dream," Nate said.

"Bingo, kid," Mozag replied. "That dream really happened."

"How did you get here?" Nate asked.

"This carnival is a crossroads between the dreamscape and the waking world," Mozag said. "I came here via the dream route. I found the menagerie and posed as a typical aardvark. I sensed when you and your friends arrived at the undercarnival. In my present state, my magic is limited, but I managed to send the flyers your way, trying to get your attention."

"It worked," Nate said.

"Listen, this carnival is evil," Mozag said. "If the owners have their way, the dreamscape will swallow reality as we know it. They must be stopped. You have to find where the sleepers are located."

"What sleepers?" Nate asked.

"Dreams must be powered by sleepers," Mozag said. "I can sense sleepers here in this carnival, trapped in a powerful dream state. Permanently dreaming. I suspect their dreams are integral to this carnival. You and your friends must find them and help them awaken. You'll need a skeleton key."

"Where do I get that?" Nate asked.

"Win it," Mozag said. "I'm not sure where. I'm telling you

what I have managed to perceive in this limited state. There are many locks in this carnival, and many keys, but the skeleton key opens all the locks. It can be obtained by winning some of the harder games. Look around."

"We have to get you out of here," Nate said.

"We're all caught in the same web," Mozag said. "You have to bring down the carnival. Start by wakening the sleepers. Now go. The roustabouts are coming."

"Who?" Nate asked.

"Enforcers employed by the carnival," Mozag said. "Tough guys in old-timey clothes and hats. Steer clear. You don't want to get linked to me. Find the lock at the bottom of the Fun House."

"I know about a coin slot on the floor of a ball pit," Nate said.

"That might be a secret passage," Mozag said. "I'm talking about an actual keyhole. You'll have to search deep. This info was difficult to obtain. Don't waste it. Tell John to bring everything he has. We're dealing with an extinction-level threat. Go."

The aardvark turned and padded to the far side of the enclosure, no longer paying any attention to Nate. Following Mozag's instructions, Nate caught up to Pigeon and the others by the okapi. He watched from the corner of his eye as three burly men in flat caps and simple clothing entered the building.

Carrying blackjacks, they marched toward the aardvarks.

CHAPTER TWENTY
UPWARD

Looking ahead at the okapi, Nate laid one hand on Pigeon's shoulder and the other on Summer's. "Mozag is here," he whispered.

"What?" Pigeon asked, looking around.

"Don't be conspicuous," Nate said, glancing over at the roustabouts climbing into the aardvark enclosure. "He's an aardvark."

Trevor moved closer. "Really?"

"Are those guys after him?" Summer asked.

"Mozag called them roustabouts," Nate said. "Keep your eyes on the okapi."

"Mozag is the most powerful magician we know," Pigeon said. "He's bailed us out in the past."

"Shouldn't we help him?" Summer asked.

"Not according to Mozag," Nate said. "He gave me a message. We have an assignment. We need to get out of here." He glanced over and saw a writhing aardvark being shoved into a coarse sack.

"I could use my Clown Lips," Summer said, reaching for the candy.

"No," Nate said. "Where do we go if we start a fight down here?"

"But we can't let them take Mozag," Summer insisted.

The roustabouts exited the aardvark enclosure. The animal in the bag had gone limp.

"He told me the way to save him and everyone else is to bring down the carnival," Nate said.

"They're looking around," Pigeon said.

"Don't return eye contact," Nate said, staring at the zebra-striped legs of the okapi.

"Two of the men are leaving," Trevor said. "One is coming this way."

"Should we run?" Pigeon asked, a tremor in his voice.

"No way," Nate whispered. "Be cool. Act oblivious."

"I'll keep the lips ready," Summer whispered.

"Yeah," Nate agreed, fingering the Cannon Blast in his pocket.

The roustabout stood directly behind Nate and tapped a blunt finger on his shoulder. He turned and looked up at the man. The guy had a square face and a nose that had been broken once or twice. His blocky build made him imposing.

"You kids found your way down here early," the roustabout said, his voice deep and a little gravelly.

"We tried a coin in the roller coaster slot," Nate said. "Seemed obvious after the bumper cars. Is there a problem?"

"You're welcome to explore," the roustabout said. "Encouraged even. But *respectfully*. Why talk to the aardvark?"

"I'm a little different from other kids my age," Nate said. "I find aardvarks adorable."

"One of those aardvarks is a troublemaker," the roustabout said. "What do you know about him?"

"He eats bugs?" Nate tried.

The roustabout glanced at the other kids.

"Why did you stuff him in a sack?" Summer asked.

"That's what happens to troublemakers," the roustabout said flatly.

"Isn't that cruelty to animals?" Summer asked. "I want to talk to your manager."

The roustabout exhaled sharply through his nostrils. "You really don't."

"I feel like we're being harassed," Summer said. She looked at Trevor. "Do you feel targeted?"

"A little," Trevor said.

"If we harass you, there will be no debate about what is happening," the roustabout said, cracking his knuckles. "Play by the rules, and we won't have to interrupt the game."

"We're just exploring," Nate said. "We paid tickets to come in here. What game are you talking about?"

"Steer clear of talking aardvarks," the roustabout said.

"I don't even speak aardvark," Nate said. "I didn't build this zoo. I didn't put aardvarks here. We got lured in by prom- ises of seeing weird animals."

The roustabout surveyed the room. "I'd say you're getting

your money's worth." He tipped his cap. "Enjoy." He turned and started walking away.

"What will you do to the aardvark?" Summer asked.

The roustabout stopped and looked at her over his shoulder. "Same thing we always do to troublemakers. We'll put it to sleep." He strolled away.

After the roustabout exited the building, Nate, Summer, Trevor, and Pigeon huddled to talk.

"I thought that was going to be a fight for sure," Trevor said.

"What do you think he meant about putting Mozag to sleep?" Summer asked. "Like, at the animal shelter?"

"He was trying to intimidate us," Nate said.

"He did a solid job," Pigeon muttered.

"What mission did Mozag give us?" Trevor asked.

"We're supposed to find the sleepers," Nate said. "People stuck in the carnival, permanently dreaming."

"Where are they?" Summer asked.

"We need a skeleton key," Nate said. "We can supposedly win one at some of the harder games. Then we have to open a lock deep beneath the Fun House. That's all I know."

"Then let's get going," Trevor said. "I saw a lot of games out there."

* * * * *

At 11:52 p.m., Nate sat hunched on a bench in the underground station, elbows on his knees. Pigeon sat on the floor, leaning into a corner, eyes drooping. Summer shuffled through a small stack of handouts and brochures she had acquired. Trevor paced back and forth.

"Pidge," Nate said. "You can't sleep."

"What?" Pigeon asked, blinking. "I'm just resting my eyes a little."

Trevor stalked over to Pigeon, seized his hand, and pulled him to his feet. "Wrong answer," Trevor scolded. "Do I have to make you do jumping jacks?"

"Sorry," Pigeon said, slapping his cheeks. "Waiting is hard."

"Then keep moving," Trevor said.

"Anything in those papers?" Nate asked Summer.

"Not much," she replied.

They had scoured the undercarnival, paying extra attention to the games, asking about a skeleton key. Some people had heard of them, but nobody knew where to obtain one. They checked on the prize at the Brawling Alley, but it was an Enchanted Carnie Coin. Summer had collected all the flyers and leaflets she could find in hopes of discovering clues.

"I really am so tired," Pigeon said. "I can't shake it off."

Nate got up and walked over to him. "We're all tired. But you know the deal. We have to stay awake."

"Maybe some French fries would help," Trevor suggested.

Pigeon grabbed his stomach with both hands and groaned. "It may be a long time before I eat fries again."

They had eaten at an establishment called the Potato Mill. Dinner had consisted of standard French fries, curly fries, steak fries, garlic fries, waffle fries, shoestring fries, tater tots, hash browns, potato skins, potato wedges, potato cakes, and baked potatoes with a stunning variety of toppings and dipping sauces. It had tasted so good, they all ate until they felt ready to burst.

"What excuse should we give when we get home?" Nate asked, hoping fear would help rouse Pigeon.

"What can we say?" Pigeon lamented. "We're doomed. It would be better if I had been kidnapped. Then at least I could blame the criminals."

"I'm going to try to sneak in," Summer said. "If my parents can't pinpoint what time I arrived, they can't be as mad."

"Won't your parents be awake?" Pigeon asked.

"Probably," Summer said. "But if I can sneak past them, eventually they just find me sleeping in bed. When they ask, I'll just pretend I don't know what time I got in and say that I was so tired I went right to my room."

"It's a stretch," Pigeon said. "But better than no plan."

"Almost makes me miss white fudge," Trevor said.

Nate chuckled. The treat Belinda White had made rendered parents oblivious to practical concerns, almost zombified. "Do we have any left?"

"We could ask Mr. Stott," Pigeon said.

"No," Nate said. "That stuff was bad news. We can't be drugging our parents to get out of trouble."

"Could we make up a story?" Trevor wondered. "I mean, we're here because the carnival is a threat. We're not just messing around. It's a crisis, but not one we can talk about. We're justified in making up an emergency."

"Like what?" Summer asked.

"Somebody's appendix burst," Trevor said.

"We were taken hostage," Nate tried.

"We got trapped in a cave," Pigeon proposed.

"The cave one isn't bad," Summer said. "And almost completely true."

They heard the rattle of an approaching train.

"Here we go," Nate said.

Several other people appeared on the platform, all of them adults. It was hard to tell whether they were carnival guests, employees, or a mix. The oncoming train got louder, then quieted as it pulled into the station and came to a stop. Every seat was empty.

The old conductor came out of the station. "Tickets, please," he called out. "Nobody rides without a ticket."

Some of the adults walked over to him and started handing him undertickets. Nate approached and asked, "How many tickets do you need?"

The conductor waved him away. "You already presented your tickets on the other end."

Riders were claiming seats. The train was about halfway full, with the most open seats toward the middle. Trevor sat by Summer and Nate sat with Pigeon.

"Pull those lap bars down," the conductor said, strolling parallel to the train. "Consider removing hats, or at least hang on to them."

A passenger toward the front of the train took off his cowboy hat.

The train lurched forward without warning, the acceleration pinning Nate back against the seat. Cool air whooshed by as their velocity increased. The track curved upward, stalactites blurring past on either side. The thunder of their passage echoed down branching caverns, multiplying the uproar. The track became nearly vertical, spiraling. They rose with an acceleration similar to falling. In one area, the track folded back on itself in a pretzel shape, threading between rock outcroppings. Some stretches of the cave were dark, others lit by flickering torches or steadily glowing blue globes.

After a particularly fast and steep ascent through the dark that made Nate think of astronauts blasting off, the train shot out of the tube. They were back on the normal wooden roller coaster! Stars shimmered overhead in a black sky.

The ups and downs of the traditional roller coaster seemed tame compared to the underground track. After some final bouncy little hills, the train slowed and clattered into the boarding area. There were no ride attendants in view.

"We made it," Nate said, turning around to check on Pigeon.

Pigeon sat with his eyes squinted shut and his lips compressed. Sweat beaded on his forehead. He held up a finger to acknowledge Nate's statement. The moment the lap bar released, Pigeon hurried from the train and ran to a garbage can, bending over it and puking violently.

Nate felt bad for his friend, but he hated the sound of somebody throwing up. On previous occasions, the smell of vomit had been enough to make him retch. After Nate climbed from the train, he covered his ears and looked away from Pigeon's heaving back. While Summer went to offer comfort, Nate and Trevor escaped through the exit.

The sky above and the fresh air helped Nate realize how claustrophobic he had begun to feel inside the cave. Although some of the caverns were enormous, everything had been enclosed, and the air had smelled of minerals.

Summer and Pigeon caught up to Nate outside the ride. Pigeon's face looked waxy, but there was no vomit around his mouth or on his shirt.

"Too many twists and turns on the way up?" Trevor asked.

Pigeon moaned. "I may never eat French fries again."

CHAPTER TWENTY-ONE

NIGHT MARKET

When Nate had initially boarded the roller coaster with his friends, the sun had been shining and the carnival was crowded. Now, more than an hour after closing time, the carnival was silent and still. No rides operated. No people milled about. No music played. And there were very few lights—just enough to dispel the worst of the darkness along the walkways.

The carnival had begun to feel familiar after multiple visits, but now that it was dark and empty, it became newly foreign. Rides that appeared entertaining in the daytime or when bedazzled with lights were now vague, sinister shapes towering in the gloom.

Nate considered the shadowy surroundings. Should he and his friends be moving more stealthily? Were there night watchmen? He didn't want the embarrassment of being escorted from the park for getting caught trespassing after hours.

But the other passengers from the roller coaster train were walking casually, which helped allay his worries.

When Nate, Trevor, Summer, and Pigeon reached the main boardwalk, they turned toward the exit. But the rest of the passengers went toward the dim, motionless carousel, deeper into the park. Laced with shadow, the elk and dolphins of the carousel looked more like goblins and sea monsters. Beyond the carousel, a deep purplish glow hung over the area.

Nate stopped one of the men from the roller coaster. "Where are you going?"

"Night market. It's open from midnight until 3 a.m." The man walked on.

Nate looked at the others. "Should we go?"

"I'm exhausted," Pigeon said. "I feel like I'm going to collapse."

"I'm dead whether I get home at 12:30 or 2:30," Trevor said. "I'm too wired to sleep anyway."

"I can make sure Pigeon gets home if you guys want to check it out," Summer offered.

"Maybe we should," Nate said.

"Don't forget we come back here on a field trip in the morning," Pigeon said. "Assuming my parents let me live . . ."

"Go home," Trevor said. "Get some rest."

Summer continued toward the exit with Pigeon. The other passengers from the roller coaster train were nearly out of view. Nate and Trevor hurried to catch up.

The plaza behind the carousel had been overtaken by a bazaar. Vendors displayed their goods on carpets spread on the ground and inside canopied booths. The deep purple glow emanated from strategically positioned globes affixed to poles or on the ground. Their size varied, and Nate could see no wires powering them. He noticed that his shoelaces shone brightly under the light, as did Trevor's teeth.

Nate and Trevor wandered down an aisle. The atmosphere was more secretive than festive. There was no music, and conversation was murmured or whispered. None of the vendors solicited customers—instead they hung back, waiting to be approached. Some booths offered food. Others held intricate artwork. One sold marionettes. Another featured a variety of fish in bowls and small aquariums.

Nate noticed Edward trading a ticket for a small reddish banana at a fruit stand. He was wearing his sword.

"Edward," Nate greeted, approaching him.

Edward turned and smiled with recognition, teeth gleaming eerily. "I see you found the night market."

"We're coming back from the undercarnival," Nate said.

"Who is your friend?" Edward asked.

"I'm Trevor."

"I didn't know about this market until tonight," Nate said.

"It occurs spontaneously," Edward replied.

"No set schedule?" Trevor asked.

Edward tapped the side of his nose. "You just listen for rumblings that one is coming up."

"I have a question," Nate said, drawing closer. "Do you know where we can find a skeleton key?"

"I've heard of them," Edward said. "But they are not in my area of expertise. If you want a friendly warning, people who go after that key tend to disappear. Then again, if you find it, the skeleton key could open a lot of opportunities. This market is a great place to hunt for clues." He indicated the surrounding stalls. "Now, if you'll excuse me, I'm searching for answers of my own."

"What are you looking for?" Nate asked.

Edward shrugged. "Whatever you come to the carnival seeking tends to show up. I wanted treasure, and after some searching, I've uncovered multiple treasure hunts. A friend of mine wanted to be famous. She's now on that path. Now I'm trying to solve the big picture. How does this place work? How is it possible?"

"We're wondering some of the same things," Nate said.

"I wish you luck," Edward said. He walked away, peeling the fruit he had purchased.

Nate and Trevor went down another aisle of the bazaar. They walked around a huge grill where fat sausages roasted over red coals. On the far side, they found an elaborately carved box bigger than a refrigerator that shone a striking white under the purple glow.

"Would you like to use my time closet?" an Asian woman asked.

"How does it work?" Nate wondered.

"One Carnie Coin gives you one hour inside the closet," she replied. "But that hour is a single minute out here."

"Time slows down inside the closet," Trevor said.

"Yes, relative to how time flows out here," the woman said.

"What's in the box?" Nate asked.

"Only what you bring," the woman said. "You can think,

read, watch a movie on your phone, do homework. Imagine getting three hours of studying done in only three minutes!"

"I need to come back here when I have a big school project to work on," Nate said.

"Do that," the woman said with a wink. "If you can find me."

Nate and Trevor passed booths and tents selling various wares. Ratan baskets nestled in towers. Journals bound in animal skins and rare secondhand books burdened sagging shelves. Hanging macramé plant holders shared space with small bunches of herbs tied with string, all dangling from rafters. One booth displayed a village of brightly painted wooden birdhouses shaped like cottages, castles, and log cabins. A withered, vulturous head protruded from one of them, withdrawing when fire flashed in a cauldron across the aisle. The boys brushed past racks of tie-dyed blouses, leather armor, flowing pants, metal helmets, and embroidered skirts.

As they browsed the fourth aisle, Nate looked ahead with excitement. "Argali!"

The cabinet containing the fortune-telling ram awaited at the end of the aisle. Trevor ran alongside Nate to the animatronic psychic.

"This worked so well for me and Pigeon," Nate said to Trevor when they reached the machine. "Though he might not answer any more questions for me. We'll have to test to find out. You try one. Be really specific."

Trevor put in a Carnie Coin. "Where can we find a skeleton key to this carnival?"

The animatronic ram came to life, blinking and waving his

hoofs over the swirling crystal ball. The jaw began to piston up and down. "A skeleton key is the main prize at Dune Hunt."

A card dropped into the opening in the cabinet. Trevor pulled it out. "Same words."

"Let me try," Nate said, inserting a Carnie Coin. "Where can we find Dune Hunt?"

The ram went into motion again. "Present a Desert Token to the Terror Castle ride operator. That is enough from you for now."

A card dropped into the opening.

Nate looked to Trevor. "I knew there was a secret way at the Terror Castle. But I never had a Desert Token. This thing is like a cheat code. Keep going."

Trevor put in another coin. "Where can we find a Desert Token?"

The psychic rocked and waved his hoofs. "Play Loot Scoop. No more questions from you tonight."

A card ejected into the opening. Trevor collected it.

"What now?" Trevor asked. "What's Loot Scoop?"

"I don't know," Nate said. "And we're out of questions." He walked over to the nearest person, a balding guy wearing a dark shirt and jeans. "Would you ask the psychic a question for us? We'll give you the coin to use plus ten tickets."

"What question?" the guy replied.

"Where can we find Loot Scoop?"

The guy chuckled. "Are you serious?"

"Yes," Nate said. "We need to know."

"Look, I would feel bad taking your tickets," the guy said. "It's right over there." He pointed toward a corner of the bazaar. "You'll see it by a couple of other games, just beyond the soup stand."

"Thanks," Nate said.

"Don't mention it."

They found Loot Scoop positioned between a game where a player could use a mechanical claw to grab stuffed animals and a game where a player could launch a Carnie Coin at little targets to win more coins.

"Pssst, hey, kid."

Nate turned around to find the purple-faced clown from the parade leering down at him. He was startlingly tall, and his shoes were enormous. His teeth, certain highlights of his makeup, and the pinstripes of his suit gleamed bright under the black lights.

Trevor gasped and backed up against the claw game, eyes wide.

The clown held a cartoonish bomb in one gloved hand—perfectly round and black with a white fuse poking out the top.

"Light this for me, will you?" the clown asked Nate in a sly voice.

"Why would I do that?"

"If you're going to play these cruddy games, you must be as bored as I am," the clown said.

"You want to set off a bomb out of boredom?" Nate asked.

"Trust me, it's a quick antidote," the clown said. "Kaboom! Fire! Screaming! Sirens!"

"Why don't you light it yourself?" Nate asked.

The clown held up a hand to hide his lips as he spoke.

"You should see the contract they made me sign to work here. Legalese. Yawnsville. Can't do this, must do that, electricity has to be under this many volts, no acid on the elderly, rules upon rules until you go cross-eyed. One of the stipulations? Can't light my own explosives."

"So you ask kids to light them for you?" Nate asked.

"Kids are usually tiresome," the clown said. "But any port in a storm."

"What do you want to blow up?" Nate asked.

The clown stomped a foot and pointed at Nate. "What is this, Twenty Questions? See what I mean? Tiresome!" He turned to Trevor. "How about the mute? Got a light?"

Eyes still wide, Trevor shook his head.

"We don't know you," Nate said.

"I prefer it that way," the clown said. "Don't you agree? Less complications. You got a name?"

"Yeah."

"Keep it," the clown said. "What I need is a light."

"I don't have a lighter," Nate said. "And I wouldn't help you if I did. You're not a nice clown."

"Since when are clowns nice? Funny, maybe. Accident-prone, sure. I've met clowns who like getting injured to amuse a crowd. Others prefer to do the injuring. I'm the latter. My pain is no joke—yours is hilarious!"

"Look, we don't have a light, and we have stuff to do," Nate said.

"Right, you have your cruddy games to play," the clown said. "You're spending worthless coins hoping to win useless trinkets. That friend of yours is scared of me. He gets it. There may be contractual limits as to how I can amuse myself—especially regarding ticket holders—but when troublemakers try to harm this carnival . . . Well, at that point, I have a very long leash."

"We're not the ones with a bomb," Nate said.

"What bomb?" the clown asked, holding up his empty hands. "You shouldn't talk about explosives, even in jest. Security comes down hard on those kind of jokes. I think your friend may have wet himself."

Nate glanced at Trevor. He did have a damp patch on his pants. "How about you leave us alone?"

"Not until I tell a joke," the clown said. "So you can find out what kind of clown I am."

"I think I know," Nate said.

"Then it will be no surprise," the clown said. "Knock, knock."

"Go away."

"Come on, be a sport, let bygones be bygones. Knock, knock."

"Nobody's home."

"Fine, I'll tell you my name. I'm Growler. Happy now? I'm no longer a stranger. Knock, knock."

"Get out of here, Growler."

Growler clenched his fists, face scrunching with barely contained rage. "Breathe, Growler. Just breathe like they taught you. In . . . out." He took several huge breaths, then smoothed his suit. "How about this? Play along with my joke, and I promise to leave you alone."

"Fine," Nate said.

"Knock, knock."

"Who's there?"

"A dead guy."

"A dead guy who?"

"A dead guy who went looking for a skeleton key."

The clown spun on his heel and strutted away, taking huge strides with his long legs, whistling as he tossed the cartoonish bomb from one hand to the other.

Nate watched Growler go. The clown did not look back.

Nate turned his attention to Trevor. "Are you okay?"

"I was right," Trevor whispered. "Clowns are evil menaces to society."

Nate folded his arms. "That was a pretty nasty clown."

"I need to sit down," Trevor said. "I feel stupid. My pants are soaked."

"You sit," Nate said. "I need a Desert Token. Then we can go."

Trevor sat with his back to the claw game. "But we've been warned by a clown."

"You can sit on the sidelines for this one," Nate said. "But we need that key."

In Loot Scoop, the player controlled a mechanical arm holding a slightly curved trowel. The game was full of little heaps of gold and silver plastic coins, interspersed with plastic bead necklaces and fake jewels. But scattered among the chintzy treasure were a handful of Carnie Coins as well as some other coins that looked to be made of actual metal. Upon closer inspection, Nate saw that a few of the quality golden coins had camels on them.

Play Until You Win promised a sign on the game.

Inside the game, partitioned off from the heaps of treasure, was a chute where players could dump the prizes they scooped up. Nate realized that the challenge would be to dump the valuable items into the chute rather than plastic coins.

Nate had twelve Carnie Coins in his pocket, some of them leftover from other days. Hopefully he could win with one or two tries.

He dropped a Carnie Coin into the slot.

Experimenting with the controls, Nate found he could move the trowel around with reasonable accuracy. Pressing the big button caused it to scoop. The problem was the trowel had a shallow surface, so it could not hold much. A lot of what it scooped up fell off as he tried to move the trowel over the chute.

But Loot Scoop rewarded patience. There was no limit to how many times he could try until something came through the chute into the bin at the base of the game.

On about his twentieth scoop, Nate got one of the camel coins to stay on the trowel along with several plastic coins. As he carefully maneuvered the trowel over to the chute, some coins slipped off. The camel coin dropped back among the treasure at the same time a couple of plastic coins fell into the chute. Nate's turn ended, having gained two plastic coins, one gold and one silver.

He wanted to kick the machine but instead inserted another Carnie Coin.

The longer Nate played, the more he realized that the hardest part was getting the camel coin to the chute before he accidentally dumped in worthless rewards. On his fourth turn, he finally moved the trowel around until only a camel coin remained on its surface.

On the way to the chute, the camel coin slipped off.

But at least no junk went down the chute, which allowed his turn to continue.

Nate repeated the strategy again and again, scooping and shaking off worthless treasure until only a camel coin remained. Most of the time the camel coin fell during the process. But he kept those efforts away from the chute, so his turn continued.

"Can we please go?" Trevor asked.

Nate had never seen his friend so distraught.

"I've almost got it," Nate said.

He tried and failed again. And again. And again. This turn had lasted at least half an hour. His eyes were feeling itchy. Could he try again tomorrow? What if the game only appeared as part of the night market? What if this was his only chance?

At last, with a single camel coin on the trowel, Nate positioned it over the chute and dumped it. The coin rattled down into the bin.

"Four Carnie Coins for one camel coin," Nate said. "I hope it's actually a Desert Token."

"Can we go?" Trevor asked.

Nate gave his friend a hand up.

"How did I pee my pants?" Trevor asked. "I hate that I lost my head like that. What's the matter with me?"

"I've never had an issue with clowns," Nate said. "But Growler is freaky."

"I hope nobody notices," Trevor said. "Especially my parents."

"You spilled some water on your lap," Nate said. "That's what I saw."

They walked through the bazaar, along the lonely board-walk, past the darkened ticket booths, and over to the bike rack. Nate and Trevor claimed their bikes and started pedaling across the empty parking lot.

"Nate. Trevor," a gruff voice called from the darkness as they reached the end of the parking lot. "Don't be afraid. It's John."

Nate and Trevor both hit the brakes.

"Are you boys all right?" John Dart asked.

"We're okay," Nate said. "I'm not sure how we'll be after we arrive home so late."

"Sandra has it handled," John said. "It's good to have a dream expert on our side. Just go home and get to bed. Big field trip tomorrow."

"What did she do?" Trevor asked.

"We'll talk tomorrow," John said. "Come to the cafeteria as early as you can. We're not serving lunch, but we'll have breakfast. We shouldn't talk too much out here. I don't want anyone at the carnival linking you to me. But I'll be watching you get home safely."

"Are Pigeon and Summer all right?" Nate asked.

"Safe and sound," John said. "I was worried that you two were taking so much longer to get back. You need rest. Get going."

Nate rode to Trevor's house first. All the lights were off.

After he made sure his friend was inside, Nate pedaled up the street to his own house. He parked his bike off to the side instead of in the garage to avoid extra noise. The front door was unlocked. He eased it open and made his way through the dimness to his room. Kicking off his shoes, Nate flopped onto his bed.

He knew he should get up and brush his teeth.

That was his last thought of the day.

CHAPTER TWENTY-TWO
CIRCUS ACT

"Ladies and gentleman!" the ringmaster cried, flecks of spittle peppering his microphone. "Children of all ages. I proudly present the high-wire daredevil you all came here to see. The one, the only, Nathan Sutter!"

The crowd in the bleachers at either side of the big top roared. Spotlights raced across the striped interior of the tent, circles of light crisscrossing until they focused on a single performer high above the circus floor.

Nate gulped.

He stood on a little platform near the top of the tent, a balance pole in his hands. Spectators in the highest bleachers were tiny below him, their features too distant to distinguish. Just beyond the tips of his shoes, a long, thin wire stretched before him, leading to another small platform near the top of another tentpole. He wore a tank top, soft shoes, and snug, flexible pants. He had chalk on his hands and held a balance pole horizontally.

The spotlights shining up at Nate from multiple directions were hot and blinding. Somewhere beneath him, a drumroll began. A hush fell over the crowd.

Nate was supposed to step out onto the high wire. Everyone expected it. Had he ever taken a single step on a tightrope before? Was there even a net down below? With the glare from the spotlights, it was impossible to tell.

Nate glanced at the rungs leading down from the platform. What if he set aside the balance pole and climbed down? At this height, that would be scary enough. Would people boo? Would they throw things?

"Nathan Sutter adores tension," the ringmaster declared. "The suspense is overwhelming. Let's give him some encouragement. Na-than. Na-than. Na-than."

The crowd took up the chant, repeating his name. The drumroll got louder and faster.

Nate took a tentative step onto the wire. It wobbled slightly, thin and taut beneath his sole. He slowly dragged his other foot off the platform. He felt unsteady, but retained his balance. The pole in his hands offered a mild illusion of security. Underfoot, the wire had very little give. The room grew quiet except for the drumroll. He managed another step. Nate's center of gravity wavered, and he leaned, eliciting a gasp from those below.

Could he leap back to the platform? Why was he doing this?

How had he gotten here?

The realization hit like a thunderbolt.

This was a dream.

There was no way he would have agreed to walk a high wire without training. The whole situation was absurd. He felt like he was going to die.

His balance gone, Nate chucked the balance pole aside as he fell. He caught the tightrope, palms stinging. The audience let out bigger gasps. One woman screamed.

Now he was dangling. Could he travel hand over hand back to the platform? It shouldn't be far. When he turned to look, he saw Growler seated on the platform's edge, legs swinging, eating a banana.

"You've gotten yourself into quite a pickle," the purple-faced clown said.

"Get out of my way," Nate demanded.

Growler casually tossed the banana peel. It landed on the high wire near one of Nate's hands. "That would have worked better if you had stayed on your feet!"

The crowd laughed.

Nate brushed the banana peel off the tightrope. It fluttered downward, splaying wide and rotating.

Growler produced a hacksaw and moved it back and forth in the air.

The crowd laughed harder.

Nate concentrated on flying. This was his dream, so theoretically he could take control. If he just believed, he should be able to do it. But the downward drag of gravity felt real and relentless. The tightrope dug painfully into his fingers. He doubted that flying was an option.

"It's fun when amateurs try to compete with the pros,"

Growler said as he started sawing. Little fibers of the metal tightrope snapped and frayed.

Nate concentrated on the hacksaw, trying to transform it into a violin bow.

"Are you challenging my saw, featherweight?" Growler said with a derisive laugh. "This is my dream too."

The hacksaw severed the tightrope, and Nate fell. The crowd gasped.

Nate knew that if he held to the high wire, he could swing like Spider-Man, except he worried about hitting the pole beneath the far platform. Catching a glimpse of the net below, Nate released the tightrope. Air rushed by as he plummeted. He turned so he would land on his back. People screamed. He smelled buttery popcorn.

His body dropped into what felt like a springy hammock. It flexed downward, absorbing his momentum, then tossed him back into the air. The next time he landed was gentler, and soon he was just bobbing in the net. Nate scrambled to the edge of the net, rolled himself over it, and dropped the final few feet to the ground.

The crowd laughed and applauded, appreciative of the spectacle.

"Get him, boys!" Growler called from above.

Roustabouts came rushing from different directions, grim-faced men in flat caps and work boots. One held a tire iron. Another had a mallet. Any empty hands were clenched into fists.

Nate faked to the left, then sprinted to the right, knifing between two of the roustabouts. "I can fly," he told himself, jumping forward, but the best he could manage was to keep running.

The audience laughed as the roustabouts gave chase. A quick glance showed six or seven angry men on his tail. A round bomb landed in his path, bouncing and rolling, fire sparking from the diminishing fuse. Nate swerved away from it. The bomb exploded, shooting confetti in all directions. The shockwave hurled Nate to the ground, ears ringing from the deafening boom.

Nate staggered back to his feet. Dust and colored bits of paper hung in the air. A huge divot cratered the floor of the big top. The roustabouts were still coming.

"He's a squirrelly one," Growler hollered from above.

The audience laughed and hooted.

"Nate!" called a female voice from up ahead.

Racing forward, wiping dust from his eyes, Nate recognized Sandra's dark hair with its distinctive silver and white streaks.

"This way!" she called, leading him under the bleachers.

Nate ran into the gloomy space striped with light. Peanut shells, soda cups, and stray popcorn littered the ground. Above him, feet, purses, drinks, and snacks could be seen through long, narrow gaps.

Sandra faced Nate calmly. "We're safe here."

Nate looked over his shoulder. "What about the roustabouts? What about Growler?"

"I secured this area for us," Sandra said. "This is mostly your dream, though the people who run the carnival are trying to stake a claim. I walled us off in here. We need to talk. I'm glad I found you."

"Me too."

"I've wanted to give you this," Sandra said, holding up a woven friendship bracelet that matched the one on her wrist. "You can only receive it in a dream. We can share dreams if you wear it."

"Sure," Nate said, holding out his hand. "Could you tie it on?"

"I have your permission?"

"Yes," Nate said. "As long as you're really Sandra."

"I am," she said, securing the bracelet around his wrist.

"Why couldn't I fly?" Nate asked.

"Doubt and fear," Sandra said. "You believed the dream more than you believed in your own power. It's all right. You'll get better at it."

"How did you find me?" Nate asked.

"It's what I do," Sandra said. "I sensed your distress. It was easy since I had your permission."

"John told me you somehow handled my parents last night," Nate said.

"I coaxed them into falling asleep before they could realize how late you were out and guided them into pleasant dreams."

"You didn't have their permission," Nate said.

"I can still exert a fair amount of influence without permission," Sandra said. "Especially if the target isn't resisting. Just like how somebody at the carnival tampered with your dream tonight without full permission."

"Did I give partial permission?" Nate asked.

"Anyone who reads the posted signs at the carnival and still attends grants access," Sandra said.

"Sneaky," Nate said. "We learned there are people trapped in the carnival who are asleep and can't wake up."

"That goes well beyond ordinary dream tampering," Sandra said. "I suspected something like it might be happening. Every sleeper they add increases their power. They must be stopped."

"What should I do?" Nate asked.

"Having the bracelet will help," Sandra said. "You received it in the dreamscape, so they can't keep it out of the carnival."

"I forgot to drink Mr. Stott's potion," Nate realized. "I was so tired."

"Which made it easier for them to access your dreams," Sandra said. "Easier for me too. That oversight may end up working for our good."

"What now?" Nate asked. "The school's field trip to the carnival is in the morning."

Sandra motioned to a bed in a dark corner. "Go rest. I'll make sure the remainder of your dreams are untroubled tonight. You'll need your strength for tomorrow."

"What should my priority be in the morning?" Nate asked.

"Wake the sleepers," Sandra said. "We must rescue them before the carnival grows too strong."

"I feel like I'm in over my head," Nate said.

"You're right," Sandra said. "But somehow you must succeed."

Nate crossed to the bed and slid under the covers. He could still hear the clamor of the circus, but it was distant, muted. He closed his eyes, and sleep enfolded him into oblivion.

CHAPTER TWENTY-THREE

FIELD TRIP

Buses clogged the parking lot when Nate arrived at school. He parked his bike and hurried to the cafeteria where John Dart sat with Summer and Trevor eating breakfast burritos. Two extra trays containing burritos, vanilla yogurt with blueberries, and orange juice waited beside them. The huge bowling ball remained in the room, having been rolled into a corner.

"Join us," John called to Nate, indicating an unclaimed tray of food.

Nate sat down. "You guys got here early. I was exhausted this morning."

"I'm just happy not to be grounded for a month," Trevor said. "It was a miracle. My parents were asleep when I got home and mentioned nothing about my late arrival this morning."

"Same," Nate said. "I forgot to take the potion Mr. Stott

gave us, and I had a weird dream." Nate shared his dream and his conversation with Sandra.

"I want a friendship bracelet from Sandra," Summer said.

"You may have to risk a dream without the potion to get one," John said.

"It disappeared when I woke up," Nate said, holding up his bare wrist.

"It's there," John said. "I have one too. It will only appear when you're dreaming."

"Hi, guys," Pigeon said, approaching.

"How do you feel?" Summer asked.

"Way better," Pigeon said. "Not sick to my stomach. Just kind of worn-out."

"Have some breakfast," John offered.

Pigeon glanced at the tray and looked relieved. "Good. No hash browns."

"We met Mozag as an aardvark," Nate told John. He explained about the undercarnival and the roustabouts who took Mozag away. "Mozag wanted me to tell you we're facing an extinction-level threat."

"I figured," John said. "But it's sobering to have that confirmed." He glanced at his wristwatch. "Sandra should arrive any minute."

"Do we know anything about Zac and Benji?" Trevor asked.

"Zac was in and out of the carnival yesterday," John said. "He and Benji left before the regular closing time."

"How will today go?" Summer asked.

"You'll travel with your homerooms to the carnival," John

said. "You have until two o'clock. I would say continue your investigations. Build on your leads. We need to make quick progress. Even viewed from outside, the carnival is significantly bigger today than it was yesterday. After you kids were settled, I spent last night catching clowns and pirates who were trying to raid the town."

Sandra approached the table and sat down. Dressed in sweats, she looked a little ragged, dark circles under her eyes. "Everything depends on you kids finding the sleepers," she said without preamble. "The carnival is gaining strength every day by recruiting sleepers. Think of every new sleeper as mass added to a black hole. The more massive a black hole becomes, the greater its power to consume all matter around it. Eventually, nothing can escape. With enough sleepers, this carnival could potentially swallow everyone and everything, pulling our entire waking reality into the dreamscape."

"How do we wake them up?" Nate asked.

"I don't believe you can," Sandra said. "The problem we must solve is one of access. First, you must find the sleepers. They will be heavily guarded. Then, Nate, you must fall asleep among them."

"Wait a second," Nate said, glancing around the table. "I thought falling asleep inside the carnival was bad."

"Normally, yes," Sandra replied. "But thanks to your dream last night, you have one of my friendship bracelets. If you dream alongside the sleepers, I should have access to your dreams. I'll wake you up and them as well."

"It's risky," John warned.

"More risky than if the carnival devours the world?" Nate asked. "I'm in."

"After attending the carnival today, all of you besides Nate should skip taking Mr. Stott's dream suppressor potion," Sandra said. "The sooner I get a bracelet on you, the safer you will be."

Trevor ran a hand through his hair. "I'm not sure I can handle being hunted by clowns. It crosses into a type of fear I don't know how to control."

"If that happens in your dream, I'll rescue you," Sandra said.

Trevor looked at John. "What if it happens in real life?"

"Do your best," John said. "For me, it helps to picture the worst-case scenario ahead of time."

"You get scared?" Pigeon asked.

"Not so much for my own life anymore," John said. "I'm content with who I am and how I've chosen to live. I've made peace with my past mistakes. I'm ready to meet my demise if needed. But sometimes I fear failing my missions. I fear what may happen to others. I fear for you kids."

"What do you mean you picture the worst-case scenario?" Pigeon asked.

"I picture the worst outcomes that could happen," John said. "I get used to how they might feel, and I decide how I will behave even if the worst results come to pass. Even if I fail. If I'm only willing to sacrifice for success, then failure becomes terrifying. Surrendering the need for a guaranteed outcome cuts the tension for me. I accept the darkest possibilities, and then work for something better. It's not a method that works for everyone."

"I might try that," Trevor said heavily. "The worst thing I can imagine is clowns dragging me off to be their eternal prisoner." He shivered. "The thought makes me want to run away screaming. But would I rather my friends were hurt or killed? Could I face clowns for a chance to save the world? I don't know . . . that might be enough to shatter my brain."

"We all have breaking points," John said. "Just do your best."

The first bell rang.

"We better go to homeroom," Pigeon said soberly.

"We can do this," Summer said. "Let's go pretend we're having fun at the carnival. And save the world while we're at it."

Nate got up from the table, as did the others.

"I'll bus the trays," John said. "Nate, a word."

Nate hung back as his friends departed. Sandra lingered as well.

John tapped his cafeteria tray. In the corner sat a small yellow gumdrop. "Mr. Stott whipped up that gumdrop this morning. It can be hard to fall asleep amid duress. The magic in that candy will help you doze if needed."

Nate pocketed the gumdrop. "Does it have a name?"

"Not yet," John said. "Dream Quick? Sleep Now? Not really my department."

Nate patted his pocket. "Thanks."

"Good luck, Nate," Sandra said.

"See you in my dreams," Nate replied.

He hurried to homeroom and slid into his seat behind Zac. The Foster Child did not turn around. "Zac," Nate said. "Hey, Zac."

After a moment, Zac looked over his shoulder. "Oh, hello there. Are we friends?"

"I'm sorry we disappeared yesterday," Nate said.

"You guys never came back to the Fun House," Zac said. "We waited for a long time. Then we looked all over for you. Not for a few minutes. Until closing."

"I'm so sorry," Nate said quietly. "We got stuck someplace and didn't make it back until long after closing."

"You got stuck someplace in the carnival?" Zac asked.

"There is an undercarnival," Nate whispered. "We didn't know what we were getting into when we went down there. The only train out left at midnight."

"Oh," Zac said, seeming less annoyed. "I guess I can't blame you for getting trapped. As long as I get to have some adventures too."

"You'll have plenty if you stick with us," Nate said. "It's going to get really dangerous though."

"It's about time," Zac said with a wink.

"How did the video go?"

"Piece of cake," Zac said. "I can generate content in my sleep."

The second bell rang.

"All right, class," Mr. Zimmerman said at the front of the room. "Today is a very special occasion. As you know, the Dreams and Screams International Carnival has invited our school for a visit. You will each get fifty tickets and five Carnie

Coins courtesy of the carnival. Secret tip? Try your coins on the bumper cars. But you didn't hear that from me! Remember to ration your tickets, because you will be responsible for your own lunches, and the tickets are your currency. If your tickets are low at mealtime, try the Last Ticket Diner. Like it stated on the permission slip, additional tickets and coins may be purchased with your own money."

Zac raised his hand. "What will the carnival teach us about history?"

"Golden question!" Mr. Zimmerman said, pointing at Zac. "You get an A in class participation for the term. Anyone who can report back tomorrow about historical influences on the attractions will get extra credit. Be sure to explore! There are secrets at this carnival. I'll admit I'm a fan. I'm working on some investigations of my own."

Mrs. Jackson's voice came over the loudspeaker. "Sixth-grade teachers, your buses are ready. Please escort your classes to the parking lot. Seventh- and eighth-grade teachers, please wait for my announcement."

"You heard the lady," Mr. Zimmerman said. "I want a single file line. Keep this orderly. Let's go have some fun, people."

Mr. Zimmerman led them out to the parking lot. Nate covered his mouth to avoid breathing fumes from the idling buses. He boarded the bus behind Zac, trying not to think of the train of buses from his dream. At least the Swindler wasn't driving.

Nate and Zac sat together.

"The Eiffel Tower showed up in our neighborhood," Zac said.

"What?" Nate asked.

"A relatively little one," Zac said. "Maybe four stories tall. It appeared overnight in the middle of our cul-de-sac."

"More dream relics."

Zac peered out the window. "Should be an epic day."

"Will you be filming?"

"Not officially," Zac replied. "Just for fun. I can always make use of good footage."

"What do you think about letting Benji know about our secrets?" Nate asked.

"You tell me."

"We have a lot to explore today," Nate said. "We could use the extra help. Is he trustworthy?"

"More than I am," Zac said. "I think he would help us."

Their bus started rolling forward. A few of the kids clapped and cheered.

Zac showed Nate the video he had made in the Fun House. He fell down several times inside a spinning tunnel. He panicked as a hallway seemed to shrink around him the farther he went. He summed up the experience with his head enormous and warped, obviously filmed in a mirror. Benji did not appear. As usual, the video was slick and reasonably funny.

Students craned their necks as the bus entered the carnival parking lot. There were already a lot of cars in the lot for a weekday morning.

"Do you get extra tickets today?" Nate asked.

"Always," Zac said. "I can get you extras too. But don't ditch me again."

"We weren't trying to ditch you," Nate said. "We just didn't know what to do about Benji."

The day was pleasantly warm. Puffy white clouds floated in the sky. It was hard to believe anything dangerous could happen on a day like this. Nate thought he counted two new ticket offices. With kids streaming off the buses, it took some time for Nate and Zac to find Summer, Trevor, Pigeon, and Benji.

"Thanks a lot for ditching us yesterday," Zac said once the six were together. "Benji and I really bonded over the pain of abandonment."

"We looked all over for you guys," Benji said. "We even split up for a couple of hours so we could cover more ground."

"They don't need all the boring details," Zac said.

"We got stuck somewhere," Trevor blurted, clearly flustered.

"I told Zac we were stuck in the undercarnival," Nate said.

"What's that?" Benji asked.

Nate lowered his voice, motioning the others closer. "Zac and I decided to let Benji in on the secrets." Nate faced Benji. "This carnival is magical. There are tons of hidden places inside of it, including an underground carnival where we were trapped until after midnight."

"Oh, come on, don't mess with me like that," Benji said.

"You'll see," Zac said. Long lines of students waited at the ticket offices. "Should I grab us extra tickets? We can go straight to the Currency Exchange."

Zac bypassed the ticket offices, leading the others inside the park to the Currency Exchange. Soon they each had a hundred tickets and ten Carnie Coins.

"What is going on?" Benji asked. "This place grew!"

Nate studied the carnival. The boardwalk was broader and longer. The games adjoining it looked like permanent installations, with elaborate signage and detailed finish work. The carousel was now three stories tall, with stegosauruses and triceratops on the upper level. The bright crests of multiple roller coasters could be seen in the distance.

"We told you," Zac said. "It's magical."

"I almost believe you," Benji said.

"We have some business at the Terror Castle," Nate said. "Let's go there first."

The Terror Castle looked much how Nate remembered it. Except was it a little taller? Were the battlements more sophisticated? Did the werewolf in the window actually look intimidating?

As his group approached the front of the line, Nate fished the camel coin from his pocket. He hoped it was the Desert Token, and that it would work as promised. When Nate reached the front, he held up the token. "This is for the six of us."

"Nice try," the attendant said. "The Desert Token is only good for one car. Four of you can experience it. The others will have to use tickets and ride normally."

Nate turned to the group. "What should we do?"

"Let Zac and Benji see it," Trevor said. "Pigeon and I will

head over to the shop above the Swindler's. Take care of business there."

"Good idea," Summer said.

Zac grinned at Trevor. "If we don't see you until tomorrow, these things happen."

Nate handed over the Desert Token. Zac and Benji took the front seats, leaving Nate and Summer in the back two.

Trevor and Pigeon hopped out of line. Then Pigeon turned back. "Where should we meet?"

"The carousel," Zac answered.

"If you're not there when we get off the ride, we'll go to the Swindler's," Nate added.

The car started forward. Pigeon called something else, but Nate didn't catch it.

CHAPTER TWENTY-FOUR
DUNE HUNT

N ate had experienced the Terror Castle multiple times, but he felt new tension as his car advanced into the dungeon torture chamber. How would the Desert Token make this ride different? Would the change be obvious? Or would it resemble their previously fruitless searches for coin slots?

The car progressed into the cemetery, weaving through tombstones. The gravediggers fighting the vampire looked just like Nate remembered.

"Do you see anything different?" Nate asked Summer.

"Not yet," she replied.

When the car entered the pyramid, it took a sharp turn and began to accelerate. They passed through an embalming room that Nate did not recall from previous rides. Was this a whole new path?

They plunged down a drop then zoomed through a

glittering room with a dozen golden sarcophagi surrounded by heaps of treasure. Nate barely had time to glimpse jade figures and ceremonial urns. He smelled musty stone and the tang of metal. Complex hieroglyphs turned the ancient walls into a stylized storyboard.

They careened into darkness, speeding for a long moment. Then a square of light appeared up ahead. The square grew until they raced into bright sunlight. Behind them loomed the enormous pyramid they had traveled through. The air was markedly hotter and dryer. Tawny dunes stretched to the edge of sight.

The car came to a sudden stop in front of an odd little island of civilization in an ocean of sand—a weathered counter surrounded by blue-and-white ceramic tiles. A young boy in a kaftan and sandals swept the tiles, keeping the surrounding desert at bay. A man with an aquiline nose, dark eyes, and a jawline beard stood behind the scarred counter. He wore a fez atop his head.

Roughly twenty people waited on the tiles, crowding under the shade of an embroidered canopy. All eyes regarded the new arrivals.

Dune Hunt was written on a freestanding sign. The desiccated wood looked almost petrified.

Beyond the edges of the tiles, sand stretched away in all directions, rising into dunes. The monumental pyramid and the tracks for the Terror Castle car were the only other signs of civilization.

Nate leaped from the car onto the hot sand and walked over to the tiles. His friends followed. The crowd parted to provide access to the counter. Nate glanced back at the Terror Castle car. Would it stay? How would they restart it when they wanted to return?

"What just happened?" Benji asked. "Where are we?"

"Magic carnival," Summer muttered as they approached the counter.

"Welcome, newcomers, to the most thrilling game at the brink of the searing sands," the man behind the counter announced in lightly accented words. He gestured to the top of the dune behind him. "Scale the dune and seize the fabled skeleton key."

"How many tickets?" Zac asked.

"No tickets," the man said. "This is a test of courage and skill."

Zac looked around. "Why isn't anyone else trying?"

"Some of us are thinking about it," a burly man replied.

"It's no small decision," a woman said.

The man behind the counter shrugged. "Not enough courage, perhaps. Or a shortage of skill."

"Then why hang around?" Zac pressed, considering the crowd.

"Spectacle, perhaps," the man said with a shrug. "Some are scheming."

"What happens to the people who fail?" Nate asked.

Zac pointed at Nate. "Good question!"

"They are claimed by the sands," the man behind the counter said vaguely.

"Meaning what?" Nate asked. "They get lost? They pass out?"

"Or else they sink into the desert never to be seen again," said a woman in the crowd.

"You must make your way carefully," the man behind the counter advised.

"How many people have tried today?" Nate asked, looking at the crowd.

A young man pushed forward. "I'm next." He wore a sleeveless shirt and running shorts. "I wish to try before these newcomers."

"You spoke first," the man behind the counter said. "The opportunity is yours."

The young man grinned and pumped a fist. He had a lean, athletic build. "I've been watching. Everybody zigzags. I bet the secret is to charge straight up."

"That would require a great deal of stamina," said the man behind the counter.

"It's not that high," the young man said. "I regularly run ten miles on the beach."

The dune was not nearly as tall as some of the others in view. From the bottom to the top was no more than thirty yards. And the slope was not terribly steep.

"You are welcome to try," the man behind the counter said.

"Why are you after the key?" Nate asked.

"Are you serious?" the young man responded. "Do you know how many doors you can open with that thing?"

"What are you looking for?" Nate asked.

The young man shared a guarded smile. "Wouldn't you like to know?"

He stepped off the tiles and onto the sand. He approached the dune, then moved sideways along the base, apparently selecting his spot. Suddenly he dashed forward, every step spraying sand. He reached the slope of the dune at a full sprint and started up.

For the first several steps, the young man flew toward the top. About halfway up, he started to flounder. Each step plunged him deeper into the sand. His progress slowed as the sand beneath him slid down the slope. Soon his legs were churning madly just to stay in the same place. When he stopped fighting, the gentle slide of sand conveyed him several feet down the slope.

He came to a standstill less than halfway up the slope, now almost to his waist in sand. As he tried to battle forward, he made a little progress, only to sink to his chest.

"Hey," the young man called. "A little help?"

"You knew the risks, friend," the man behind the counter yelled to him. "Are you abandoning your strategy? Straight up the side, I believe it was?"

The young man lurched forward with determination, then sank to his shoulders. He spread his arms out over the surface of the sand to stop himself from sinking, but soon all that remained was his head.

"Bad idea!" he called out. "Somebody help me!"

His head disappeared beneath the sand. The smooth surface of the dune looked as it had before he churned it up.

"Who is next?" the man behind the counter asked.

The crowd stared gravely. An older man in Bermuda shorts crossed himself.

"Why do we need the skeleton key?" Benji asked Nate.

Nate moved closer, drawing Zac and Summer into the huddle. "It opens the secret locks at the carnival. This carnival is pulling the real world into the realm of dreams, and if the carnival keeps growing, the whole world could be destroyed."

Benji looked to Zac. "How much do you know about this?"

"Only a little," Zac said. "But the description fits. Could be true."

Benji squinted up at the dune. "I bet I can do it."

"Really?" Summer asked.

"I'm small for my age, but I have big feet," Benji said. "I'm light and quick. Like a jackrabbit. But I have a few questions for the guy running the show."

Benji emerged from the huddle. "What's your name?"

"Khabib."

"I'm Benji. This can be done?"

"It can. Others have won."

"There is a route that would let me climb the dune without sinking?" Benji asked.

"Yes. Multiple routes."

"Is there quicksand around the dune?" Benji asked. "Or just on the dune?"

"The sinking sand is only on the dune," Khabib said. "The surrounding dunes are made of more traditional sand."

"Could I walk around the dune and go up the back side?" Benji asked.

"You could," Khabib said. "Although it would make it more difficult for us to track your progress."

251

"After I get the key, I still have to make it down," Benji said.

"Naturally," Khabib agreed.

"Let me talk to my friends," Benji said. He beckoned the others back into a huddle.

"Do you really think you can do this?" Zac asked.

"The secret is patience," Benji said. "I'll probe the ground ahead and back off if I start to sink. Change direction as much as needed."

"Sounds promising," Summer said.

"When I get to the top, I'll throw the key down, just in case," Benji said. "I have a good arm." Turning, he raised his voice. "I'll go next."

"Excellent," Khabib said. "The opportunity is yours!"

Benji plodded over to the base of the dune. He prowled along the base, going partway around it before starting up. Benji had gone far enough around that Nate watched his profile as he climbed.

Benji took cautious steps, testing his weight on the sand before committing. The practice made for slow going. A third of the way up the dune, his methodical steps started limiting his progress, because he backslid almost as much as he advanced. At least he wasn't sinking.

He made his way laterally instead of climbing, still testing the sand as he went, coming back toward the front of the dune rather than looping around to the far side. After traveling sideways, he began slowly advancing upward again, apparently having found a firmer slope.

He came to a standstill about halfway to the summit. He

moved laterally again, sliding down a little as he edged sideways. Every time he tried to ascend, rivulets of sand trickled down beneath him, undermining his efforts.

Benji backed down the slope a few steps, then began to sink. Until now, the sand had only been ankle-deep, but suddenly it was up to his knees.

"Careful, Benji!" Zac shouted. "You've got this."

Slowly and deliberately, Benji edged to the right. The sand was now at mid-thigh. He tried to gingerly move forward and sank to his hips. "I think I'm in trouble," Benji cried, an edge of panic in his tone. "It's like the sand went soft everywhere."

"Keep perfectly still!" Zac shouted.

Benji complied, not moving a muscle. "I'm still slowly sinking!"

"Lay flat," Zac coached.

Benji tried to retreat down the hill but sank to his waist. "I'll try to lay flat," he yelled, panic overtaking him. He leaned back into the sand, and it closed around him until only his head remained above. "Didn't help! Not a great technique! Oh, no. This was a mistake! Once the sand starts to feel like liquid, you're trapped. The more I strain, the tighter it grips, always pulling me downward."

Only part of his face was above the sand. He was still sinking. "Sorry, guys. Tell my mom and da—"

His lips sank beneath the sand. A moment later, no part of him was visible.

"Benji!" Zac screamed. "No! Benji!"

Nate watched silently, feeling sick inside. Where had

Benji gone? How long could Benji breathe under the sand? Would any air filter through?

Zac turned to Nate and Summer. "We have to help him."

"If we try to climb the dune, won't we sink just like he did?" Summer asked.

"What can we do?" Zac cried. He wheeled on Khabib. "Where did he go?"

"He is now part of the desert," Khabib said.

"How many tickets for a rope?" Zac snapped. "How many coins?"

"There is no rope," Khabib said.

"We have to dig him out," Zac demanded.

Khabib gestured at the dune. "You are welcome to try."

Zac stood panting, tears in his eyes. He shuffled over to Nate and Summer. "We can't help him. There's nothing to do."

"I don't see how to rescue him," Nate said, his eyes stinging.

Zac sat down on the ceramic tiles and buried his face in his hands.

Summer crouched and wrapped an arm around him.

"He might not be dead," Zac mumbled. "This is a carnival. How long could it stay open if it kills customers? Preston told me the carnival is designed to feel like a grand adventure. He mentioned traps that seem lethal but really just mean you're out of the game."

"What are you saying?" Summer asked.

"Kind of like your turn is over," Zac said. "I didn't really understand what he meant."

"So Benji might be safe in some underground room?" Summer asked. "With other contestants who lost?"

"I don't know," Zac said, eyes teary. "Maybe. I hope so."

"Or he's dead," Nate said.

"Roller coasters are meant to scare you, not kill you," Zac said. "I hate not knowing. We shouldn't have come here. It wasn't worth the risk."

"We had to come," Nate said. "And we still have to get that key."

"I can try it with the Clown Lips," Summer offered.

"No," Nate said. "I should try with the Cannon Blast. I should have thought of it earlier. Maybe I can shoot all the way to the top."

"You don't know the range," Summer said. "You might fall short. If you hit a soft spot in the sand, you'll probably disappear instantly."

"The candy gives me a better chance than trying to run up the slope," Nate said.

"Why did you let Benji try?" Zac asked bitterly.

"He seemed confident," Nate said. "Taking it slow was a good idea."

"Until it wasn't," Zac said.

Nate went to the counter. "Khabib, is the key that little black line poking up from the top of the dune?"

"Yes," Khabib said.

"I want to walk around the whole dune before I try," Nate said. "Make sure there isn't a better approach."

"Be my guest," Khabib said. "If I were taking the risk, I would do the same."

Nate ventured onto the scalding sand. He stepped carefully, keeping away from the base of the dune. Hiking in the sand was plodding work, but at least he generally stayed on the surface. It took several minutes to get all the way around the dune. The back side was roughly the same steepness as the front. The sides were a little less steep, which was presumably why Benji had started there.

When Nate returned to the canopied area, he approached Khabib. "I want to try next."

"The opportunity is yours," Khabib replied.

Nate took the Cannon Blast from his pocket. He looked at Summer. "I'm going to try to clear the dune. There are more dunes behind it. If make it over the top, I'll grab the key as I go by. I only have one shot. If I fall short, I'll do my best to scramble up the rest of the way."

"Be careful," Zac said. "We already lost one of us."

"This strategy is the opposite of careful," Nate said.

He popped the candy in his mouth. It was sweet with a hot tang. His body tingled with energy, as if all his cells were vibrating. The feeling intensified as Nate moved toward the dune. Nate remembered Preston's instructions: aim, bite down, launch.

Finding the angle he wanted, Nate halted a few paces from the base of the dune. He stared up at the thin black key projecting from the top. He visualized himself flying just over the skeleton key, within reach, but clearing the summit. Staring at the space just above the key, Nate bit down.

He shot skyward, accelerating instantaneously, the passing air a hurricane in his ears. The face of the dune blurred beneath him as he rocketed upward, reaching the summit with alarming abruptness. Arms outstretched, he intended to grab his target with both hands, but he barely got one hand around the key as he soared over the apex, stealing it from the sandy peak.

Having overtopped the dune, Nate continued to climb, soaring in a long arc toward a larger mountain of sand. He almost cleared the second dune but clipped the top with an explosion of sand. He tumbled wildly down most of the far side.

When Nate came to a rest, the skeleton key remained in his grasp. The shaft of the key was six inches long, with complicated teeth at the end.

For another moment, his body felt heavy and strong. Striking the top of the dune had not hurt, nor had flipping and cartwheeling down the far slope. Every detail had seemed sharp and vivid. His senses and reflexes must have sped up during the flight, because he could now sense them returning to normal. Or maybe it was just the adrenaline subsiding.

Nate sat up. Walking back to his friends would be a slog. He had better get started. The others would be worried.

He stood up and brushed copious amounts of sand off his clothing. Striding along the slope of the dune parallel to the ground, Nate planned to walk around the sand heap rather than over the crest. He could barely hear Summer and Zac shouting his name, so he yelled an answer.

"I'm all right! I got the key!"

CHAPTER TWENTY-FIVE

LUX

Trevor and Pigeon were waiting at the three-story carousel when Nate, Zac, and Summer arrived. The carousel spun behind them, music chiming, animals rising and falling like pistons. Despite the bright sun overhead, the day seemed cool compared to the desert heat.

"Where's Benji?" Trevor asked.

From the look on his face, Nate thought Zac might start crying again, but he held it together.

"We lost Benji," Zac said. "He drowned in quicksand."

"Wait," Pigeon said. "He's gone? Like, dead?"

"We hope not," Zac said. "It isn't like we saw a body. He might still be alive. I heard there are traps in the carnival that aren't as deadly as they seem. Sort of a way to weed out contestants."

"Sounds demented either way," Trevor said.

"There was nothing we could do to save him without getting sucked under too," Zac said.

"Wow, this just got heavy," Trevor said.

"I think it was always heavy," Nate said. "Reality is finally catching up with us."

"Reality?" Zac laughed bitterly. "Benji went into some secret desert dimension at a traveling carnival and disappeared. How is anyone supposed to believe that? There is no good explanation for what happened. He's probably just going to be listed as another 'missing person,' and we might never really know what happened to him."

"I hope he's going to turn up," Pigeon said.

"You were in a desert dimension?" Trevor asked.

"Yeah," Summer said. She explained how they'd gotten to the Dune Hunt game, and Nate showed them the skeleton key he'd pulled from the sand.

"I wish I'd used my Cannon Blast before Benji had tried to hike up the side," Nate said.

"I think I'm done," Pigeon said, taking a few steps backward. "I don't want to be at a carnival where kids vanish."

Summer nodded. "This place is twisted. No game should kill people—or pretend to kill them."

"Maybe we should tell John what we've learned and let the pros take it from here," Trevor said.

Zac stared stoically.

Nate studied his friends. They looked tired and scared. He was in turmoil as well. It was one thing to have risky adventures. It was something else to lose a friend. Maybe they were right.

Nate rubbed his forehead. He had tried not to think about how hard Benji had fought to stay above the sand. But now the horror returned. Benji had gone under because he went first. They lost him because he was brave.

Would similar bravery get them all killed? Nate scowled. If they hadn't taken some risks to resist Belinda White and her brother, Jonas, their town would have been destroyed. Maybe even the world. Was quitting the best way to honor Benji's memory?

They had the skeleton key. But John and the other pros couldn't enter the carnival. If Nate couldn't do it, the Council would have to recruit some other kid.

Would any other kid see it through?

Nate sighed. "Pidge, guys, you've already risked so much. We're not playing games here. This is life and death. We got the skeleton key, and one person might be enough to fin-ish this. Mozag gave me a job to do, and I'm going to see it through, even if it gets me killed. If we don't stop this carnival, it'll be everywhere soon. And others will die or be lost or go missing. Losing Benji is a nightmare. But if I don't put that out of my head for now, I could lose everybody I care about."

Summer looked at Trevor, Pigeon, and Zac. "I'm staying with Nate."

"If anyone is staying, I'm here too," Zac said.

"Your chances go up with more help," Trevor said. "I'm in."

"There isn't much of a choice," Pigeon said heavily. "I don't want this for any of us. But if we don't do it, who will?"

"It's going to be rough," Nate said. "What are our assets?"

"Pidge and I got some candy!" Trevor said. "Preston sold

them to us for three Carnie Coins. Mine is a Drip Drop. When I use it, I'll be able to turn my body to liquid so I can fit through tight spaces while also avoiding damage. Sounds pretty cool."

"I got a Statue Stick," Pigeon said. "When I eat it, I turn into a statue of myself. The material of the statue will match whatever I'm holding in my left hand. I remain a statue until I drop what's in my hand."

"You eat the candy and just stand there?" Nate asked.

"No, it's a living statue," Pigeon said. "I can move around."

"Let's hope the statue can move fast," Zac muttered.

"Are we ready for the Fun House?" Summer asked.

"Almost," Nate said. "Sandra warned that the sleepers are guarded. We'll need to be prepared for anything. I want to buy another Cannon Blast. And Zac should get something too."

"You're talking about the shop above the Swindler?" Zac asked.

"Yeah," Nate said.

"I know a better place to get candy," Zac said. "Have you heard of the Lux Lounge?"

The other kids shook their heads.

"I met with some of my sponsors at the carnival yesterday while you guys were gone," Zac said. "They're really jazzed about my videos and how attendance is growing because of them. As a perk, they told me about the Lux Lounge. I checked it out without Benji. It's the luxury club inside the carnival. They have a bunch of magic candy available, and it's only one Carnie Coin each."

"Whoa, why didn't you mention this earlier?" Summer asked.

Zac smiled. "I was going to, but you guys never came back, remember?"

"Did you already buy some candy?" Trevor asked.

"A little," Zac said. "I think Nate is right that going after the sleepers will be dangerous. We should load up."

"Where is this lounge?" Nate asked.

Zac glanced at the carousel. "Why do you think I wanted to meet here?"

Zac led the others to get in line.

"Do they have Cannon Blasts at the Lux Lounge?" Nate asked.

"I'm not sure," Zac said. "There seemed to be a big variety, but I'm new to the world of magical candy. If they don't have what you want, we can always go back to the other shop."

The carousel stopped. After the riders got off, the line surged forward. When the gate closed, Nate and his friends stopped about twenty riders from the front.

"Next go-round," Trevor said.

"It's good we're toward the front of the line," Zac said. "We need a specific booth."

"A booth?" Summer prompted.

"See the four booths on the second floor?" Zac asked. "Decorated kind of like carriages?"

"Sure," Nate said. "Behind the animals against the inner wall of the carousel."

The carousel started turning, music playing.

"There are two benches inside each booth," Zac said.

"They'll sit four—six, if you squish. We'll fit fine. I think they're for old people who don't want to go up and down on an animal. You can see there's a red booth, and also blue, yellow, and green. We want the green one."

"Let me guess," Pigeon said. "Coin slot."

"Coin slot plus a trick," Zac said. "Even then you can be turned away. But I have official access. Same with anyone I bring inside."

The carousel slowed to a standstill, and the riders exited. The gate at the front of the line opened. Everyone who went through paid three tickets. Most people rushed to claim horses, frogs, storks, or honeybees on level one. Zac hustled up to the second level and went to the green booth. Nate was pretty sure they were the first riders to choose a booth over an elk or a dolphin.

The interior of the booth was cozy, if a little hot and stuffy. Zac produced a Carnie Coin and inserted it into a slot down by their feet. A jester's face was embossed on the wall of the booth adjoining the inner wall of the carousel. When Zac pressed both eyes of the face, a door swung inward, revealing a small room and the top of a staircase.

Zac went first into the room, then, after the others came through, he closed the door. Posh red carpeting softened the floor and continued down the stairs, where white walls and a shiny brass railing curved downward.

"No point in waiting," Zac said, leading the way down.

"How many secrets does this carnival have?" Summer muttered.

The staircase circled down through at least ten full

corkscrews before opening into a lavish lobby. Rich carpeting cushioned every step. An intricate coffered ceiling and paneled walls added sophistication. Stately busts gazed out from niches lined with ornate molding. Water babbled in numerous small fountains. One looked like a floating pitcher pouring endlessly into a basin.

Wearing a tuxedo, Preston Wilder stood behind a podium on the far side of the lobby. Zac escorted the others to him.

"Hello, Zac," Preston said warmly. "I see you brought some familiar faces."

"You just sold us candy above the Swindler's place!" Pigeon said.

"I get around," Preston said, tugging on one sleeve of his coat. "Some people wonder if I have a twin."

Nate could see a large, elegant room beyond Preston. People were dressed fancy. "Do we need reservations?" he asked.

Preston rolled his eyes. "Reservations are so middle-class. But the boys do need jackets." He eyed the four boys, sizing them up. "Just one moment." Preston stepped away and promptly returned with four sport coats on hangers. He handed one to each of them.

"Do I need something?" Summer asked.

"You're perfect just as you are," Preston replied smoothly.

Nate put on the sport coat. Not only did it fit comfortably but it also worked with his jeans and T-shirt. The same appeared true for the other boys.

"Come right in," Preston said. "Leave the coats in the lobby when you're done."

The red carpet ended at a seamless marble floor. The wide, bright room had enormous paintings on the walls depicting sailing ships, battlefields, and hunting parties, all in gilded frames. A huge mural covered the high ceiling, depicting godlike beings enjoying a sumptuous feast. Well-dressed diners ate Italian food and conversed in the upscale restaurant that dominated much of the room.

Through oversized doorways in the far walls, other rooms could be seen. One held a ballroom with people dancing to live music. Another contained a casino, where participants crowded around tables lined with green felt.

A lovely woman in a cocktail dress approached Trevor. "Bruschetta?" She held out a platter of little pieces of toasted bread topped with cured meat and diced tomatoes.

Trevor glanced at Zac.

"The food is free," Zac said.

Trevor, Nate, and Pigeon each took one.

A handsome man in a formal white shirt with a black vest approached Summer carrying a platter. "Cream puff?"

She grabbed one for each hand. Zac took one as well.

"I feel like a high roller," Trevor said, trying to catch falling tomato fragments with his free hand as he took a bite of his bruschetta.

"Kids are allowed to gamble here," Zac said. "But only at tables that risk tickets and Carnie Coins."

"That still sounds illegal," Summer said.

Zac shrugged. "Not in here. Hey, there's a soda fountain over this way. They'll make just about any soda you can dream up."

"What about the magical candy?" Pigeon asked.

"Right," Zac said. "We want the Emporium. This way."

Zac ushered them out of the restaurant, past a security station, and across a small marble lobby. Off to one side, Nate noticed a spiderweb insignia on a door with the word Dormitory beneath it. He tapped Trevor, who nodded in recognition.

Coming around a corner, they encountered two tough-looking roustabouts wearing black leather flat caps, white dress shirts with the sleeves rolled back over beefy forearms, and cummerbunds. Beyond them, the word Emporium was emblazoned above an entrance, each letter a mosaic of glittering, mirrored tiles.

"The stuff in the Emporium isn't free," Zac explained. "Some things are really expensive. But the candy is reasonable. You guys go ahead and check it out. I have a question for the security guys."

"What question?" Pigeon asked.

"I might have dropped my earbuds in here yesterday," Zac said. "I want to check if somebody turned them in. The candy counter is off to the left."

Nate, Trevor, Summer, and Pigeon entered the Emporium. Nate didn't usually like shopping, but much of what he saw inside the Emporium caught his interest. There were full suits of armor standing upright, a half-sized bejeweled carousel horse, a stuffed polar bear, an old-fashioned jukebox, the mounted head of a rhino, a big Harley Davidson motorcycle, a narwhale horn, and a perfect replica of C-3PO.

Walking toward the candy counter, Nate passed a

mannequin in dark, rubbery apparel. Breathing tubes connected to the blank face.

"It's a stillsuit like you might find on Arrakis," a middle-aged salesperson said in efficient tones. "This other figure is modeling an approximation of shardplate from Roshar."

Nate studied the ornate armor. "How much is it?"

"One hundred thousand tickets and five thousand Carnie Coins," the salesman said. "Display mannequin included."

Nate whistled softly. "I might have to save up a little."

"Nate," Pigeon called with some urgency. "Get over here!" He had reached the candy counter.

"Excuse me," Nate said to the salesman, hurrying over to his friend.

The candy was laid out atop the counter in different sections. A discreet little sign dubbed one subset the Belinda White Collection. Another section was attributed to Jonas White. Camilla had her own candy as well. The final category was labeled Assorted Favorites. Nate noticed some Cannon Blasts in that final group.

A young saleswoman approached them and said, "Please let me know if you have any questions."

"They have Moon Rocks," Trevor said to Nate, studying the Belinda White Collection. "Shock Bits. Dizzy Fizzers. And some I don't know."

Zac caught up to them. "Lots of candy, right?"

"Jackpot," Pigeon said.

"There's a problem though," Zac said. "Camilla White wants to talk to you."

"What?" Nate asked. "She's here?" He looked around the Emporium.

"No," Zac said. "But there are a bunch of security guys waiting to take you to her."

Nate felt stunned. "Why?"

"Because I told them you're planning to wake the sleepers," Zac said.

Nate felt blood rushing to his face.

"What?" Summer asked, wheeling around to face him.

"Camilla hired me," Zac said. "Not only for the advertising. I was supposed to keep an eye on you guys since day one. You weren't described as villains, but I guess some people you know kidnapped her sister and brainwashed her. Does that ring a bell?"

"No, Zac, no," Nate said, trying to keep his voice under control. "You are messing up big-time."

"Camilla warned me there are rivals who want to destroy her carnival," Zac said. "The same enemies who abducted her sister and ran her brother out of town."

"Her siblings were trying to destroy Colson," Pigeon said.

"That's your story," Zac said.

"Lindy is under our protection," Summer said.

"Nobody here wants to harm Belinda," Zac said. "I already rescued her from Mr. Stott. You're too late. Yesterday, while you guys were trapped or whatever, I delivered a letter to Belinda from her sister. Belinda came to the carnival this morning."

"Zac, you have no idea the harm you're causing," Nate said.

"I hope the same is true about you," Zac said. "Security doesn't want a scene. They sent me in as a flag of truce. If you come quietly, they'll be lenient. They have a place prepared where you can get some rest. I didn't want it to come to this. I was trying to play along with you guys, but then you decided to cross this line. You can't plan acts of terrorism against the carnival and expect me to keep quiet."

"Isn't it obvious the carnival is bad?" Summer exclaimed. "Look what happened to Benji!"

"I'm sure Benji is fine," Zac said. "And if not? You guys led him to look for things that are meant to stay hidden."

"Then why make a game of finding them?" Summer pressed.

"Ask Camilla," Zac said, backing away.

Nate looked to Summer. "We have to get out of here. Right now the candy is free. Grab what you can."

CHAPTER TWENTY-SIX

FUGITIVES

Nate went straight to the Cannon Blasts. After feeling the power of that candy, he had wondered what he could do with a lot of it.

"Stop them!" Zac shouted to the saleswoman. "They're stealing magical candy!" He turned around and ran off.

"Put those down," the saleswoman said.

"Don't mess with us," Nate replied, stuffing Cannon Blasts into his pockets, but keeping one in his hand. Other salespeople ran toward them. Nate glanced at his friends. "We have to go."

After snatching candy of their own, Summer and Pigeon ran with him. Trevor was a few steps behind.

The salespeople seemed content to herd them toward the exit.

"Think there's another way out of here?" Summer asked.

"Maybe," Nate said. "But it's not a big store. We should get back up to the carnival as fast as we can."

Six security men waited in a loose semicircle on the marble floor outside the Emporium. They looked like they had come off the same assembly line as the roustabouts, with small variations. All had hard faces that might have been hastily sculpted from clay. Their blocky bodies were heavy with muscle. These six wore black leather flat caps and dress shirts. A couple had tattoos on their bulging forearms. Two held nightsticks. One carried a stun gun.

"We don't want a disturbance," one of the security men said. He had a no-nonsense voice and was clearly the leader.

"Then get out of our way," Nate replied.

"Not going to happen," the leader replied.

"I hope the carnival has good medical insurance," Nate said, tossing the Cannon Blast into his mouth.

Summer put on the Clown Lips. Instantly, she wore white face paint with a big red smile and blue highlights around her eyes. Her rainbow hair was tied into two floppy pigtails. She wore orange pants with white polka dots and a green shirt under a blue-checkered jacket with a big yellow flower on the lapel. Her red shoes were absurdly huge.

Nate stifled a laugh.

"She's a clown," one of the security men said to another with trepidation.

"Get 'em, boys," the leader commanded.

The security men rushed forward.

Pigeon grabbed a cow figurine in his left hand, instantly

271

turning into a statue of himself crafted from white plastic with large black splotches.

Trevor tossed something into his mouth.

Every nerve and sinew vibrating at a fever pitch, Nate aimed between two of the security men and bit down on the Cannon Blast. As he launched forward, Nate stretched out his arms so he could grab the chests of the men. When his hands struck the security men, the two roustabouts burst apart in a massive spray of sand.

Nate shot forward, swiftly covering the distance back into the Italian restaurant. He plowed through a line of tables, fine wood shattering into matchsticks. Plates and food went flying, diners shrieked, and Nate finally struck the marble wall on the far side of the room, leaving a dent laced with cracks at his point of impact.

Unshaken by the wild ride, Nate rolled over and looked back at the path he had cleared. Diners stared at him in shock, some still holding utensils. Beyond them, his friends fought the four remaining security men.

Summer dodged swings from a nightstick, then slipped around her attacker and kicked him in the back of his knees, putting him on the ground.

Another security guy wrestled with Pigeon before flinging him across the marble floor. His hard plastic body slid to a stop, undamaged.

Another man grabbed Trevor only to be flung back with a brilliant flash. Apparently, Trevor had opted to use Shock Bits.

Nate put another Cannon Blast in his mouth. He waited until two security men lined up, then bit down. His trajectory took him back over several restaurant tables before he slammed through one security man, releasing a blizzard of sand, and knocked the head off a second roustabout. Nate continued onward, crashing violently into a marble pillar, spewing stone fragments.

A growling security man brought his nightstick down on Summer's head. For a moment, her skull squished flat, folding like a taco around the short club, but then her cranium rebounded to its normal shape as if made of rubber.

The headless roustabout remained on the floor, sand spilling from his gaping neck.

"They're just big bags of sand," Nate said.

The lead security man looked at his headless comrade with puzzlement. He then held up his own hand and wiggled his fingers. It seemed evident to Nate that the roustabout didn't know he was artificial. His flesh looked perfectly real. But when his colleagues crumbled to sand, they left behind no skin, blood, or bones. Even as Nate watched, the headless security guy dissolved into sand and clothes.

Dropping the cow figurine, Pigeon returned to his normal form. He snatched a fragment of marble with his left hand, then opened another paper tube and dumped flavored sugar into his mouth, promptly becoming a marble statue of himself.

Reaching into an inner pocket of her gawdy jacket, Summer produced a large wooden mallet and bashed the growling security guy with it. He fell under her blows and became a heap of sand on the marble.

Pigeon charged the leader, wrapped stone arms around

him, then squeezed and twisted until the startled roustabout burst open and dissolved into particles.

"What did you do to them?" Zac asked. He crept out of the security office, staring at the scene with frightened eyes.

"What we had to," Nate said.

"We have to get out of here," Summer said.

"What should we do about Zac?" Pigeon asked. His voice sounded normal despite his stony form.

Trevor stalked over to Zac and held up a yellow, crystalline candy. "Suck on this."

"No way," Zac said, backing up.

"I'm trying to be nice," Trevor said. "Eat this candy, or we'll make it worse."

As Summer, Pigeon, and Nate closed in, Zac accepted the candy and popped it into his mouth. He wobbled, features drooping, then slapped down to the floor like the hammer of a mousetrap.

"Sun Stone," Trevor said. "It increases gravity for a while. The opposite of a Moon Rock. Enjoy."

"Let's go," Summer urged.

Nate, Trevor, Summer, and Pigeon ran toward the entrance, Pigeon clomping heavily, marble on marble. Back at the lobby, they found Preston barring their way.

"Halt!" Preston demanded. "You children should be ashamed of your behavior. We invited you here as guests, and you tore the place apart."

"It was a trap," Summer said, still dashing toward him.

"I will not let you hooligans run wild through this carnival," Preston stated.

"Out of our way," Nate said, drawing near, Cannon Blast in hand. "Unless you want to find out if you're made of sand too."

Preston stepped aside, and the kids charged past him. They raced across the plush red carpet and started up the winding stairs. Soon Nate was breathing hard. Running up multiple corkscrews of stairs required a lot more energy than walking down them!

"This is exhausting," Nate said after about five complete spirals.

"Hop on piggyback," Pigeon offered. "I don't feel tired at all. Being made of rock seems to have that advantage."

Nate climbed onto the marble back of his friend.

"I can take you, Trevor," Summer said. "I guess clowns don't wear out either."

Trevor touched Summer's mouth. "Where did your Clown Lips go?"

"They merged with my face," Summer said. "But I can still feel them. I don't think taking them off will be hard."

Pigeon never broke stride as Nate rode him the rest of the way. In her clown gear, Summer matched Pigeon step for step. Neither of them were breathing hard.

At the top of the stairs, they faced the door leading out to the carousel booth. Nate dropped from Pigeon's back, and Summer set down Trevor. The door had no handle or knob, and it refused to budge when they pushed on it.

"I've got this," Pigeon said, punching a marble hand through the wooden door with a crunch. A couple more punches and Pigeon had torn the splintered door apart.

Beyond the mangled door, the booth was empty. The carousel was at a standstill as riders disembarked.

Pigeon slipped the fragment of marble he was holding into his pocket and returned to his normal self. "A walking statue might draw too much attention," he said. "I can always transform again."

Summer remained in her clown apparel as they hustled through the demolished door and down the stairs in time to join the last people exiting the ride.

Nate kept an eye out for more roustabouts, but all he saw was the typical bustling crowd. He noticed several kids from school, but he was too on edge to greet anyone.

"Fun House?" Trevor asked.

"Might be now or never," Nate said. "If we leave the carnival, I don't think we'll be welcomed back."

"Just because we smashed up their fancy secret club and bashed their security people into sand?" Summer asked.

"What was with the sand?" Pigeon asked. "Did that make sense to you guys?"

"Says the kid who can turn into marble," Trevor joked.

"Making henchmen out of sand kind of makes sense," Summer said. "Isn't it the sandman who sends you to dreamland?"

"We have to move," Nate said, heading toward the Fun House. "Keep your candy ready in case they attack again."

"Marble is solid, but not the hardest stone," Pigeon said to Trevor. "It's around a three on Mohs' hardness scale."

"Still better than a plastic cow," Trevor said.

"I had to go with what I could find on short notice,"

Pigeon said. "But trust me, I have my eye out for some steel or titanium."

"What about a diamond?" Nate asked.

"If you see one, let me know," Pigeon said. "That's a ten on the hardness scale."

"I like having a lot of candy again," Trevor said. "It raises my confidence in a fight."

"It should," Nate said. "I only grabbed Cannon Blasts. It all happened so quick."

"I only have Clown Lips," Summer said.

"I mostly have Statue Sticks," Pigeon said. "And a few Moon Rocks."

"I went with a broader sampling," Trevor said. "Moon Rocks, Shock Bits, Frost Bites. It slowed me down, but I also snagged a few trick candies like Sun Stones and Whisker Cakes. Along with a bunch of Drip Drops."

"I wish I had more variety," Summer said.

"We can always share," Trevor said. "But I have a hard time seeing myself in Clown Lips."

"I can't believe Zac backstabbed us," Pigeon said.

"Yeah, ouch," Trevor said. "Camilla must have tricked him."

"I'm mad he lured in Lindy," Nate said. "Mr. Stott must be freaking out. We should watch for her."

"Do you think she would turn on us?" Summer asked. "After what we've been through?"

"Who knows?" Nate said. "She has tried to destroy us before."

"Do you still have the skeleton key?" Pigeon asked.

"Safe and sound," Nate said, patting his thigh. "It's pretty long, but these jeans have deep pockets."

"We've got roustabouts at nine o'clock," Pigeon warned. "Two of them."

"Don't stare at them," Nate said.

"I don't think it matters," Pigeon replied. "They're openly tracking us."

"Why don't they make a move?" Trevor asked.

Nate glanced around the crowded plaza. "I don't think they want a fight where everyone will see it."

"Stick to the crowded walkways," Summer suggested.

"Maybe the Fun House is a bad idea," Trevor said. "They could corner us in a tunnel or hallway there."

"We have to get to those sleepers," Nate said. "If the security guards want a fight, I'll give it to them. We finally have some firepower."

"How do we get deep into the Fun House?" Pigeon asked.

"My guess is we start with the ball pit," Summer said. "The secret way we got from Edward hopefully leads to deeper places."

The Fun House came into view up ahead, windmills spinning. Several clocks of different sizes had been added to the exterior, all showing different times.

"We're not waiting in line to get in, are we?" Pigeon asked.

Summer shook her head. "Every minute we delay gives them time to prep their defenses."

"And organize a counterattack," Nate said.

Bypassing the line, Nate marched up to the ticket taker at

the front. He noticed two kids from his English class watching him from the line.

"Fun House emergency," Nate said hastily, handing over more than enough tickets. "We're on an urgent mission for Preston Wilder."

"Nice try," the ticket taker said, stifling a yawn. "There's a line."

"Call security if you want," Nate said, pushing through the turnstile.

"I will," the ticket taker said, reaching for a walkie-talkie.

Nate waited as Summer, Pigeon, and Trevor went through the turnstile, then he pivoted and waved at the roustabouts who had been following them at a distance. "Give Preston my regards!" he called.

Then Nate followed his friends through the gaping clown mouth and into the Fun House.

CHAPTER TWENTY-SEVEN

FUN HOUSE

The Fun House was designed to disorient visitors. With multiple routes through the experience, it was possible to travel to the end and miss many interesting detours. At the moment, Nate knew they needed to reach the ball pit quickly.

Might security guards ambush them on the way? How long could he keep a Cannon Blast in his mouth without biting it? That was untested. He did not want to accidentally trigger the candy and slam into a bystander. He felt lucky he hadn't hurt any innocent people back at the Lux Lounge. He'd just wrecked some tables and scared some diners.

Assuming the diners were all authentic. How many of the individuals at the carnival were made of sand like the roustabouts? There had been so many people at the undercarnival, but so few trains came and went. Were they all people who had been following the carnival and opted to live down there? Or were some of them fake?

Nate decided to keep a Cannon Blast in his hand. Pigeon and Trevor clutched candy as well, and Summer was unabashedly remaining a clown.

Beyond the entrance, there were three main options: ramps to the right snaked up to the potato-sack slides, the mirrored hall to the left led to the teeter-totter floors, and straight ahead were the rope swings. Nate felt sure the swings were the best route to the ball pit, and Summer apparently felt the same way, because she charged ahead without consulting anyone.

Nate suspected the Fun House had been designed by someone unfamiliar with lawsuits. At the rope swings, participants had to cross padded trenches to reach one platform after another. If swingers fell at the wrong time, they could easily sprain an ankle.

Nate pocketed his Cannon Blast and seized the nearest rope above a knot. Then he stepped into the noose at the bottom and swooped to the first platform alongside others penduluming over the trench.

Summer was having a blast on the swing, holding on with one hand, her feet running in midair. When she reached the far side, she pretended to stumble and swung back across, then back again, spinning and flailing. Several onlookers laughed. Nate had to admit she was a pretty good clown.

"Don't forget we're in a hurry," Nate muttered to her.

"I know," Summer replied. "I'm testing my clown powers."

"How did you pull that mallet out of your jacket?" Nate asked. "Back at the Lux Lounge?"

"I have no idea," Summer said. "I needed a weapon. I reached. It was there. Call it clown instincts."

Nate swung to four more platforms before completing the course. He felt bad for the people who lost momentum and had to drop into the trenches, but he was glad not to join them. He didn't have time to climb ladders for second tries.

Beyond the rope swings, they passed into candy-striped, turning tunnels. Nate walked along the first one, stepping to the left to avoid being flipped over. He emerged to find that more tubes had appeared since his previous visit. In one of the narrower tunnels, Summer planted her feet and braced her hands against the ceiling, circling through a handstand until she was upright again.

"No roustabouts yet," Trevor said at the far end of the last tunnel.

They advanced into a huge room where tangles of climbable nets stretched from wall to wall and floor to ceiling. Nate remembered that heading up and to the right would take them to the ball pits.

Nate did his best to move quickly, but the nets had some give, and distracting shockwaves arrived through the movements of other people. Summer raced along like a monkey, despite shoes that could barely fit into the available holes. The most precarious times came when Nate had to transfer from one net to another, but he managed to stay on the course.

Having navigated the nets, they crossed to a room with several pits filled with plastic balls of every color. Some older kids from Diablo View waded around one of the pits, chucking balls at one another. The largest pit was the size of a respectable swimming pool.

"We need the big one," Summer said. "There should be a coin slot on the ground in the deep end."

Nate, Trevor, Summer, and Pigeon jumped into the huge pit, displacing balls all around them. The balls in the shallow end came up to their waists. As they pushed forward to the deeper area, the balls almost reached their necks.

"This could take a while," Nate said, the balls crowding his face enough to make him claustrophobic as he tried to feel for irregularities on the floor with his feet.

"We should post a guard," Summer said. "How about Pigeon?"

"You got it," Pigeon said, laboriously advancing through the deep balls. "This feels too much like drowning."

Summer ducked under the balls. "Try diving down," she said to Nate. "You can breathe fine. It's just kind of hard to move."

Nate burrowed down toward the floor of the pit. Bright reds, blues, yellows, greens, oranges, and purples filled his vision, and he realized that plastic balls had a distinct smell. The resistance of the balls was strange. When he leaned forward, they supported his weight. It had been easier to touch bottom when he was upright. But by angling downward, he found he could work his way to the floor, like a slow form of swimming. He still couldn't see much, so Nate proceeded by feel, rubbing his hands against the smooth floor of the pit.

"I found it!" Summer's muffled voice called. "A coin slot. I'm getting out a Carnie Coin. Okay, here goes nothing."

Suddenly Nate was falling.

With no warning, he dropped straight down, surrounded by a cloud of light, plastic balls.

Unsure how far he would fall, Nate tried to twist in the air so his feet would hit first. He landed sideways on a huge, springy net with plenty of give. It absorbed his momentum, then tossed him up into the air, a deluge of balls around him. Nate could not help thinking of the dream where he had plunged from the tightrope.

Tremors went through the net as Summer and then Trevor landed next to him. Looking up, Nate could see that the entire floor of the ball pit had dropped away like a giant trapdoor. Pigeon jumped through the opening moments before it closed up, his body crushing many balls and making the net wobble wildly. Above, the trapdoor latched shut, forming a ceiling.

Like a giant spiderweb, the net spanned the entire room, anchored to all four walls. The blank white confines offered few options. One wall had a single opening leading into a stark hallway, so Nate scrambled through the ocean of balls in that direction. The balls flowed toward him as his weight warped the net. The springy give beneath him made his footing less certain. He bounced, lunged, and stumbled over to the opening, stepping off the net just after Summer. Turning, Nate helped Trevor and Pigeon escape the unstable net as they crawled near. Hundreds of balls had spilled through the gap into the hallway.

"That might have been the biggest jump scare of my life," Trevor mused.

"It wasn't scary with clown skills," Summer said. "I did two flips on the way down. Maybe you should all put on Clown Lips. I have plenty."

"I'll stick with my Cannon Blasts for now," Nate said, getting the candy out again. "They're very useful for destroying roustabouts."

Moving down the long, white hallway, Trevor stomped the stray balls that crossed his path. A red door awaited at the end of the hall, flanked by two more on opposite walls of the corridor. Nate and the others paused at the dead end.

"Forward, left, or right?" Pigeon asked.

"Do you think one is a trap?" Trevor speculated.

"Or two?" Nate added. "Or all three?"

"They might take us to different places," Summer said. "Let's split up."

Nate gaped at her in surprise.

"Just kidding," Summer said.

"You're really getting into this clown act," Nate said.

"We can't waste time," Pigeon reminded them. "Our enemies are hunting us."

"Or setting up an ambush," Trevor said. "They may have secret ways to access anywhere in this fun house."

"How about this one?" Summer asked, opening the door on the left-hand wall to reveal a square white room with three yellow doors, one on each wall.

"This gives me a bad feeling," Nate said, trying the door at the end of the hall. Peering inside, he saw a square white room with a green door on every wall. Then he went to the door on the right side of the hall and found a room of blue doors.

"Let me check something," Nate said. "Hold this one open?"

Summer placed her hand on the knob. Nate entered the room with the blue doors and opened one to reveal a white square room with orange doors.

Nate returned to his friends. "It's some kind of door maze. Does anybody know a strategy for this kind of thing?"

"I vote we go fast," Trevor said.

"That might get us super lost," Pigeon said.

"Who cares if we can't return here?" Trevor asked. "The way back is sealed."

"I'll lead," Summer said, reaching into her coat and producing a birdcage with a canary inside. She paused. "I was hoping for another mallet, but I guess this fits an exploration."

"Like in a coal mine," Pigeon said.

She set the cage down and entered the room with yellow doors.

"Are we just going through doors at random?" Nate asked.

"We should go straight as far as we can," Pigeon said. "At least that way we won't travel in circles."

Summer nodded, walking to the door across the room. The next one had purple doors. They followed her through rooms with orange doors, green doors, blue doors, yellow doors, and black doors. Deeper into the maze, the colors of the doors in each room varied. They reached a room with doors in yellow, brown, red, and purple. Then a room with doors in orange, black, green, and gold.

As they progressed from room to room, Nate became increasingly amazed by the scale of the labyrinth. Summer went straight across rooms, and whenever a door opened on a brick wall, they turned right. Behind one door, they found a staggering drop, as if they had emerged from the side of a canyon.

Summer kept charging forward. Pigeon began breathing hard, then ate a Statue Stick and turned himself to marble. Before long, Nate and Trevor were the ones panting and lagging.

Then, in a room with two green doors and two yellow doors, they found a tall stack of couplets embossed in gold on the wall from ceiling to floor. They paused to read.

GO THROUGH RED
WIND UP DEAD
GO THROUGH BLACK
NEVER COME BACK
GO THROUGH BROWN
SURE TO FROWN
GO THROUGH BLUE
STEERING TRUE
GO THROUGH GREEN
NOT TOO MEAN
GO THROUGH YELLOW
HAPPY FELLOW
GO THROUGH GOLD
MUCH TOO BOLD

GO THROUGH ORANGE

UM . . .

BETTER THAN PURPLE

"This is the key to the puzzle," Pigeon said. "The rhymes establish a hierarchy of door colors."

"Red and black are obviously bad," Trevor said.

"Brown and gold are bad too," Summer said. "Maybe less bad though. Dying is worse than frowning."

"Which is better?" Nate asked. "Yellow or blue?"

"'Happy fellow' sounds more enthusiastic than 'steering true,'" Pigeon said.

"What about orange?" Trevor asked.

"It didn't have a rhyme," Summer said.

"Neither did purple," Pigeon said. "I think we have to assume those are in the middle."

"So from best to worst," Summer said, taking her time as she continued to study the rhymes. "Yellow, blue, orange, purple, green, gold, brown, black, red."

"Or it could be blue, yellow, purple, orange, green, brown, gold, red, black," Pigeon said.

"Or it could all be meaningless," Trevor pointed out.

"It's not written in marker," Nate said. "Somebody chiseled it into the wall with gold letters."

"It's way better than flying blind," Summer said. "We have to choose an order to use."

"Yours was good," Pigeon said. "We can refine as we go if something feels off."

"Do we have it memorized?" Summer asked. "We may not see this again."

"I think so," Nate said.

"Yodeling Buffalo Organize Proud Goose Grillings Before Baking Radishes," Pigeon said. "The first letter of every word matches a color."

"That's way harder to memorize than the colors," Trevor complained. "Even if I forget some of the middle ones, I'll remember the best are yellow and blue. And red is danger."

"I've got it," Summer said. "Let's go."

They proceeded through a yellow door. From that point forward, they avoided passing through a black, red, brown, or gold door. If they reached a room with only red or black doors, they backtracked. Going through yellow doors was the priority.

They raced through one room after another. Eventually, they reached a room with doors of yellow, red, black, and green. The same rhyming couplets were embossed on the wall.

"Did we loop back to the same room with the poem?" Trevor asked.

"No, the other room had different door colors," Summer said. "I remember it was two of one, and two of another. We took a yellow door out of that room."

"Is this the same poem?" Pigeon asked, studying the words.

"Exactly the same," Nate said, scanning it from top to bottom. "Let's keep going."

On they went, through dozens more doors, then hundreds. They trudged onward, Summer and Pigeon carrying Nate and

Trevor piggyback. At length, they reached a room with three red doors and one yellow.

Summer opened the yellow door and stood still for a moment instead of rushing through. "This one is different," she announced. "No more doors. It's a . . . courtyard."

She took a step forward, and Nate peered around her to see a vast enclosure with large gray tiles on the ground, each about five feet square and marked with a distinct symbol at the center. There was no ceiling above the lofty walls, leaving the blue sky visible.

Nate kept his Cannon Blast ready. He had held it for so long that some of the black dye had rubbed off on his palm. "Where's the obstacle?" he asked Summer. "This looks too easy."

"I don't know," Summer said, studying the area. She walked forward, and dark clouds immediately crowded out the blue sky, a light rain falling. Summer turned back to Nate.

"Wasn't the sky just blue?" she asked.

"Yes," he said, gazing up, droplets rushing toward him from a cloudy backdrop.

She took a couple steps forward, and a heavy wind began to blow. Nate leaned into the gust to avoid getting pushed sideways. Summer looked back at him, her rainbow pigtails fluttering like flags. "It's getting worse the farther we go."

"Back up," he shouted, returning to the doorway.

When Summer retreated as well, the wind subsided, and the rain stopped. Leaning out of the doorway, Nate looked up at a blue sky.

"That's bizarre," Pigeon said. "Is the weather changing outside too?"

"I have no idea," Summer said. "But it gets worse the farther I go."

Pigeon crouched, looking at the first tile beyond the doorway. "That tile has a symbol like the sun. When you stood on it, the day was fine, right?"

"I guess," Summer said.

Pigeon walked out onto the tile. The sky remained clear and bright. "This next one has a symbol of a rainy cloud."

"Genius point," Summer said. "You're an absolute legend." She walked out onto the first tile with Pigeon. "Let me guess. The next one is wind?"

"Looks that way," Pigeon said.

"So we have to watch where we step," Nate said. "Avoid the harshest weather."

"Everyone back through the doorway," Summer said. "We need to experiment."

The other kids retreated from the room, and Summer moved to the rainy tile. Immediately rain poured down. Summer tilted her face upward. Her makeup didn't run. "It's raining harder than before."

Nate stepped through the doorway onto the sunny tile, and the rain became gentler. "Maybe that's because last time some of us were on the sun tile."

"They all add together," Summer said. "Wind and rain if we stand on the rainy tile and the wind tile."

"We should keep people on sun tiles when we find them," Pigeon said. "It should soften the other weather."

"Magicians should make more stuff like this," Trevor said, gesturing to the area. "Weather rooms. I'd play here."

"I'll settle for getting through this," Nate said.

"If I go forward one more I land on wind," Summer said. "Diagonal right looks like a tornado, which we should avoid no matter what. Diagonal left appears to be an especially bright sun. It's bigger with extra rays. Heat wave? Drought?"

"We can handle a little heat," Trevor encouraged. "Try it."

She stepped diagonally left, and the rain went away, replaced by an oppressively hot sun. Nate, Trevor, and Pigeon advanced together to the rainy tile, and a humid mist percolated down. The day remained hot.

"The tile straight ahead has a hurricane symbol," Summer narrated. "I see lightning to one side of it. And squiggly lines to the other."

"We don't want hurricanes or lightning," Nate said.

"That leaves squiggly lines," Summer announced, going diagonally forward.

Icy wind blasted Nate from the side, forcing him down on one knee. Frigid pinpricks of snow needled his bare skin. Pigeon moved to the drought square, his marble body untroubled by the storm. The gusting winds became warmer, the snowflakes slushier. Summer advanced again, and the blizzard was replaced by a dense fog.

They made their way across the room, experiencing a sandstorm, slippery frost, sleet, dust devils, moderate hail, a thunderstorm, and various combinations of wind, rain, and snow. They avoided tiles with icons representing hurricanes, tornados, lightning, tsunamis, and earthquakes.

"Is an earthquake considered weather?" Pigeon asked.

"Sure looks like it," Summer replied. "Unless maybe the symbol indicates a rockslide."

The final tile in front of the far doorway produced a bright rainbow arching down to the opposite side of the enclosure. Clothes damp, the kids paused to admire the sight before exiting the courtyard into a short hallway.

A lone roustabout awaited. He wore the standard outfit of a white shirt, black vest, a flat cap, and work boots. He held up both hands. "I'm not looking for a fight. I came here with a proposal."

It was weird to see the tough-looking guy acting a little nervous.

"What's the offer?" Summer asked.

"Growler is not a patient clown," the roustabout said. "Since you made it this far, he sent me with an offer. He's anxious to have his fun with you, and doesn't like waiting. If you're willing to trust me, I'm here to speed up the process. Save everyone time. Growler understands where you want to go. He knows you have the skeleton key. I'm under orders to lead you to the keyhole that accesses the sleepers."

"What's the catch?" Nate asked.

The roustabout shrugged. "Growler will be waiting for you. Nobody gets the best of him. But he will also be there if it takes you ten times as long."

"Is Growler your boss?" Nate asked.

"He's head of security," the roustabout said with a nod. "Also Master of Mayhem. Among other things."

"How do we know you won't attack us or double-cross us?" Pigeon asked.

"You have my word," the roustabout said. "I'm under orders to convey you safely." He held out his arms. "I have no weapons. Pat me down if you like."

"What if this is misdirection?" Trevor asked. "Leading us to the wrong place to keep us from the right one."

"I guess anything is possible," the roustabout said. "My offer is genuine. I can lead you through the mirror maze and down to Growler in a matter of minutes. Without my help, it could take hours. It's up to you."

"Let's go with him," Nate said. "Sounds like we have to face Growler sooner or later."

"Do we want to reach Growler if he is luring us in?" Trevor asked.

"If that clown is between us and the sleepers, yes," Nate replied. "And if the roustabout leads us astray, we can always backtrack."

"All right," Summer said. "But stay at the front, roustabout. Do you have a name?"

"Steve," the roustabout said.

"Do all the roustabouts go by Steve?" Summer asked.

"What? No. We go by our names," Steve said. "I'll give you one guess what I call my friend Dennis. Come on. This way."

At the far end of the hall, Steve stopped outside a mirror maze. "Stay close in here. There's no gravity, so you can easily forget which way is up."

He jumped forward lightly and drifted down a hallway

mirrored on every surface, including the floor and ceiling. Summer went next.

"If you're made of rock, you might break the mirrors," Trevor whispered to Pigeon.

"Same with being too ugly," Pigeon replied. "But they let Steve in. I don't care if I damage this carnival."

Nate hopped forward into the null gravity. Having mirrors on all sides created the illusion of corridors extending toward infinity in multiple directions. Nate kept an eye on Summer, trying not to be fooled into following one of her hundreds of reflections. When she reached the end of the corridor, she pushed off in a new direction. Nate stayed on her tail.

"Try not to touch the glass," Steve called from up ahead. "It's a pain to wash."

"Then how do we turn?" Nate called back.

Steve chuckled. "I'm joking. The glass stays clean by magic or something."

Many of the turns were not right angles, and he soon lost all orientation of up and down. If Nate didn't have Summer to follow, he could imagine going crazy in a place like this. His only hope was keeping Summer in view.

What if Steve abandoned them in here? It would be a great trap.

"Can you imagine Mirror Mints in this place?" Trevor asked. "Slipping deeper and deeper into mirror dimensions? You really could be lost forever."

"The thought gives me vertigo," Nate replied.

"I have some pretty good vertigo going already," Trevor said. "I'm not taking my eyes off of you."

In some places, mirrors rotated or oscillated, making reflections lurch and sway. Nate tried to focus on Summer despite the distraction of reflected tunnels shrinking, elongating, and reorienting around him. Elsewhere, warped mirrors created impossible shapes out of Nate's reflections or flipped them upside down. Illusory corridors branched and curled in kaleidoscopic chaos. Nate felt if he looked away from Summer for a moment, he would never find her again.

Eventually, a rectangular doorway appeared in front of him. Steve stood beyond it, upside down. Nate twisted so he would be right side up when he returned to gravity. After stepping through the doorway, he helped Trevor and Pigeon come through.

"We're getting there," Steve said. "You're lucky I know the shortcuts."

"Is that a joke?" Nate asked.

"Try it without me and you'll see," Steve said.

He led them into a new room filled with clashing colors and patterns. Stripes and polka dots mingled with geometric shapes and fluorescent swirls.

Steve pointed to a ladder stretching up through a hole in the ceiling. "That's the escape hatch, if you want to return to the regular carnival." Then he indicated the opening on the wall where a tube slide descended into darkness. There was a slight sheen to the slide, as if it had been greased.

A sign on the wall above the slide read

DO NOT RIDE IF A LOT OF PEOPLE WOULD MISS YOU

"This is the Speed Slide," Steve said. "Keep your ankles

crossed and lay flat. If you try to slow yourself, you could lose a hand. Just relax."

He grabbed the top of the slide and slung himself into the opening.

"Sounds like a rush," Summer said, crossing her feet and scooting in after him.

Nate was a little jealous that her Clown Lips would protect her. Same with Pigeon's Statue Sticks.

Pigeon went next.

"Might be time to try a Drip Drop," Trevor said, producing what looked like a piece of red licorice. "I imagine it would be hard to tear the hand off a liquid person. Do you want one?"

Nate hesitated. He did. But he also wanted a Cannon Blast ready when he got to the bottom.

"How long does a Drip Drop last?" Nate asked.

"A thousand breaths," Trevor said. "Preston said it usually lasts roughly an hour."

Nate knew that overlapping candy could be disastrous. And he needed his Cannon Blasts available. "I'll pass."

Trevor ate the treat. He held up a watery hand, then it suddenly severed at the wrist and splashed on the ground in a little puddle. Just as quickly, the puddle jumped up and became Trevor's hand again.

"This is awesome," Trevor said. "It's more intuitive than I thought. I was worried it would be complicated."

His entire body, including his clothes, collapsed into a pool on the floor. After laying still for a moment, he reformed quickly. "It isn't all or nothing," Trevor explained, pushing one liquid hand through his own chest. "I can liquify myself to varying degrees."

"That *is* awesome," Nate said. "We better catch up."

"Right!" Trevor splashed into the slide and took off.

Nate briefly considered launching himself down the slide using a Cannon Blast. The candy would protect his body, and he would almost certainly break the speed record on the slide. But what about his friends at the bottom? He didn't want to hurt anyone.

Nate put his legs into the slide, crossed his feet, then bucked forward and laid back. He gained speed quickly, the slick slide angling downward. His body slid up the walls on the turns, and the g-forces became almost painful. How would he stop at the bottom? If it was an abrupt ending, he would be smashed like a bug.

But the slide kept going, winding deeper and deeper into the Earth.

Would he emerge inside the undercarnival? Beneath it?

Finally, the slide leveled out. He emerged from the complete enclosure of the tube into a long, open straightaway that produced slightly more friction than the rest of the slide. Gradually his body slowed. Eventually the spongy sides of the narrowing straightaway squeezed him to a stop.

This new room was crafted from dark, polished wood. Nate climbed out of the slide and caught up to his friends. They stood with Steve beside one of the several doors leading out of the room, each one a different shape or size.

"This is as far as I go," Steve said. "Growler awaits behind this square door. I have never seen anyone voluntarily pay him a visit, but that is your business. Mine is finished."

Steve walked across the room and exited through an oval door.

Nate stared at the others in silence.

Trevor gave a nervous laugh. "You know, with all the difficulty getting here, I sort of lost track of the fact that I was voluntarily going toward an evil clown. Is it too late to go back?"

CHAPTER TWENTY-EIGHT

GROWLER

I'm not happy about facing Growler either," Pigeon said. "But we have to brace ourselves and do what we came here to do."

"Summer and I will stay in front," Nate said. "You guys be ready to help."

Trevor's fingers were trembling. He drew in a shaky breath. "We're just going to open that door—on purpose—and talk to an evil clown?"

"Pretty much," Nate said. "Sometimes you have to rip off the Band-Aid."

Trevor held up a finger. "And sometimes, you soak the Band-Aid in water so it isn't so sticky, and then you peel it back a little at a time, so the shock isn't so extreme."

"The more you think about it the worse it will be," Summer said, grabbing the doorknob. "On three. One."

Instead of counting the other numbers, she opened the door and stepped inside. Nate followed closely.

He found a plain room with a hardwood floor and white walls.

Keyholes of various sizes pocked the walls.

Growler stood in the center of the room, showing them his profile. He wore his pin-striped suit and pulled out a large alarm clock as they entered. The sinister clown tilted his head. "You made good time. I have a low tolerance for waiting. Is any chore more tedious?"

Trevor and Pigeon came timidly into the room.

With a gesture from Growler, the door slammed shut.

Nate jumped and almost put the Cannon Blast in his mouth, ready to attack.

Growler held up a hand. "You four have been causing mischief in my carnival. You mowed down the whole security detail inside the Lux Lounge, stole a bunch of candy, and made a mess of my favorite restaurant. Part of me wants to take you under my wing. You're like the children I never had but always wanted! Especially you with the pigtails! And especially if that one kid can stop wetting himself."

Growler turned to face them. "The problem is, these offenses happened in my house, among my people. It would be hilarious if you busted up some other chump's luxury lounge. But not mine, see? The gag gets old fast when you play it on me."

"So what now?" Nate asked.

Growler cackled. "Very direct! I like a kid who gets to the point. Let's talk this out. Nobody communicates anymore. Not about the things that matter. How's Grandma? Has she taken any falls lately? It's bound to happen. Those bones aren't getting any stronger."

"I don't follow," Nate said.

"What do you kids have against this carnival?" Growler challenged.

"You have people trapped in sleep who can't wake up," Nate said.

Growler rested an elbow in his hand and tapped his cheek. "Valid point. People are asleep." He stabbed a finger at Nate. "Counterpoint. They all chose to be asleep. Every one of them is sleeping voluntarily. Who made it your job to rouse them?"

"If the carnival keeps growing, it will swallow the world," Summer said.

Growler pressed a fist against his forehead. "What's so great about the waking world? How's it going out there lately? Have a lot of your dreams been coming true? Or is it still mostly people living in squalor, surrendering their imaginations to a machine that keeps very few on top?"

"I like my life," Pigeon said. "The world isn't perfect, but we keep trying."

Growler held up a finger. "Why not try for something better? A place that offers what you actually want. A place with room for everyone to be a king, an adventurer, or a gangster, or to find romance, or to live out whatever most excites them."

"We can do that in the real world too," Nate said.

Growler shook his head. "Seems that way when you're young. The real world is limited, kid. If you make it to the top, it will be by climbing over the corpses of your competition."

"We don't need to be at the top," Pigeon said. "We just want good lives. Real lives."

"Do you kids like observational humor?" Growler asked, folding his arms. "You're all going to grow old, get sick, and die. Same with everybody you know. Unless they die young in some unfortunate way." He stared at them. "What? It's funny because it's true!"

"Life is a lot more than that," Nate said.

"Fine, we can agree to disagree," Growler said. "Nothing wastes time like philosophy." He cracked his knuckles. "I know what you kids really want. You passed my tests, so I'm prepared to give it to you. A hundred Carnie Coins each, ten Enchanted Carnie Coins, the Veteran's Map, and a discount coupon for the Last Ticket Diner. Congratulations! You all win!" He took out a kazoo and blew it, producing a squawk.

"We're going to use the skeleton key to visit the sleepers," Nate said. "If they want to stay asleep, they can."

Growler chuckled darkly. "Oh, some of them may want to wake up. That's possible. But that would be reneging on our deal. They chose to sleep. End of story. No sequels." He walked to the far wall and tapped a keyhole. "This is the one you want."

"Why would you tell us that?" Nate asked.

Growler shrugged. "I can't attack any ticket holders unless they attack me first. It's a public relations thing. Comes down from the top. But I'll tell you what—none of you are going to see those sleepers with me standing in the way."

"So we have to fight?" Nate asked.

"That's up to you," Growler said. "You can clip my toenails

instead. Or I could give you haircuts. Maybe we could have a picnic. Did anyone bring Takis? I love those things!"

"I could eat," Nate said.

Growler laughed explosively. "You're wearing me down, kid. You're a tough negotiator." He put his hands on his hips and tapped one foot. "Okay, final offer. We reserve this option for the toughest stalemates. I will bequeath each of you a VIP passport. We're talking unlimited tickets and coins. Lux Lounge access. Full private suite on the premises. Membership in our vacation club. Let's face it—this carnival is growing, and you'll want to go everywhere it reaches."

"Are you full of sand?" Nate asked. "Like the roustabouts?"

"Aren't we all created from the dust of the Earth, kid?" Growler asked, placing a hand over his heart. "I once heard what little boys are made from—snakes and snails and puppy dog tails. Little girls? Sugar, spice, and everything nice. But clowns? What are we full of? Comedy, maybe? Tears? Cream pies and seltzer bottles? I haven't broken open the old piñata to find out! Think you're man enough to try?"

Nate put the Cannon Blast in his mouth.

"There we go!" Growler exulted. "His favorite trick, folks! Heroism by blunt force trauma!" He produced a catcher's mitt, squatted, and held it up as if ready for a pitch. He pounded a fist into the glove. "Come on, buddy boy. What are you waiting for? Some folks say you're washed up. They call you a bum. Let's show them your best stuff. Bring the heat!"

Aiming at Growler's chest, Nate bit down and rocketed

forward. The instant before he struck the clown, Nate heard Growler's voice.

"Good night."

Nate blasted through the clown and slammed into the wall riddled with keyholes, rebounding sharply but feeling no pain. The massive impact did no visible damage to the wall, but Growler had burst apart. No flesh and blood were evident. No sand either. Just his crumpled suit and a catcher's mitt.

And purple gas.

The mist plumed out across the room, flowing over the kids even as Nate felt his senses downgrading from the heightened state induced by the Cannon Blast.

Summer was coughing. Trevor too. The gas smelled good. Like grape bubble gum. Nate began to cough.

"What is this stuff?" Pigeon asked. "It smells like cough syrup." He plugged his nose and mouth, then after a moment, released his hold with a gasp. "I tried to stop breathing, but I guess even as a statue I need oxygen."

"I feel drowsy," Summer said, staggering.

Nate felt the effects of the candy fading away. His eyes got heavy, and he slapped himself to stay alert.

"Growler said good night!" Nate yelled, standing up. "This was the plan all along! To knock us out! Put us to sleep!"

"Good plan," Trevor said around a yawn.

"Turn to water," Nate urged his friend, groping for the skeleton key. "We can't fall asleep here!" He coughed.

"I, um, I can't . . . um . . . feel how," Trevor said, speech slurred, eyelids drooping.

Nate had the key out. Gritting his teeth, he stomped toward the keyhole Growler had indicated, jabbed the key inside, and turned it. Something in the wall clicked, and a previously indiscernible door swung inward.

"This way," Nate said, a hand over his mouth to filter the gas. "Let's get to better air."

Pigeon was already unconscious on the ground, his body flesh again, the fragment of marble beside his left hand. Summer stumbled toward Nate. Trevor came as well, feet dragging.

"Stay awake," Nate hollered, blundering forward. He bumped against something. It looked like a glass coffin out of a fairy tale. There was a person sleeping inside. He looked up. The enormous room was filled with rank upon rank of glass coffins. Dozens of sleepers. Hundreds.

His vision became blurry. Nate pinched himself and slapped his cheek. He took a deep breath of the cleaner air. The edges of his vision were black, and the floor seemed to tilt underfoot.

Summer made it through the doorway but crashed to the ground. She was no longer a clown. Her red candy lips lay a couple feet from her head.

"Wait," Trevor said, walking up to one of the coffins and tapping on the glass. "I know her. Isn't that . . . what's her name?"

The question helped Nate cling to consciousness. He approached his friend. The lady inside the coffin was older, and her long straight hair was violet at the tips.

"Camilla," Trevor said. "What's she, um, doing . . ." He

slumped down to all fours, trying to raise his head, then collapsed.

Nate attempted to scream. He couldn't even muster a whimper. He dropped to his knees, barely noticing when his cheek slapped against the floor.

CHAPTER TWENTY-NINE

ASLEEP

"Welcome, my boy!" the Swindler said grandly, spreading his arms wide, his immaculate straw hat at a jaunty angle. "Congratulations are in order. You made it to the grand prize!"

Frowning, Nate took in his surroundings. He was outside, under a blue sky, at the foot of an ascending golden staircase. Long flights led upward from one landing to the next. The Swindler stood above him on the first landing. The gilded steps continued beyond the con man until they reached a pearly gate.

"Is this supposed to be heaven?" Nate asked, glancing behind him at a field of brilliant wildflowers in full bloom.

The Swindler chuckled through a grin. "We may be toying with that imagery a little, but no, son, this is where the carnival quest ends. Only winners reach this place, and you made it! This is the entrance to Dreamland. Now the real adventure begins."

Nate scrunched his face. How did he get here? The staircase seemed disconnected from the world he knew. Was he dreaming? A memory stirred. "I was fighting a clown."

"You defeated him," the Swindler said. "Very few have. That's how you earned your way here. You survived Screamland. Welcome to Dreamland!"

"My friends were with me," Nate said. "What happened to them?"

"The same thing that happened to you," the Swindler said. "They fell asleep."

"What is this place?" Nate asked.

The Swindler blinked. "Do you really not know? It's where everyone wants to be! This is the place where your dreams come true. Anything you can imagine will materialize in this realm. Would you like to alter reality so candy is healthy for you and makes you stronger? Want to add six inches to your height? How would you like to become the greatest basketball player who ever lived, able to make any shot you can imagine? Anything you can envision comes to life inside of Dreamland. Literally."

Nate narrowed his eyes. "What if I want to wake up?"

"Have you ever felt more awake?" the Swindler asked, bouncing his cane off the landing. "You won't have to sleep ever again. Not here. Not unless you want to."

"Can I wake up?" Nate asked.

The Swindler shrugged. "I can't help you there, kiddo. I'm not here in that capacity. I help successful dreamers get out of limbo and into Dreamland. Beyond those gates are the building blocks to anything you want. Would you like to be a king? A treasure hunter? A space explorer? Want to create your own theme park? Design your perfect mansion? It all comes true inside of Dreamland."

"It sounds too good to be true," Nate said. "What's the catch?"

The Swindler showed a shocked expression. "No catch. Just a few formalities, and you're on your way."

"You sound like a used car salesman," Nate said. "If I go into Dreamland, can I leave?"

"Who would want to leave Dreamland?" the Swindler asked. "What would you do? Try to follow your dreams in the waking world? Good luck."

"I like dessert, but I wouldn't want to eat it all the time," Nate said. "I'd get sick."

"You can have anything you want in Dreamland," the Swindler said. "Fruits and vegetables alongside hot fudge sundaes. Or hot fudge sundaes more nutritious than broccoli. The Dreams and Screams International Carnival is a doorway. The Screamland before the Dreamland. We're talking about having everything you can envision and amending those wants as you go."

Nate walked up the few steps to the landing where the Swindler waited. The higher position afforded a better view of the expansive wildflower field, with trees at the outskirts. Above him, pearlescent walls and gates kept Dreamland unseen.

"You want to make an agreement," Nate said.

"Just a formality," the Swindler said, producing a contract written in golden ink on creamy white paper. "Standard agreement for admittance to Dreamland. In short, you will spend the rest of your life living out your dreams. In return, you offer to share your dreams and the power to create them with others."

"Sharing dreams sounds like more than a formality," Nate said.

"Think about the advantages," the Swindler said. "Somebody builds a ten-story skatepark you would never have imagined. In Dreamland, you can picture a skateboard and sufficient skills and then enjoy skating in a park someone else dreamed up. Dreamland already has amazing cities, caves, islands, landscapes, even entire planets for you to explore. And if you add something of value, you can share it as well."

"I see what you mean," Nate said.

"Who wants to live like a hermit?" the Swindler asked. "In a community, you can find leisure time. Focus on what interests you most. Enjoy your life. In Dreamland, we share the load of creating and sustaining our magical kingdom. No one person does all the heavy lifting." He slapped the contract. "This is your promise to share the load while you benefit from the efforts of other contributors."

"And if I don't sign it?" Nate asked.

The Swindler shrugged. "Everybody has to participate or the system falls apart. If you refuse to sign, you would be left to make your way alone in limbo."

"Where is limbo?" Nate asked.

The Swindler pointed with his cane. "See where the field fades into nothing? That's where limbo begins."

"Is it bad?" Nate asked.

The Swindler huffed. "It's bewildering. There's no infrastructure. Zero resources. You never quite know where you're going or where you've been. You're on your own in limbo. "

Nate gazed beyond the tree line. It was strangely barren. Not dark, not bright. Just kind of beige.

Nate looked back at the Swindler. "Do you remember me?"

"Sure, you're the kid who had me guessing numbers. Nate. You came in with Summer."

"We lost to you."

"I took a few tickets off your hands. All in good fun."

"I don't want to get conned again."

"This is no con," the Swindler protested earnestly. "My persona is a carnival act. It's entertainment. Dreamland is my life's work. Many people seek this place their whole lives and never find it."

"All I do is sign the paper?" Nate asked.

"And lose the bracelet," the Swindler said.

Nate looked down at his wrist, surprised to see Sandra's friendship bracelet had appeared—another confirmation he was dreaming. "Why do I have to give up the bracelet?"

"Standard policy," the Swindler said. "Kind of like no outside food or drink. House rules. No foreign merchandise."

"That makes it easy," Nate said. "No deal."

The Swindler spread his hands apologetically. "If that's the way you want to play your hand."

"You couldn't give me the first thing I asked for," Nate said. "To actually wake up."

"You won't wake up, regardless of what you choose here," the Swindler said. "You already decided to sleep."

"No, I didn't," Nate protested.

The Swindler smiled. Nate thought it almost looked pleasant, until he paid attention to the Swindler's eyes.

"Welcome to my turf. You're inside a dream inspired by the carnival. You chose to sleep when you destroyed the clown. He didn't spray you or spike your drink. You demolished Growler and put yourself to sleep. End of story. No sequels. Remember the signs at the entrance?"

"By the ticket booths?" Nate asked.

"When you came into the park after reading the posted signs, you forfeited any dreams inspired by the carnival."

"I'm inside the dreams you own," Nate said numbly. He felt empty. And foolish. And deeply frustrated. "What can I do?"

"You already paid the price of admission by sleeping inside the carnival," the Swindler said. "You might as well claim the reward. Dreamland is the ultimate prize, son. It's a place for winners. A nonstop victory lap. You did well getting here. Seems like a shame to pay the price and miss the prize. Spending the rest of your days in limbo wouldn't be my choice."

"It's not my first choice either," Nate said. "But it beats losing my bracelet and signing away more of my rights and maybe leaving my friends behind. Plus, I don't trust you. And I don't deal with people I don't trust."

"So be it," the Swindler said, glancing up at the pearly gate then back to Nate. He held up his thumb and forefinger, the tips almost touching. "You came this close to having it all. Reminds me of a guy I heard about who lost his winning lottery ticket. You two should go bowling. You'd have a lot to talk about."

"If I'm stuck in dreams for the rest of my life, I've already lost it all," Nate said.

"I hope that brings great consolation through the long, lonely years ahead," the Swindler said. "Good luck, my boy. You're going to need it."

The Swindler snapped his fingers.

And Nate was someplace else.

He was sitting in a desert of beige under a beige sky. The only interruptions to the bland emptiness around him were silvery blobs on the ground, like smooth clumps of mercury, some of them quite large.

There was nothing unpleasant. If anything, the surroundings were rather peaceful in their simplicity. But it was a place of absences—little variety in color, a neutral smell, no particular sounds.

"Good job resisting the Swindler," a voice spoke from behind him.

The words didn't scare him. In fact, hearing them was a relief. Nate turned to find Sandra standing there. He felt sure she had not been present a moment ago.

"Where did you come from?" Nate asked.

"I've been watching you," Sandra said. "I had to wait to reveal myself until you left the Swindler. I'm not strong enough to confront him directly. Not here on his home field. You did well in retaining the bracelet. Had you lost it, you would have passed beyond the range of my help."

"He offered to make all of my dreams come true," Nate said.

Sandra laughed darkly. "Of course he did. I'm sure he wanted the bracelet gone. Though I doubt he fully realizes what a problem it will cause."

"What can we do now?" Nate asked.

"So many things," Sandra promised. "You realize the Swindler left out a lot of the fine print, right?"

"You followed the whole conversation?" Nate asked.

"Yes, thanks to the bracelet," Sandra said. "Nate, he offered to let you enter Dreamland and make your dreams come true, as if it was his gift to bestow. But you already have that power. He was offering something that was already yours."

"Can my dreams come true in limbo?" Nate asked.

"Limbo is the Swindler's term for uncreated dreamspace," Sandra said. "There is much more here than he led you to believe. You see those pockets of silver?"

"How could I miss them?" Nate replied.

"That's dream batter," Sandra said. "There is an infinite supply. And you can turn it into anything."

"Really? How?"

"It responds to your intentions. Imagine the batter becoming whatever you want," Sandra suggested. "For beginners, it sometimes helps to touch it."

Nate walked over to the nearest metallic blob of batter.

He imagined a sword inside of it, then he reached into the material until he felt a hilt. Pulling out his hand, he withdrew a sword exactly like he had imagined it, with a fancy cross guard and a sharp, straight blade. No, it was better than he had envisioned, as if an expert swordsmith had filled in the details he had incompletely pictured.

"That's amazing," Nate said.

"And limitless," Sandra replied. "This uncreated dream-space has much more potential than the Swindler led you to believe. By contrast, his Dreamland behind those gates has a lot of ready-made features. Handy tools for beginners. Sort of like training wheels on a bike. But once you learn how to ride, who wants training wheels?"

"Great point," Nate said, swishing his blade through the air.

"Now that I'm inside this dreamspace, I can find your friends and offer them friendship bracelets as well. I know Summer and Pigeon also denied the Swindler. They sensed not to trust his offer. Trevor remains in conversation with him. The Swindler is unaccustomed to losing so many prospects in a row. Wait here for me."

The air rippled, and Sandra stepped into the shimmer, disappearing.

"I need to learn to travel like that," Nate muttered.

He walked over to a large blob of dream batter, touched it, and focused his intention. The batter reformed into a perfect replica of the couch in the family room that he used when watching TV. It was his favorite couch—a little worn, but incredibly comfortable.

Nate sat down, his thoughts spinning as he waited.

Would he have ever tried to turn the silvery blobs into anything without instruction? Probably not. Most likely he would have avoided them in case they were hostile or poisonous.

What else could he make? A robotic friend? A fortress? What if Sandra returned to find him racing around in a Ferrari?

Nate set to work.

CHAPTER THIRTY

SURPRISE VISITORS

Trevor stared at the plain and beige landscape around him, empty except for some reflective silvery globs. Maybe he should have taken the deal from the Swindler. Having his dreams come true seemed a lot better than hanging out here forever. This dreary landscape was nearly as bleak as the mirror dimension.

Would any of his friends have taken the deal? What if they were all inside of Dreamland waiting for him? No, Nate would never go for it. Trevor doubted Summer or Pigeon would either. The guy had to be called the Swindler for a reason.

"Hello?" Trevor tried experimentally.

The surrounding emptiness swallowed the word, making it feel insignificant. What was he supposed to do now? He could lay down on the ground. What if one of those silver globs crept up to him? They looked like they could be dormant predators, ameboid monstrosities that absorbed their prey.

Could he walk out of this endless wasteland? Or would he walk forever?

The Swindler had called this place limbo. Maybe the secret was finding a bar he could shimmy under. If he heard steel drums playing, he decided he would head in that direction.

Suddenly Sandra appeared in front of him, as if she had removed an invisibility cloak. Summer and Pigeon were with her.

"Whoa," Trevor said. "Where did you guys come from?"

"Other parts of limbo," Pigeon said.

"The Swindler deliberately mislabeled this place as limbo," Sandra corrected. "But you're not trapped here unless you believe him. This is simply undeveloped dreamspace. Like a computer disk with no programming on it."

"Except those silver blobs," Trevor said.

"Those are where we write the programs," Sandra said. "Great job denying the Swindler, Trevor. You stayed outside his main trap."

Trevor pumped a fist. "I knew it." He glanced at Summer. "I was doubting a little though."

"May I give you a friendship bracelet?" Sandra asked, holding one up. "It will help us remain linked within the dreamscape."

"Sure," Trevor said, taking a step toward her and holding out his wrist.

"We already have ours," Summer said.

Sandra tied on the bracelet. "Now I'm even more firmly

anchored in this dreamspace. We have a lot to do. Do you mind if I take us to Nate?"

"Let's go!" Trevor said.

A slight shimmer appeared in the air. Sandra motioned for the others to follow and stepped into it, vanishing. Summer and Pigeon went next, then Trevor crossed through. No physical sensation accompanied the act, but he abruptly emerged into a different beige wasteland with a new arrangement of globs.

A large military tank was coming toward them, treads grinding noisily, the big cannon in front pointing in their direction. Trevor also noticed a brown couch, a fully decorated Christmas tree, and a few sports cars, including a sick version of the Batmobile.

The tank rumbled to a halt, the hatch on top swung open, and Nate emerged with a huge grin on his face. "You're all here!"

"They each denied the Swindler," Sandra reported. "Finding them was easy. You've been busy, Nate."

"I'm experimenting," he said, emerging from the tank with a sword in his hand. "I don't have to understand how a car works. Or even a tank. I just imagine them and something fills in the blanks."

"Imagination can be very powerful," Sandra said. "Especially here."

"You made this stuff?" Trevor asked.

"Out of the dream batter," Nate said, gesturing to a nearby silver blob. "I'm so glad you guys are all right."

"That depends how you define 'all right,'" Pigeon said. "Considering we're trapped in some weird dream landscape."

"Was Growler full of sleeping gas?" Summer asked. "It's all kind of fuzzy."

"Yeah," Nate said. "The skeleton key worked. We made it to the sleepers. There were lots of them."

"Do you remember seeing Camilla there?" Trevor asked.

"Yes, right before I went down," Nate said.

"Wait," Sandra said urgently. "Camilla was among the sleepers? Are you sure?"

"Unless it was her twin," Trevor said.

Sandra furrowed her brow. "That is unexpected. Give me a moment." She closed her eyes, a look of concentration on her face. After a moment, her eyelids flew open. "She's part of this dreamspace." Sandra shook her head. "I don't understand."

"What do you mean?" Summer asked.

"This place functions more like a prison than a dream-land," Sandra said. "Camilla should be running this dream-space, not falling victim to it. We should start with her—see what's going on."

"Can we get to her?" Summer said.

"Let me see," Sandra said, closing her eyes again. "If she hasn't deliberately walled herself off . . . Yes, here we go." She opened her eyes. "Ready?"

"Can we bring the tank?" Trevor asked.

"It might send the wrong message," Sandra said. "We can always make a new tank. You'll find that winning battles in the dreamscape depends less on having the biggest gun, and more on having the stronger will."

A portion of the air nearby began to tremble. "Keep your guard up. We're going into part of the Swindler's Dreamland. A portion designated for Camilla. Her body is with the sleepers, but her mind is in here. I'm not sure what to expect. Stay close to me, in case we have to retreat." Sandra stepped through the shimmer. Trevor entered after Nate.

He emerged on a suburban street. The houses were of an older style than Trevor was used to seeing. The parked cars looked like they came from a period movie. Were they in the 1950s? Maybe the sixties? The mature maples along the street were ablaze with bright reds, oranges, and yellows. Not many leaves had fallen.

"We're in Burlington, Vermont," Sandra announced. "A dream version of the place, obviously."

"This feels so real," Nate said. He slapped his cheek. "I could be awake."

"It's highly realistic," Sandra said. "I'm not sure I could fly in this particular dreamspace. We're visitors here, and Camilla's control over the physics is masterfully secure."

"Camilla made this place out of the silver blobs?" Trevor asked, impressed.

Sandra nodded. "She created this place within the dreamspace the Swindler allotted to her. She's a master dreamcaster."

"Where is she?" Summer asked.

Sandra pointed at the nearest house. Modest in size, it had colonial architecture with blue walls and white framing around the windows. A white picket fence enclosed the tidy front yard.

Sandra led them through the gate and up to the front porch. Trevor came last, closing the gate. The wood felt real, the paint slightly peeling in places. He bent down and brushed his palm over the grass. Camilla had been meticulous in her details.

Sandra knocked on the front door. A moment later, a man answered. Trevor started. He was a younger version of the Swindler, but without the straw hat, and wearing a sweater vest over a white shirt. "How can I help you?"

"We're here to see Camilla," Sandra said.

"Some of her friends from school, are you?" the man said. "Well, any friend of Camilla's is welcome. She's playing out back. I'm her father, Carl." He shook hands with Sandra. "Come inside."

Carl stepped away from the door, and they entered a clean, conservatively decorated home. He escorted them to a back door. "She has about an hour before dinner," he said. "Have fun."

The backyard had a large wooden deck. Beyond it spread a spacious lawn, with a circular, above-ground pool taking up much of one side. At the back of the lawn perched a solidly constructed tree fort with two swings beneath it. A tire swing hung from a high, thick limb on a neighboring tree.

A few paces from the tree house swings, three kids huddled around a game of marbles. They had drawn a circle in the dirt and were using shooters to knock smaller marbles out of the ring. The youngest looked to be about Trevor's age. She had auburn hair with a slight curl and was quite pretty. Her older sister looked like a teenage version of Lindy. The oldest of the three was recognizable as a young Jonas White.

The game of marbles broke up as the kids noticed the newcomers.

"Hey, guys," Jonas said in friendly tones. "Have we met?"

"We're friends of Camilla's," Sandra explained. "We need to talk with her."

Camilla looked the least excited to see them. "About what?"

"It's important," Sandra said. "It might be best if we talk in private."

"Is this about school?" Camilla asked.

"Let's go with that," Sandra said.

"Could we have a few minutes?" Camilla asked her older siblings.

"Sure thing," Jonas said.

"Should we save the game?" Lindy asked, glancing at the marbles.

"Yeah, we'll finish later," Camilla said.

Trevor thought it was odd the way the older siblings were deferring to the youngest. Lindy and Jonas walked into the house.

"I don't usually have visitors from outside," Camilla said, her intonation more mature, though she still looked like a kid. "What are you doing here?"

"Your carnival is causing major problems," Sandra said.

Camilla gave a little nod. "I suspected your visit might have something to do with that."

"These four children have been imprisoned in sleep," Sandra said. "Alongside hundreds of others."

Camilla nodded, tears glimmering in her eyes. "Including me."

"We were surprised to find you among the sleepers," Sandra said.

"Trevor and I talked to you at the carnival just a day ago," Pigeon said.

"Then we saw you in a glass container," Trevor said.

Camilla nodded. "My mother is impersonating me. She is skilled at that kind of magic."

"That wasn't you inside the wagon?" Pigeon exclaimed.

"No," Camilla said.

"How long ago did your mom take your place?" Trevor asked.

Camilla scrunched her face. "Almost two years."

"And your father is the Swindler?" Nate asked.

"Makes a girl proud, right?" Camilla said, shaking her head. "I'm not a fighter. I don't do confrontations. Especially not with my parents. I can't fix this."

"Other people can do the fighting," Sandra said. "Tell me why you made this carnival."

"To help people realize their dreams," Camilla said. "Individuals in my family have done a lot of evil in the world. I was trying to accomplish some good."

"How did your dream evolve into a prison?" Sandra asked.

Camilla sighed. "In a word? Mutiny."

"What happened?" Sandra asked.

"I don't want to talk about it," Camilla said. "It's too

painful. You have intruded upon my coping mechanism. It's easier here. I can shut out the disappointment. Distract myself. This place is my painkiller."

"You recreated your childhood?" Sandra asked.

Camilla laughed. "No. This is the childhood I wanted. The childhood I needed. It is my attempt to fix my life, beginning where it went wrong."

"You had a difficult life," Sandra said.

"My parents were magical criminals," Camilla said. "They did their best to raise criminals. I guess you could say I was the white sheep of the family. My mother and father worked to stifle my creativity and destroy my integrity. I endured my upbringing without them breaking me, but it was a nightmare."

"They are doing their best to share that nightmare with the world," Sandra said. "Through your carnival."

"I know," Camilla said. "Even as I hide here in my counterfeit childhood, I can't help checking in on what they are doing to my masterpiece, my greatest creation, my life's work. I may be stuck here, but when I focus, they can't stop me from seeing out. You are trying to stop them? Are you willing to fight?"

"I'm a dreamwalker," Sandra said. "I'm the best the Council managed to send against this threat. And these kids are experienced at resisting evil. They have been doing a remarkable job. Every one of them turned down the Swindler's offer to enter his dreamspace."

Camilla lowered her gaze, shaking her head. "I sure didn't." She looked at Nate, Summer, Trevor, and Pigeon. "Good job, kids. I mean it. That shows great character." She turned her attention back to Sandra. "I can't help in the fight. It isn't who I am. But I'm happy to give you information that could assist."

"What went wrong?" Sandra asked. "How did the mutiny happen?"

"My parents fell on hard times," Camilla said. "Too many of their plots unraveled. They lost credibility in the magical community and ended up penniless. My siblings and I surpassed them in almost every way. We were more powerful magicians, and we were having a bigger impact on the world. In my youth, our parents taught us to be merciless, and in return they got ruthlessness from Jonah and Belinda. Careful when you make a weapon; it may end up pointed at you. My parents wound up with nothing."

"You took them in," Sandra said.

"It seemed harmless," Camilla said. "Mom and Dad were old and washed up. Out of options. They had used magic to slow the aging process, but not very well. I decided to let them assist at the carnival."

"That was kind of you," Sandra said.

Camilla shrugged. "I believe at first they were sincerely grateful. They had been so desperate. Literally homeless. No lair to protect them. Mom and Dad really tried to contribute for the first couple of years. My carnival provided shelter, and the work they performed helped them recover their confidence. Eventually they marshaled their strength, and I realized nothing had really changed. They weren't reformed—they had just been too weak to wreak havoc.

"I created the carnival to do good, but they warped it to do evil. When I tried to stop them, they imprisoned me. I was too heartbroken to fight back."

"How did this carnival gain so much strength?" Sandra asked. "Dreams are being manifested directly into reality inside the carnival and even around town."

Camilla hesitated, then said, "Before I started the carnival, I found the Dreamstone, quarried from the same vein of silica used to craft the original dreamcatcher. It was the quest of my lifetime. I didn't win it by bloodshed or duplicity. I researched and I explored and eventually I succeeded."

Sandra gasped.

Camilla nodded. "The talisman is real, and supremely powerful. Its capacity to transfer dreams into the waking world is the engine powering my carnival."

"The carnival your parents wrested from you," Sandra said.

"It's difficult to define ownership of this carnival," Camilla said. "The Dreamstone cannot be owned by an individual. Its power is shared by all. It truly belongs to everyone. If the dreamers knew that and believed it, they would be free.

"My father is not a very impressive magician, but he is a truly gifted con man. By falsely claiming ownership of the Dreamstone, he has convinced people they have lost the power to awaken from this dreamspace. He tells them they chose this, insisting they have signed away their rights. Once they believe him, it becomes true."

"Can you wake up?" Sandra asked.

"I'm not sure," Camilla said. "I was crushed by my father's betrayal and tired of fighting him, so I chose to enter his

Dreamland. Even though I know it's a trick, it feels like I have lost the power to wake myself up."

"It's not true," Sandra said. "If you made a choice you regret, you always retain the power to choose differently in the future, no matter what anyone claims."

Camilla nodded. "Intellectually, I know you're right. Fear plays a part too." Her voice got quiet. "Deep down, I'm terrified of my parents."

"That's very self-aware," Sandra said.

Camilla looked around. "I've had time to reflect."

"Do you know where we can find the Dreamstone?" Sandra asked.

"Yes," Camilla said. "I'm deeply connected to it. I worked with it for years. I like to think we had an understanding. Father has hidden the Dreamstone away and has placed many safeguards around it. But my parents could never hide it from me. Not in the carnival I constructed."

"Where should we look?" Sandra asked.

"There are two carnivals," Camilla explained. "One exists in the dreamscape, the other in the waking world. The dreamscape carnival is much grander and more elaborate, and it grows much more quickly. But as Father adds sleepers, he is gaining power to pull the dreamscape carnival directly into physical reality."

"He is breaking the barrier between the dimensions," Sandra said. "He could overwrite and destroy this physical world."

"Exactly," Camilla said. "Unthinkable destruction. One of the properties that makes the Dreamstone so special is that it exists simultaneously in waking reality and the dreamscape. It is a physical object made of ethereal dreamstuff. And Father has hidden it in both places."

"So there is a tangible Dreamstone in the physical carnival, and an ethereal one in the dream carnival," Pigeon summarized.

"Yes," Sandra said. "Like two halves of a whole, they must be brought together. And both halves are accessible, because the carnival is a crossroads."

"Yes," Camilla said. "When anyone enters the carnival, they are already partway into the dreamspace. Certain dream principles apply. For example, most of the traps that appear deadly in the carnival simply move the victim into the dreamspace. Their physical body joins the sleepers."

"Wait," Nate said. "Is that true for the sand around Dune Hunt?"

"Yes," Camilla said. "If you sink in the sand, you end up as a sleeper."

"Then Benji is alive!" Trevor exclaimed.

"I think Zac knew that," Summer said.

"Do you know Zac Foster?" Pigeon asked Camilla.

"I don't," she said.

"He must have dealt with her mom," Nate said.

"We can't die in the carnival?" Pigeon asked.

"You could die," Camilla said. "If you jumped off the top of the roller coaster, you would die. If somebody stabbed you with a sword, you could die. But many specific traps would actually just put you to sleep."

"Did you make the traps?" Summer asked.

Camilla shook her head. "My parents."

"You were telling us about the Dreamstone," Sandra prompted.

"The Dreamstone has a consciousness," Camilla said. "It exists to serve humankind. Physically, the Dreamstone rests inside the vault at the Swindler's carnival attraction."

"Behind the door where he stores the prizes?" Summer asked.

"Exactly," Camilla said. "The ethereal portion of the Dreamstone is hidden in the dreamscape, tucked away in the deepest reaches of the mausoleum within the Terror Castle cemetery. Look for the crypt marked Growler."

"Is Growler dead?" Trevor asked.

"The original Growler was a carnival clown who scared my father when he was a boy," Camilla said. "Father patterned the current Growler after him."

"Nate smashed the current Growler into sleeping gas," Pigeon said.

Camilla nodded. "That is one of his tricks. Growler is a denizen of the dream realm. You destroyed the body he was using in the physical carnival. Given time, he will develop a new physical form."

"Once we find the ethereal part of the Dreamstone, what do we do?" Nate asked.

"Bring it to the Swindler's vault in the dream carnival," Camilla said. "It must be matched with the position of the Dreamstone in the physical carnival. Only then will the Dreamstone become fully accessible in the physical carnival. Once you take the completed Dreamstone outside the carnival, you will undo most of the magic sustaining the operation."

"That is what we needed to know," Sandra said gratefully.

"Be careful," Camilla said. "The moment the Dreamstone becomes activated inside the Swindler's physical vault, he will move to protect it."

"We need to steal it right when it gets placed there," Nate said.

"That would be ideal timing," Camilla said. "Remember, you're not stealing it. We all have a claim to the Dreamstone. Anyone who tries to keep it for themselves misunderstands it. I hope you succeed. I would much rather see my carnival destroyed than used to do evil."

"We'll do our best," Sandra said. "Come on, kids. We have a lot to do."

CHAPTER THIRTY-ONE

PREPARATIONS

S andra produced a shimmer in the air, and Trevor stepped through first, returning to the beige wasteland. He glanced at the nearest mass of dream batter. What could he make? A flamethrower? A crate of hand grenades?

Sandra came last, breaking his concentration. She asked the kids to gather around. "We need to act swiftly. Once the Swindler knows our plan, he will move to stop us."

"Sounds like we need two teams," Nate said. "One team to get the ethereal portion of the Dreamstone from the dream carnival cemetery and bring it to the Swindler's vault. At the same time, the second team will need to raid the Swindler's vault at the physical carnival."

"Once the Dreamstone is whole, we must take it beyond the boundaries of the carnival," Sandra said.

"That might be a job for Cannon Blasts," Nate said.

Summer nodded. "And Cannon Blasts could get us into the vault if its defended."

"Think we could tackle the cemetery?" Trevor asked Pigeon.

"Somebody has to do it," Pigeon said. "In marble form, I'm good at pounding stuff open, and with your Drip Drop, you can slip into tight spaces."

"The Swindler can sense my presence," Sandra said. "So if I go with either team, he will figure out what we're doing. Instead, I'll try to waken some of the sleepers. I sense there may be several people of interest to revive. If the Swindler thinks waking people is the point of my attack, it will distract him and buy you time for your efforts."

Sandra turned to Nate and Summer. "Our plan depends on you two escaping this dreamspace. You'll have more power in the carnival if you're physically awake than if we try to project you there. Growler's sleeping gas should have worked through your system by now, but you and Summer must believe the Swindler has no claim on you in order to wake up."

"He doesn't have a claim on me," Summer said. "I agreed to nothing."

"Bashing a clown isn't exactly a contract," Nate said. "I should be able to wake up."

"Good," Sandra said. "I'll also try to bring John Dart into this dreamspace. Magical enforcers normally have no access to the carnival, but now that I'm in, the defenses are breached."

"Weren't we at the carnival when you gave me the friendship bracelet?" Nate asked.

Sandra shook her head. "That was a version of the carnival

you had dreamed up. Growler and others were intruding into your personal dreamspace."

"Is John asleep?" Pigeon asked.

"I hope so," Sandra said. "I gave him a friendship bracelet in a dream several nights ago. I also sent him a message to go to sleep before I came here."

"That would be great to have his help in here," Nate said.

"What's the next step?" Trevor asked.

"Wake Nate and Summer so they can return to the physical carnival," Sandra said.

"How will we know when to attack the Swindler's vault?" Nate asked.

Sandra scrunched her brow. "I will send something from the dreamscape as a signal. How about a cloud shaped like a poodle in the sky above the Swindler's attraction?"

"That should work," Summer said.

"And it won't draw too much attention to us," Nate said. "I mean, the connection shouldn't be obvious."

"Once you get back to the room where you battled Growler, take the circular door," Sandra said. "Go to the shaft with the ladders."

"All right," Summer said.

"Before we go back to the normal carnival, I have a question," Nate said. "Why are the roustabouts full of sand?"

"The carnival is a crossroads between the waking world and the dreamscape," Sandra said. "Much like how physical objects can pass out of dreams into the waking world near the carnival, so can certain people. But since humans are more complex, the projections that appear are synthetic, essentially puppets controlled by minds inside the dreamscape. The roustabouts and many other characters at the physical carnival are not actually living people."

"Creepy," Summer said.

Sandra studied the beige landscape. "There are unseen barriers here meant to keep you asleep. Barriers of the mind, intended to hold you captive. Shall we demolish them?"

"Yes," Nate said. Summer nodded.

Sandra closed her eyes. "Your sleeping bodies have been placed inside containers. When you awaken, just push upward—the lids are on hinges."

"What should we do?" Summer asked.

"Stay confident," Sandra said. "Remember that you deserve to awaken." She pointed at a nearby blob of dream batter. It divided in half, and two wooden chairs took shape. "Sit."

Nate and Summer each claimed one of the chairs. They watched Sandra expectantly.

"I need you to balance on the two rear legs," Sandra said.

"That's random," Nate said.

"Trust me," Sandra said.

Nate tipped his chair back until only the back legs were in contact with the ground. "Like this?"

"That's right," Sandra said.

"For how long?" Summer asked.

"As long as you can manage," Sandra encouraged, coming around behind them. "Find the point of perfect equilibrium, then pick up your feet."

Nate and Summer complied, their chairs wobbling as they endeavored to stay balanced. Sandra grabbed the backs of the chairs and yanked, tipping them over. When the backs of the chairs struck the ground, the chairs were empty.

"Where did they go?" Trevor asked.

"The feeling of losing one's balance is a great way to jolt people awake," Sandra confided. "They both succeeded."

"What should we do?" Pigeon asked.

Sandra reached into a blob of dream batter and removed a metal cylinder the size of a roll of quarters. "This is an alloy made from steel and nickel. One of the hardest substances I know." She reached back into the dream batter. "And here is a diamond as an extra option."

Pigeon accepted the gifts. "Isn't my candy back with my body?"

"Try your pockets," Sandra said.

Trevor checked as well, finding his candy there.

"I already replicated it for you," Sandra said. "You also have plenty of tickets and Carnie Coins. While you are inside the dreamscape, I can help you more than I can the others. Is there any candy you wish you had?"

"A candy we've used before?" Pigeon asked,

"Any candy you can dream up," Sandra said. "In the dreamscape, I can produce just about anything."

"Can you just teleport us right to the Dreamstone?" Trevor asked.

"Sadly, no," Sandra said. "The cemetery is surrounded by powerful shields. But you can enter the dreamscape version of the Terror Castle ride and reach the mausoleum that way. Just exit the car inside the cemetery."

"Can we give ourselves powers since we're in a dream?" Pigeon asked. "Reshape things to our advantage?"

"In theory, yes," Sandra said. "Doing so in your own dreams is relatively simple. However, the carnival is a shared dreamspace, and the physics of the dream carnival are firmly established. It would be hard to completely defy them. But the physics allow for manipulation by magical candy."

"How about a candy that lets me shoot lightning out of my eyes?" Pigeon said. "It could target whatever I'm looking at."

"How would you determine when the lightning fires?" Sandra asked.

"When I hold my breath and clench both fists," Pigeon said.

"What would you call it?" Sandra asked.

"I don't know," Pigeon said. A grin played on his lips. "Stormfire."

Sandra reached into dream batter and handed Pigeon five blue suckers. "The effect will persist as long as the lollipop is in your mouth."

"They're already magical?" Pigeon asked.

"It isn't difficult for me here," Sandra replied.

"How about a variation of animal crackers?" Trevor proposed. "Each cracker could give me some of the best attributes of the animal. An eagle would give me the ability to fly and have keen eyesight. A monkey would grant me amazing climbing abilities. Call them Hybrid Crackers."

"Good concept," Sandra said, plunging a hand into the dream batter and withdrawing a small box. She handed it to Trevor.

Trevor turned the container over in his hands. Red with

white stripes, it featured images of several animals on the front beneath the words Hybrid Crackers. The packaging looked professional.

"Anything else?" Sandra asked.

"Can you do Peak Performance gum?" Trevor asked. "It optimizes whatever you're doing."

"Like Sebastian Stott makes?" Sandra said. "Sure." She extracted several sticks of gum from the dream batter and passed them to Trevor. "Ready to go?"

Trevor and Pigeon shared a look. "Let's do it."

Sandra extended her hand, creating a shimmer in the air. "This portal will take you to the line for the Terror Castle. Don't dawdle. I'll distract the Swindler for as long as I can, but there is always the risk he will sniff out what you're doing and move against you."

"Once we have the Dreamstone, we'll have to run to the Swindler's attraction in the dream carnival?" Pigeon asked.

"Is it in the same place as in the normal carnival?" Trevor asked.

"Yes," Sandra confirmed.

"Can you give us something to make us fast?" Pigeon asked.

"Your shoes," Sandra said, waving a hand. "Say 'super-speed,' and your shoes will do the rest."

"That will work in addition to the candy?" Trevor asked.

"It will," Sandra said. "One caution. Use these items only in an emergency. There's a good chance the effects of the candies and the shoes will draw unwanted attention. But once you're embattled, go for it."

"Good advice," Trevor said. "We'll stay safe."

CHAPTER THIRTY-TWO

CEMETERY

Trevor stepped through the distorted air and into the shadow of a massive castle. Tattered banners hung limply from worn battlements. Armored knights patrolled the walkways above, and ravens circled overhead against the background of a yellow haze that seemed to hover over the castle like a sickness.

Pigeon came through and stood beside Trevor. "Wow," he said. "Now *that's* a castle!"

The line of ticket holders went over a drawbridge and below a raised portcullis. Torches burned on the walls inside, where riders embarked. Trevor and Pigeon got into the line.

The other individuals in the line looked like ordinary people. One kid complained to his dad that the castle looked scary, but his father reassured him that it was all pretend. Trevor wondered how many of them were from the physical world, and how many had been created to populate the dream. He could perceive no way to distinguish between real people and dream personages.

Trevor wondered whether the other people in line could tell he and Pigeon were out of place. Nobody seemed to pay them special attention.

The queue advanced at a good pace. Soon Trevor was walking over the solid wood of the drawbridge. In the moat below, crocodiles teemed, overlapping one another, jaws snapping, as if hoping for a careless bystander to fall.

At the front of the line, the once-boxy cars of the real carnival had become dune buggies made from bones and chrome. Nate and Trevor handed their tickets to a tall, pale man with a glowering expression. They climbed into a dune buggy, the lap bar came down, and the car zoomed forward.

A rancid smell hit as they rushed into the dungeons. Clutching slimy strands of meat, rats scurried away from the dune buggy headlights. A scrawny, disheveled man cowered in a corner, weeping, filthy hands hiding his face.

After his first glimpse of the torture devices, Trevor closed his eyes. Desperate screams echoed off the moist walls.

The dune buggy advanced into the laboratory. A hulking man lay on a table, partly covered by a thin sheet, his physique stitched together from many different bodies. The skin tones were markedly different where the crude seams met. A white-haired scientist dragged a corpse into the room as lightning flashed outside the window. The goliath on the table stirred and groaned, the sheet falling further down his scarred, hairy torso.

Trevor closed his eyes again. The ride felt too real. He took a deep breath, trying not to get freaked out.

The dune buggy exited the laboratory into the graveyard, a huge moon providing bone-white light. As they approached the front gates, Trevor's heart froze at the wrought iron sign arching above the entrance.

CLOWN CEMETERY

"No way," Trevor said. "Not fair."

Pigeon went rigid.

The dream carnival graveyard was much larger than the one in the physical carnival. Here, headstones and statues extended to the edge of sight, covering distant hills. Low fog crawled over the dew-spangled turf, swirling around the bases of the monuments. A few fireflies winked in the dimness like errant sparks. A dark sign had Mausoleum embossed in gold alongside an arrow pointing left. In the distance, near the base of a hill in the indicated direction, stood a stately structure of black stone.

"That's where we need to go," Pigeon said, scooting out from under the lap bar and jumping from the dune buggy.

Trevor followed, rolling to a stop on the wet grass, fog churning around him. He stood up, the fog rising to his thighs. "Are you all right?" he asked, helping Pigeon to his feet.

"Except for being in a clown graveyard," Pigeon replied. "I'm trying to wait to use my candy."

"Another car," Trevor said. He and Pigeon crouched behind headstones as another dune buggy came along, headlights brightening the mist as they swung across it.

Once the dune buggy passed, Trevor and Pigeon started running through the crowded graveyard toward the mausoleum. The fog left only patches of the ground visible. What if there was a low tombstone? Or an open grave? The possibility convinced Trevor to slow down a little.

After gaining distance from the path of the dune buggies, the glare of headlights no longer reached them, allowing Trevor and Pigeon to stop hiding from the vehicles. They passed tight groups of statues of clowns and obelisks with names like Bobo, Zippy, and Drivelsnipe. The grander headstones had images of clowns and circus tents engraved on the surfaces, accompanied by epitaphs like "The show will go on" and "Who got the last laugh?"

Trevor stumbled and realized one of his shoes was untied. As he hastily crouched to retie it, the silence of the graveyard was shattered by a prolonged, goofy laugh from up ahead.

Pigeon slid to a halt, dropping to his knees. "How long before we can use the candy?"

"Might be about time," Trevor said, voice quavering. "What should I go with?"

"Turning to liquid could help us get through the mausoleum doors," Pigeon said.

Trevor nodded and got a Drip Drop ready, the licorice waxy in his hand.

Another laugh answered the first, from off to the side. Then a deeper, more menacing laugh came from behind.

Turning, Trevor saw a clown in full makeup dragging himself out of his grave. Orange hair clotted with soil, striped outfit streaked with grime, the clown shoved a heavy stone out of his way. The clown stared into Trevor's eyes, grinning and chuckling as he hobbled to his feet.

Trevor wanted to run, but instead remained rooted where he stood. He tried to call out a warning to Pigeon, but only managed an exhalation coupled with a reedy squeal.

Standing upright, the clown shuffled toward him, his nostrils flaring in little pulses as if tracking Trevor by scent.

Trevor heard the honk of a bugle horn, followed by high-pitched giggling. He glanced over his shoulder, his thoughts in disarray. On some instinctive level, he knew that if he ran, the clown would charge. What would the clown do if it caught him?

A metal arm reached behind Trevor's knees and scooped him into the air. Cradling him, Pigeon started running. Trevor put an arm around Pigeon's steel shoulders. They were inhumanly hard, as if his friend had become a robot.

Another slovenly clown dragged himself from the ground by clutching a headstone. A badly burned clown crawled on charred arms and legs. Clowns in various stages of decomposition were approaching from multiple directions, wading through the mist.

Pigeon dodged around them in a frantic dash toward the mausoleum.

The clowns did not hurry. There were dozens of them, and more kept rising out of the fog all over the cemetery. Overlapping giggles and laughs assailed Trevor's ears. One clown used a loop of string to blow huge bubbles. Another tried to ride a miniature tricycle, but it was missing a back wheel so he kept tipping over. Most trudged implacably toward them.

"If I eat my Drip Drop, I can run," Trevor managed to say.

"Do it," Pigeon replied.

Trevor put the licorice into his mouth and chewed it up. They were nearing the mausoleum, but the clowns ahead of them rose up to block their way. A hefty clown, his mouth a maroon rictus, stood at the front, flanked by many others.

"We're trapped," Trevor said.

"What should we do?" Pigeon asked, setting him down.

Trevor could find no words, overwhelmed by fear.

"I'll get us out of this." Pigeon's voice was unsteady but determined. "I doubt these bozos ever fought a kid made of pure steel."

The clowns continued to encroach from all sides.

The hefty clown inflated a long, slender balloon. "What kind of animal do you want?"

"You're not funny!" Pigeon stammered, clenching his fists. "And you're not scary! You're like a bad joke that won't die!"

Pigeon rushed at the hefty clown and seized the front of his shirt. The clown tried to grab him back, but Pigeon swung him around like a club, bashing the neighboring clowns. Having bludgeoned a hole in their line, Pigeon charged forward, tossing the hefty clown aside.

Trevor followed closely, the remaining undead clowns turning slowly to follow him.

Moonlight reflected off the glossy dark stone of the dignified mausoleum. Pigeon reached for the large bronze doors, bracing to pull them from their hinges.

"Stop!" Trevor shouted. "It's better if we keep them intact so we can lock out the clowns."

The crack between the double doors was only a finger-breadth wide, so Trevor turned to liquid and slurped through the narrow gap. Solidifying on the far side, he undid two latches and pulled the doors open. Pigeon came through and slammed the doors on the mob of undead clowns staggering in their direction. Trevor refastened the latches.

Inside the mausoleum, globes of light near the ceiling shed a faint blue glow. Pigeon pointed at a wall of crypts labeled Ventriloquist Dummies.

"This isn't fair," Trevor mumbled numbly. "Dummies too?"

Pigeon led the way down a corridor between two walls of crypts, steel feet noisy against the stone floor. Based on the markers, both clowns and dummies were interred within the walls, stacked six high at either hand.

"Let's do our job and get out of here. We're supposed to go deep."

The crypts on both sides of the aisle began to rattle. Pigeon and Trevor broke into a run.

"Say," an annoyed voice called from inside a crypt. "Let me outta here! Nobody packs away Chuckles before his time!"

"A fella can't breathe in here," a different voice cried. "A fella can't stretch!"

Trevor tried to block out the voices as he ran alongside Pigeon. A staircase came into view ahead, broad stone steps flowing down from one landing to the next. The top was chained off, but Pigeon charged through the feeble barrier and raced down the stairs. Trevor remained a couple of steps behind him.

At each landing, more rows of crypts were visible, but Pigeon continued downward until the stairs reached the bottom.

"Don't read the wall," Pigeon suggested, turning down the only available aisle.

Trevor could not resist looking.

DEEP PLACES ARE FOR BAD CLOWNS

"I could have done without that," Trevor scolded himself. He pelted down the aisle behind Pigeon. Stacked crypts rose high on either side, below the arched ceiling. The crypts began to rattle, and voices grumbled.

"Who's out there?" one female voice called harshly. "Open this up! I've got a surprise for you!"

Pigeon and Trevor kept running. The aisle ended at a large burial vault with a heavy stone lid. A single word was etched in the side of the stone box.

GROWLER

"This is it," Pigeon said. "The Dreamstone should be inside."

Pigeon grabbed the edge of the granite lid with his metal hands and heaved it off the box. The substantial lid slammed down with a boom. Trevor felt the floor vibrate.

A skeleton wearing Growler's pin-striped suit sat up inside the burial vault. "What are you slackers doing here?" the skull asked in Growler's voice.

Trevor wanted to reply. He just couldn't get any words out.

"We need the Dreamstone," Pigeon said.

"Over my dead body," Growler replied.

"Exactly." Pigeon reached for the skeleton, but his hands passed through the ghostly figure without physical contact.

Growler laughed. "You can't hurt what you can't touch."

"Then you can't hurt us either," Pigeon countered.

"Don't be so sure," Growler said. "The second you lay one of your grubby fingers on that Dreamstone, I'll have every clown corpse in this cemetery on you like a school of piranha."

"Then there are going to be a lot of broken teeth," Pigeon said, reaching into the vault and withdrawing a glossy, spherical stone swirled with fine, colorful lines that shimmered and shifted as they caught the light.

"You asked for it," Growler said, his voice rising to a wail. "We've got a couple of bandits in here! To arms! To arms!" The skeleton flew out of the burial vault and raced along the crypts, tearing them open. Apparently, Growler could interact with physical material when it suited him.

"Superspeed," Pigeon said. "Say it, Trevor."

"Superspeed," Trevor whispered.

Everything around them seemed to slow down. Crypts opened with syrupy sluggishness. Dead clowns tediously clambered out of their enclosures, moving at less than one-tenth normal speed. Laughter and words stretched deeper and lengthier.

Trevor and Pigeon started running. At their high speed, dodging the emerging clowns was easy. They made it up the stairs with hardly any interference, but at the top, clowns and animated ventriloquist dummies flooded the aisle.

"Follow me," Pigeon said.

He charged forward, shoving clowns to either side and

kicking ventriloquist dummies out of the way. Some of the more decayed clowns broke apart as Pigeon bullied past them. Trevor followed, dodging around slowly grasping hands. At the end of the corridor, Pigeon hastily unlatched the mausoleum doors, only to find a mob of cackling clowns awaiting them outside.

Lowering his head, Pigeon rushed forward like a running back. Clowns dominoed away from his brutal charge, and Trevor darted through the gap. After several steps, they broke through the decomposing crowd and began weaving their way through the crowded tombstones ahead of them.

When they reached the track for the dune buggies, Pigeon turned to follow it. They ran so fast that they easily caught up to the nearest dune buggy.

"I'm getting tired," Trevor said. "Let's not pass them."

"Want to ride piggyback?" Pigeon offered.

Trevor hopped onto his friend's back. Pigeon stayed right behind the dune buggy as they entered a pyramid. The aroma of ancient stone and unknown spices, the faded hieroglyphs on the walls, and the first shambling mummy, bandages loose around a dislocated jaw, convinced Trevor to focus on the dune buggy. He didn't need more scary images in his mind right now, so he did his best to ignore the roaring.

When the dune buggy reached the end of the ride, Pigeon raced through the exit, heading away from the Terror Castle. They ran under blue skies through the crowded carnival, still moving at least ten times faster than the people around them.

The dream carnival had the same layout as the physical carnival, but the rides were all larger and grander. Perhaps most notably, in places where the physical carnival ended, the dream carnival kept going, covering neighboring hills as far as they could see.

"Our speed is clutch," Trevor said as they blew past people in the crowd. "It gives us a real chance."

"I'm just happy to leave the cemetery behind," Pigeon said. "I'd much rather fight roustabouts than clowns."

The Swindler's shop looked exactly like the building in the physical carnival down to the font on the glittering sign. But there was no barker out front, and a small notice in the window declared the establishment closed.

After climbing the ramp to the front door, Pigeon set down Trevor, lowered his shoulder, and rammed the door down. The room beyond was still and empty, games on the counter waiting to be played. There was only one other door in the room, so Pigeon crashed through that one as well.

The vault they entered had beige walls, floor, and ceiling. A large blob of silver dream batter occupied one corner of the room. A pedestal rose in the center of the room, and on it rested a shadow in the exact shape of the Dreamstone.

Pigeon approached the pedestal and set the Dreamstone over the shadow. The Dreamstone immediately vanished, and the shadow turned from black to gold.

Pigeon turned to Trevor. "I think we did it."

The door to the Swindler's establishment gradually opened. Trevor and Pigeon turned to see an orangutan standing there, filling most of the doorway, backed by several roustabouts.

"You kids are in enormous trouble," the ape slowly said.

CHAPTER THIRTY-THREE

DREAMSTONE

N ate jerked awake inside a glass container. He checked his pockets and was relieved to feel his Cannon Blasts there. He flattened his palms against the glass lid above him, then pushed, and the clear covering hinged open. He climbed out, then closed the lid.

Summer emerged from her own case several containers away.

Rows of glass coffins filled the room. There were hundreds, and aside from a few empty containers, each one held a sleeper.

"Look," Summer said. "It's Edward. Looks like he finally fell asleep in the wrong place."

Nate crossed to where she was standing. Inside a glass coffin, Edward reclined on his back, hands folded across his chest, rapier at his side.

"Or got knocked out," Nate said. "Trevor and I just saw him last night. This must be recent."

Summer rushed down the row, then the next. "I've got one of the Battiato twins."

"Which one?" Nate asked.

"Take your pick," Summer said.

Nate explored a different row. "Here's the other one," he announced. "Victor or Ziggy. I thought magical enforcers couldn't enter the carnival."

"Maybe they were brought in already sleeping," Summer said, browsing another row. "Mr. Stott has invited Mozag into his lair."

"Hopefully they weren't stripped of their powers to get inside," Nate replied. A few more rows yielded no familiar faces. Then Nate stopped again. "This lady lives in our neighborhood. She's two houses up the street from me."

"Here's Benji!" Summer exclaimed. "He really is just asleep."

"That's a relief," Nate said, trotting along another aisle and stopping abruptly. "I found Mozag! No hat."

"Should we try to wake him up?" Summer asked, running over.

Nate shrugged. "Could be a game changer." He lifted the lid.

Summer reached inside and shook the mage's shoulder. "Mozag!" she hissed. "Wake up! It's an emergency. Mozag!"

His body remained completely inert, his features blandly unconscious. Was he even breathing? Nate held a hand above the mage's nose and mouth. Breath came very faintly. Hoping it might startle him awake, Nate temporarily covered the mage's mouth and nose, but he remained still.

"I don't think we can wake them up like this," Nate said.

Summer poked Mozag one more time. "Use your magic! Come back to us!"

"Not a twitch," Nate said, closing the lid. "He's down for the count. Should we head up to the carnival?"

"We better," Summer said. "Who knows how long it will take Trevor and Pigeon to do their part?"

They dashed for the front of the room, Nate a few steps ahead of Summer.

"Oh, no!" Summer exclaimed, skidding to a stop.

Nate slowed, glancing back.

"Lindy," Summer said.

"Really?" Nate asked, halting. "Man, she got caught fast."

"She looks so peaceful," Summer said.

"I wonder what she's dreaming about," Nate said. "We should go."

"Yeah," Summer said.

Nate and Summer went through the door into the room where they had confronted Growler. It was empty. Growler's clothes were gone, and Nate detected no trace of the fumes that had put them to sleep. They went through the square door, returning to the room where the slide had deposited them.

"Sandra told us to take the circular door," Summer said.

She and Nate hurried to the round door and entered what looked like the bottom of an empty elevator shaft. Looking up, Nate could see no end to the shaft—it simply shrank to a point. A ladder leaned against each wall of the shaft. The ladders were of equal height, but all ended after about twenty rungs.

"Looks like up is the only way out," Summer said. "But these ladders are way too short."

"I could Cannon Blast upward," Nate said. "See what I find."

"And ditch me?" Summer asked.

"You could eat one too," Nate said.

"True," Summer said. "But Sandra specifically mentioned the ladders. Maybe they are important?"

"There could be a secret hidden at the top," Nate said.

"Let's find out," Summer said. She stepped onto the first rung of one of the ladders, and it immediately telescoped upward at least a hundred feet, leaving Summer only nineteen rungs from the top of the ladder.

"Are you all right?" Nate called up to her.

"I think so," Summer said. "I'm glad I had a good hold. But I'm going to put on my Clown Lips before I go any higher."

Nate walked over to a different ladder, firmly gripped the sides, and stepped onto the first rung. With a disorienting rush, the ladder extended a hundred rungs taller. Nate was still nineteen rungs from the top. He looked over to find Summer dressed as a clown. She took another step, and the rungs below her doubled in number.

Nate continued upward, the ladder stretching a hundred rungs for every step he took. He got used to the sensation of the expanding ladder, but he still clung tightly. When Nate reached the top, the ladder ended in the center of the floor of an empty pink room with a glittery ceiling. Glancing down, the shaft shrank to a vanishing point.

Summer hopped off her ladder and came around to help Nate, her oversized shoes in his face. The floor of the room was rubbery and had some give, as if they were walking on the surface of a water balloon. Nate stomped and sent a wave rippling across the floor.

"Where do we go from here?" Summer asked.

"I only see one exit," Nate said, pointing to a revolving door made from horizontal metal bars.

"Can you see what's on the other side?" Summer asked.

"It's too dark," Nate said. "That might be deliberate. I'll keep my candy ready."

Nate started to push through the revolving door, then experimentally tried to pull it the other way. The door resisted his efforts—it was a one-way passage. The bars of the door slotted through the horizontal bars of a barrier, blocking a return trip. Beyond the revolving door, Nate found several other revolving doors, turning on their own.

"I hope this is the right way," Nate said over his shoulder. "I doubt we can backtrack."

A series of revolving doors continued to sweep Nate and Summer forward. They must have passed through ten or more revolving doors before they emerged at the top of a greasy, plastic slope.

"More one-way travel," Summer said beside him. They braved the long slide into a sponge pit.

Nate clambered through the sponges until he regained a solid floor. Again, this room had a one-way revolving door.

"Keep going," Summer urged.

They whirled through the revolving door into a circular room where the entire floor was spinning. Below the red walls and ceiling, a blue-and-yellow spiral remained in constant motion. The room had multiple entrances, and for the first time since returning from the dreamscape, other Fun House participants were present.

"We've been here before," Nate said.

"We're right by the Fun House exit," Summer said.

The floor carried Nate, Summer, and a few other people along an endless circular route, like a record on a turntable. Nate knew from experience that it sometimes sped up or slowed down. He also knew where to jump off to pass through the curtain of tinsel that led to the exit.

Summer went first, and Nate followed her into the afternoon sun. Outside the Fun House, it looked like an ordinary day at the carnival. Nate smelled caramel popcorn and saw a clown juggling boxes for a circle of onlookers. Groups of kids moved about, some taking their time and enjoying snacks, others scampering to the next ride.

"Let's hurry to the Swindler's place," Summer said, taking off her Clown Lips and returning to her normal form. "We need to find a spot nearby where we can watch for the cloud."

"The roustabouts are probably still hunting us for busting up their special club," Nate said.

Summer glanced at the sky. "No poodles yet."

They set off toward the Swindler's attraction. After his intense experiences over the past few hours, Nate found it strange that people were still going about their day. He stayed vigilant as they crossed the park. He noticed no roustabouts, but he did see several kids from school.

"What time is it?" he asked.

Summer pointed out a clock. "One thirty."

"We only have half an hour before we're supposed to bus back to the school," Nate said.

"Looks like we'll be finding our own way home," Summer said.

"Sure," Nate replied. "We'll have to watch out for teachers rounding up stray kids."

When they reached the Crafts Tent, Summer pointed out a little stand selling smoothies. "We can probably kill time at those tables until the cloud shows up if we drink our smoothies slowly."

"It has a good view of the Swindler's place," Nate said.

They approached the counter, and Nate ordered a berry smoothie while Summer went with peach. They chose a circular table set back from the walkway. As they waited, Nate's attention alternated between the crowd and the sky.

"What if the cloud doesn't show up?" Nate asked.

"I don't want to think that way," Summer said.

"We'd need a new plan."

"We'd need to rescue Trevor and Pigeon first."

When the smoothies came, Nate was disappointed by the taste of the artificial flavoring. Mr. Stott's smoothies and shakes always used real ingredients. At least the drink was cold. He was thirsty enough to ignore the tang of chemicals. He made an effort to take it slow.

Summer grabbed his arm. Nate looked to the sky first,

then saw a troop of at least thirty roustabouts forming up in front of the Swindler's attraction. Most carried weapons of some sort—tire irons, chains, blackjacks, baseball bats. The strongman was with them, curly brown hair brushing against muscle-bound shoulders.

Some onlookers backed away, seeming concerned by the show of force. Others watched curiously, as if expecting a performance to begin.

Nate and Summer turned away from the mob to avoid getting spotted.

"They know something is up," Summer whispered. "Trev and Pidge must be doing well."

Nate noisily slurped the last of his smoothie.

Summer glared at him. "Are you trying to draw attention?"

"Sorry."

The roustabouts remained alert, but nobody noticed him or Summer. Nate rolled a Cannon Blast between his fingers. "Can we handle that many?"

"We have to find a way," Summer said. "We don't have to beat them. Just get through them. In and out."

Nate nodded. Glancing up, he saw a large cloud shaped exactly like a poodle in a sitting position.

"There's the signal," he said.

"Not very subtle," Summer remarked.

The strongman had taken up a position right outside the Swindler's front door. Roustabouts flanked him and filled the ramp. Many others patrolled the walkway in front of the establishment.

"Should I blast at the door?" Nate asked.

"You'll hit it at a sharp angle from here," Summer said. "I wish we were straight across from it."

"At least it would surprise them."

"The strongman is enormous," Summer said.

"I hope he's full of sand," Nate said. "Otherwise, I could seriously hurt him."

"If he's protecting the guy who is trying to destroy the world, that's the risk he takes," Summer said.

Nate put the Cannon Blast in his mouth. "I see no reason to wait."

"They'll just bring more reinforcements," Summer agreed. "Keep extra Cannon Blasts ready to go. You'll have to keep moving."

Nate knew she was right. When in motion, nobody stood a chance against him, but between the blasts, he would be vulnerable. "Ready?" he asked.

Summer put new Clown Lips up to her face and transformed into a clown.

With three Cannon Blasts in his hand and more in his pocket, Nate focused on the strongman. His best bet would be to aim directly at him and try to ram him through the door.

Nate bit down and launched. He streaked forward above the heads of the roustabouts milling out front. His knee clipped the railing of the ramp, crunching the wood to splinters. The strongman looked right at Nate and caught him in a big bear hug. The impact of the collision lifted the strongman off his feet, his huge body glancing off the door, then rolling to a stop on the platform out front, Nate still in his embrace.

Nate struggled, but his arms were pinned to his sides,

which meant he couldn't get another Cannon Blast to his mouth.

"I have him," the strongman declared in a deep voice. He stood up, Nate firmly in his arms.

Summer charged the roustabouts, and they swarmed her. She produced a baton from inside her jacket and swatted at the security men, nimbly dodging until they overwhelmed her.

As Nate thrashed, the strongman squeezed him painfully in response. His magical durability was gone, and the embrace felt like it could break bones, so Nate went limp. At least the candy was still in his grasp. All he needed was a moment of freedom.

The strongman carried Nate down the ramp. Summer was pinned to the ground by four roustabouts. Her clownish body stretched and contorted in their grasp, but she failed to wrench free. The strongman brought Nate to a roustabout wearing a brown corduroy suit coat with a heavy pipe wrench resting against his shoulder.

"Where do I take him, boss?" the strongman asked.

"Follow me," the jacketed roustabout said.

Unexpectedly, an arm reached around the roustabout from behind, a hand grabbed his face from the other side, and the assailant twisted in opposite directions. The roustabout's neck cracked, then his head came off, dumping sand. When the body dropped, John Dart stood behind him, a Battiato brother at either side.

"Hi, Nate," John said. His hard gaze went to the strongman. "Set down the boy."

"You tore his head off," the strongman said.

"Ordinarily I can't play so rough," John said. "But like you, I'm a physical projection from Dreamland. For the first time in a long time, I can do my work unrestrained."

One of the Battiatos leaned his head to one side and popped his neck. "Now?"

"Almost," John said. "Last warning. Release the kid."

The other roustabouts watched, weapons ready. They seemed to be waiting for a signal.

"Stay back," the strongman said. "I can crush the boy at my leisure."

"You know what the problem is with big, strong guys?" John asked, stepping forward so he was within reach of Nate, looking up at the strongman.

"What?" the strongman asked.

"Joints," John said, crouching and whipping his leg into the side of the strongman's knee. The big man buckled. John struck the guy's elbow and yanked Nate free.

"Get them!" bellowed the strongman from the ground.

John brought his elbow down on the big guy's neck, and sand poured everywhere. "Now!" John said.

The Battiatos waded forward eagerly. One had retrieved the pipe wrench, the other wore brass knuckles. The roustabouts charged, but the Battiatos met them with gruesome efficiency, staying close, working together, dodging swings, then busting the roustabouts open like sandbags.

"Use your candy," John reminded Nate. "Go. I've got Summer." John joined the Battiatos. The roustabouts were clearly amateurs trying to challenge professionals.

Nate glanced to the Swindler's shop, then back at

Summer. He saw an opportunity that would let him nail several roustabouts and take him above Summer. It would also leave him with a better angle to attack the door.

He popped a Cannon Blast into his mouth, focused on his destination, and bit down. He rocketed forward, roustabouts exploding like piñatas, spraying sand instead of treats. Tearing through so many of them slowed his progress enough that Nate continued only about twenty feet beyond the crowd, rolling to a stop against a cinder block wall.

Nate put another Cannon Blast into his mouth. His flight had freed Summer from the roustabouts holding her down. She was now on her feet, bashing one with a croquet mallet while the others fought John and the Battiatos.

Nate was directly across from the Swindler's front door. He bit down on the candy and zoomed forward, crashing through the door and slamming into the back wall of the room beyond.

The Swindler stood alone at the counter, games spread out before him, his cane in one hand.

"Hello again," the Swindler said casually. He snapped his fingers and both the door Nate had penetrated and the door leading to his vault vanished, leaving blank walls. "You need to work on your manners."

Nate moved to put another Cannon Blast into his mouth, but the Swindler snapped his fingers again and the candy vanished. Nate patted his pockets. There was more candy inside.

"I can get rid of it all," the Swindler said, his fingers poised to snap again. "Why are you here?"

Nate held his hands away from his pockets. "I think you know. I came for the Dreamstone."

The Swindler whistled. "You're aiming high. I can respect that. Do you realize what will happen when the Dreamstone is reunited with its dreamscape half?"

"It means I can take it," Nate said.

"In theory, yes," the Swindler said. "It also means I'll become more powerful than ever. This room, so close to my power source, is the wrong place to challenge me. We're technically in the physical world, but I can manipulate it almost as easily as a dream."

"Is that how you win your contests?" Nate asked.

The Swindler shrugged. "One of the ways." Cocking his head, he looked around. "We're being watched."

"All of the dreamers see you," Sandra's voice said.

Nate scanned the room for her, but she did not appear to be present.

The Swindler spread his arms wide, cuff links glittering. "I love an audience," he exclaimed warmly. "My boy! The Dreamstone would be quite a prize, and I would be reluctant to part with it. But I've always been a sporting man. How about we resolve this with a contest?"

CHAPTER THIRTY - FOUR

CONTEST

Nate weighed his options. If he reached for a Cannon Blast, the Swindler would make it vanish. The doors were gone. And the Swindler made a career out of winning every game he played.

"A contest would represent your best chance at this point," said Sandra's unembodied voice.

"Hear that, son?" the Swindler pressed. "Let's give the people what they want!"

Nate swallowed. "Fine."

"Standard format," the Swindler said. "You pick the game, then we agree to rules and terms."

"All right," Nate said.

"That's my boy!" the Swindler exclaimed. "I've been longing for some truly high-stakes action. What will be the nature of the contest?"

Nate scoured his mind. If there was a way for the Swindler

to win, he would. What kind of contest would let Nate win even if he lost? Sandra had made sure this interaction would be seen by many others. Was that to prevent the Swindler from just killing him? Or was there an advantage in having an audience for the contest?

"We're all waiting," the Swindler said.

A possibility entered Nate's mind. There wasn't time to study every potential implication, but he had a question that might put the Swindler in a tight spot. How would he phrase it? He would have to keep planning as they conversed.

"I'll ask a question," Nate said.

The Swindler gave a slow nod. "Interesting. Trivia. Or a riddle. I agree—provided it has a factual, definitive, verifiable answer."

"That's fair," Nate said.

"An impartial judge would be useful," the Swindler said. "Under the circumstances, that might be hard to come by."

"What about the Dreamstone?" Nate proposed.

The Swindler pursed his lips. "That could work. It has a consciousness. I can hear it. Some on your side can hear it. I accept. Rules and terms. You want possession of the Dreamstone. If I fail to answer your question, or if I answer incorrectly, it is yours. If I supply a correct response, you voluntarily enter Dreamland. How's that for a fortunate deal? If you lose, all your dreams come true."

Nate knew that a loss would mean imprisonment in the dream realm, maybe forever. But what else could he offer? He had to win. "Let's do it."

"As to the rules," the Swindler said. "You must acknowledge

that there may be acceptable answers to your question that you fail to anticipate. Any answers that our judge deems accurate still count as a win."

"I agree," Nate said.

"And I should have three tries at answering," the Swindler said.

"I only get to ask one question," Nate pointed out.

The Swindler cocked his head. "All right. One question. One answer."

"There should be a time limit," Nate said. "You have one minute to respond. If you don't answer, I win."

The Swindler chuckled. "That one works in your favor. If you ask me a puzzler that takes me more than a minute to figure out, you deserve the victory. Can we also agree that once we begin the contest, you have one minute to pose the question? All in good faith, mind you. We can't be blamed if the other person somehow silences us."

"Sounds reasonable," Nate said.

"Any other provisos?" the Swindler asked.

"I can't think of any," Nate said.

The Swindler held out a hand. "Let's shake on it. This is a simple contest, but we have a lot riding on it."

Nate crossed to the Swindler and shook his hand.

"Are you ready?" The Swindler produced a stopwatch from an inner pocket of his jacket.

Nate took a deep breath. "Sure."

"You have sixty seconds," the Swindler said. "Once you pose your question and I confirm that I understand it, I will restart the timer for my answer. Ask away." The Swindler clicked a button, and the stopwatch started ticking.

Nate did not want to flirt with disaster by taking up most of his sixty seconds, but he checked and double-checked the question in his mind. Was there a better way to phrase it? Were there multiple, unforeseen answers that would avoid the trap he was setting?

After thirty seconds went by, Nate cleared his throat.

"Who owns the Dreamstone?" he asked.

Something behind the Swindler's eyes faltered. For a moment, surprise cracked his polished façade. Then he was back in control. The Swindler stopped the timer. "You mean who owns the Dreamstone right now? Presently?"

"Yes," Nate said. "Who currently owns the Dreamstone?"

The Swindler started a fresh minute on the stopwatch. "Allow me to muse before I answer. Ownership of mystical objects can be a counterintuitive subject." He scratched the side of his jaw. "Do I have the Dreamstone in my possession? Is it under my control? Do I function like an owner for all practical purposes? Yes, absolutely. But what would the Dreamstone accept as an accurate answer?" He drummed his fingers on the counter. "I'll admit this much—that was a more penetrating question than I expected. And I'm almost out of time."

The stopwatch showed ten final seconds.

"Technically, everyone owns the Dreamstone," the Swindler said at last.

"Wait, everyone owns it already?" Nate asked, emphasizing the answer. "Then was it yours to offer as a prize in the contest?"

The Swindler chuckled. "You agreed to it. We con men have a proud tradition of selling things we might not technically own to suckers willing to buy them. Care to put a down payment on the Brooklyn Bridge?"

"You're talking about a lie," Nate said. "This was supposed to be a fair contest."

"We made an agreement," the Swindler said. "You asked your question, and I answered it correctly. Now you have to fulfill your end of the bargain."

"No, I don't," Nate said. "Your prize was a fraud. If your answer is right, the Dreamstone wasn't yours to give. Also, it means there is nothing to prevent me from taking it. Either way, you've kept it for yourself long enough."

"You're right, Nate," Sandra's voice said. "The Swindler's hold on the carnival is all pretense. None of his claims or bargains are valid. The Dreamstone founded and supports the carnival, and it does not belong to him. It belongs to everyone."

The walls of the room began to tremble. The floor quaked.

The Swindler steadied himself against the counter. "Now wait a minute," he said, panic in his voice. "You're taking this too far! If that contest was invalid, let's establish a new one."

"There can be no competition for ownership of the Dreamstone," Sandra's voice maintained. "As you said, it belongs to everyone. Go get it for us, Nate."

An opening in the wall appeared where the door to the vault had been. Nate rushed through and saw the Dreamstone on a pedestal in the center of the room. He picked it up, and the Swindler's entire building disappeared.

Nate and the Swindler now stood in a vacant lot sur-rounded by tents and carnival attractions. The Swindler looked around in disbelief. In front of the lot, John Dart waited with Summer in her clown costume and the Battiato brothers. All that remained of the roustabouts were clothes and sand. One of the Battiatos cupped a wound in his shoulder where sand was leaking out. Nate hadn't realized the Battiatos had ap-peared as dream people just like the roustabouts.

"Give that back," the Swindler cried nastily at Nate, strid-ing toward him, all veneer of calm control gone.

"I'm taking the Dreamstone outside the carnival," Nate said. He pulled a Cannon Blast from his pocket.

The Swindler snapped his fingers, but nothing happened.

Nate popped the candy in his mouth, turned toward the front of the park, and blasted off. He soared in a long, high arc. As he plummeted downward, he shouted a warning and people scattered. He landed in the plaza near the carousel, bouncing and rolling on the pavement, leaving a crack where he first landed.

The crowd pointed at him and commented in amazement.

"Where did he come from?"

"How is he getting up?"

"He should be dead!"

Nate bit down on another Cannon Blast and traveled in a long trajectory over the carousel and most of the Grand Boardwalk, curving down toward the Currency Exchange.

"Out of my way!" Nate yelled as he hurtled downward. "Out of my way!"

He crashed into the octagonal booth, smashing through

the front and bursting out the back, narrowly missing the employee inside. Nate got back on his feet, put another Cannon Blast into his mouth, and, Dreamstone still in hand, he took flight into the parking lot.

CHAPTER THIRTY-FIVE

LINDY

With the orangutan filling the doorway, Pigeon hesitated. Could they retreat into the Dreamland vault and close themselves in? No, they had broken down the door. Their best bet was to charge out of here. Sure, the talking red ape was intimidating, but Pigeon had many options.

He pocketed his piece of steel, turning back into his regular self. Then Pigeon put a Stormfire lollipop into his mouth. His whole body felt charged, the little hairs on his neck standing upright. The orangutan shuffled forward, roustabouts behind him. Glaring at the ape, Pigeon held his breath and clenched his fists.

A thick streak of white-blue lightning streaked from his eyes, tearing through the orangutan and the roustabouts behind it. Clouds of sand released into the air as the bodies burst apart. Rootlike tubes of vitrified sand clunked to the ground, marking where the lightning had passed. The scent of ozone lingered.

"My Drip Drop ran out," Trevor said, shaking animal crackers into his palm. "I don't want a dolphin. What's this? A grasshopper? Why not?" He put one cracker back in the box and ate the other.

Pigeon charged out the front door to find roustabouts stampeding up the ramp. Clenching his fists and holding his breath, lightning sizzled through the long line of beefy men before scorching the ground behind them. A blizzard of sand surged outward from where the roustabouts had ruptured, and fulgurites clattered against the ramp.

Pigeon glanced back at Trevor. "Come on!"

His friend sprang forward, crossing the room and passing through the doorway in a single leap, landing in a crouch. Pigeon realized the carnival was too crowded with innocent bystanders for more lightning, so he tossed the Stormfire lollipop aside, removed the steel from his pocket, and ingested another Statue Stick.

The remaining roustabouts hung back. Pigeon stomped down the ramp, and Trevor soared over the ramp in one enormous jump. Soon Pigeon and Trevor were in the clear, running side by side. The roustabouts had no way to compete with their speed.

"Where should we go?" Trevor asked.

"Let's head for the exit," Pigeon said. "Our job is done. I don't think we're welcome in the dream carnival anymore."

Pigeon and Trevor raced along the walkway between the Crafts Tent and Livestock Central. Pigeon watched for more roustabouts, but they seemed to have left them behind.

"Check out the carousel," Trevor said.

On the far side of a plaza teeming with elaborate fountains, Pigeon saw a towering cylinder. The carousel in the dream carnival was nine levels tall, topped with tubes that emitted showers of colored sparks. The menagerie of animals to ride included lobsters, moose, dragons, snow leopards, rams, crickets, unicorns, jackalopes, elephants, polar bears, and griffins. Jewels refracted light from gilded casings as the tower gradually spun. The music it played was eerily slow.

"Pigeon, Trevor—halt!" called an authoritative voice. The words were not slowed by Pigeon's heightened speed.

Turning toward the speaker, Pigeon saw Preston Wilder dressed in his formal ringmaster apparel. Behind him stood Camilla White, face grim, arms folded. Pigeon realized it was really Camilla's mother in disguise. Three sad-faced clowns stood nearby, one holding an oversized butterfly net, the second clutching a straitjacket, and a third gripping a tubular firearm.

Preston waved. Why weren't Preston or the clowns moving slowly? Pigeon knew he still had superspeed because the carousel remained sluggish and the fountains in the plaza splashed in slow motion.

"Final warning, Pigeon," Preston said. "Halt or we'll stop you."

"Keep running," Trevor urged.

There came a boom like a gunshot, and a weighted net enveloped Pigeon, slamming him to the ground with a resounding clang. He tried to rise, but he was entangled in the mesh and it would hardly budge.

"Be glad Dipsy is a good shot," Preston called. "The weight of that net would have killed Trevor. Who gave you permission to wear those enhanced shoes?"

"Your Mom," Trevor replied.

Preston pointed at their feet, then snapped his fingers. "Your footwear is no longer enchanted, so my colleagues and I can return to normal speed as well."

Pigeon saw the water flowing regularly in the fountains. The music from the carousel no longer dragged.

"Trevor, run," Pigeon said. "I'm pinned."

"I'm not ditching you," Trevor said, tugging at the heavy net.

"You might as well cease struggling, Trevor," Preston said offhandedly. "Sure, you could try to hop away, or maybe turn to liquid to avoid straitjackets and nets, but a barrel would do the trick. I am much more powerful than my counterpart in the material world. Don't force additional demonstrations."

"What do you want?" Pigeon asked.

"Justice," Preston said. "You disturbed the peace here. You tried to steal from us. So you must join the sleepers and help rebuild what you have harmed."

"Not likely," said a strong female voice.

Pigeon peered up through the mesh of the net at an adult version of Lindy, now in her early twenties. She wore her reddish hair long and was quite pretty.

Preston looked confused. "What are you doing here?"

"I'm the sister of the owner," Lindy said. She waved a hand, and the net confining Pigeon crumbled to dust. "She doesn't approve of how you're managing things. You're fired."

"On whose authority?" Preston sputtered, waving his hands as if casting a spell. His motions generated no results.

"Camilla's," Lindy said.

"I'm right here," the woman who looked like Camilla declared.

"You're not my sister," Lindy accused. "You're the person who should have protected her. You should have protected all of us."

The woman who looked like Camilla gestured with her hands, as if summoning magic.

"Are you two trying to work dream magic against me?" Lindy asked. "Do you have any idea how powerful I am? Camilla already brought me up to speed."

"Get her!" Preston ordered the clowns.

Lindy clenched a fist, and the ground beneath Preston, the fake Camilla, and the clowns liquified. They sank to their chests, as if they had been dropped into the shallow end of a pool. Lindy opened her hand, and the ground solidified again, leaving them trapped and struggling.

"Impossible," Preston complained.

"Quite easily managed," Lindy said. "Don't pick fights above your weight class." She turned to Pigeon. "Are you okay, Pidge?"

"I am now," Pigeon said. "You got older."

"This is how I chose to project here," Lindy said. "My physical body is resting with the other sleepers. Including you two."

"Do you remember being Mrs. White?" Trevor asked.

"Finally, yes," Lindy said. "An advantage of journeying into the dreamscape is that I could access parts of myself that had been walled off."

"You're not working against us?" Pigeon asked.

"Did you think I would help my father?" Lindy asked incredulously. "Are you kidding? I wouldn't trust him to manage a fish tank. He has betrayed me and my siblings more times than I can count. And here he is, abusing Camilla again. If I had fifty enemies in a room, I'd neutralize my father first."

"The last time you were Belinda, you tried to take over our town," Trevor said.

"Fair point," Lindy said. "But then I got an unexpected gift."

"What?" Pigeon asked.

"A fresh start," Lindy said. "I got to see life from a new per-spective, inhabit a different viewpoint. We had been true en-emies, but once Mr. Stott had the upper hand, all I felt from him was forgiveness and real concern for my best interests. The same was true of you kids. I lost an eye fighting you, but you replaced it with a better one. What do you call an enemy who defeats you in self-defense, then legitimately takes care of you?"

"A friend?" Trevor guessed.

"At least that," Lindy said. "I'm not sure who I am anymore. Not the woman you knew, nor the little girl Mr. Stott tried to raise. I do know that he was a better father to me in the year we have spent together than my real dad was over a lifetime. And I made many new friends. Especially you, Pigeon."

"If you're rescuing us instead of trying to kill us, let's call it a good start," Pigeon said.

Lindy smiled. "Nate has the Dreamstone."

"He does?" Trevor asked.

"In the physical carnival," Lindy said. "I'm keeping an eye on him."

"You can sense Nate?" Trevor asked.

"I'm not new to magic," Lindy said. "Much is visible from the dream realm."

"Is he all right?" Pigeon asked.

"He's charging for the exit like a human cannonball," Lindy said. "He's going to undo this place."

"What will happen?" Trevor asked.

"This will no longer be a crossroads," Lindy said. "The physical carnival and the dream carnival will fully separate."

"Will the physical carnival explode?" Trevor asked.

"Nothing so dramatic," Lindy said. "My guess is anything powered by magic will be unplugged. Any secret ways into the dream carnival will be disconnected. The rest will remain. Relics of a grand misadventure."

Sudden thunder roared, and a tremor ran through the dream carnival.

Lindy's eyes widened. "Nate is out. He did it."

Trevor pumped a fist. "He's so clutch."

"Can we get back to the real world?" Pigeon asked.

"The gulf between the dreamscape and the waking world may be growing wider," Lindy said. "But we are not native to this place. We need only wake up."

"There have been issues with that," Trevor said.

"Camilla will help," Lindy said. "As will your friend Sandra."

"What will you do?" Pigeon asked.

"First on my agenda is reconnecting with my dear sister," Lindy said. "We have lost too many years. Shall we go?" A brisk motion of her hand created a shimmering portal.

"I'm game," Trevor said, glancing over at Preston and his entrapped comrades. "There are way too many clowns in this dream."

CHAPTER THIRTY-SIX
DESSERT

The Lux Lounge beneath the carousel had been cleaned up since Nate, Trevor, Summer, and Pigeon had fought the security team there, but the walls still bore some scars. Tonight, Nate was visiting under happier circumstances. Five days after the Dreamstone had left the carnival, Camilla was hosting a dessert party for everyone who had helped overthrow her father.

Nate sat at a central table nearest to Summer, Trevor, Pigeon, Lindy, and Benji. Also at the long table was Sandra, John Dart, Mozag, and Camilla. Mr. Stott sat with them too, outside his lair under special protection from Mozag. In front of them a decadent selection of cakes and pies were arrayed, together with all the ingredients they could want to build their own ice cream sundaes.

Mozag tapped his fork against a crystal goblet, and when the room quieted, he climbed up on his chair. He had been reunited with his battered Cubs hat, and he looked around the room with a smile, making eye contact with Nate and many others.

"Welcome, friends," Mozag began. He gestured to the dessert buffet. "Please feel free to begin if you haven't already."

"Don't miss the key lime," Victor called out.

"I'm on my third sundae," Ziggy announced.

A general chuckle passed through the room.

Mozag waited for the room to quiet again. "I would like to begin by thanking a few people. First of all—Camilla, would you mind standing?"

Camilla rose to her feet, looking somewhat uncomfortable.

"I owe you an apology," Mozag said. "I initially suspected you were the mastermind behind the disappearances at the carnival. Instead, your father was pulling the strings, leaving you a prisoner within your lovely creation. You provided key assistance at a crucial time. Without your help, Carl White may have emerged victorious. You have our thanks."

The room applauded.

"How are my father and mother?" Camilla asked. "I haven't seen them since the carnival separated from the dreamscape."

"Your parents have been very cooperative," Mozag said. "We have them in a secure facility where they can dream about whatever they want until they are rehabilitated."

"Be slow to believe they've changed," Lindy called out.

"We'll take precautions," Mozag said. "Though I will mention that once the Dreamstone left the carnival grounds, neither of them had much fight left. It seems that artifact was the crutch Carl depended on for power."

Camilla nodded and sat down.

"Onward," Mozag continued. "Would John Dart, Sandra Lafond, Victor Battiato, and Ziggy Battiato please rise?"

The four of them stood, Victor and Ziggy at a neighboring table. Ziggy had some whipped cream at the corner of his mouth. His brother gestured with a napkin, and Ziggy wiped it off.

"These are four of the finest magical enforcers you will ever meet," Mozag declared. "John and Sandra played key roles in protecting the town of Colson when the carnival arrived, and Sandra used her dreamwalking abilities to open the carnival to us. All four risked life and limb to protect us from tyranny. I am professionally and personally indebted."

The room applauded. The four enforcers waved. The Battiatos wore big grins. John was the first of them to sit.

"Belinda White," Mozag said. "Would you please stand?"

Lindy got up.

"On the chair, perhaps, so people can see you?" Mozag suggested.

Lindy climbed onto her chair.

"Any magical enforcer would tell you that Belinda White has given our community some scares in the past," Mozag said. "But on this occasion, she was instrumental in protecting Trevor and Pigeon, and in bringing her parents to justice after the carnival fell."

Everyone clapped. Pigeon whistled. Lindy watched calmly.

"Belinda, now called Lindy, is an old soul in a rejuvenated body," Mozag said. "Now that Lindy has regained her memories, Sebastian Stott has agreed to transfer custody to her sister, Camilla, though he will remain in her life as a friend and mentor. I know this comes with mixed emotions for everyone involved."

"Sebastian Stott will always feel like a second father to me," Lindy said. "I can't see him any other way."

Mr. Stott cleared his throat. "I feel similarly. My door is always open."

Mozag nodded appreciatively. "The Council has approved of this change, with the precautionary protocol of annual interviews with the sisters to check up on the situation. May our burgeoning friendship with the White sisters expand and deepen in the years to come."

Cheers and applause greeted this statement. Lindy got down off her chair.

"And now would Summer, Nate, Benji, Trevor, and Pigeon please arise."

Nate stood up along with his friends.

"These five kids went above and beyond once again to protect the world from magic gone awry," Mozag said. "Benji is new to the group but made no smaller sacrifice than the others. All confronted perilous threats and endured extreme hardship to obtain the Dreamstone and remove it from the carnival. Through their bravery, disaster was averted and peace restored. I consider each of them an important member of my inner circle."

Uproarious cheers and applause followed. Nate felt a little silly but also appreciated the acknowledgment.

"No event like this is complete without a surprise," Mozag said. "Would Zac Foster come forward?"

Nate craned to find Zac. He had not seen him since they parted ways unhappily.

Zac approached from a far corner of the room, looking uncomfortable.

"Zac was duped by Carl and Ellen White," Mozag said. "He advertised for the carnival under the mistaken belief that he was protecting it from unscrupulous attackers. He tried to help Belinda, who he understood was a kidnapping victim. I have talked with Zac extensively, and considering the information he was given, I have concluded that he acted with courage. He asked to be here tonight." Mozag held out a hand to Zac.

"I wanted to apologize in person," Zac said, looking at Nate and those seated near him. "I had everything backward. I thought you had gotten mixed up with the bad guys. I feel like a fool for almost ruining everything."

"Why haven't you come to school?" Benji called.

Zac flushed. "I've been wrestling with some tough feelings. Mostly guilt and shame. I was overconfident with what I thought I knew about the carnival, and I got burned. My face might be all over the Internet, but I haven't wanted to show it at school. Guys, I'm really sorry."

"It's okay," Pigeon said. "Everybody loves you."

Zac broke into a smile.

"We'll make room," Trevor said, scooting his chair. "Come have dessert."

The room applauded as Zac wedged a seat between Trevor and Pigeon. Nate waved and Zac waved back.

"One last matter before we enjoy our food," Mozag said.

"Camilla, would you mind elaborating on the future of the park?"

Camilla stood again. "As many of you know, when the dream carnival separated from the physical carnival, we lost most of the major ancillary locations, including the Undercarnvial, the Overcarnival, the Lost Moors, the Black Water Rapids, the Grotto, the Pirate Fleet, Enigma Island, and the Gemstone Mines, rendering them unrecoverable. But we are left with a significant quantity of permanent attractions and some of the minor ancillary locations, like the Lux Lounge."

"Thank heaven for that," Victor said.

"And for whoever made these desserts," Ziggy added.

The comments were seconded by several shouts.

"Some of the sleepers were visitors to the carnival who became entrapped," Camilla said. "They came from near and far, and were disoriented when they awoke from their prolonged dream. The majority of them have already returned to their former lives. But nearly half were staff members who remained involved with the carnival in their dream state. Many of them helped prepare the treats tonight, as did several members of the regular staff."

Nate clapped and got another burst of applause going.

"Aside from exerting influence through dreams, my father used an old family recipe to make the town more open to accepting the carnival," Camilla said. "This substance was in the bubble-gum gas during the parade, as well as in the cotton candy. His efforts yielded interesting results. This carnival now owns the ground on which it stands, and we have permits from the city and the state to operate for a minimum of twenty-five years."

This drew surprise from the audience. Nate looked at his friends. Pigeon shrugged. None of them had heard this news.

"With help from my sister and a few loyal members of the management team, and after some new hires, the Dreams and Screams International Carnival will reopen as Dreamland, a permanent Bay Area amusement park. We'll no longer augment the experience with the Dreamstone or any other magic, but we will instead use our imaginations to make it an enjoyable destination for all."

The audience clapped again.

"Anyone seated with us tonight will enjoy free lifetime memberships to Dreamland," Camilla said. "And if you would ever like to work here, just ask. Enjoy the desserts."

Nate had already scooped some vanilla ice cream into a bowl, and now he added gooey hot fudge. He loved the combination of hot and cold. The fudge had steam coming off it.

"Can you believe the carnival will keep running?" Trevor asked.

"I'm glad," Summer said. "There is so much here now—it would be a shame to waste it."

"Nate, I never heard what you did with the Dreamstone," Benji said.

"I started a rival theme park across town," Nate said, grinning. "Insomnialand. You can't dream if you don't sleep."

"Sounds good to me," Trevor said. "I've seriously had clown dreams all week."

Pigeon patted Trevor's back. "They still scare me too."

"Answer his question," Summer prompted.

"The real story is boring," Nate complained. "After I escaped the carnival, I took the Dreamstone to the candy shop. Mr. Stott passed it to Sandra and the Council."

"So she's going to make the rival theme park?" Zac asked.

"I'm part of a team that will preserve and protect the Dreamstone," Sandra said.

Zac blushed a little. "I was just kidding."

"Did we ever find out what Edward was doing?" Nate asked.

"I talked to him," Summer said. "He was part of a secret movement inside the park. They were trying to solve the mystery of the sleepers, while finding as much treasure as possible. He got caught not long before we did."

"Zac, will you come back to school?" Pigeon asked.

"Sure, if you guys accept my apology," Zac said. "Otherwise I'll probably move to Madagascar."

"Why punish Africa?" Benji asked.

Everyone laughed.

"We forgive you," Nate said.

"Some of our best friends have been people who initially worked against us," Pigeon said, glancing down the table at Lindy.

"Next time I'll advertise for the right cause," Zac said. "And maybe help fight against the actual bad guys."

"How did it feel to knock around some villains for real?" Summer asked John.

He wiped his mouth with a napkin before responding. "I really don't enjoy violence. But since I was trying to rescue you kids, it felt pretty good to skip the tranquilizer darts. The whole experience seems dreamlike. I mean, I was asleep, but a physical version of myself materialized out of my dream and into the carnival. That magic is over my head."

"It's nearly over mine," Sandra said. "It was only possible while the Dreamstone powered the carnival."

"You guys have to try the chocolate cream pie," Pigeon gushed.

"Victor was right about the key lime too," Trevor enthused.

Nate glanced at the pies. He felt content with ice cream drenched in hot fudge and sprinkled with nuts. There were too many desserts to sample everything.

"John," Nate asked, "what will you do now?"

John stretched, the sleeves of his jacket pulling up his thick arms. "Me? I found somebody to take over at the cafeteria. She'll start full time on Monday. Then I'll try to hide from trouble for a while. Maybe someplace tropical."

"Will that work?" Summer asked.

"Historically speaking?" John replied. "No. Not as long as I know that guy." He jerked a thumb at Mozag. "With him in my life, my calendar stays full of problems."

"At least you'll get a vacation first," Trevor said.

John shrugged. "It's what I tell myself. Sometimes the dream can be enough."

"What if another villain comes to town?" Pigeon asked.

"I'd be here in a heartbeat," John said earnestly. "It's at the top of my priority list. But between you kids, and Sebastian Stott, and now the White sisters . . . I have a feeling word will get out that Colson is protected."

ACKNOWLEDGMENTS

When I wrote the first Candy Shop War book, I did not intend to start a series. But many of my readers really wanted another one, and they were vocal about it. Several years later, I came up with an idea I liked and wrote *Arcade Catastrophe*. Now, several years after that, I have written this third book to complete the series. If you were a little kid when I wrote book one, you are now an adult. Sorry about that. Kids today can read all three as quickly as they choose! Children of previous years would be jealous . . .

Am I positive this is the final Candy Shop War book I will ever write? Considering how the series came about, I would be foolish to proclaim absolute surety. I'll just say I currently intend for this to be the last book.

Finishing this series puts me in an odd position. For the first time since writing the first Fablehaven book, all of my series are complete. At every other point in my career, at least one of my series was unfinished.

ACKNOWLEDGMENTS

That means it's time to start a new series. I have been saving my favorite idea, and now I finally get to write it. More information will be coming as the plans solidify. Follow me on Instagram @writerbrandon, on Facebook, or at BrandonMull.com for updates.

For now, I need to thank the brilliant people who helped me with this novel. My lovely and talented wife, Erlyn, edited every chapter before anyone else saw the story, and she improved the book significantly through her efforts. My one-of-a-kind agent, Simon Lipskar, helped as always. Brandon Dorman did another awesome cover.

My thanks go to the entire Shadow Mountain team. Chris Schoebinger offered great advice as usual. My editor Lisa Mangum has a real talent for streamlining language. She improved the flow of the story and helped correct other problems. Thanks, also, to Heidi Gordon, Richard Erickson, Breanna Anderl, Troy Butcher, and Callie Hansen.

I also owe thanks to my family for their patience and their help with ideas and editing. This includes Clark Baker, Brock Baker, Chet Baker, Ava Baker, Anika Baker, Erlyn Baker IV, Fiona Baker, Sadie Mull, Chase Mull, Rose Mull, and Calvin Mull. Other early readers who helped with feedback include Jason and Natalie Conforto, Tara McKinney, Pamela Mull, Cherie Mull, Lila Mull, Charan Prabhakar, and others.

And of course I have to thank *you*, the reader! Because you read my books, listen to my books, share my books, buy my books, and request my books from libraries, I get to keep writing more! I hope to bring you even better stories in the years to come.

READING GUIDE

1. The carnival in this story could move dreams into reality. In what ways can we make our dreams become real? What is required to make that happen?

2. Do you find clowns funny, scary, or both? Explain your reasons.

3. If you could dream anything into existence, what would you make? Would you ever get tired of having that ability? Why or why not?

4. A theme park can be a fun escape from daily living. Would it stay as fun if you went to the same theme park every day? Why or why not?

5. There were layers to the Dreams and Screams International Carnival. The more the kids explored, the more they found hidden eateries and attractions. Would it be practical to design a real carnival that way? Explain your answer.

6. If you could add new attractions or lands to the carnival in this book, what would they be? Describe your ideas.

7. Mr. Stott was worried that if he let Lindy interact with her sister, Camilla, she might revert to her evil patterns, so he wanted to keep her away from the carnival. In what ways was he justified in his parenting? In what ways was it unfair to Lindy? Do you agree with Mr. Stott's position on the matter? Why or why not?

8. Why did Camilla White hide from her troubles inside of Dreamland? Do you think she had a responsibility to stand up to her parents? Why or why not?

9. Zac ended up working against some of the main characters in this story. Why did he want to stop Nate, Trevor, Summer, and Pigeon? What convinced Zac to change his position?

10. Would you want to visit an amusement park exactly like the Dreams and Screams International Carnival while it was powered by the Dreamstone? Why or why not?